LO

In the world of Warhammer, no race is more feared than the dark elves, and no member of this race is more cunning and treacherous than Malus Darkblade. Tricked by the foul daemon Tz'arkan, Malus has a single year to find five artefacts and return them, or his immortal soul will be forfeit. After many months of hardship and adventure, Malus has just one artefact left to find - the Amulet of Vaurog. On the run from Har Ganeth, the rogue dark elf is captured and taken to Naggarond, where he is ordered by the Witch King to lead the defence against a Chaos invasion. As battle rages around him, with assassins and traitors dogging his every move, what chance does Darkblade have of ever finding the amulet, let alone getting back to Tz'arkan before his time runs out?

Lord of Ruin is the thrilling conclusion to first saga of Malus Darkblade, the epic dark fantasy series that has taken the Warhammer world by storm.

In the same series

Book 1: THE DAEMON'S CURSE
Book 2: BLOODSTORM
Book 3: REAPER OF SOULS
Book 4: WARPSWORD

A WARHAMMER NOVEL

LORD OF RUIN

A Tale of Malus Darkblade

DAN ABNETT & MIKE LEE

Dedication: For my mother, Johnnie Lee – my best and most dedicated fan. Without you, none of this would have been possible – M.L..

A Black Library Publication

First published in Great Britain in 2007 by
BL Publishing,
Games Workshop Ltd.,
Willow Road, Nottingham,
NG7 2WS, UK

10J 9J 8J7J6J 5J4J 3J 2J

Cover illustration by Clint Langley.
Map by Nuala Kinrade.

A CIP record for this book is available from the British Library.

ISBN 13: 978 1 84416 195 9
ISBN 10: 1 84416 195 1

Distributed in the US by Simon & Schuster
1230 Avenue of the Americas, New York, NY 10020.

THIS IS A dark age, a bloody age, an age of daemons and of sorcery. It is an age of battle and death, and of the world's ending. Amidst all of the fire, flame and fury it is a time, too, of mighty heroes, of bold deeds and great courage.

AT THE HEART of the Old World sprawls the Empire, the largest and most powerful of the human realms. Known for its engineers, sorcerers, traders and soldiers, it is a land of great mountains, mighty rivers, dark forests and vast cities. And from his throne in Altdorf reigns the Emperor Karl Franz, sacred descendant of the founder of these lands, Sigmar, and wielder of his magical warhammer.

BUT THESE ARE far from civilised times. Across the length and breadth of the Old World, from the knightly palaces of Bretonnia to ice-bound Kislev in the far north, come rumblings of war. In the towering Worlds Edge Mountains, the orc tribes are gathering for another assault. Bandits and renegades harry the wild southern lands of the Border Princes. There are rumours of rat-things, the skaven, emerging from the sewers and swamps across the land. And from the northern wildernesses there is the ever-present threat of Chaos, of daemons and beastmen corrupted by the foul powers of the Dark Gods. As the time of battle draws ever nearer, the Empire needs heroes like never before.

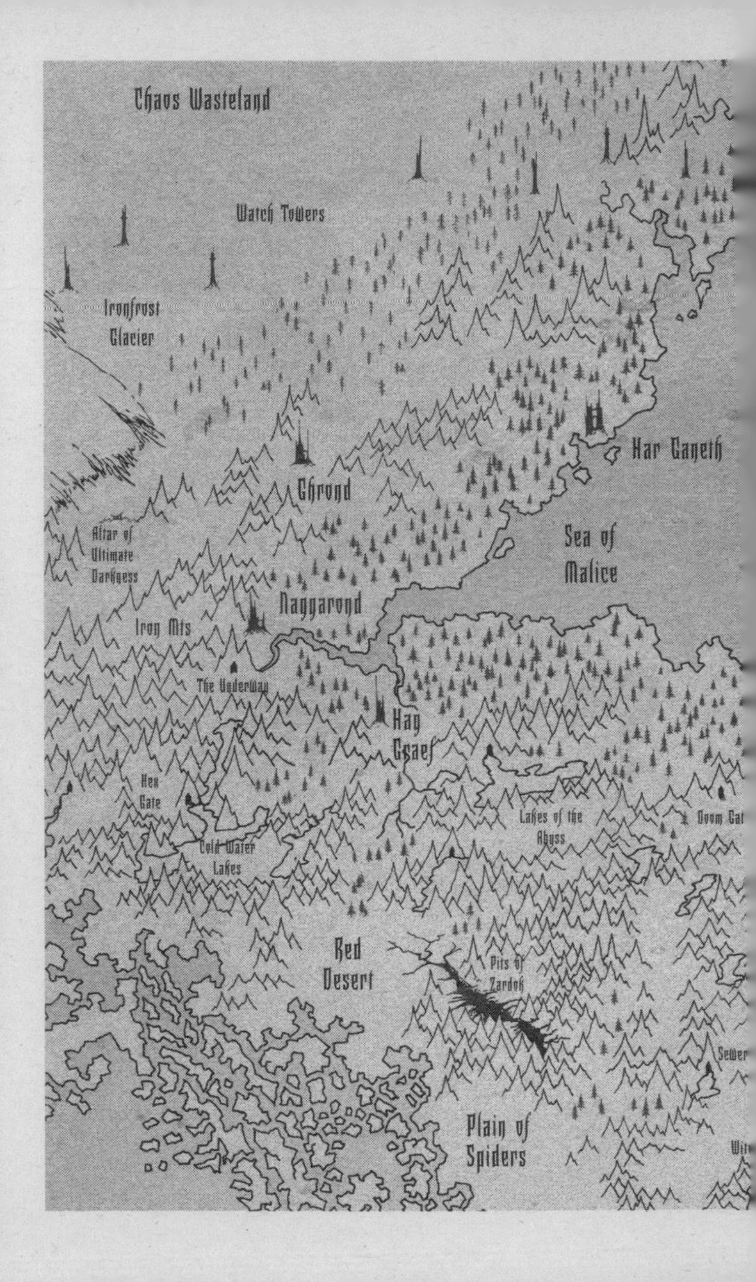
Chaos Wasteland
Watch Towers
Ironfrost Glacier
Ghrond
Har Ganeth
Sea of Malice
Altar of Ultimate Darkness
Naggarond
Iron Mts
The Underway
Hag Graef
Hex Gate
Lakes of the Abyss
Doom Ga
Cold Water Lakes
Red Desert
Pits of Zardok
Sewer
Plain of Spiders

Naggaroth
Karond Kar
Sea of
Chill
The Monoliths
Granite Hills
Hotek's Column
Black Forests
N
Clar Karond
Vaul's Anvil
Doom
Glades
Sea of
Serpents
Grasslands
Arnheim

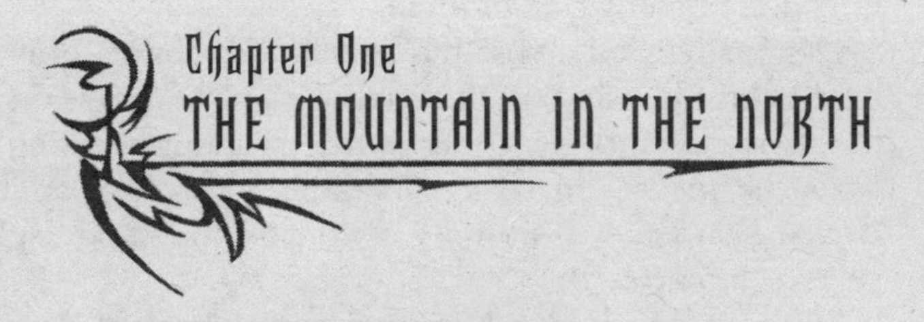

Chapter One
THE MOUNTAIN IN THE NORTH

The Chaos Wastes, first week of winter

THE COLD WIND shifted, blowing gusts of snow from the southeast and whispering in torment through the topmost branches of the trees. Urghal froze in place, settling on his haunches amid the snow-covered undergrowth. The beastman's nostrils flared, scenting prey, and his thin lips pulled back in a rictus of feral hunger.

Urghal swung his horned head left and right, catching glimpses of his two fellow hunters, Aghar and Shuk, as they split up and slid into concealment as well. The dense mountain forest had gone deathly silent save for the keening wind, and the beastman's long, tufted ears twitched restlessly as he strained to hear signs of movement from farther down the long slope. Heavy muscles bunched and relaxed along the beastman's broad shoulders, causing the dark, spiral tattoos etched into his thick hide to roll and shift in unnerving patterns. He breathed slowly and deeply, his clawed fingers flexing around the knotty grip of the rough-hewn club resting in his broad hands. The hunting had been poor since the herd had crept back to the cleft mountain and reclaimed their former territory. Soon the new master of the herd would begin culling out the weak and the slow and butchering them for the cook fires. Urghal had no intention of being one of them.

Silence stretched across the dark wood, broken only by the shrill buzzing of flies circling the open sores on the beastman's bony snout. Then without warning came the rustle and crash of bramble and fern, and Urghal heard the drumming sound of hooves racing over the loamy earth.

The beastman listened intently as the herd of deer stampeded up the slope directly at him. Ferns and thick shrubs were trampled and torn as the panicked animals forced their way through the dense undergrowth. Urghal could smell them now, perhaps as many as a dozen, the scent of their fear burning in his nostrils. He ran a thick, black tongue over his jagged teeth, lusting for the taste of hot, salty blood.

Twenty yards. Ten. Urghal caught glimpses of swaying branches now as the herd drew near. He heard the slight sounds of his fellow hunters readying themselves to strike. The beastman's muscles tensed like coiled springs just as the herd crashed over him like a wave.

A doe burst from the undergrowth to Urghal's left, dodging nimbly around the bole of a dark oak tree in a blur of frenzied motion. The beastman caught a glimpse of wide, terrified eyes as he sprang from his crouch and lashed out with his heavy club. The length of hardened oak smashed into the doe's side, splintering ribs and snapping the animal's spine with a brittle *crack*. The deer squealed in agony and plunged headfirst onto the ground.

Howls and hungry roars shook the air as Aghar and Shuk joined in the bloodletting, slashing at the plunging, leaping bodies with dagger and claw. Urghal smelled bitter blood in the air and bellowed cruel laughter as a huge stag burst from the foliage to the beastman's right. The stag saw the beastman at the very same moment; consumed with terror the deer tossed its antlered head and tried to spring away, but Urghal swept his bloodstained cudgel in a whistling arc, shattering the stag's gleaming antlers and smashing its skull. The deer hit the snowy earth with a heavy thud, its legs thrashing in the throes of death, and Urghal dropped his club and fell upon it, tearing at its warm throat with his teeth. The beastman ate greedily of its flesh as it trembled and died, tearing away ragged bites and choking them down whole in an effort to sate his frenzied hunger.

It was several long moments before Urghal realised how quiet the forest still was, and as the all-consuming hunger began to ebb he wondered what could have panicked the woods-wise deer in the first place.

The beastman raised his gore-smeared snout, licking his nostrils clean and tasting the frigid air once more. The wind rose and fell; over the rich scent of blood and spilt entrails he caught the faint whiff of something strange and bitter that sent a thrill down his knobby spine. His companions ate on, oblivious to everything except the steaming feast laid before them.

A premonition of fear tightened Urghal's throat. Baring his blood-slicked teeth, the beastman looked about frantically for his club and saw it lying on the bloody snow a dozen paces away. He lunged for the weapon, barking out a warning to his herd-mates just as the air shook with a thunderous roar and a huge shape leapt from the shadows beneath the trees.

The beast was massive, shaking the earth as it landed on two taloned feet among the surprised beastmen. Nearly thirty feet long from snout to tail, it filled the small clearing where the hunters had ambushed their prey. Its hide was dark green and scaled like a dragon's, and its muscular haunches were covered in scars from hundreds of deadly battles. Long, skinny forelimbs were tucked in tight against the beast's narrow chest; the creature's muscular, cable-like tail balanced its lunging motion as it snapped up a pair of deer carcasses in its huge, lizard-like jaws and swallowed them in a few crunching bites. Rivulets of blood mingled with tendrils of ropy spittle that drooled from between the creature's dagger-like teeth. Eyes the colour of spilled blood rolled wildly within deep, bony oculars as the beast searched about for more prey. Quick as a snake it lunged again, tossing the body of a deer into the air and eating it in a single gulp.

Shouts and bellows of fright echoed across the clearing as the hunters reeled from the beast's sudden assault. Urghal snatched up his club, snarling in rage. Hunger warred with fear as he watched the monster feed upon their kills. As the creature lunged for another deer, Urghal realised that it was oblivious to the three beastmen surrounding it. Its long, powerful tail now drooped, partly dragging the ground, and the flesh covering its bony head was shrunken, stretched across the skull like thick parchment. As it ate, Urghal saw its ribs standing out sharply from its flanks. It was starving, the beastman saw. He understood that madness all too well.

The beastman noticed the empty, weathered saddle strapped around the monster's back, just behind the sloping shoulders. Ragged saddlebags were strapped down behind it, their sides tattered and frayed by hard use and indifferent care. Silver rings glinted in the beast's leathery cheeks where reins had once been fitted. Then he saw the long, black-hilted sword buckled to the side of the saddle and knew that its rider had to be long dead.

Urghal bared his blackened teeth and barked commands to his fellow hunters. The creature was weak and stupid with hunger, he said. They could leap upon its back and kill it while it fed and feast off its acrid flesh for many days. Aghar and Shuk listened, and their shrunken bellies lent them courage they might not otherwise have possessed. Gripping their weapons tightly, the beastmen circled around the creature's flanks. Aghar sidled up along the creature's right side, raising his dagger for a deep thrust into the monster's neck. Shuk crept near the base of the creature's tail, ready to throw his massive bulk onto the appendage and weight it down, hampering its movement. Urghal crept up along the left side, drawing closer to the saddle. He would leap up and draw the black blade, then plunge it into the back of the monster's neck. The beast would be dead before it realised it was in danger.

Grinning viciously, Urghal turned to Shuk – and, too late, saw a dark shape leap from the depths of the forest and land upon the beastman's back with a terrifying shriek. Urghal heard the clatter of metal as the attacker pounced upon Shuk's bare torso, then saw pallid hands reach around the beastman's broad chest and plunge claw-like fingers through scarred hide and slab-like muscle. Shuk bellowed in terror and pain, throwing back his horned head and reaching over his shoulder to try and pry free his assailant, but the pale-skinned attacker clung to his victim like a cave spider, pressing close to the beastman's back.

Urghal caught a glimpse of a pale, angular face framed by loose, matted black hair as the armoured attacker lunged for Shuk's throat. Eyes as dark as the Abyss burned into Urghal's own. Bluish lips skinned back over perfect white teeth, and the figure tore open the beastman's muscular throat. Blood burst from Shuk's lips as he tried to staunch the fountain of crimson jetting from the ragged wound in his neck. Urghal watched the black-eyed monster bury its face into the gaping wound, tearing away mouthfuls of flesh like a frenzied rat.

The dying beastman fell to his knees, choking on his own blood. Urghal gripped his cudgel and bellowed a challenge – just as the scaled beast beside him turned and lunged for Aghar. The creature's whip-like tail slashed in the opposite direction, crashing into Urghal's chest. Ribs snapped like twigs beneath the powerful blow; Urghal was flung backwards across the clearing and dashed against the bole of a towering oak tree. Stunned by the double impact the beastman toppled onto his side, feeling broken bones grate together in his chest.

As his breath rattled wetly in his throat, Urghal saw Aghar charge at the black-armoured attacker. The hunter bellowed in berserk fury, and the lithe figure responded with a bestial growl of his own. Bloody mouth agape, the armoured warrior leapt to his feet with disquieting speed and met the beastman's rush head-on.

Aghar was head and shoulders taller than his foe and half again as wide. Urghal expected the armoured attacker to be smashed to the ground by the hunter's furious charge, but instead the two crashed together in a clatter of flesh and steel. A pale hand reached up and took hold of the beastman's throat, and the pair grappled for the space of several heartbeats. Savage snarls and guttural growls rose from the desperate struggle; Urghal could not say for sure from which throat the terrible sounds came. Then, with a sudden, convulsive wrench Aghar pulled his dagger-arm free and stabbed at the armoured figure again and again, the blows ringing against the smaller assailant's steel breastplate and pauldrons.

There was a muffled heavy thud and a crunch of broken bones. Aghar shuddered at the blow, his cloven feet lifting off the ground from the impact. The beastman doubled over, choking in agony from a shattered breastbone, and the black-eyed attacker grabbed Aghar's ridged horns and wrenched them around in a neck-snapping twist.

Urghal felt the cold gaze of the killer settle on him. Growling in pain, the beastman struggled to rise onto his knees. Without warning an armoured boot crashed into his shoulder, flipping him back onto the ground. The pale-skinned warrior had crossed the dozen yards between them in the blink of an eye. The beastman growled defiantly, hefting his club one-handed – but as he met the warrior's face the weapon tumbled from his stunned grasp.

Depthless black eyes, without iris or pupil, regarded Urghal with the soulless hunger of the Abyss. The warrior's mouth and pointed chin dripped with clotted gore, spattering the ornate gilt-work of his plate armour. Trickles of red flowed into the crevices and corners of three golden skulls affixed to the foe's breastplate, and a thick torc of red-gold enclosed his wiry neck. Just above the burnished gold curve of the torc jutted the rusty hilt of Aghar's dagger. The long blade had been driven clean through the warrior's throat, its broad point emerging at an angle just below the warrior's right ear.

As Urghal watched, the warrior reached up with a red-stained hand and slowly pulled the dagger free. A trickle of thick, black ichor leaked from the gruesome wound. Ropy black veins pulsed and writhed like worms beneath the skin of the warrior's throat and along the back of his hands.

The warrior let the dagger tumble slowly from his dripping fingers. It landed right beside Urghal's head, but the beastman made no move to pick it up. With a ghastly red grin, the black-eyed warrior opened his mouth and uttered a sound no living throat could possibly make, and the beastman's fevered mind shattered at the sound of it.

Urghal's cry of terror shook the black-limbed trees as the killer reached for him with claw-like hands.

LITTLE BY LITTLE, as the beastman's raw flesh filled his wasted belly, a measure of sanity returned to Malus Darkblade. His body, withered like a shrunken root by the nightmarish ordeals of his journey, began to shudder and ache as the daemon relaxed its remorseless grip. The shock of consciousness was so intense that for an agonizing moment the highborn was certain that he was going to die. He fell onto his back, still clutching tattered scraps of flesh in his hands, and howled his wretched hate to the roiling northern sky.

Part of him was certain he was already dead. His mind recoiled from the few memories he had of the past few weeks, driven ever northwards by the daemon's merciless will. No sleep, no food, no rest for weeks on end, driven to lengths no living body ought to endure. Even Spite's near limitless stamina had been driven to the breaking point and beyond.

But they had reached the broken mountain. Nearby lay the pale road and the dreadful temple. Many times in the last few weeks he hadn't thought such a thing possible, but now, so close to his goal he wanted nothing more than to die. He wept bitterly at the thought, feeling icy tears course down his hollow cheeks.

Rise, Darkblade, the daemon said, and his body responded to the implacable command. Ravaged muscles tautened painfully, propelling Malus upright with a groan of helpless rage. *Your final hour approaches.*

Malus's body lurched across the clearing towards Spite. His mouth worked silently, trying to utter dark curses from his ruined throat. From somewhere farther up the wooded slope came a chorus of howls and the rolling, mournful notes of horns. The clamour of the battle had reached as far as the beastman camp, and now the herd was on the move.

As he approached the saddle the cold one groaned and cowered, snapping at him fearfully. The daemon lashed the nauglir with its black will, and the cold one whined in submission, allowing the highborn to clamber jerkily onto its back. Still groaning, the nauglir rose wearily onto its feet and was mentally lashed into motion, beginning the last leg of its long, hellish odyssey.

The horn calls faded but the howls of the beastmen drew nearer as the daemon led Spite around the flank of the mountainside. Darkness fell as they rode. Malus swayed in the saddle, his gaze drifting to the black-hilted sword resting by his left knee. With all his might he tried to force his hand to reach for the sorcerous blade, but Tz'arkan's will held him fast.

All for nothing, he thought, as the daemon drove him onward to the temple like a sacrificial lamb. He thought of Hauclir, and the fields of the dead. He thought of the daemon-haunted shade and the soul-shattering screams of his sister. All for nothing.

Hatred and loathing burned like a seething coal in his ravaged chest – and the little finger on his left hand twitched.

Malus scarcely dared to breathe. He couldn't bring himself to hope, but even in the depths of privation and despair there was always room enough for hate. With hate all things are possible, he thought. His bloodied lips trembled in a palsied smile.

Half-formed memories dogged in the highborn's wake as they plunged on through thicket and fern. The echoes of the hunting beastmen called to mind a desperate flight through these same woods exactly one year before. Every now and then they passed a stand of trees or a wooded hollow that seemed familiar to him, though part of him knew that it was only a trick of the mind.

The shouts of the beastman herd were close now – perhaps a half-mile further upslope, hidden by the depths of the forest. Without warning the ground suddenly levelled out, and Malus found himself on a road of pale, snow-covered stones untouched by the passage of millennia. It was a road built for the tread of conquerors, with each stone carved in the shape of a skull and standing stones set at intervals along its length, praising the Ruinous Powers and exalting the deeds of the Chaos champions who ruled there. A year before, the blasphemous runes of the standing stones held no meaning for Malus; now he looked at them through daemon-tainted eyes, and the names carved on the menhirs burned themselves into his brain. Malus could feel his sanity crumbling with each passing moment as they drew nearer to the temple; desperately he turned to his hate, stoking it with all the bitterness and rage his year of servitude had wrought in him. The highborn focused on the hilt of the sword and prayed to every cursed god he could name for the strength to tear the unholy blade from its scabbard.

The air hummed and crackled with unseen energies as the daemon within Malus drew closer to the temple. Unearthly power crackled over his tortured skin, and the black-limbed trees lining the road rattled and shook in an invisible wind. Spite's pace quickened steadily, as though the nauglir was being drawn forward like iron to a lodestone. A strange, buzzing hum began to build in the back of Malus's skull.

By the time they swept around the final bend of the winding road Spite was nearly at a gallop. His drumming feet echoed off the close-set trees, and for a dizzying moment Malus felt as though he'd been cast back in time, riding with a troop of armoured retainers at his back. He thought of Dalvar, the dagger-wielding rogue, and Vanhir, the haughty, hateful knight.

He thought of Lhunara, riding quietly at his side, her fierce smile gleaming in the darkness. Choking back bitter bile, the highborn pushed the memory away.

And then the air trembled with the shout of a hundred furious voices as the beastmen raised their weapons and challenged the lone rider bearing down the road towards them. The herd had guessed where he was headed and had cut him off just short of his goal, exactly as they'd done just twelve months past.

But there were no armoured retainers to open the way for him this time. The beastmen stood in a roaring, bellowing mob that filled the tree-lined avenue before him. Axes, cudgels and rusty two-handed swords were brandished by the light of guttering torches. Spite stumbled to a halt, hissing and screeching in agitation as the mob surged forward.

Malus sensed his chance. The daemon would have to let him draw the warpsword before they were overwhelmed. With all his hate-fuelled will he tried to force his hand to reach for the blade.

But just a few yards short of the cold one the howling mob fell to their knees and pressed their horned heads to the skull-faced stones. In the midst of the mob a shaman with a single red eye gleaming from the middle of his narrow skull bleated: 'The prophecy is fulfilled! The Drinker of Worlds is come! Bow before the blessed Prince of Slaanesh, and let the dirge of Eternal Night be sung!'

Once again the daemon lashed at the nauglir's beleaguered mind, and the warbeast lurched forward, trotting down a path that opened through the centre of the prostrate mob. Malus trembled with impotent rage as they passed unchallenged through the herd and rode on a short way until the trees parted before them. Beyond rose a square, tiered structure of sheer, black stone, windowless and devoid of ornamentation, as cold and soulless as the Abyss itself. Surrounding the temple was a wall formed of similar stone, and a square-arched gateway. A desperate battle had been fought there a year before; skeletons of beastmen and misshapen Chaos beasts still littered the ground where they had fallen to druchii crossbows and swords. They crunched beneath Spite's heavy tread as the cold one walked beneath the gateway and came to a halt within the courtyard beyond.

There were more bones here, speaking of another scene of slaughter. Huge skulls and piles of dark bones that once had been nauglir, and druchii skeletons in rusting armour. They lay in the white snow where he'd slain them almost twelve months before.

He'd killed his own retainers out of shame, unable to bear having them see how the daemon had enslaved him. Now he met their black, empty stares and wished he could grind their grey bones into dust.

Malus's body lurched into motion, sliding awkwardly from the saddle. His face contorted into a rictus of thwarted rage, the highborn could only watch helplessly as his hands unbuckled the warpsword from the saddle and then collected the frayed bag containing the rest of the daemon's relics. As he pulled the sack free, Spite collapsed onto its side, as though unburdened at last of a terrible weight. Its flanks shuddered and heaved, and its breath came in ragged gasps.

It is time, the daemon said, its cruel voice reverberating in Malus's skull. *Quickly now! Carry the relics to the crystal chamber, and soon your curse will be at an end.*

Filled with dread, Malus turned his back on the dying nauglir and marched like a condemned man into the shadow of the daemon's temple.

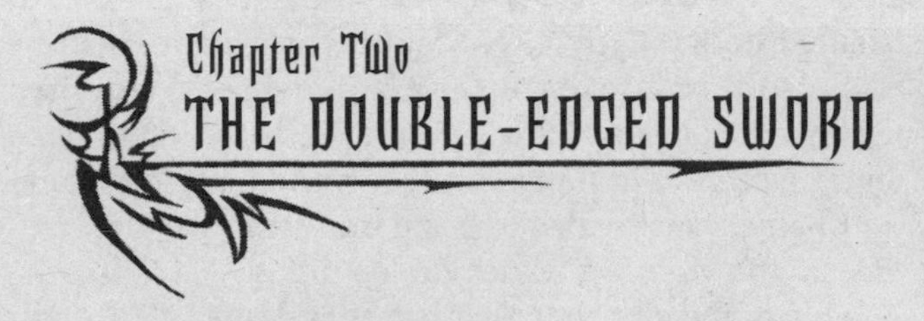

Chapter Two
THE DOUBLE-EDGED SWORD

The city of Har Ganeth, eight weeks before

SMOKE HUNG LIKE a pall over the City of Executioners, wreathing the broad hill in streamers of grey that tasted of cinders and the grease of cooked flesh. High in the blade-like towers of the temple fortress the sacrificial bells were ringing, calling to the faithful to bare their blades and give thanks for Har Ganeth's deliverance. Tortured screams and the howl of hungry mobs rose like a paean into the cloudy summer sky.

The fighting had raged for more than a week, and the lower quarters of Har Ganeth had suffered the worst. Two days after the riots had ended the narrow, maze-like streets were still choked with corpses and the charred remains of burnt-out buildings. Fresh splashes of vivid red painted the rust-coloured walls of the White City, and the shadowy avenues reeked of the charnel stench of the battlefield. Shopkeepers and tradesmen picked their way carefully amongst the piled debris, looking for useful bits of salvage. Groups of young children ran along the cobblestone streets, brandishing tiny, stained knives and rawhide cords strung with severed fingers decorated with rings of silver and gold. Axes and meat cleavers flashed and *thunked* into dead flesh, separating vertebrae with a wet crackle as the druchii collected severed heads to stack outside their blood-stained doors. Only a few days before, many of those same folk had taken up torch and blade and risen against the priests of Khaine's temple, believing that the apocalypse was at hand. But the would-be Swordbearer of Khaine was revealed to be an impostor, and the leaders of the uprising either driven off or slain, so the people of the city bent their heads and piled skulls outside their shops and homes, praying that the vengeful shadow of the temple executioners would pass them by. At the sound of tramping feet they hunched their shoulders and lowered their gaze to the bloody stones, fearful of attracting the attention of the temple executioners, or worse, the hungry gaze of Khaine's bloodthirsty brides.

Thus, when the heavy tread of a nauglir and the dull clatter of armour echoed down the narrow streets the people of Har Ganeth hid their eyes and paid no heed to the highborn rider – or the black-hilted blade buckled at his side. Only the city's ravens took notice of his passage, raising gore-stained beaks from their bloated meals and flapping great, glossy wings. *'Blood and souls!'* they croaked exultantly, regarding Malus Darkblade with lantern-yellow eyes. *'Scourge! Scourge!'*

Damned nuisances, Malus thought, his scowl deepening the hollows of his sunken cheeks and drawing dark lines around his thin lips. Spite, sensing its master's irritation, tossed its blocky head and snapped at the capering ravens, scattering venomous drool from its toothy maw. The highborn settled the cold one with an expert tug on the reins and guided the warbeast around the burnt wreckage of an overturned wagon. More black shapes circled overhead, floating like shadows in his wake. The ravens were sacred to Khaine, he'd learned. Is it the sword that stirs them so, he thought, or is it me?

Something cold and hard slithered serpentine around Malus's heart. A voice hissed like molten lead along his bones, setting his teeth on edge. *A meaningless distinction,* Tz'arkan sneered. *You and the burning blade are now one and the same.*

The highborn jerked upright in his saddle, armoured fists clenching the thick reins hard enough to make the leather creak as a wave of freezing pressure swelled behind his eyes. He bit back a savage curse, blinking at the black spots that drifted like ashes across his vision. His pulse throbbed turgidly in his temples, veins thick with oily, black ice.

Tz'arkan's hold over him was nearly complete.

It was the daemon's damnable curse that had brought him to Har Ganeth in the first place, seeking one of the five arcane relics that would free Tz'arkan from his crystal prison in the Chaos Wastes – and allow Malus to reclaim his stolen soul. The Warpsword of Khaine was one such relic, but in the millennia since the daemon's imprisonment the weapon had found its way into the possession of the Temple of Khaine, where it was kept in anticipation of the day when the Lord of Murder's chosen one would claim it and usher in the cataclysmic Time of Blood. According to the elders of the temple, that chosen one was none other than Malekith himself, the merciless Witch King of Naggaroth, but Malus knew that to be a convenient fiction, a lie told in the pursuit of temporal wealth and power.

The truth, as it often happened in the Land of Chill, was rather murkier than that.

Malus managed a bitter chuckle. 'Could it be that the great daemon has wound himself up in his own webs of deceit?' he growled. 'Are you sorry now for making me your catspaw? It was your own machinations that put the blade into my hands, after all. My *fate*, as you so gleefully put it.'

He'd learned a lot about fate in the ten months since he'd entered Tz'arkan's chamber in the far north. Fate was the word that puppets used to describe the tugging of invisible strings. It hadn't been fate that had drawn Malus to the north in search of power and wealth; he had been pointed at Tz'arkan's temple and loosed like an arrow, manipulated into undertaking the expedition by his half-sister Nagaira. Yet she herself was being manipulated in turn by Malus's own mother, the sorceress Eldire. Eldire had known of the daemon and its ages-old schemes somehow. She had learned of the prophecy and the Time of Blood, and had spent untold years shaping people and events to bring about their fruition. Not to serve Tz'arkan, but to usurp the daemon's machinations for her own secret purposes. It was an act of towering ambition and ruthlessness that culminated in the birth of her son, Malus. She had shaped him to be the lever that would set the daemon's inscrutable designs into motion.

But prophecies, by their very nature, were slippery, treacherous things.

Others had tried to bend him to their will, or claim the mantle of prophecy for their own. Nagaira had tried to bend him through deception and sorcery, seeking to turn the daemon to her own purposes. Worse still, his twisted half-brother Urial, poisoned in the womb by Eldire herself and given to the temple as a sacrifice, had survived the Cauldron of Blood and been initiated into the mysteries of Khaine's cult. Dissident members of the cult who refused to accept Malekith as Khaine's Swordbearer believed that Urial was the chosen one, and the circumstances of the prophecy fit well enough. He was secretly groomed to claim the sword when the time was right, and after his beloved half-sister Yasmir was revealed as a living saint of the Bloody-Handed God he betrayed Malus and fled to Har Ganeth, where he summoned the temple zealots to cast down the heretical elders of the cult.

For a week the City of Executioners tore itself apart as the zealots led its citizens in a bloody uprising. Urial had come very close indeed to achieving his aims. Too close for comfort, Malus admitted to himself, absently raising a hand to his breastplate where Urial's sword had slipped between his ribs. But for the daemon's power, he would have died.

Tz'arkan had sunk its talons deep into his body, spreading its corruption a little more each time Malus had drawn upon its infernal strength. Even now, his skin felt like ice, his muscles shrivelled and weak, aching for another taste of daemonic power. He had only a few months left to claim the last of the daemon's five artefacts and return them to the temple in the north or his soul would be forever lost, but Malus couldn't help but wonder if he wasn't already too late. Had he fought for the last ten months to reclaim his soul only to become a daemonhost once Tz'arkan was free?

Malus had good reason to believe that had been the daemon's plan all along.

Foolish druchii, the daemon spat, *The warpsword was not meant to be wielded by the likes of you. You see it as nothing more than a sharp blade, but it is a talisman of supernal power. As ever, you trifle with forces beyond your ability to contemplate.*

The highborn caught Spite sniffing at the bloated corpse of a dead horse, still trapped in the overturned wagon's traces. Malus put his spurs to the warbeast's flanks and startled the nauglir back into a heavy-footed trot. 'Oh, but you are mistaken,' he replied. 'I see it as a fine weapon *and* a talisman of great power – one I have every intention of using as I see fit. What do you care, so long as I am doing your damned bidding?'

In truth, Malus suspected he knew the source of the daemon's concern. The warpsword radiated power like a burning brand – even now he could feel its heat, seeping from its scabbard and sinking into his bones. Power enough to supplant the daemon's icy gifts and resist Tz'arkan's will, or so he hoped.

You imagine that you carry a mere blade on your hip? No. That is Khaine's own hunger given form, the daemon hissed.

'Then I will see that it is kept well-fed,' Malus replied.

Of course you will, Tz'arkan said mockingly. *You have no choice. The sword has claimed you, and like all those who wielded it before you it will one day turn in your hand when you fail to give its due.*

Something in the daemon's voice gave Malus pause. He glanced down at the warpsword's black hilt and felt a sudden chill.

It's just another lie, he told himself. Malus laid a hand on the sword's black pommel and savoured its warmth. It's the only chance you have against Tz'arkan, and the daemon knows it. 'Best for you then if we part ways before the blade gets the better of me,' the highborn said.

The daemon's laughter etched itself like acid into Malus's bones. *No, best for* you, *Darkblade. Bad enough that your allotted time is running out – now you trifle with an eldritch artefact that hungers for your life's blood. Don't you understand? Your doom is sealed! The best you can hope for now is to find the Amulet of Vaurog and return to my temple in the north before you are undone. Otherwise your soul will belong to me until the end of time.*

With the daemon's mirth echoing jaggedly in his head Malus kicked Spite into a canter, no longer caring what the cold one caught between its snapping jaws or crushed to paste underfoot. His thoughts roiled like the murderous brew in Khaine's own cauldron as he contemplated his next move.

The farther down the wide hill Malus went the worse the devastation became. The highborn districts around the temple fortress near the summit had been largely untouched; each home was like a small citadel unto itself, ideally designed to fend off all but the most determined assaults. The lowborn districts further down the slope had suffered far more, first at the hands of the temple warriors and then the successive riots that had raged across Har Ganeth for days on end. Many of the stone structures had been blackened by fire and several had collapsed completely, spilling their charred contents onto the streets.

But it was the merchants' quarter and the warehouse districts at the base of the hill that had suffered worst of all. Many shopkeepers had shut their doors and hoped to weather the storm, but as the riots gave way to open warfare between the zealots and the temple loyalists the quarter became a no-man's land caught between the warring factions. Shops were pillaged or burned in the riots, then had their bones picked clean by scavengers as the fighting wore on.

Beyond the merchants' quarter the slave market and the warehouse district were in ruins. It was here that the fighting raged hottest, once Urial and his zealots seized the temple and trapped the loyalists out on the streets. Large warbands of blood witches and executioners had been isolated by mobs of frenzied citizens and forced to take refuge in slavekeepers' stables or shipping houses. Fires touched off by the vicious street fighting had raged unchecked for days, and the air around the wreckage was thick with tendrils of turgid, stinking smoke. When the wind shifted Malus could catch glimpses of the city walls, rising untouched above the devastation. If anything the walls had only served to hem in the carnage, turning Har Ganeth's rage back upon itself as the city tore itself apart.

He was still within the warehouse district, less than half a mile from the city gate when he heard the first stirrings of the mob. Their bloodthirsty roar shook him from his bitter reverie, their cries of *'Blood for the Blood God!'* echoing weirdly along the ruined streets. The sounds seemed to be coming from just up ahead, though he couldn't be certain of anything in the shifting smoke. For a fleeting moment he contemplated altering his course, but with a flash of irritation he pushed the thought aside. He could guess what the mob was after, and it didn't include the likes of him. The highborn spurred his mount on through the smoke, the nauglir's broad feet crunching cinders and scorched bones with every step.

The sounds of the mob ebbed and flowed, muffled by the wreckage and the shifting wind as he continued down the rubble-strewn avenue, until Malus began to believe that the druchii were heading away from him, moving off to the west. The cries tapered off, and after he'd ridden on in relative silence for a few minutes he finally allowed himself to relax. Just at that moment, as though stirred by the laugh of a capricious god, a gust of wind banished the concealing smoke that surrounded the highborn and the mob erupted in a bloodthirsty cheer less than a dozen yards to Malus's left.

There were thirty or forty of them, filling a broad side street next to the wreckage of a long, single-storey warehouse. Most of them were lowborn citizens in soot-stained robes, clutching swords or axes in their grimy hands, but the ringleaders of the band were a pair of young blood witches and a handful of temple executioners. The servants of the temple were standing on a broad pile of fallen stones to give the crowd a better view of their efforts. The white stones beneath them were stained in patterns of red: striations of vivid crimson bled into a dull brick red, then to a dark reddish-brown where the congealing gore had settled into crevices and cracks among the stones. Headless bodies sprawled down the rockslides, spilling their contents onto the gritty cobblestones.

Several druchii squirmed and hissed in the grip of the mob, awaiting their turn before the drachms of the executioners. They had made the mistake of siding with the zealots during the revolt and had lacked the wit to switch sides again once the uprising had failed. Or perhaps they had simply been caught in the wrong place at the wrong time; one of them, Malus noted, looked more like a trader from Karond Kar, with his indigo-hued kheitan and a set of slaver's chains hanging from his hip.

For the moment, the hapless prisoners had been granted a short reprieve. The servants of the temple had far sweeter offerings to occupy their attentions.

Two druchii swayed atop the stone pile, held upright in the iron grips of the executioners. They had been stripped to the waist, but Malus noted the filthy white robes and torn sleeves that were bunched around their hips. Their muscular chests and arms were severely bruised and blackened; looking at them the highborn could well believe they'd been hauled from the rubble of one of the buildings nearby. Tellingly, neither man bore the mark of sword nor axe on their bodies, despite the days of hard fighting that had raged across the city.

They were zealots, members of the renegade splinter cult that worshipped Khaine's true faith. Killers without peer, they wore no armour in battle and clothed themselves in white to better show the red favours of their god. Hundreds of them had flocked to Har Ganeth at Urial's call and had taken a fearful toll of the temple warriors during the uprising. Once it had become clear that the uprising had failed, most of the survivors had scattered back into the countryside – which made zealot prisoners all the more enticing to the vengeful blood witches. These two would suffer for weeks under the witches' expert hands before their remains were given to the Cauldron of Blood. It was the worst fate possible for the true believers, who prayed to Khaine daily for a glorious death in battle.

Malus eyed the doomed men coldly and thanked the Dark Mother for the distraction. Better you than me, he thought, then frowned irritably as Spite slowed to a near stop as it caught the scent of fresh blood. The highborn glared at his scaly mount and made to spur the beast back into a canter when suddenly an anguished cry rang out from the rock pile.

'Deliver us, holy one!' the zealot cried to Malus. 'Draw your sword and slay us, in the Blessed Murderer's name!'

Heads turned. Malus felt the predatory stares of the blood witches against his skin and felt his hair stand on end. All at once the air seemed charged with pent-up tension, crackling with furious energies like the moments before a summer storm. Spite sensed the change, too, and rumbled threateningly at the crowd.

Of all the damnable luck, the highborn cursed. He didn't recognize either of the zealots' pleading faces. Malus had fallen in with the true believers by accident when he'd first made his way into the city, looking for his own secret path into the temple fortress. He had even taken a hand in stirring up the early riots, hoping to distract the temple elders further, and had wound up with far more trouble than he'd bargained for.

The mob eyed Malus like a pack of feral dogs. In his worn robes and scarred plate armour, he had the look of a landless knight or an exiled noble rather than a wild-eyed heretic. The highborn's face was gaunt, emphasizing his sharp cheekbones and pointed chin. Eyes the colour of brass shone from sunken eye sockets, marking him as one of Khaine's chosen. More forbidding still was the grey pallor of his face, like a druchii in the grip of a terrible sickness.

'No one is going to save you from your sins, heretic,' Malus spat, wrenching at Spite's reins. 'Khaine has no cold mercies for the likes of you.'

The nauglir shook its massive head and sidestepped, unwilling to turn away from the mob. It clashed its massive jaws and growled menacingly, and the mob hissed in reply.

One of the temple witches levelled her sword at Malus. Lines and loops of fresh blood glistened on her muscular arms and her long, bare legs. 'You are not a temple priest,' she said in a throaty voice, like cold air rising up from a tomb.

'I have never claimed to be,' Malus said tightly, trying to get the cold one under control. Spite circled and stamped, pacing away and then angling back towards the crowd like iron drawn to a lodestone. The tension in the air continued to build, setting the highborn's teeth on edge. What in the name of the Dark Mother was going on?

'Coward! Apostate!' the zealot screamed, surging against the grip of the executioners.

'Seize him,' the witch said coldly.

The mob erupted into lusty shouts, brandishing their weapons as they rushed at the highborn, and Spite lunged at them with an answering roar, nearly jerking Malus out of the saddle.

He could feel the pent-up tension burst in a rush that crackled through the air and sizzled across his bare skin. It was like the seething flare of an open flame or a lash of summer lightning. Malus cried out in bewilderment and anger, struggling to stay upright as Spite tore into the mob. Bones crunched and blood sprayed in the air as the cold one caught a man by the shoulder and bit off his right arm. The druchii's anguished scream set Malus's nerves on fire.

Spite roared and lunged at another man running past the cold one's flank, catching the druchii by the hip and flinging him into the air. Malus cursed and pounded the beast's flanks with his spurs, but the nauglir had gone berserk, tearing at its foes with reckless abandon.

The mob surged hungrily around the snapping beast. A sword blade rang off Malus's breastplate. Pale, blood-streaked faces glared up at him, their dark eyes burning with battle-lust. Bare hands seized his mail fauld and his right leg, trying to pull him out of the saddle. Snarling like a wolf, Malus pulled his leg free and planted his heel in a man's upturned face, but more hands closed about his ankle and dragged him downwards.

He felt himself sliding inexorably from his seat. Rage and desperation seethed through his veins. Without thinking, Malus reached for the warpsword. Its hilt was hot to the touch, and the long, eldritch blade seemed to leap from its scabbard with an ominous hiss.

Roaring blasphemies, Malus raised the ebon blade to the stormy sky. Above the cacophonous shouts of the mob, the highborn heard a horrified shriek from one of the temple witches, then he swept the sword in a vicious arc through the arms and heads of the grasping crowd. Flesh blackened and withered as the sword drank deep of hot blood and mortal pain.

Roars of bloodlust turned to screams of terror and despair. The mob reeled back from the smoking corpses of their brethren, crying out Khaine's name. Malus leapt after them, his face set in a mask of berserk rage.

Overhead, the croaking laughter of ravens echoed across the stormy sky.

THE BLOOD WITCH'S face was oddly serene. Malus admired the alabaster perfection of her high cheekbones and the subtle curve of her elegant jaw. Her brass-coloured eyes were calm, her round lips slightly parted and vivid with the blush of youth. In another time she could have been a violet-eyed princess of lost Nagarythe, about to whisper her secrets into the ear of a lover.

Close enough to kiss those perfect lips, Malus drew a shuddering breath and pulled the warpsword free. The ancient blade scraped against stone as it slid from the pile of rubble at the witch's back, leaving her body to slip from the long blade and slump lifelessly to the ground.

For a moment the highborn blinked drunkenly at the witch's body, as though seeing it for the first time. His skin was hot, as though flushed with fever, and his nerves still sang with fading notes of bloodlust. His gaze drifted to the drooping tip of the warpsword. A faint curl of crimson vapour rose from its razor edge.

With an effort of will Malus raised his head and beheld the trail of slaughter that stretched the length of the long, broad street.

Ruptured bodies and severed limbs lay in a tangled carpet across the cobblestones. Many bore their wounds upon their back, cut down as they tried to escape. Broken weapons glinted in the weak sunlight, showing where others had tried to fight the hunger of a god. Every face Malus could see was twisted in a rictus of terror and pain – all but the two zealot prisoners. Their headless bodies still knelt upright on the cobblestones, their arms outstretched in a gesture of religious ecstasy.

'Blessed Mother of Night,' Malus whispered in horrified awe. 'What have I done?'

You have slaked the thirst of the burning blade, Tz'arkan hissed. *For now.*

Dozens of people, the highborn thought, unable to tear his eyes away from the carnage. *Dozens* of damned people. The last thing he remembered clearly was drawing the sword. After that... only laughter and terrible screams. The thought of such a loss of control terrified him.

Shouts echoed in the distance, back in the direction of the merchant's quarter. The highborn looked for the temple executioners and found their bodies at the base of the rock pile just a few yards away, surrounding the corpse of the second blood witch. He tried to count the bodies of the lowborn, but gave up in disgust. There was no telling how many there were for certain, or if any might have escaped the slaughter and run for help.

Malus forced his body to work, weaving his way quickly among the fallen bodies. He noted absently how little blood there was – just blackened flesh and shrivelled organs.

Spite was not far from where Malus had dismounted, feeding warily on one of the dead men. The nauglir shied away at the highborn's approach. Malus snarled irritably at the warbeast. '*Stand,* damn you!' he shouted – and caught his hand tightening slowly around the hilt of the warpsword.

Malus froze. Eyeing the black blade warily, he slowly and deliberately slipped the sword back into its scabbard. Twice it seemed to get caught in the scabbard's mouth, forcing him to draw it out slightly and try to sheathe it again. When the weapon finally slid home the highborn breathed a sigh of relief.

Within moments the heat suffusing his muscles began to fade, like an iron plucked from the fire, leaving him feeling wretched and cold once more.

Caught between the dragon and the deep sea, Malus thought, fighting a wave of black despair. Which was the worse fate?

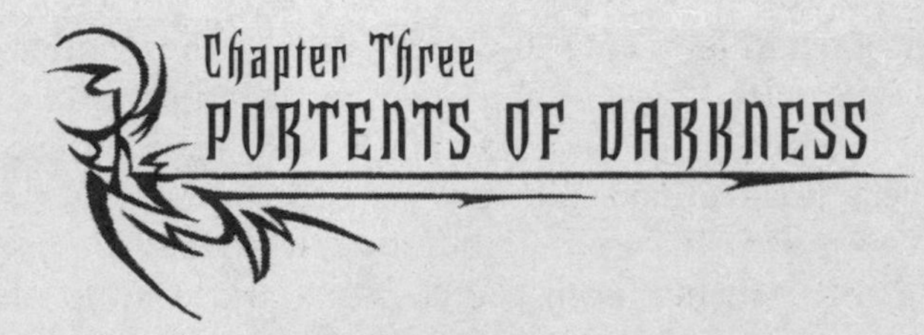

Chapter Three
PORTENTS OF DARKNESS

MOONLIGHT GLEAMED ALONG the gold fittings of the warpsword's scabbard and kindled a dusky fire in the depths of the oblong ruby set at the juncture of hilt and blade. Malus admired the relic fearfully for a moment, holding the sheathed weapon carefully in both hands. He fancied he could feel its heat, pulsing softly like a sleeping heart. He licked his cold lips nervously, then with a deep breath he laid the weapon on the fabric spread across his knees and wrapped it tightly from end-to-end in layers of frayed and dirty sailcloth. With each turn of the cloth he felt a bit colder, a bit smaller and more withered than before. When he was done, Malus tied off the bundle with loops of rough twine and then carried the wrapped weapon over to Spite. The cold one was crouched beneath the trees on the opposite side of the small forest clearing, watching its master warily with its red-ember eyes.

His face set in a mask of grim determination, Malus stowed the warpsword with his saddlebags, securing it tightly to his saddle beside the bag where the rest of the daemon's relics were kept. Reluctantly, he took his hands from the blade and patted the nauglir's flanks. 'No hunting tonight,' he said quietly, eyeing the dark depths of the surrounding wood. 'There's no telling what you might run into.'

It was only a few hours past sundown, and they were almost ten miles from Har Ganeth, deep in the wooded hills north and west of the city. The clearing was one he'd used often in the two months he'd prowled the Slaver's Road outside the City of Executioners. There was even a small lean-to built from pine boughs to provide some shelter from the elements and a store of firewood laid by. Lighting a fire was out of the question, however. The last thing he wanted to do was to advertise his presence, and he doubted the flame would warm his cursed bones anyway.

He'd escaped the city without further incident, though by the time he'd reached the wide city gate he could hear the first cries of alarm from the scene of the massacre. Malus trusted that the citizens would blame the attack on a band of zealots but he had no intention of putting his theory to the test. The highborn had all but galloped through the open gateway, relieved to find the Slaver's Road nearly empty of traffic. For the next few hours he'd worked his way westward along the road, keeping a wary eye out for plumes of dust rising on the horizon.

Malus had a very good reason for wanting to get out of Har Ganeth as quickly as he could: there was every chance that Malekith was on the way to the city with an army at his back, alerted by news of the temple uprising.

Though he'd personally ended Urial's coup, the highborn doubted that the Witch King would show him any gratitude. Malus had been a fugitive since early summer after murdering his father at Vaelgor Keep, scarcely twenty miles to the northeast. He'd done it to gain possession of the Dagger of Torxus, another of the daemon's damned relics, not that the motive made any difference according to the laws of the land. Malus's father had been the Vaulkhar of Hag Graef, one of the Witch King's lieutenants, and no one slew one of Malekith's vassals without his leave. He hoped that the Witch King thought him dead, slain along with thousands of druchii in a confused night battle outside Hag Graef several months before, though it wasn't something he was willing to bet his life on. His half-brother Isilvar, now Lurhan's only heir and Hag Graef's Vaulkhar, almost certainly knew the truth. The question was what would he do with the knowledge? Isilvar had very good reasons to want him dead, the least of which was a nasty scar across his throat that Malus had given him in a battle beneath their sister Nagaira's tower a few months ago.

Frowning in thought, Malus combed through his saddlebags and pulled out an oil-stained cloth bag and a small bottle of wine. Then he drew the heavy battle-axe from a loop on the nauglir's saddle and sank wearily to the ground beside the cold one's armoured flank. As he leaned back against the nauglir's side the great beast shifted, its blocky head swinging around to fix him with a beady glare. Malus gave the beast a haughty glare. 'Settle down,' he warned, and tried to get comfortable once more. Again, the nauglir recoiled from his touch, rising to its feet and giving its master a warning hiss.

'All right, all right!' Malus snapped, snatching up his axe and his store of food and stalking to the other side of the encampment. He sat down heavily with his back to a rotting log and fixed the warbeast with a murderous look. 'See if I let you eat the next dead horse we come to.'

After a few moments Spite lowered carefully back onto its haunches and rested its snout on the ground so that it could keep a wary eye on Malus. The nauglir had been acting very strangely ever since they'd returned from the City of the Ageless Kings, far north in the Chaos Wastes. He'd gone there in search of the real warpsword, only to fall into the clutches of the power-mad druchii zealots who'd stolen it. They had intended to kill him and feed upon his life essence, and so they'd crucified him in the broad plaza outside their temple.

He'd had no choice but to call upon Tz'arkan's power to escape. Events after that were somewhat hazy. The next thing he recalled clearly was standing on the bridge of stone outside the Sanctum of the Sword in the temple fortress in Har Ganeth and watching his half-sister Yasmir eating their brother Urial's still-beating heart.

The prophecy of the Scourge maintained that he was destined to marry Yasmir, now considered a living saint of the Bloody-Handed God. After witnessing what she'd done to Urial the very idea of wedding her made his blood run cold. *Perhaps if I'm lucky the warpsword will kill me before that becomes an issue*, Malus thought bleakly.

It was getting colder in the clearing as the moons climbed into the cloudy sky. Even in late summer the Land of Chill was true to its name. Malus unwrapped his meagre bundle of salted fish and yellow sauce and began to eat, chewing doggedly at the tough flesh and washing it down with swigs of vinegary wine. He took his time with the meal; as wretched as it tasted, it was still better than the hardtack that he would be eating come the morrow.

By the time he was done the moons were shining almost directly overhead and his breath made a faint mist in the cold air. Malus doggedly finished off the terrible wine and summoned up his nerve. The other reason he'd chosen such an isolated campsite was because he was in sore need of information, and some conversations were best kept private.

He also had a dreadful feeling that he wasn't going to like what he was about to learn.

Malus wiped his face and put away the cloth and empty flask, then sat cross-legged with his back to the fallen log and his stolen axe within easy reach. The highborn pulled off the armoured gauntlet covering his left hand. A plain silver ring glinted on his finger like a band of purest ice. He held it up to the moonlight, noting with a grimace that the veins on the back of his hand were black with the daemon's corruption.

The highborn made a fist, focusing his remorseless will on a single thought.

Eldire.

A faint, familiar breeze ghosted across Malus's face – and the daemon inside him writhed in anger. His muscles seized and his guts curdled; Malus toppled onto his side with a groan, doubling over with the sudden wave of nausea and pain. Pressure built within his head, as though the daemon had his brain in a vice, causing sparks to dance before his eyes. Malus rolled onto his stomach and vomited his meal onto the cold, hard ground, his breath coming in shallow gasps timed to the pounding in his skull.

The highborn rolled back onto his side, fetching up against the side of the log. He caught the scent of ashes, and then suddenly the pain and sickness was receding like a black, oily tide. The pounding in his skull eased, and Malus thought that he heard the daemon's angry voice receding into an infinite distance. When it was gone he was left trembling with a leaden cold that seemed to radiate from his very bones.

'What have you done?' spoke a woman's voice, hard and cold as carved marble. The words had a peculiar echo to them, as though spoken from deep within a well. 'You fool! Malus, what have you done?'

The highborn's eyes flickered open. Above him loomed a glowing apparition wreathed in pale silver light. 'Hello, mother,' he said, managing a bitter laugh. 'How I've missed your loving voice.'

She was statuesque and regal, clothed in the heavy, dark robes of the witches' convent. Her pale hands were clasped before her and her braided white hair seemed wrought from moonlight, haloing the cruel angles of her face. Her form was insubstantial – the highborn could see through her as though she were made of fog, picking out Spite's sloping form and red-ember eyes on the other side of the clearing. For all that, Malus felt the weight of Eldire's stare like a dagger-point against his skin.

'Impertinent wretch!' Eldire snapped. 'Your body belongs wholly to the daemon now. Your veins pulse with foul energies. I can even see the daemon itself, sliding like a leviathan beneath your pallid skin!'

'Does it coil about my heart like a nest of serpents?' Malus sneered, wiping his mouth with the back of his hand. 'Does it clutch my shrivelled brain in its dripping jaws? Your gifts are wasted in this case, mother. I've known this every minute of every day for nearly a year.'

Eldire's ghostly face blazed with fury. 'This is far worse than mere possession, child! You have taken the final step. I warned you of this, back in the dwarf tombs!'

'Do you imagine I did this by choice?' the highborn shot back. Grimacing against the pain in his guts, he pushed himself wearily upright and rested the back of his head against the moss-covered log. 'The damned warpsword wasn't in the temple after all. I had to go into the Chaos Wastes to claim it.' His gaze fell upon the back of his black-veined hand and his anger faded in a wave of disgust. 'It was either this or death; there were no other choices open to me. For now, I live, and while I live, I can fight.' He met the seer's forbidding gaze. 'And now I have the sword.'

Eldire's dark eyes widened a fraction of an inch. The fury ebbed from her alabaster face. 'You drew the burning blade,' she said, her voice slightly more hollow than before.

'There were very compelling reasons at the time. I won't bore you with the details,' Malus said darkly. 'Tz'arkan was even less pleased than you. It makes me wonder if perhaps the warpsword's power is strong enough to counteract the daemon's influence.'

Eldire frowned at her son. 'Perhaps,' she allowed, with a sigh like a wind seeping from a tomb. 'Khaine's hunger cares little for the schemes of other beings, even daemons as potent as Tz'arkan. In fact,' she said, her expression turning angry again, 'the warpsword is likely the only reason you have any consciousness left. Looking at you, it's a wonder that the daemon isn't able to make you dance like a puppet.'

The idea sent a chill down Malus's spine. His gaze drifted to the wrapped bundle of the warpsword. Could he afford to keep feeding its hunger? Could he afford not to? 'The daemon may possess my body, but I assure you, my will remains intact,' he said. 'I dance for no one, least of all that damnable fiend.' He paused, watching the black veins throb beneath his skin. 'What I want to know is what will happen once the daemon is freed.'

The seer's lips pursed in thought. 'That is an interesting question,' she said. 'By rights, your soul would be snuffed out like a candle flame as Tz'arkan claims your body as its host. Now, however...' After a moment Eldire made a faint shrug. 'I cannot say. It is possible that the sword might counteract the daemon's claim over you, but you may be certain that until the moment arrives Tz'arkan will take whatever steps it can to help decide the matter in its favour.'

Malus gave his mother a hard look. 'So you're saying all is not lost.'

'I'm saying that if you are very clever and very lucky you might manage to trade one doom for another,' the seer replied archly. 'The warpsword will kill you sooner or later, Malus. Now that you've drawn it you can't turn it loose.'

The highborn let out a weary sigh. 'All of us die, mother,' he said, staring into the darkness. 'So it's not much of a price to pay, now is it?'

'Bold words for someone who has never spoken with the dead,' Eldire replied. 'Nevertheless,' she said, raising a hand to pre-empt a retort from her son, 'what's done is done. You have the sword, and that is what is important. That leaves just one relic to reclaim.'

'The Amulet of Vaurog,' Malus said ruefully. 'I've no idea where it is and precious little time to look for it. As near as I can tell I have two months left to return to the temple and set the daemon free, and the trip alone takes almost a month and a half.' He shot Eldire a sidelong glance. 'So unless you've got the power to make me fly, I've only got two weeks left to find the last relic.'

Eldire hitched up the ghostly hem of her robe and bent close to Malus, so that mother and son were almost nose-to-nose. 'Would you like a pair of wings, Malus?' she asked, her voice dangerously sweet.

Malus's sarcastic reply turned to ice at the tone in his mother's voice. 'That's... generous...' he said carefully. 'But perhaps I should worry about finding the relic first and making the trip afterward.'

Eldire smiled a wolf's smile. 'A very wise decision,' she said, straightening once again. 'My time grows short,' she announced. 'Speaking to you in this way is very taxing, especially now that the daemon has grown so strong. Is there aught that you wish of me?'

'I was hoping you knew something about the amulet,' Malus said quickly, forcing himself to sit up straight. 'That was why I called you in the first place.'

'The amulet?' Eldire said. Already her form was losing its nebulous consistency, melting like morning fog. 'It is a potent talisman, wrought from meteoric iron in ages past. No weapon can harm the warrior who wears it.'

'Never mind what it does!' Malus cried. 'Do you know where it is?'

Eldire's image began to blur, dissolving into formless mist. Her answer was little more than a sigh.

'The path to the fifth amulet leads to Naggarond,' the seer replied. 'Seek the amulet in the lightless halls of the Fortress of Iron.'

By the time Malus had recovered his wits, Eldire was gone. He looked to Spite. The nauglir raised its massive head and let out an irritated snort.

'I couldn't have said it better myself,' the highborn said darkly, folding his arms tightly across his chest. 'The Witch King's own fortress. I should have known.'

One doom for another, he thought bitterly to himself, feeling the daemon's corruption rise like a black tide from his bones and spread beneath his skin.

MALUS AWOKE TO aches and pains from head to toe. The clearing was bathed in the pearly light of false dawn, and wisps of fog curled along the ground. He was laying on his side, wrapped tightly in a heavy cloak sodden with morning dew. A few feet away Spite slept with its head tucked behind its long, whip-like tail, hissing like a boiling kettle.

Long fingers teased gently at his scalp, the tips warm against his clammy skin. His sleep-fogged mind savoured the sensation as the fingers brushed against his right ear, sending a trickle of warmth flowing along its curved outer edge.

Another rivulet of heat flowed across his cheek and over the top of his lips. It tasted of salt and iron.

The highborn's eyes went wide. He opened his mouth to speak, but the words were blotted out by a crushing wave of agony that radiated from his skull. Malus writhed within the tight confines of his cloak, but try as he might he could not pull himself free.

Blood ran in a freshet across his face and down his neck. It flowed into his right eye and he gasped at another, fiercer wave of pain.

Helpless, blinking away the drops of blood catching in his eyelashes, Malus turned his head and looked up to find an armoured figure crouching at his shoulder. More blood poured down the back of his head as though his skull were a broken jug of wine.

Bright blood painted Lhunara's pale grey hands, pooling beneath torn black fingernails and running in jagged courses along her wrists. Her blue lips parted in a lunatic smile, and her one good eye shone with a fevered gleam. The other eye, swollen and black with rotting blood, rolled aimlessly in its socket.

'We are of one mind, my lord,' she said, her voice bubbling from liquefying lungs as she raised her hands to the awful wound on the right side of her skull. With a wet, slithering sound she pressed the grey matter in her palms deep into the maggot-infested cavity.

'One mind,' she said, then reached for his face. 'One heart. One eye...'

MALUS AWOKE SCREAMING, thrashing about in slick, dewy loam.

His heart lurched in terror as he found that his arms and legs were wrapped tight. Still half-blind and witless, he writhed and kicked, sputtering and howling like the damned. Then with a convulsive heave he tore one leg free and realised that he was tangled in his heavy cloak.

Panting furiously, Malus forced himself to close his eyes and rest his head against the damp earth. When the hammering in his heart had eased, he slowly and purposely untangled his limbs and spread the cloak open, heedless of the early-morning chill.

Finally, when his breathing had slowed, the highborn opened his eyes. It was well past dawn, and weak sunlight was streaming through the close-set branches of the tree over his head. A thick root bulged up from the ground under his back, pressing hard against his spine.

Frowning, Malus raised his head. He was lying on an animal path between stands of tall oaks. Green, dripping ferns brushed against his cheeks, making him shudder.

He was nowhere near the clearing he'd camped in.

Cursing blearily, he clambered to his feet. The forest stretched away in every direction. Bits of foliage were caught between the plates of his armour, and the palms of his hands were caked with dirt. Blessed Mother of Night, he thought. How did I get here? Memories of the night before were fuzzy at best. He remembered sitting in the darkness, trying to envision a way into Naggarond of all places... and then things became vague. Did I get drunk on that damned vinegary wine, he thought?

He did a slow turn about, casting his gaze frantically about in an attempt to get his bearings. The game trail looked familiar and at least headed south towards the edge of the forest. Rubbing his face with a grimy palm he started walking down the trail, suddenly conscious of the fact that his battle-axe was nowhere to be seen.

Malus followed the trail for nearly a mile through the dense foliage, growing more confused and apprehensive by the moment. As he went he began to notice signs that he might have followed the path previously. From the shallow footprints and broken branches it looked as though he'd been reeling along like a drunkard in the darkness. It was a wonder he hadn't impaled himself on a low branch or cracked open his skull against the side of a tree.

After walking a mile and a half he found himself fighting back a rising tide of panic. Then, off to the southwest, he heard a familiar steam-kettle hiss. With a sigh of relief the highborn left the path and made for the sound, thrashing impatiently through the undergrowth. After about a dozen yards the trees began to thin out, until finally he stumbled onto the edge of his campsite. Spite rose to its feet at his sudden appearance, wide nostrils flaring as it tasted his scent.

Malus stopped dead at the edge of the clearing, scanning the small space warily. His axe was still where he left it. Even the folded parcel of cloth that had contained his evening meal was still where he'd left it. Moving carefully, he crossed the campsite and approached the nauglir. 'Easy, Spite,' he said, reaching for his saddlebags. The cold one snorted at him, one red eye regarding him balefully as the highborn searched through his gear.

The three remaining wine bottles hadn't been touched. He checked each wax seal and found them perfectly intact.

Spite shifted on its broad, taloned feet and grumbled irritably. 'All right, all right,' Malus said, securing the saddlebags and slapping the cold one on the flank. 'Go. Hunt. I need to think.'

The highborn stepped away as the huge warbeast slipped with surprising stealth into the thick undergrowth. Then he turned and once more scanned the ground near where he'd sat. There was no sign of a disturbance. It was as though he'd simply stood up and walked off into the darkness.

Malus settled wearily against the log and tried to clean some of the dirt from his hands. Try as he might, he couldn't remember much of the night after he'd spoken with Eldire. Could she have done something to him? If so, why? He shook his head irritably. The idea made no sense.

Then there was the nightmare. He'd heard of druchii who cried out, even got up and moved about in the grips of a powerful nightmare. Had there been more to the dream that he didn't remember? Had the ghastly vision of Lhunara sent him fleeing into the depths of the forest? 'I may have to start drinking myself to sleep again,' he muttered sourly. 'Or hobbling myself at night like a horse.'

From off to the north came a sudden eruption of frenzied movement – something huge thrashed through the forest, snapping branches and slapping heavily against tree trunks. Malus grunted softly. Spite had already found a morning meal.

Then, as if in answer, came sounds of movement to the south, back in the direction of the road.

Without thinking, Malus snatched up his axe and rolled quietly into a crouch, peering warily over the top of the fallen log. Scarcely daring to breathe, he held perfectly still and strained his senses to the utmost. Moments later he heard a much fainter rustle in the undergrowth, perhaps twenty yards to the southeast. The highborn closed his eyes and tried to picture the surrounding terrain in his mind. Whatever it was, it sounded like it was working its way up the game trail he'd recently been following.

Then came another crackle of broken branches – this time directly to the south. The highborn bared his teeth.

It sounded like a hunting party. And it was coming his way.

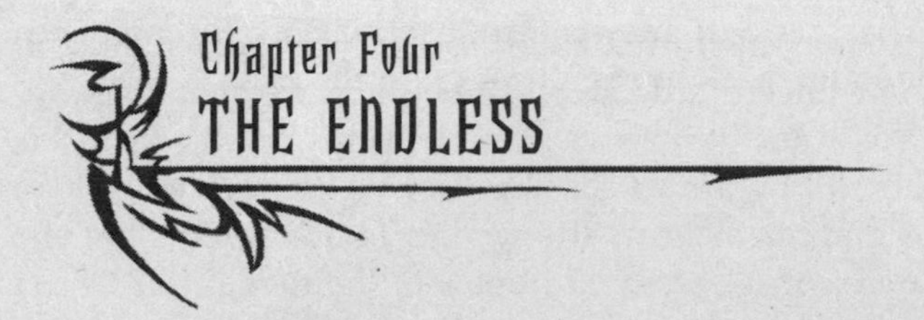

After everything he'd been through in the last ten months, Malus no longer believed in luck. Whoever the hunters were, they hadn't simply stumbled onto him by accident. He doubted they were city folk from Har Ganeth – the camp was too far away and too deep in the woods to catch the attention of a band of refugees. An autarii hunting party was a possibility. The Shades claimed the entire mountain range and hill country north of the Slaver's Road, and it wasn't unheard of for small raiding bands to find their way to the southern foothills to steal from westbound slave caravans. But no autarii worth his salt would be so clumsy as to give away his position, particularly in the deep woods.

That left only one possibility: they were men from Malekith's army.

Malus's hands tightened on the haft of his battle-axe and peered over the top of the log into the shadows beneath the thick trees. It was possible they were just a foraging party, hunting for deer or pheasant to feed the Witch King's warband. It was also possible that they were hunters of a different kind, combing the woods in search of him. But how could they have found me? Malus thought. He reckoned he knew these woods better than any soldier from Naggarond, and he'd been careful to cover his trail the evening before.

Undergrowth rustled off to the highborn's right, still some fifteen yards away. The hunters were moving cautiously and swinging a little further to the west. He turned his gaze to the east, hoping to catch some sign of movement from the second hunting party, but the dense foliage stymied him. Still, he thought, if I can't yet see them, they can't see me.

Then came the sharp sound of a branch snapping near the game trail. Ten yards away, he reckoned, and also a bit farther east. The two groups were swinging around the edge of the campsite. What was more, he suddenly realised that he'd heard no indications of movement from directly south. They know where the campsite is, he thought, feeling the hairs bristle on the back of his neck. They are trying to surround it, cutting me off from fleeing further northward.

He had to move now, before the noose closed around him. Fortunately Spite was somewhere north of him now, feeding on his morning meal. If he could reach the nauglir he was sure that he could outpace whoever was stalking him, fleeing northward into the foothills. Of course, that meant he'd be trespassing on autarii land, but first he had to survive to get there.

Still crouching low to the ground, Malus turned and scuttled across the campsite. As he did, the sounds of movement erupted from east and west. The hunters were making their move.

Malus ducked his head and followed the path that Spite had taken upon leaving camp. At least, he tried – not two feet beyond the edge of the clearing he crashed headlong into a briar thicket that the iron-skinned cold one had simply muscled its way through. Thorny branches lashed at the highborn's face and neck, eliciting a strangled hiss of pain. Malus lashed at the hedge with his axe, hoping that a few good strokes would be enough to hew his way past, but the thin, green branches rebounded from the weapon and lashed back at him like whipcords. Worse, the attempt made considerable noise, causing him to feel dangerously exposed. Malus gave up after a handful of noisy strokes and rushed to the west, looking for a clearer path through the undergrowth.

He heard someone burst from cover and dash into the clearing only a half-dozen yards behind him. Not waiting to see who it was, Malus ducked and dodged past thin saplings and drooping ferns, reaching the end of the thicket and cutting back northward again. His tense gaze scanned left and right, hoping to catch some sign of the nauglir's trail, but the cold one's path was almost invisible to his unskilled eyes. *The damn thing is almost thirty feet long and weighs a ton,* he thought irritably, *yet it can move like an autarii in the woods when it wants to.* For a moment he contemplated whistling for Spite – easier to bring the cold one to him than the other way around – but he was certain the hunters would hear him as well. He had no idea what would happen then, and didn't want to find out.

Malus strained his ears for the sound of pursuit and kept to the parts of the wood that offered the least amount of resistance, trading concealment for speed. The ground began to slope gently upward, starting the slow climb to the low foothills that were still more than a mile distant. Within a few minutes he came upon a small wooded hollow and on impulse he headed inside rather than skirt it.

The shadows beneath the close-set trees were deep, but at least it meant that there was less undergrowth to fight through. Almost immediately Malus found a narrow game trail winding through the centre of the hollow and followed it without hesitation. Seconds later he came upon a large pool of fresh blood splashed across the trail and found a pair of large, familiar footprints nearby.

Malus settled into a crouch, breathing heavily. He'd found the spot where Spite had ambushed his prey but the damned cold one was nowhere to be seen. Nauglir, like many predators, preferred to drag their food somewhere more secure before they felt safe enough to eat. Which meant that the warbeast could have gone off in nearly any direction.

A flicker of movement in the shadows to Malus's left brought him around, weapon at the ready. No one was there. The highborn turned in a slow circle, looking for any signs of danger. As near as he could tell, however, he was alone.

Branches crackled perhaps a dozen yards behind him. The hunters had reached the south end of the hollow.

Malus sank into a crouch, quickly sizing up the surrounding terrain. Did he dare make a stand here, or keep running? Now he regretted leaving the warpsword bound to Spite's saddle!

Moving as quietly as he could, Malus swung around the bloodstain so as not to leave a trail his enemies could follow, and sidled into the dense woods to the west of the path. Vines and brambles tugged at his hair and scraped against his steel armour, but he resisted the temptation to swipe them away with his axe. Instead he burrowed deeper, hoping to draw the vegetation behind him like a cloak.

A few yards further on the highborn came to the burnt and blasted trunk of an old oak tree. Clearly felled by lightning years ago, the shell of the old tree rose less than ten feet and terminated in a jagged, moss-covered stump. A cleft in the wide trunk ran from root level up to about waist height. Thinking quickly, Malus hurried to the cleft and carefully wormed his way inside.

Rotten, pulpy wood and squirming insects rained down on him as the edges of his armour plates scraped the inside of the tree. Malus closed his eyes and clamped his mouth tightly shut against the dank-smelling debris and braced his back against the far side of the tree. Then, moving carefully, he raised a foot and felt about for a toehold a few feet off the ground. Within moments his boot found a ridge that would support his weight. Gritting his teeth, the highborn pressed his back against the trunk and heaved upward. As his other foot came off the ground he fumbled quickly for another foothold and found one just above the cleft.

Working quickly, Malus forced his way three more feet up into the hollow trunk and hung there, scarcely daring to breathe.

No sooner had he stopped moving than he heard faint sounds of movement in the woods outside. The highborn stifled a bitter curse. He heard the swish of branches and the crackle of dead wood, and for the first time he heard hushed voices speaking in what sounded like druhir. From what he could tell there were at least three of them, but he couldn't quite make out what they were saying.

The voices drew nearer. The highborn heard the muted rattle of plate harness and the faint clatter of sword scabbards. Malus looked down at the narrow shaft of pale light shining through the cleft. As he watched, a shadow passed across the opening. He held his breath, expecting to see a head peer into the opening at any moment.

For several long moments the conversation continued. The words were strangely muffled; again, Malus couldn't quite divine their meaning, but he could guess from their cadence and tone that they were discussing where to look for him next. At length, one of the hunters seemed to arrive at a decision. With a grunt, the hunters moved off, apparently continuing to head farther west. The highborn let out a slow breath. Once he could no longer hear any sounds of movement he counted slowly to one hundred, then carefully eased himself back to earth.

Getting out of the cleft proved much more difficult than getting in. In the end he was forced to turn about and sink to his knees, then crawl backwards out of the hole. At any moment he expected blades or crossbow bolts to bite into his back, but within a few moments he was free. Brushing rotted wood and insects out of his hair, Malus regained his bearings and headed off east as fast as he could manage.

He hadn't gone more than a few yards when he heard a familiar growl some ways to the north. Now at least he knew which direction the cold one had gone in. The question was whether or not the hunters had heard the same thing, and what they would make of it.

Malus continued west, heading back to the game trail. He could follow the faint trail as far north as he could, hopefully making better time than his pursuers, but if they were now heading in Spite's direction as well he was sure to cross their path. Unless he continued west, crossing the game trail and then doubling back in a wide circle to come at Spite from the east. But doing so would take time. Which risk was more worthwhile?

Caught up in his internal debate, Malus almost missed the flicker of movement to his right. Certain that this time it wasn't his imagination, he fetched up against the bole of a tree and dropped to a crouch, scanning the deep shadows all around him.

Nothing moved. There were no sounds save for the restless wind. Malus waited for ten seconds, seeing nothing, then took a deep breath and started off once more. He went for ten yards and then abruptly stopped, whirling to the right.

There! He saw a shadow flit from the darkness beneath one tree to the next. It was the size of a raven, and darted through the air at shoulder height. The hair on the highborn's neck stood on end. He was being hounded by a shade, no doubt reporting his location back to its master. Even now, Malus imagined the huntsmen he'd encountered were doubling back, following the call of their unearthly hound.

The time for stealth was past. Malus turned and ran for the game trail as fast as he could. With the weight of his armour his footfalls echoed through the dense wood, but all that counted now was speed. Such was his haste that he ran full-tilt into the same thicket he'd encountered earlier. Needle-like thorns raked his face and hands, but with a savage snarl he hacked wildly at the branches with his axe and bulled his way through.

Panting like a dog Malus stumbled onto the game trail – and saw at once that he was not alone.

Three figures stood in a tight group a few yards down the trail to Malus's right. They wore black, woollen robes over breeches and boots, and their torsos were protected by silver steel breastplates engraved with elaborate designs and sorcerous runes. Their bodies were wrapped in heavy, hooded cloaks, and their faces were hidden behind masks of polished silver. Three female faces worked in cold metal regarded him curiously, their polished features seeming to float within the black depths of their hoods. One of the figures raised a black-gloved hand, and Malus turned and ran northward as fast as his feet would carry him.

'Spite!' Malus called, throwing all caution to the wind. Fortunately for him, the game trail twisted and turned, quickly carrying him out of sight of the three shade-casters. Had he run afoul of the autarii after all? The three women he'd seen were witches, of that he had no doubt, but no witches he'd ever seen wore masks and archaic armour over their robes.

Shouts and sounds of movement rang out from Malus's left; the hunters he'd met by the tree were closing in. Off to the north he thought he heard another low growl from Spite. He tried to gauge how far off the sound was when he turned another corner and an armoured figure stepped onto the path directly in front of him.

For a fleeting second Malus thought one of the witches had somehow flown ahead to cut him off. The figure wore black robes and silver steel armour, but the ornate, archaic plates covered the hunter from neck to toe like a proper knight. Two swords hung from the hunter's belt and his face was hidden behind a mask worked in the shape of a leering daemon. A hadrilkar of polished gold glinted from the depths of the man's hood.

The hunter raised a gauntleted hand. Malus was too close to swing the axe, so instead he held the haft out before him and crashed directly into the man. With a crash of wood against steel the masked figure fell backwards and Malus leapt over him without breaking stride.

More shouts sounded behind him, and then he heard a whickering sound slice through the air behind him. Something heavy struck him between the shoulder blades and then a steel web wrapped his chest and arms in a fearsome embrace. Barbed hooks scraped across his armour and locked inside its crevices, and suddenly Malus was off-balance and stumbling forward. With a furious effort he tried to regain his balance, but then his foot struck a protruding root and he crashed headlong to the ground.

The highborn thrashed and rolled, wrestling with the implacable grip of the net. Footfalls sounded behind him as he struggled, and three masked figures loomed into view over him. One grabbed his ankles, flipping him expertly onto his back, while another grabbed the folds of the net that laid across his chest. The third warrior stood a few feet away and slowly drew his sword.

With a snarl Malus pulled one foot free as the man holding the net began to straighten. On impulse the highborn kicked the warrior in the side of the head, and he fell sideways with a muffled curse. As he did he inadvertently pulled part of the net with him, freeing Malus's right arm. The warrior who had been holding his feet let go and lunged for the highborn, but Malus rolled quickly to his left and unrolled himself from the barbed trap. Driving the second warrior back with a savage sweep of his axe, Malus struggled to his feet – just as the masked swordsman lunged in from the highborn's left.

The warrior's blade was just a silver flicker in the forest gloom. Battlefield instincts alone spared Malus; without thinking he pivoted on his right foot and blocked the sword stroke with the haft of his axe. As it was, the force of the blow nearly drove Malus back to his knees, and before he could recover the swordsman pressed his attack, landing two more solid blows that nearly knocked the highborn off his feet.

Whoever the warriors were, they were tough and skilled opponents. Without a word shared between them the masked men fanned out in a loose semicircle, clearly working to hem him in. The other men kept their swords in their scabbards, however, leaving the lone swordsman to batter Malus's failing guard. The highborn gave ground quickly, retreating further north up the path, but within moments one of the hunters was going to cut behind him and seal off his retreat.

Malus suffered another ringing blow to the haft of his axe and risked a hurried feint at the swordsman's face. The short swing checked the warrior's advance for half a second, but it was enough for the highborn to spin on the ball of his left foot and then lunge at the masked hunter who had circled around behind him. Caught off guard, the warrior tried to retreat, but the highborn charged him with a bestial roar and caught him with a vicious blow that struck sparks from his ornate breastplate. The force of the blow knocked the man from his feet, and the highborn charged past him and continued along the path.

'Spite!' Malus called again, and immediately was answered with a sharp hiss just ten yards off the path to his right. Without hesitation the highborn plunged into the undergrowth, hacking bushes and saplings out of his path with wild sweeps of his axe. If he could just get to the nauglir's side he could turn the tide of the battle in his favour.

Malus caught the sharp smell of spilled blood. Up ahead he caught sight of the nauglir's scaled back and grinned fiercely. The cold one had dragged his kill to another clearing almost a hundred yards farther up the hollow.

'Up, Spite, up!' he cried to the crouching warbeast. Malus could hear the sounds of the masked warriors in close pursuit a scant few yards behind him. As he plunged into the clearing his looked for the wrapped bundle of the warpsword on the cold one's back.

Instead he saw a black-robed figure standing close to the nauglir's saddle. One gloved hand rested on the side of Spite's neck, and the nauglir's eyes were downcast in submission. The witch regarded him impassively from the depths of her silver mask as Malus ground to a sudden halt.

Two more witches glided silently from the shadows to Malus's left and right, attended by two warriors each who advanced with swords in hand. The highborn's three pursuers charged into the clearing directly behind him, completing the encirclement.

Malus turned slowly in place, regarding each of the hunters in turn. His gaze passed from masked face to masked face, dismayed and bewildered by their strange appearance. These were no autarii, he realised. No group of shades would be so regimented.

The highborn stopped in his tracks. Each of the warriors wore the same golden collar. *Gold*, not silver or even silver steel. Peering closely at one of the hadrilkars, Malus saw that it was worked in the shape of a pair of twining dragons.

His breath caught in his throat. These were no mere hunters, Malus realised. He knew who they were, though few had ever seen them face-to-face.

They were the personal bodyguards and agents of the Witch King. They were the Endless.

Chapter Five
FORTRESS OF IRON

BLACK ICE POURED from Malus's veins as the seven warriors closed in around him.

The rush of daemonic power shocked him, drawing a horrified cry from the highborn's throat. Time stretched like a bowstring; the movements of the Endless slowed to a turgid crawl, even as Malus's own body seethed with merciless vigour. Inwardly the highborn recoiled in terror and disgust from his unexpected salvation.

'I did not ask for this, daemon,' he hissed. 'You cannot force your damned gifts upon me!'

Things have changed, Darkblade, Tz'arkan said. His laughter trembled along Malus's skin. *I am now free to protect you as I see fit. I would think you would be grateful. Do you imagine that Malekith despatched his chosen with orders to kill you? Had he wanted you dead he could have sent ten thousand spearmen into the woods to root you out like a boar. No, they are here to drag you back to Naggarond in chains, where you will suffer torments that no sane druchii can imagine.*

'Take it back!' Malus snarled. 'Take your cursed ice from my veins. I neither want nor need it!'

You cannot turn back the seasons, Tz'arkan replied coldly. *You had your spring and your summer, little druchii. Soon it will be autumn. Winter cannot be far behind. The ice will come whether you wish it or not.*

Malus clenched his fists around the battered haft of his axe and roared like a wounded beast. The masked warriors were still gliding towards him, poised between one step and the next. Were he able to see their faces he imagined that they would be stretching like melted wax, surprise registering by degrees as the highborn seemed to blur before them. Then, like a butcher, he settled on his first victim and prepared to drown his misery in a tide of hot blood. Yet before he could take a single step a cold, melodious voice spoke in his ear.

'Your sorcery is impressive, Malus of Hag Graef, but in the end it changes nothing.'

The highborn whirled, fear tightening his throat. His axe sang through the air, angling for the witch's neck, but she moved as though he were standing still. She reached forward without apparent effort and touched her fingertips to his armoured chest.

Blue fire exploded behind his eyes. He felt himself falling, the silver face of the witch receding into darkness. Her voice tolled after him like a bell.

'You belong to the Witch King now.'

NIGHT HAD FALLEN by the time he woke again. Malus opened his eyes to the shifting hues of the northern lights in an unsettlingly clear late-summer sky. The stars were cold and pitiless as diamonds, and the twin moons cast strange shadows across the foggy landscape. Black-robed figures moved silently at the corners of his vision, and he heard people speaking in terse, hushed tones.

He was stretched out like a corpse on the hard ground, still cased in his battered armour. He wasn't bound in any way, but his body felt like lead. With a grunt, he tried to sit upright. It was all he could do just to prop himself up on his elbows.

Malus saw at once that he was in the middle of a small camp, somewhere along the Slaver's Road west of Har Ganeth. There were no fires, only small globes of witchlight resting on low, iron tripods, and perhaps a dozen tents set in orderly clusters around the spot where he lay. Masked warriors were busy dismantling and stowing the tents as the highborn watched, while another group saddled a score of coal-black horses hitched to a picket line a dozen yards away. Grey sea fog curled around the steeds' glossy black hooves, and their eyes glowed green in the reflected witchlight.

The Endless went about their tasks all around Malus, paying him as much attention as they might give to a bedroll. A quick check showed that his axe was nowhere to be seen, and they'd plucked his two daggers from his belt. There were no irons to bind his wrists or ankles, which implied a great deal about his captors' capabilities. If he tried to run, the Endless and their witches were certain he would not get far.

'You are awake,' spoke an unearthly, musical voice. It was cold and sweet as a trumpet or a silver bell, and sent shivers down the highborn's spine. He tried to turn his head to glance at the witch, but the effort left him exhausted. Malus sank back to the ground as the masked druchii circled around him and knelt gracefully at his side. She held a narrow decanter of cut red glass in one hand and a polished silver cup in the other. 'That is good. We will be leaving soon.'

She poured a small measure of a black liquid into the cup and held it out to Malus. The highborn studied her eyes warily. They were wide and dark within the gleaming oculars of the mask, and reminded him of nothing so much as the frank, earnest stare of a child. Setting his jaw, he lifted himself up on one elbow and slowly reached for the cup. 'Where is the army?' he asked wearily.

The witch cocked her head to one side. 'Army? There is no army.'

Malus frowned, his dark brows furrowing in consternation. He studied the black liquid at the bottom of his cup and took a small sip. The potent liquor seared his tongue and flowed like molten iron down his throat. Tears sprang to his eyes. 'Then where is Malekith?' he gasped, fighting the urge to cough.

'The Witch King is in Naggarond,' she said, as though it explained everything. 'We have been commanded to bring you to him.'

The liquor seethed inside Malus's guts, but it also returned a small measure of strength to his limbs. Steeling himself, he finished off the cup. 'Reminds me of the time I drank some lamp oil as a child,' he said hoarsely. 'Honestly, the oil had more flavour.'

'It is a dwarf liquor called barvalk,' the witch said, taking the cup from him. 'Dark riders carry it on cold winter nights. It keeps the blood hot and the mind sharp.'

'Probably takes the tarnish off silver as well,' he muttered, but silently admitted that his limbs had begun to loosen and his mind was alert and awake. With a rueful grin he levered himself fully upright and stretched his arms and shoulders.

The witch was well within reach. Her stare was guileless and her manner relaxed. It would take no effort at all to seize her and close his hands around her neck. But what then, Malus thought? Was she the witch that had felled him in the wood with but a single touch? He could not tell. And even if he did slay her, what then? He was surrounded by more than a dozen warriors, and even if he could somehow fight his way free, the Endless had already demonstrated they could track him easily with their magic.

Malus's shoulders slumped within the confines of his armour. Putting him in irons was redundant. There was nowhere he could go, and they knew it.

Then he remembered what Eldire had told him: *the path to the fifth relic leads to Naggarond.*

It was just possible that falling into the clutches of the Endless was a blessing in disguise.

'All right,' Malus said, trying to sound resigned to his fate. 'What next?'

The witch rose to her feet. 'There is food prepared in the tent yonder,' she said, pointing over Malus's shoulder. 'If you are hungry, eat. We will be riding through the night and will not pause again until midday tomorrow.'

Malus nodded. In truth, food was the last thing on his mind at that point, but better to fuel mind and body while he could. 'Where is my mount?'

The witch turned and inclined her gleaming mask towards the line of trees to the north. 'Your cold one is being tended to there, beyond the camp,' she said. 'Go to it after you have broken your fast, and wait for the order to depart.'

Without so much as a farewell the witch began to walk away. 'Wait!' Malus called. 'What is your name?'

The druchii paused. Her head turned slightly, moonlight glinting on one rounded cheek. 'I have no name,' she said, childlike amusement in her voice. 'I am Endless.' Without waiting for a reply she joined a group of figures packing saddlebags nearby. Soon Malus couldn't tell for sure which of the identical figures was her.

The highborn shook his head wearily and clambered to his feet. Malekith's bodyguards continued breaking camp swiftly and efficiently, hardly sparing their prisoner a sideways glance. Not twenty yards to the south a caravan of flesh merchants were driving their wheeled cages northward up the Slaver's Road, heading for Karond Kar. He listened to the drovers curse the stolid oxen as they went, harangued in turn by the slave master and his sons. One of the young druchii slavers looked up at that moment and stared curiously at the small encampment. He saw Malus watching him and raised his coiled scourge in salute.

Malus raised his hand in return, and the young slaver spurred his horse and cantered to the head of the caravan. Still shaking his head, the highborn headed for the tent that the witch had indicated, hoping that the bodyguards had brought some meat and cheese, and perhaps a bit of decent wine.

ONCE CAMP WAS broken and the baggage packed the Endless set a gruelling pace as they bore their prisoner back to Naggarond. Mounted on their preternatural steeds the masked druchii rode all through the night and half of the following day before finally calling a halt in the middle of a cold and desultory rain.

Horses snorted and stamped, their breath pluming in the chilly air as they were led off the road into the tall grass. The animals paid no heed at all to the cold one in their midst; sired from thoroughbred stock brought from drowned Nagarythe, the dark steeds were foaled in the sorcerous stables of Naggarond itself, and feared neither man nor beast. Cousins to the dark steeds that the kingdom's messengers rode, they were fleet as storm winds when given their head, and could run for days without tiring.

For Spite's part, the nauglir paid little heed to anything, including Malus himself. Since the encounter with the Endless near their camp in the woods, the cold one had been strangely subdued and passive, following commands as meekly as a whipped slave. On the road the cold one loped along at the same pace as the rest of the party, ignoring the highborn's subtle commands.

The nauglir followed the horses off the road and settled onto its haunches, its head perking up a bit at the welcome caress of the rain. Malus slid from the saddle and tried to stretch the kinks out of his hips and shoulders. Though no stranger to hard riding, more than fourteen hours in the saddle left him feeling as though he'd been beaten with a club.

Masked druchii slid effortlessly from their saddles and silently inspected their mounts, checking hooves, muscles and tendons with expert hands. Malus did the same for Spite, although the highborn was checking for telltales of a very different kind.

He found the cluster of magical runes within moments, painted with some kind of indigo dye onto the nauglir's bony skull. The rain had no effect on them, nor did they blur when he rubbed them with his thumb. Malus patted Spite's neck resignedly. The

Endless had usurped his control over his own mount and effectively turned Spite into a jailer of sorts. He couldn't spur the cold one to turn on the riders even if he wanted to.

With nothing else to do, Malus leaned against Spite's flank and waited. After a few minutes one of the warriors made his way down the line, holding a bottle of barvalk and half a sausage. Malus steeled himself and took the proffered cup when his turn came, then wolfed down a thick slice of sausage. As soon as the warrior had finished making his rounds he jogged back to the head of the line and without a word the Endless climbed back into the saddle. Their midday break had lasted little more than fifteen minutes.

They rode through the rest of the day and well into the night. Ahead of them went the dragon banner of the Witch King of Naggaroth, and slave caravans travelling in either direction pulled aside and waited with heads bowed as the black riders thundered past. It was nearly four hours past sunset when the Endless finally called a halt, leading their mounts off the road and preparing a cold meal by witchlight. Cold, wet and aching from head to toe, Malus pulled his bedroll from the saddle and fell wearily to the ground beside Spite.

No sooner had he closed his eyes than one of the witches was kneeling beside him with a handful of salted fish and a hunk of bread wrapped in a greasy square of cloth. He took the food without thinking, his exhausted brain only dimly aware that it was close to midnight and the warriors were climbing back in their saddles again. Groaning, the highborn stowed his bedroll and climbed back onto his mount. He ate his meagre rations as they rode.

By the end of the second evening the black riders had reached the western end of the Sea of Malice, and were within a day's ride of the great crossroads where the Slaver's Road met the Spear Road as it headed north to the Wastes. The ration of barvalk at each rest stop had grown more generous, and Malus found himself growing accustomed to the taste. It didn't relieve the aches and pains of the endless ride but it made them slightly more tolerable. As the riders ate and rested, Malus resisted his body's demand for sleep and spent the time carefully arranging his bags. He dug into the pack where three of the daemon's relics were hid and fished out the wrapped bundle that contained the Idol of Kolkuth. He could feel the coldness of the brass figure through the layers of frayed cloth as he set it atop the rest of the bag's contents. During the day's travel he'd worked out a plan of escape. Once the Endless had got him inside the Iron Fortress he would wait until the last moment before seizing the idol and using its power to transport himself away from his captors. He felt certain that once he was inside the fortress he could find ample hiding places from which to begin his hunt for the Amulet of Vaurog.

Providing, of course, that the witches couldn't simply use their shades to locate him once more – and that their sorcerous hold on Spite didn't force the nauglir to turn on his own master.

The Endless rotated their riders through different points in their formation as they travelled; Malus wasn't sure of the reason why, unless perhaps it was to limit their exposure to him as much as possible. After the second day he thought to start a conversation with one of the witches riding beside him, and was surprised when she answered every question he put to her. She told him how the

Endless were given to the Iron Fortress as babes, taken as a sort of tithe from each of the highborn families in Naggarond. The witches received training by Morathi herself, while the warriors were taught by a highborn named Lord Nuarc, the finest warlord in the Witch King's warband. They served Malekith until death, at which point their mask and gear were given to a waiting neophyte. There were always a thousand of the Endless, guarding the precincts of the Iron Fortress and marching with the Witch King when the druchii went to war.

From what Malus could determine, the bodyguards wanted for nothing and possessed not a shred of independent thought or ambition. They were essentially incorruptible, a realization that both frustrated and horrified him at the same time.

Tempted by the witch's loquacity and her apparent lack of guile, Malus asked her how they'd managed to find him. 'It must have been sorcery,' he said offhandedly. 'How else would you have known to look in a nameless clearing in the middle of a vast forest?'

'We are all trained in shade-casting,' the witch replied. Her childlike voice was tinged with surprise, as though it were the most obvious question in the world. 'It is nothing to summon a fetch and have it search for you, providing you have the subject's name.'

'A fetch?' Malus asked.

The witch giggled behind her silver mask. 'The weakest of shades; little more than a fragment of spirit essence, intelligent enough to command but utterly devoid of will or initiative. They can be set to simple tasks, but their reach isn't very long.' She regarded Malus with a condescending shake of her head. 'I'm surprised you know so little, given your demonstration in the forest.'

'My knowledge is... specialised,' Malus replied. 'You say their reach is short?'

She nodded. 'Yes. They have little strength of their own, and must depend upon the energies of the summoner to remain active in the physical realm. A shade-caster can command a fetch over a few dozen miles, perhaps, but no more.'

The highborn looked away, pretending to study the faint line of Dachlan Keep in order to mask his frown of dismay. A dozen miles, he thought? Not much distance for a sorcerer, perhaps, but that would mean he would have to use the idol to leave Naggarond completely in order to escape their reach. Perhaps if he could find a place to hide somewhere in the nearby hills and then use the idol to come and go from the fortress...

Suddenly he straightened in the saddle. Malus turned to the witch. 'You said that a fetch couldn't reach for more than a few dozen miles?'

'Of course,' she replied.

'Then how did you know where to look for me? I could have been in Har Ganeth, or on the road to Karond Kar – I could have been at sea aboard a corsair, for the Dark Mother's sake.'

The witch shrugged. 'We were told to look for you along the Slaver's Road,' she said.

And how did Malekith know that, Malus thought? He was certain that he wasn't going to like the answer.

THEY CAME UPON the crossroads at well past midnight of the fourth day. The air was cool and clear, and the highborn shivered in the saddle from exhaustion as much as dread as the riders slowed their mounts to a walk and passed among the forest of burning souls.

The last time Malus had been this way was at the head of a small army, marching south to conquer Hag Graef in the name of Balneth Bale. The withered figures, wired to tall iron poles all around the crossroads and set alight with sorcerous fire, had held little terror for him then. Now he found himself listening to their faint, maddened cries and dreading the sight of the empty stake that the Witch King had set aside for him. Only those highborn who'd broken Malekith's laws were sentenced to burn at the crossroads, some lingering in agony for years as the elements wore away their bodies inch by inch. As Malus rode among the guttering lamps that used to be powerful men he could not help but tremble at the fate that awaited him. He reached back and checked the bag where the idol was kept, making certain he could reach it quickly when the time came.

On the other side of the crossroads lay a narrow ribbon of road that gleamed ghostly white under the moonlight. The Hateful Road led to Naggarond alone, and was paved with the skulls of a hundred thousand elves. The hooves of the dark steeds clattered hollowly on the magically treated bones and the riders sat straighter in the saddle as they drew closer to home.

The road wound among dark, lifeless hills and through echoing hollows dense with oak and ash, while in the distance the high walls and pointed towers of Naggarond rose ever higher into the indigo sky. Glimmering witchlight shone like a thousand eyes from the buildings of the fortress city, lending it a kind of cold, brooding life. This was not a place built upon ruthless power like Hag Graef, or stained with bloodlust like Har Ganeth – Naggarond was black, eternal hate quarried from cold marble and unyielding iron. It was the implacable heart of the druchii given form.

They travelled the Hateful Road for another hour, until finally they crested a rocky ridge and came upon a flat, featureless plain that stretched between the curving arms of a bleak mountainside. Naggarond curled upon itself like an enormous dragon upon the plain, surrounded by a gleaming wall nearly sixty feet high. Tall towers bristling with iron spikes rose from the wall every mile or so along its length, sited to rain clouds of arrows and heavy stones upon any invader. Ahead, Malus could see a massive gatehouse that was a small fortress unto itself, looming over a double portal wrought from slabs of polished iron nearly twenty feet high. The highborn shook his head in wonder. He'd once thought that Hag Graef's fortifications were fearsome, but nothing compared to Naggarond's forbidding bulk.

The dark riders led their steeds directly across the plain and approached the iron gates. No challenge issued from the gatehouse's jagged battlements; evidently the mere sight of the gleaming silver masks of the Endless was sufficient. With a terrible, echoing groan one of the massive gates swung open and the column trotted down a long, wide tunnel that ran beneath the gatehouse. Darkness pressed in from all sides, and the highborn fought to keep from hunching his shoulders at the thought of the murder holes and oil flues that doubtless pierced the stone overhead.

Malus expected to emerge from the tunnel into a large, open square, much as in the style of other druchii cities. Instead he found himself in a narrow lane overlooked by tall, stone buildings with deep-set oaken doors. Witchlights glowed from sconces hanging over many of the doorways, creating pools of flickering light amid a twisting path of abyssal shadow. The hooves of the dark steeds struck sparks from the grey cobblestones and sent up a thunderous clatter that reverberated from the close-set walls.

All druchii cities were treacherous, labyrinthine places, full of blind alleys and confusing turns designed to entrap and kill the unwary, but Naggarond was unlike any living city Malus had ever seen. Once inside the walls there were no landmarks to navigate by; nearly every street ended at a crossroads that connected to three other narrow lanes, all leading off in unpredictable directions. None of the buildings he saw bore signs or sigils that told what they were, and if there were market squares anywhere he never saw them. Within minutes he was utterly lost, and he knew full well they had only just entered the outer wards of the city.

They rode for more than an hour through the labyrinth, alone but for the echoes of their passage. Malus saw not a single living thing along the way: no citizens or city guards, no drunkards or thieves, penny oracles or cutthroats. It reminded him of nothing more than the houses of the dead, that city of crypts in the east where the ancient dead of Nagarythe were bound fearfully in vaults of stone.

There were three more defensive walls that subdivided the city, closed by three more heavy gates of iron. Tall, silent houses pressed hard against either side of these inner walls; as the first of the six cities, Malus had the sense that it had grown in fits and starts as the kingdom prospered, expanding beyond its own walls again and again until it was ringed like an old, gnarled tree.

Thus, when they paused before a fourth wall of gleaming stone it took several long moments before Malus's exhausted mind registered the narrow, arched gate and the gatehouse formed of blades of forged iron.

Witchlights shone from the oculars of iron dragons that rose to either side of the formidable gate, their spread wings formed of hammered iron plates as sharp-edged as swords. Beyond the gatehouse rose a profusion of close-set towers like a thicket of polished spear-blades, pierced by slitted windows that glowed with sorcerous fire. Tendrils of vapour rose from behind the walls of the iron fortress, rising among the towers and reaching for the twin moons with claw-like fingers.

They had come at last to the Fortress of Iron, citadel of the undying Witch King.

Chapter Six
THE WITCH KING

A RATTLING BOOM reverberated from the iron gatehouse, startling Malus from his exhausted stupor, and the arched gate swung inward on ancient, dwarf-wrought hinges. The highborn felt a chill race down his spine as the black gate swung open and he stared into the blackness beyond. He feared to tread any deeper into the Witch King's domain, but he knew that he had to get at least a glimpse at the fortress grounds to allow the Idol of Kolkuth to get him inside. As the first of the riders nudged their dark steeds forward Malus reached back and loosened the flap on the bag where the idol was kept.

The passage through the gate was shorter than he expected, barely twelve feet from one end of the tunnel to the other. Beyond lay a small courtyard paved with flagstones of polished slate and bounded by statues of imposing druchii knights and rearing dragons. Above them loomed the sharp-edged towers of Malekith's citadel and the vassal lords of his warband, casting a deep shadow over the weary travellers. As Malus led Spite into the courtyard he felt the weight of a terrible gaze fall upon him; for a moment he felt like a rabbit caught in the shadow of a swooping hawk, and cold, unreasoning terror seized his heart and turned his muscles to ice. Even Spite felt it, causing the massive warbeast to sink onto its haunches and snap its jaws at the empty air. Just as quickly as it struck, the terrible pressure eased, and Malus caught the hint of a sinuous shifting amid the thick shadows that lay across the paving stones. He stole a glance upwards and caught a faint hint of motion, as though a great serpent were coiling about one of the citadel's tallest towers. Then he glimpsed the outline of a long, narrow head silhouetted against the moonlight, and a pair of glowing red eyes that brooded over the dark city with lordly disdain. A black dragon, Malus realised with a shudder. His jaw gaped at the terrible sight.

Malus was so caught up with the sight of the fearsome beast that he paid no heed whatsoever to the highborn that awaited them in the middle of the courtyard until he spoke. 'Are you certain you have the right man?' the highborn rasped in a powerful, commanding voice. 'He looks like a corpse.'

The highborn's tone snapped Malus out of his reverie. He saw the Endless sliding from their saddles and watched the masked warriors bow their heads respectfully to the druchii lord, who returned the gesture with a disapproving scowl. Exhaustion and spite emboldened Malus's tongue. 'Lord Nuarc, I presume?'

'Did I give you leave to open your damned mouth, boy?' Lord Nuarc snarled. He was a tall and powerfully built druchii, clad in enamelled plate armour ornamented with gilt etchings and potent runes of protection over a skirt of shining ithilmar mail. His paired swords were masterworks, their pommels set with rubies the size of sparrow's eggs and resting in scabbards decorated with ruddy gold, and a cloak of glossy black dragonscale hung about his broad shoulders. Even without the thick gold hadrilkar circling his neck it was clear that he was a powerful noble and a member of the Witch King's personal retinue. His sharp nose was scarred in two places by sword-strokes, and a star-shaped dimple of scar tissue on the side of his neck spoke of the spear thrust that had ravaged his voice. The druchii's black eyes shone with keen wit and hinted at a will stronger than steel. His black hair, streaked with grey, was pulled back from his lean face and bound with a band of gold.

'He can be no other, my lord,' said one of the warriors, speaking in a voice eerily identical to the witch Malus had spoken with in their time on the road. 'We found him in the forest near Har Ganeth as you said. By his name the shades knew him.'

Malus leaned back and reached his hand beneath the flap of his saddlebag. The idol's icy surface burned against his fingertips. He tried to visualize a spot back along the road, someplace near woods and hills where he could lie low and plan his next move.

Nuarc looked Malus over again and shook his head. 'I wouldn't have believed it.' He looked the highborn in the eye. 'How did a shrivelled wretch like yourself kill Lurhan of Hag Graef?'

'With a sword. How else?' Malus sneered, his ire getting the better of him. If Nuarc was expecting excuses or snivelling pleas for mercy he was going to be disappointed. 'People have a habit of underestimating me, Lord Nuarc. I tend to make them regret it.'

Nuarc studied Malus for a moment, then nodded appraisingly. 'Brave but stupid,' he declared. 'I suspected as much.' He frowned at the highborn. 'Take your hand out of your bag, boy,' he snapped. 'We didn't bring you all this way to steal your trinkets.'

'No, you brought me here to hang me at the crossroads,' Malus shot back. 'Am I supposed to feel grateful that you won't steal my possessions until after I'm dead?'

'Dead?' Nuarc exclaimed. 'If the Witch King wanted you dead you and I would be having a very different kind of conversation right now.' His lip curled in disdain. 'For the moment, Malekith simply wishes to speak to you.'

Malus had to stop and replay Nuarc's words in his head. 'He wants to speak to me?' he echoed. His exhausted mind couldn't make sense of what he'd been told.

'I'm not in the habit of repeating myself, boy,' Nuarc growled. 'Now get out of that damned saddle. The Witch King knows you've arrived, but I won't send you to the Dragon Court looking like some flea-bitten autarii.'

Nuarc's iron-tinged rasp galvanized Malus's near-senseless body into motion. Before he was fully aware of it he was climbing down from Spite and standing uneasily on the slate paving stones. As if on cue, a pair of beastmasters with ornate kheitans and beast prods appeared from the shadows, ready to take charge of the sullen nauglir.

'Follow me,' the warlord commanded, and turned on his heel. Malus, his mind reeling from the sudden change in circumstances, quickly cinched up the saddlebag containing the relics and stumbled after Nuarc.

What was going on, he thought as he followed the warlord through an ironbound door into the citadel proper. Again, the words of his mother echoed in his mind. *Seek the amulet in the lightless halls of the Fortress of Iron.*

What did she know that he didn't?

NUARC LED HIM to a cold, austere apartment in one of the citadel's towers – it might have been the warlord's own keep, as far as Malus knew – where a trio of silent, efficient servants waited to make him presentable for an audience with the Witch King. They stripped away his battered armour and kheitan, as well as his stained and tattered robes, and laid out food and wine while they drew a steaming bath to wash away the dust of the road. He ate like a wolf while he waited for the hot water to be poured, eyeing the wine wistfully but leaving the bottle untouched. His wits were addled enough as it was.

While he waited a pair of masked warriors slipped silently into the apartment with his bags piled in their arms. Malus masked his fear with a curt nod and quickly checked them after they'd gone. For a wonder, nothing had been disturbed.

Perhaps I've fallen asleep in the saddle and this is all a bizarre dream, he thought. Nothing else makes much sense.

The servants scrubbed him industriously and said nothing about the fresh scars on either side of his torso where Urial's sword had run him through, nor did they show concern for the web work of black veins that ran from his right hand all the way across his shoulder and up the side of his neck. No doubt the servants were spying on behalf of someone – or several someones – but there was little Malus could do about that. Let them make their report. He doubted it could make his situation any more precarious than it already was.

The food and the hot water preyed upon him, making his eyelids droop. Malus splashed a bit of water on his face and tried to concentrate on the facts at hand. In retrospect, his treatment at the hands of the Endless now made a bit more sense. He hadn't been their prisoner at all, just a highborn who had been summoned to the Witch King's court with all dispatch.

And now this, Malus thought, his weary gaze sweeping around the apartment. He wasn't being treated like a guest, necessarily, but certainly as something more than an outlaw. So what could possibly account for that, the highborn thought?

The obvious answer was that Malekith wanted something from him. Something that couldn't be got using the end of a red-hot iron or a torturer's knives.

He waved the servants away and leaned back in the tub. He eyed his bags piled near the door. Was it the warpsword? He tugged thoughtfully at his lip. From all indications it appeared that Malekith had never received word of the uprising at Har Ganeth, so as far as he knew the blade still rested in the Sanctum of the Sword back at the temple. And even if he did know the truth, it wasn't as though the Witch King needed his permission to take it.

Or did he? Since he'd drawn the sword, did that mean no one else could claim until so long as he lived? Malus grinned ruefully. It wasn't as though that would be much of a problem for Malekith either.

What then did he possess that Malekith couldn't simply take from him? He went over everything Nuarc had said in the courtyard outside the citadel, looking for clues as to why he'd been summoned. All Nuarc had seemed to care about was Lurhan's death. The high-born's brows knitted in thought. Could that be it?

Other than his half-brother Isilvar, who now held their father's rank and properties, Malus was Lurhan's only male descendant. And while he was now an outlaw and stripped of any claim to Lurhan's legacy, Isilvar had secretly broken the Witch King's laws as well. Both Isilvar and their sister Nagaira had been members of the cult of Slaanesh; indeed, Malus strongly suspected that Isilvar had been the cult's Heirophant inside the city. After the cult had been exposed and most of its members killed, Malus suspected that Lurhan had discovered his son's involvement and covered it up.

Had Malekith found out? If so, there was no one left who could offer proof… except for him. Malus steepled his fingers beneath his chin. That was an intriguing possibility indeed.

The door to the apartment banged open and Nuarc swept inside like a storm wind, scattering cowed servants like leaves. 'This isn't some damned flesh house, boy,' the warlord growled disdainfully. 'Get dressed. The Witch King is waiting.'

Gritting his teeth, Malus rose from the tub and did as he was told. He heard Nuarc let out a surprised hiss as the warlord got a look at the daemon's handiwork, but the druchii lord asked no awkward questions.

The servants had laid out a fine set of black robes and a court kheitan of soft human hide. Hands plucked at his head; he rounded on the servants with a snarl, belatedly realizing the servants were trying to comb his long, tangled hair. Frowning irritably, he let them finish their work and bind the hair back with leather and gold wire.

There was no armour to replace his old harness, and certainly no paired swords to wear at his hip. It was clear that Malekith's interest was entirely conditional. The new outfit he wore would look just as fitting hanging from an iron pole as it would at court. 'All right,' he said grimly, pulling on a pair of new boots. 'Lead on.'

On the way out the door, Malus spared one last look at his piled baggage. He tried to reassure himself that if Malekith wanted him dead the Witch King wouldn't have bothered to give him the opportunity to unpack.

MALUS FOLLOWED NUARC through a maze of dark, empty corridors, each one as silent as a tomb. Witchlamps set in iron sconces cast solitary pools of light along the way, making the darkness seem even deeper and more oppressive. Before long the silence began to prey upon Malus, setting his nerves on edge. There was none of the hectic bustle he was accustomed to at the citadel of Uthlan Tyr, drachau of Hag Graef. Though it was the centre of power for the entire kingdom, the Iron Fortress was cold and still, filled only with echoes.

At first he'd tried to memorize their route, but after a quarter of an hour's worth of twists and turns he gave it up as a lost cause. Like the city outside the fortress, there were no landmarks by which to navigate; only those who belonged there had any hope of finding their way. Malus couldn't imagine how long one had to wander these funereal halls before they gave up their secrets.

Lord Nuarc found his way effortlessly. Within half an hour they passed through an archway into a long, empty chamber lit by massive witchlamps suspended by chains along the arched ceiling. Here Malus began to notice the furtive movements of other druchii: masked Endless, nobles going about the business of state, temple bureaucrats and scarred, nervous servants, all gliding quietly through the shadows to and from the Witch King's court. All made way for the brisk, commanding stride of Lord Nuarc, who swept past them without so much as a nod.

One long chamber led to another. In most druchii cities a drachau's audience chamber was divided into two spaces: the throne room proper and the lower room, where lesser highborn and common folk waited in hopes of a brief audience with their overlord. Here Malus counted no less than four lower chambers, each one large enough to hold a thousand druchii or more. Each room was slightly more ornate than the first; bare walls of polished black marble gave way to statues of druchii princes clad in the raiment of lost Nagarythe, which in turn gave way to titanic columns of red-veined basalt and bas-reliefs of mighty battles between the druchii and their foes. The final lower room was dominated by a tremendous flame that rose in a hissing, seething pillar in the centre of the chamber. The shifting light picked out threads of silver and gold in ancient, enormous tapestries that told of Malekith's suffering in the fires of Asuryan and the Seven Treacheries of Aenarion.

At the far end of the fiery vault stood a pair of iron doors twenty feet high, engraved with the sinuous forms of rearing dragons. The twin drakes seemed to glare down at Nuarc and Malus as they approached the Witch King's throne room. Four of the Endless stood watch at the doors with bared blades in their hands. They bowed as Nuarc approached and gave way before their master. With a single backwards glance at Malus, the warlord placed his hands on the great doors and pushed. The massive iron panels swung open on perfectly balanced hinges, throwing a rectangle of shifting blue light across a floor of gleaming black marble.

Nuarc stepped into the chamber, head held high. As Malus crossed the threshold he felt Tz'arkan contract fiercely around his heart, his power drawing back from his limbs like a swiftly receding tide.

Step carefully here, little druchii, the daemon hissed. *And remember that there are worse things than death.*

Beyond the doorway the Court of Dragons was all but devoid of light. The change brought Malus up short, leaving him near blind and intensely vulnerable in the space of a single step – an effect that of course could only be deliberate. As his vision adjusted to the gloom he saw that he was standing at one end of a surprisingly small octagonal room, barely thirty paces across. Again, after the lofty space of the previous chambers Malus couldn't help but feel the weight of the dressed stone walls pressing in on him. All around the perimeter of the room stood huge dragons carved cunningly from onyx, their wings spread like cloaks as they bowed in obeisance before the tall dais at the far end of the room. There, in shadows as deep as the eternal Abyss, glowed a pair of red-orange eyes that shone with the banked fire of a furnace.

The huge iron doors swung silently shut behind Malus, plunging the chamber into darkness. Malus felt the burning gaze of the Witch King upon him and bowed his head in genuine fear and dread.

Nuarc's voice rang out in the blackness. 'As your dread majesty commands, I have come with Malus the outlaw, formerly of the house of Lurhan the Vaulkhar, late of Hag Graef.'

The voice that replied sounded like nothing formed from a living throat – it was as hard and unyielding as hammered iron, the words rumbling out like the hot wind from a forge. *'I see you, kinslayer,'* the Witch King said. Malekith shifted slightly in the darkness, causing red light to seep from between the seams of his enchanted armour. *'Did you think to escape my wrath, Malus Darkblade? Your father was sworn to my service, and lived and died by my command alone. There can be no forgiveness for such a crime.'*

Silence fell. Malus blinked owlishly as he considered the Witch King's words. Was this some kind of test? He shrugged, wondering if Malekith could see the gesture. 'As you wish,' he replied.

There was the sound of steel rasping against steel, and more ruddy light outlined the segments of the Witch King's form. *'Will you not beg for mercy, kinslayer? Will you not bow down before my throne and treat with me, offering all that you possess if only I would stay my wrath?'*

The suggestion took Malus aback. 'Am I to believe that you would be moved by such a pathetic display? Do I seem so foolish as that?' he said, his tone indignant. 'I think not. You are the Witch King. Who am I to persuade you of anything? If you mean to exact your vengeance upon me, then so be it.'

'Kneel, then, and show your fealty to me.'

Malus gave the Witch King a bitter smile. Part of his mind gibbered in terror at his effrontery, but he'd suffered enough humiliation at the hands of Tz'arkan to last a dozen lifetimes. 'Only a vassal bows his knee,' the highborn said. 'But I am a vassal no longer. I am an outlaw now, by your own decree.' He squared his shoulders, drunk on suicidal defiance. 'So I believe I would rather stand.'

The red eyes narrowed, and Malus knew he'd gone a step too far. He drew a deep breath, believing it to be his last – when suddenly a woman's laughter, rich and cruel, rang from the darkness beside the throne.

Pale green light flickered to life across the throne room, kindled in the depths of witchlamps set in iron stands arrayed around the chamber. Again, Malus was momentarily disoriented, his defiance forgotten. Through slitted eyes he dimly perceived a tall, black throne at the top of the dais, and upon that seat of barbed iron he glimpsed the terrible visage of Malekith himself.

But it was the laughter that drew the highborn's eye. A woman was gracefully descending from the dais, clad in black robes as befitted a druchii witch or seer. She was tall and regal, with features that seemed cruel even in the depths of her mirth. White hair fell past her waist, wound with gold wire and delicate finger bones. Her dark eyes flashed with a cold, draconic intellect, her stare cutting through him as cleanly as an obsidian knife.

'Tell me,' she said, her voice belling out in the same cold tones as the witches of the Endless, 'do you come by such reckless courage naturally, or does it come from the daemon curled around your heart?'

Chapter Seven
THE EMISSARY

THE WITCH KING leaned forward upon his barbed throne. Visible heat radiated from the seams of his armour, blurring the air around him. '*Daemon?*' Malekith hissed, his burning eyes narrowing further. Behind Malus, just a few steps from his left shoulder, he heard the cold rasp of steel sliding from its scabbard.

Malus felt sharp talons sink into his heart. It might have been a warning from the daemon or it might have been a sudden rush of fear. Regardless, he took a few moments to master his composure before he answered the seer's question.

'My recklessness is the very reason there is a daemon inside me, Lady Morathi,' he said. He kept his gaze focused straight ahead, fearful of what else the seer might unearth from the depths of his eyes.

Morathi glided past him, circling him slowly. He could feel her icy gaze sweep over him, reminding him of the passing stare of the dragon in the courtyard outside. 'You are no sorcerer,' she declared, 'despite your parentage and the rumours of forbidden practices performed by your siblings.'

'It is a curse, dread lady,' Malus said quickly. 'The daemon entrapped me while I was on an expedition into the Chaos Wastes.'

'Entrapped? To what purpose?' the seer asked, as lightly as if she were inquiring of the weather. Her cold, unnatural voice was sweet, but like any polished tone it was brittle. If it broke, Malus dreaded to hear what lay beneath.

'It is entrapped in turn, dread lady, inside a crystal far to the north. I have been given a year to perform certain tasks to gain its freedom, or else my soul is forfeit.'

'Did one of those tasks involve killing your father?' Nuarc growled.

Malus glanced over his shoulder at the warlord, glad for any excuse to look away from the throne. 'Not directly, no,' the highborn said. 'Lurhan simply got in my way.'

'The daemon forced you to do this?' Malekith inquired.

Malus couldn't help but frown. Where was all this leading? 'Forced? Certainly not, dread majesty. I am master of my own fate. But the circumstances were... complicated.' The highborn tried to think of a way to explain things, but gave up with a shrug. 'Let us just say it wasn't my choice. I did what I had to do.'

Lady Morathi appeared on Malus's left side, still studying him intently. They were close enough to touch and the force of her presence was tangible, like a cold razor being drawn delicately across his skin. She radiated power in a way that not even his mother Eldire did. Her face was youthful, her features regal and severe; she was handsome rather than classically beautiful, with a broad face and a rounded chin that was almost square rather than pointed. Her eyes were like windows onto the Abyss, drinking in everything around her. 'Does this daemon have a name?' she asked, her lips quirking in wry amusement.

She knows more than she's letting on, Malus thought. She's testing me, seeing how much I know. Again, he affected a shrug. 'If it does, it hasn't shared it with me,' he said. 'Why would it? Wouldn't that give me power to control it?'

'Daemons go by many names,' Morathi said. 'But only one true name, which they hide as best they can.' She stepped forward, pinning him with her gaze. 'What does this daemon call itself when it speaks to you?'

'Itself? Why, nothing,' Malus replied sourly, 'although it has more than a few choice names for *me*.'

Malus heard a harsh bark of laughter from Lord Nuarc. Morathi stared at him for a moment more, a faint smile quirking the corners of her mouth. 'I have little trouble believing that,' she said, then turned back to the dais. 'It explains much,' she said to the Witch King as she climbed the stairs to take her place beside the iron throne.

The highborn shook his head in consternation. 'From my perspective it explains nothing, dread majesty. Why have I been brought here, if not to answer for my crimes?'

A rumbling hiss escaped from Malekith's horned helmet. *'Oh, you shall answer for what you have done, Darkblade,'* the Witch King said. *'But the payment shall be of mine own choosing.'* Malekith stretched an upturned hand to the ceiling. *'Observe.'*

There was a ponderous groan of machinery overhead. Malus glanced upwards and saw a dark, circular opening in the centre of the domed ceiling. With a thunderous rattle of heavy iron links a spherical shape descended from the opening. First the witchlight picked out curved bars of polished iron, formed into a cage or basket large enough to hold a grown druchii. At first Malus thought the cage was meant for him, but as it sank closer he saw the greenish light reflecting on a huge, uncut crystal held within the iron frame. Suddenly the highborn realised what it was. 'The Ainur Tel,' he hissed.

Malekith nodded slowly. *'The Eye of Fate,'* he said. *'One of the few relics of power brought with us out of Nagarythe millennia ago, carved from the root of the world in aeons past.'*

The great crystal was lowered on four massive chains, sinking into the room until it hung directly before Malus's eyes. With a clash of gears the chains locked in place, and a mote of faint, white light began to glow within the crystal's depths. Slowly the light began to pulse, like the beat of a tremendous heart. The glow intensified with each beat, growing in strength until the huge crystal shone like a pale sun. Malus could feel its energies washing over his skin in turgid waves, setting his nerves on fire. It was all he could do not to recoil from the legendary relic. Only by a supreme effort of will did he manage to still his shaking limbs and look unflinchingly into the light.

Morathi's voice called out to him from the dais. 'Stare into the eye, son of Lurhan,' she said. 'Cast your gaze a hundred leagues to the north.'

Frowning, Malus stared fixedly into the white glare. At first he saw nothing. His eyes grew weak and his lids fluttered – then all at once the harsh light faded and Malus saw blurry images take shape within the crystal. He saw a single, blackened watchtower rising above a bleak and desolate plain. The walls of the keep were blasted and broken and the single gate had been smashed aside, buried beneath a mound of twisted, misshapen bodies. Moonlight shone on the armoured bodies of druchii warriors in the tower's courtyard, and Malus imagined many more in the burnt-out shell of the citadel itself. Hundreds of horned beastmen and savage, tattooed marauders lay among the fallen defenders, struck down by crossbow bolts or pierced by axe or sword. It was clear to him that the watchtower had been taken by storm, its warriors overwhelmed in a single, savage assault.

Within moments the vision blurred and reformed again. The image showed another watchtower, this one standing atop a rocky hill above a swift-flowing river. Again, the walls of the keep were blackened by fire, and the fortifications were gouged and torn as though clawed by monstrous hands. Armoured corpses were splayed across the battlements, and Malus could see a knot of charred corpses where the last of the citadel's defenders made their final stand at the foot of their burning tower.

The image shifted again. Malus was shown another ruined watchtower. His bemused frown deepened into a look of genuine alarm. He glanced worriedly at Morathi – and by the time he looked back at the glowing crystal it was showing yet another border keep that had been put to the torch. This one had been attacked within only a couple of days; tendrils of smoke still rose from the fires smouldering in the wreckage of the tower. Malus's eyes widened as he saw the rubble of the watchtower gate, crushed beneath the weight of a giant whose naked body had been riddled by the tower's powerful bolt throwers.

'What is the meaning of this?' Malus exclaimed. Raiding parties of Chaos-tainted savages riding out of the Wastes was an ever-present threat, which was why there was a line of watchtower keeps along the northern frontier. But raiders went out of their way to avoid the towers as much as possible rather than spend their strength against them. 'I've never heard of a border keep being overrun, much less *four* of them,' he said. A sudden thought sent a thrill down his spine. 'Is this an invasion?'

The Witch King pointed at the relic. *'Behold.'*

This time when the vision cleared Malus saw a sky full of fire. A dark tower stood against the backdrop of a burning forest, and beneath that roiling, flame-shot sky raged a horde of howling monstrosities that crashed in a frenzied wave against the watchtower's battered walls. Spear tips glinted atop the battlements and axes flashed as the beleaguered defenders hacked at scaling-ropes or fended off ladders thrown up by maddened beastmen and furious, blood-soaked barbarians. Crossbow bolts flickered in a black rain from the tall watchtower, wreaking havoc among the ranks of the enemy, but for every attacker that fell it seemed that three more rushed to take its place.

Huge shapes waded through the raging horde: hunched, misshapen trolls and terrible giants dragging clubs made from gnarled tree trunks. As Malus watched, twin streaks of light sped from the top of the watchtower and struck one of the giants squarely in its muscular chest. In an instant the huge creature was wreathed in unnatural green flame – the terrible, liquid dragon's fire both prized and feared by druchii alchemists and corsairs alike. The giant reeled in agony, beating clumsily at the hungry flames consuming its body and throwing off gobbets of sizzling, burning flesh that fell upon the Chaos marauders swirling about its huge feet. Malus imagined the furious cheer that no doubt rose from the battlements as the giant staggered, its face melting and its mouth open in a roar of mortal agony as it toppled onto a herd of onrushing beastmen with an earth-shaking crash.

But the assault did not falter. Other giants lumbered to the watchtower gate and began to batter it with their clubs, seemingly heedless of the stinging bolts that prickled their thick hides. Sorcerous lightning rent the burning sky and flocks of hideous, winged daemons swooped over the battlements, plucking spearmen from the ramparts and dropping them to the stones fifty feet below. Packs of snarling trolls reached the base of the walls and began to climb atop one another to reach the defenders, their beady black eyes glinting hungrily.

Another bolt of dragon's fire arced from the watch-tower, striking one of the giants at the gate and setting it alight. The monster dropped its club and stampeded back through the oncoming horde, sowing carnage with every step, but the damage had already been done. Pulverized stone and shattered fittings spun through the air as the remaining giant smote the gate with its club and smashed it to the ground in a cloud of dust and debris. Into the breach swept the tide of savage marauders, and Malus snarled with impotent rage as he saw that the keep was doomed.

'Bhelgaur Keep has fallen,' Morathi declared, and the vision within the crystal faded to darkness.

Malus's mind raced as he tried to make sense of what he'd seen. 'I'm not familiar with Bhelgaur or any of the other keeps you showed me, but if they neighbour one another then that horde has torn a hole in our frontier defences more than *sixty leagues* across,' he said darkly. 'There must be tens of thousands of them.' He shook his head in terrible wonder. 'Such a thing isn't unheard of in the so-called Old World of the humans, but here? It's unimaginable.' The highborn turned to the Witch King, his former defiance and suspicion momentarily overcome by the glamour of war. 'What more do we know of these invaders, dread majesty?'

But it was not the Witch King who replied. 'Their scouts crossed the frontier almost a month ago,' Nuarc said tersely. 'Then came a flood of raiding parties, perhaps twelve or eighteen in number. Four of the watchtowers were struck within days of one another and their defenders put to the sword. Then the raiding parties came together into a single warband and marched on Bhelgaur Keep, the western anchor of our border defences.'

'That puts them within a few days' march of the Tower of Ghrond,' Malus exclaimed. If they made it past the Black Tower then the Chaos host would be at the northern end of the Spear Road and less than two weeks' march from the walls of Naggarond itself.

It was a full-scale invasion the likes of which Naggaroth had never seen before, the highborn realised at once. And it had struck the Land of Chill at the worst possible time, with the campaign season still underway and at least two-thirds of the nobility at sea or away from home. Now Malus understood why the Witch King hadn't marched on Har Ganeth when he'd learned of the uprising. What was more, he knew all too well how badly weakened the armies of the druchii were after the fighting in the City of Executioners and the brief but savage feud between the Black Ark and Hag Graef.

'But why now?' Malus said. 'Other than small raids the tribes of the Wastes have never warred against us. Who is leading this horde, and what does he want?'

Morathi eyed the highborn coldly. 'What, indeed?' she said.

At some unspoken command the doors to the throne room swung open, and Malus heard limping, shuffling footsteps slide across the polished floor. He turned – and his pale face twisted into a grimace of revulsion at the horrid figure lurching towards him.

The highborn's pallid skin was greenish-grey in the witchlight, darkening to a purple-black around the deep wounds in his forehead and neck. His armour had been savaged by blows from axe, sword and talon, scoring deep lines across his breastplate and tearing his right pauldron completely away. The noble's mail skirt was rent in a half-dozen places, and the robes beneath were stiff with rotting blood. Half of his left hand had been shorn away by a heavy blade, and his right arm ended in a chewed stump just above the elbow. Malus reckoned by the stench that the highborn had been dead for almost a fortnight.

Every inch of the noble's battered armour was covered with intricate runes, apparently inscribed with the druchii's own blood. His eyes were a ghostly white – no pupil or iris could be seen, and they glowed with sorcerous life under the gleam of the witchlights. The corpse, escorted by a pair of masked warriors, shambled towards Malus, apparently heedless of his presence. Hissing in disgust, the highborn backed away – and the revenant stopped, his head turning at the sound. Blind white eyes searched for Malus. The corpse's slack lips twitched as it tried to form words.

Malus's hand went to his hip, reaching instinctively for a blade that was no longer there. He glanced over his shoulder at Nuarc, who glared balefully at the animated corpse. 'What in the name of the Dark Mother is this?' he cried.

'This,' Nuarc growled, 'is Lord Suharc. His watchtower, near as we can tell, was one of the first to fall. Eight days ago a patrol found him stumbling along the Spear Road, and they followed him all the way to the gates of Naggarond itself.' The warlord's hand tightened on the hilt of his drawn sword. 'He came bearing a message from the master of the Chaos horde.'

Before Nuarc could speak further Morathi's voice rang across the hall. 'We have done as you wished, revenant,' she said. 'Malus of Hag Graef has been found and stands before you. Now deliver your message.'

The seer's command left Malus dumbstruck. But the revenant was galvanized by the news. With a sudden burst of energy the corpse stumbled towards him, reaching for the highborn's face with what remained of his ruined hand. Malus recoiled from the creature with a startled cry – only to fetch up against Nuarc, who grabbed the highborn by the back of the neck and shoved him rudely at the oncoming creature.

Cold, stinking flesh closed about Malus's face. He felt the splintered bones of the highborn's hand dig into his cheek as the revenant clumsily studied the shape of his features. With a savage cry the highborn wrenched free of Nuarc's grip and shoved the corpse away. It staggered backwards a few steps but did not fall, turning instead to face the iron throne. Air whistled through the pulped gristle of the revenant's throat as it filled its shrivelled lungs. When the corpse spoke its voice was a bubbling, croaking hiss, and Malus reeled in terror at the hideous sound. Bad enough that the words issued from the throat of a man long dead – worse still was the awful realization that the voice was one he knew all too well.

'You hold your salvation in your hands, Witch King,' Nagaira said, speaking through the revenant's ruined throat. 'Even now your watchtowers lie in ruins, and my army marches on the Black Tower of Ghrond. The power of the Black Ark is broken, and Hag Graef has been dealt a crippling blow. Your kingdom lies upon the brink of ruin – unless you give this outlaw to me.' The revenant raised its mangled hand and pointed to Malus. 'Deliver my brother, and the war ends in a single stroke. Otherwise the Tower of Ghrond will burn, and Naggarond will follow. Make your choice, Witch King. Naggaroth will burn until you do.'

A rumbling hiss echoed from Malekith's sealed helm. *'I have heard enough.'*

There was a rustle of movement and a flash of steel. The Endless drew and struck the emissary at the same moment, their swords slicing the revenant apart. As the head and the severed limbs struck the floor they burst into hissing flame, filling the chamber with a searing stench.

Malus swayed on his feet, still thunderstruck at all that had transpired. His half-sister had worshipped Slaanesh in secret for many years, but after he'd betrayed her to the Temple of Khaine months before she had escaped and sworn revenge on him. She had made obscene pacts with the Ruinous Powers that had granted her daemonic powers, but now this...

'Now the matter is clear,' Morathi said, fixing Malus with an appraising stare. 'It is not you she wants, son of Lurhan. She is after the daemon inside you. No doubt she believes that she can bend it to her will.'

With supreme effort the highborn got hold of himself. 'No doubt you are right, dread lady,' he said shakily. And who knows, he thought fearfully. Perhaps Nagaira can.

But that mattered little to Malus just then. His eyes darted about the throne room, taking in the position of the Endless and trying to gauge where Nuarc was standing. He had to escape, and quickly. Could he reach the warlord and take the druchii's sword? Could he call upon the daemon's strength to fight his way free? If he could somehow reach Spite he might have a chance...

Malus heard footsteps close behind him, crossing slowly from right to left. 'The Endless can be ready to ride within the hour,' Nuarc said, sounding near enough to be speaking in the highborn's ear. 'Now that we know where the Chaos horde is, we can give this witch what she wants and see them on their way.'

The highborn whirled, reaching for the warlord – only to find Nuarc's sword point less than a finger's width from his throat. Nuarc chuckled cruelly, shaking his head. 'Not so fast, boy,' he said. 'The witch didn't say anything about you getting to her in one piece, so if you want to keep your hands and feet you'll hold as still as a statue.'

Malus glared hatefully at Nuarc, but his reply was directed at Malekith instead. 'You cannot give her what she wants,' he snapped. 'It won't turn aside the horde. Nagaira will simply use me and the daemon to further her own plans of conquest.' He turned slowly to face the throne. 'She means to supplant you, dread majesty. Why else would she have raised so large an army?' How she'd managed to raise such a horde was another question altogether, the highborn thought.

The seer pursed her thin lips thoughtfully. 'Unless we could master the daemon ourselves,' she murmured. 'We could command it to slay the witch, then give Malus to her.'

'You can't control the daemon without its name,' Malus said quickly, trying to keep the desperation from his voice.

Nuarc stepped forward and seized a handful of Malus's hair. 'Then I say we send the witch his head and show her that the daemon will forever be out of her reach!'

'Enough!' Malekith roared, his armour flaring like an open furnace. *'No one makes demands of the druchii,'* he rumbled, leaning forward on his barbed throne. His red gaze burned against Malus's skin. *'She will get nothing from us but wrack and ruin.'* He stretched out an armoured hand and pointed imperiously at the highborn. *'You will see to this. When you slew the great Lurhan you deprived me of my rightful property. Now you belong to me instead.'*

Malus tried to tug his hair free, but Nuarc held him fast. 'I live to serve, dread majesty,' he growled through clenched teeth. 'What is your command?'

'Go to the Black Tower of Ghrond,' the Witch King said. *'Lord Kuall is the Vaulkhar there. It is he who failed to turn aside the Chaos horde, and you will express to him my displeasure.'* Malekith's armoured gauntlet clenched into a fist. *'Your exploits against Hag Graef are well known, son of Lurhan. Take command of the forces at Ghrond and lead them against the invaders until I arrive with the army of Naggaroth. You will hold them at the Black Tower until I arrive. Do you understand?'*

The highborn took a deep breath. He understood all too well. 'Your will be done, dread majesty,' he said without hesitation. 'I will serve you with all the vigour I possess.' As he considered the situation, his predatory mind saw a possible opportunity. 'There is one matter to consider, however,' he said carefully. 'The people of Naggaroth still consider me an outcast and a criminal. That will make it difficult to speak with any authority.'

Malekith glared implacably at the highborn. *'You are a member of my retinue now, Darkblade,'* he hissed. *'You will ride to Ghrond with the Endless and bear a writ signed with my name.'*

For the first time, Malus essayed a smile. 'Then I may reclaim my rights and status as a highborn?'

The Witch King paused, considering Malus carefully. *'In time, perhaps. Serve me well and you will be rewarded in kind.'*

'Yes. Of course, dread majesty,' Malus said, bowing deeply. 'Then, with your permission, I will return to my chambers and prepare to depart.' The sooner he got away from the iron fortress the better, he thought.

The Witch King dismissed Malus with a wave of his gauntleted hand. The highborn turned on his heel and strode swiftly for the chamber doors, giving Nuarc a defiant glare as he swept past. Already his mind was racing, contemplating all that he had to do when he reached the Black Tower.

For a short while at least, he would command an army again. He never dreamed such a day would come again. And I have you to thank, dear sister, the highborn thought with a feral grin.

As he reached the iron doors Morathi called after him. 'The daemon has sunk its roots deep into your flesh,' she said. 'What do you think is going to happen once you set it free?'

The highborn laid his hand on the iron panel. 'If I serve the daemon well it promises to reward me in kind,' he said, and then was gone.

Chapter Eight
THE BLACK TOWER

THE PAIN BUILT steadily as Malus stalked down the echoing corridors of the Witch King's palace, pressing against the backs of his eyes like steam swelling in a kettle. Blood pounded in his temples like a funeral drum, reverberating across his narrow skull until he swore he could feel it in his teeth. The highborn's thin lips pulled back in a feral grimace of pain, drawing uneasy glances from the nobles and state servants who stepped hurriedly out of his path as he swept by.

His limbs worked mechanically as his exhausted mind struggled to come to grips with his latest change of fortune. How had Nagaira managed to take command of an army? It had only been three months since he'd faced her in the tunnels beneath Hag Graef, when she'd attempted to destroy the city in an act of bloodthirsty vengeance. He had given her a terrible wound with the Dagger of Torxus, a magical weapon that severed the tie between body and spirit and pinned the soul to the spot where it was slain, to suffer as a tormented spirit for all time. Yet his half-sister had not died; like Malus, she had no soul for the dagger to steal. She had entered into a blasphemous pact with the Chaos Gods, receiving unimaginable powers in exchange for her service. Perhaps she had used her newfound might to subjugate some of the northern tribes, or perhaps they had been given to her as part of her arcane pact. The Ruinous Powers were free with their gifts, he'd learned bitterly, so long as their own interests were fulfilled as well.

And yet the sheer scope of Nagaira's actions staggered Malus. What were her true motives? It had to be more than mere revenge, surely. Was it Tz'arkan she was after, as Morathi believed? Could the daemon alone be worth so much effort? Malus felt a chill course down his spine as he considered the possibility. No less than five Chaos champions, mighty warlords and sorcerers all, had combined their fearsome powers to summoning and entrapping the daemon in the temple far in the north. As potent as they were, the champions knew that the daemon would make them more powerful still, and as far as the highborn had been able to determine, Tz'arkan had done just that. For a time the champions had bestrode the earth like gods themselves, causing the world to tremble beneath their feet.

Nagaira would know the tales far better than he, Malus knew. His cold hands clenched into fists as he stalked the twisting corridors. She would understand the awesome potential of the being lurking beneath his skin, and would know how to bend it to her will.

Once I'm in her clutches she'll bargain with the daemon through me, Malus realised. His expression turned bleak. She might even let the daemon take my soul as a token of good will, then use the five relics to bargain with Tz'arkan for even more power. She would have her revenge upon him and grow vastly more potent in the bargain – the very sweetest sort of revenge, as far as he was concerned. And then? Who knew? Perhaps she would march on Naggarond anyway, coming to grips with Malekith himself. With Tz'arkan bound to her, Nagaira might just overthrow the Witch King and claim the Land of Chill as her own.

The pain continued to worsen as he left the Court of Dragons behind. The pressure behind his eyes sharpened into needle-like points that pricked out white pinholes of light at the corners of his eyes. After ten minutes it hurt just to breathe. The air seemed to rasp like a file over his lips and teeth. He staggered, throwing out a hand to steady himself against the bare stone walls as he forced his legs to carry him onward.

He reached the door to his chambers without realizing it, fetching up against the oaken panels and fumbling for the iron ring in a blind haze of pain. How he'd found his way back from the court through the maze-like passageways of the fortress was a mystery that he hadn't the wherewithal to consider. The door banged open and he staggered into the brightly lit room, startling a trio of slaves who were busy laying out new clothes and arranging a set of polished plate armour on an arming stand at the foot of the bed. His stolen axe had been cleaned and sharpened, and lay gleaming on a tabletop nearby.

'Out, all of you,' Malus snarled, waving angrily at the blurry shapes that bowed uncertainly on the other side of the room. He staggered to the table and closed his hands on the hilt of the axe. 'I said *out*!' he roared, brandishing the terrible weapon, and the slaves fled from the room in a silent rush, their hands thrown protectively over their heads. As the door thudded shut he let the axe tumble from his hands and lurched to the bed, burying his face in the sheets with a bestial groan.

And then he heard the voice, hissing in his ears like a serpent. *You disappoint me little druchii,* the daemon whispered hatefully, and then he felt the nest of vipers coiled about his heart suddenly contract.

The pain was like nothing he had ever felt before. All the air went out of him; Malus gasped like a landed fish, his eyes wide and his hands clawing futilely at his armoured chest. The highborn slumped to the floor, rolling onto his side in a clatter of steel as he struggled for breath.

What foolishness is this, bending the knee to that parody of a king and playing at war when you and I have unfinished business, Tz'arkan continued. *Have you grown too accustomed to my presence these last few months? Did you forget the bargain you and I made? I assure you Darkblade that I have not.*

There was a roaring in his ears, and his vision was turning red, like a tide of blood rising from the edges of his vision. Trembling with effort, Malus drew in a thin gulp of air. 'The relic...' he gasped. 'My... mother...'

The grip on his heart drew sharply tighter; for half an instant Malus was certain that it would burst. All he could see was red; with a faint groan the highborn squeezed his eyes shut.

What does that witch have to do with this? the daemon growled. Malus could feel the cold touch of Tz'arkan's anger in his bones. *Is this another of her pathetic schemes?*

'She said... she said the path to the relic lies here,' the highborn moaned. 'Perhaps... it's... in the Black Tower...'

Perhaps? The daemon seethed. *You would hang your very soul from so slim a thread?*

'For now it's... all I have,' Malus gasped. There was a roaring in his ears, growing stronger by the moment. Darkness beckoned, and he sensed he lay closer to death than he'd ever been before. 'Whatever she plans... I'm a part of it,' he whispered. 'So... she would not lead me... astray. Not yet at least.'

The daemon didn't reply. For a single, agonizing instant, Malus felt Tz'arkan's grip continue to tighten – and then without warning it was simply gone. He sucked in air like a drowning man, rolling onto his stomach and biting his lip to keep from crying out. The daemon coiled and slithered within his chest, sliding black tendrils up the back of his neck and across his skull.

Pray that you are right, little druchii, Tz'arkan said. *Whatever her motives, she is not the one you should be wary of. I grow stronger with every beat of your miserable heart. Soon I'll be able to hurt you in ways you can't even imagine. And I will be watching every move you make, Darkblade. Step carefully.*

He could feel the daemon's presence dwindle. The pressure in his head began to fade. It was several minutes before he could push himself upright and blink owlishly in the glow of the pale witchlights. Every muscle in his body ached. With a groan he slowly rose onto his knees. Heavy drops spattered on the stone beneath his head, and he realised that his upper lip was damp. Malus touched it with trembling fingertips, and they came away stained with a cold, black ichor.

There was a looking glass over by the now-empty bathtub. Malus staggered over to it, peering intently into the silvered pane. The face looking back at him was one he only barely recognized. His face was even more drawn and haggard than he remembered, the grey skin pulled tight over corded muscle and fine, white scars to create a fevered mask of cruelty and hate. Streams of ichor ran from his sharp nose, his pointed ears and the corners of his eyes.

His eyes! Malus realised with a start that they were no longer the colour of heated brass – instead the irises were orbs of polished jet, so large that almost no whites were visible. When had Tz'arkan's disguise faded? The thought that the daemon could now alter or change his body at its whim frightened Malus to the core.

Behind him, he heard the chamber door creak open. Hurriedly, Malus snatched up a damp cloth hanging from the edge of the bathtub and pressed it to his face. 'Take another step and I'll split your skull,' he snarled at the intruder.

'You're welcome to try,' came Nuarc's familiar rasp. 'But daemon or no, I think you'd regret it.'

The highborn masked his surprise by scrubbing fiercely at his cheeks. 'Your pardon, my lord,' he said. 'I thought you were one of those damned servants.' After checking to make sure he'd cleaned away the last of the ichor he quickly wadded up the stained cloth and tossed it into the tub. He turned to face the general, gesturing tiredly at the clothes and armour laid at the bed. 'Give me a moment to change and I can leave the fortress at once.'

Nuarc gave Malus a penetrating stare, his expression doubtful. 'You don't look fit to pull off your boots, let alone manage another forced march,' he growled, but then grudgingly nodded. 'Not that I expect you'd let such a thing stop you. You're a hard-hearted, spiteful bastard, right enough.' The warlord pulled a metal plaque from his belt and walked over to the highborn. 'Here is the Witch King's writ,' he said, offering it to Malus as casually as though he were sharing a bottle of wine. 'I'd caution you to use it wisely, but what's the point? With that piece of paper in your hand you can do damn well whatever you please and no one will look sideways at you.'

Malus took the plaque from Nuarc's hand. It was very like the Writ of Iron he'd once been granted by the drachau of Hag Graef. This one was a bit longer, perhaps eighteen inches long, and the protective metal was unpolished silver instead of steel. He opened the hinged plaque and studied the parchment within.

He had expected a lengthy statement detailing his rights and privileges in exacting detail. Instead there were just two simple sentences. *The bearer of this writ, Malus of Hag Graef, belongs to me and acts solely in my name. Do as he bids, or risk my wrath.*

Below the archaic line of druchast was pressed the dragon seal of Malekith, Witch King of Naggaroth.

Malus closed the plaque carefully, savouring the feel of the cool metal on his fingertips. This is what absolute power feels like, he thought. With that writ in hand there was very little he could not do within the borders of the kingdom. Only the highest nobles in the land were immune from his authority, and he answered to no one but the Witch King himself. A slow, hungry smile spread across his face.

'It's a trap of course,' the warlord said, reading the look in Malus's black eyes. 'You realise that I'm sure.'

The highborn paused, his smile fading. 'A trap?' he replied, setting the plaque carefully upon the bed.

Now it was Nuarc's turn to smile. 'Of course it is. Consider the situation,' he said, pacing slowly around the room. 'This sister of yours has attacked the kingdom at a time when we are at our most vulnerable. She knows this – her remarks about Hag Graef and the Black Ark tells us that she is well aware of how weakened we are. The only way to stop her is to keep her occupied long enough for Malekith to scour the cities for every warrior he can lay hands on and form a large enough army to match her.' The general pointed a long finger at Malus. 'And you are the one thing guaranteed to hold Nagaira's attention.'

Malus thought it over. 'If so, why not simply send me to the Black Tower in chains? Nagaira would still tear the city apart trying to get at me, writ or no writ.'

Nuarc gave Malus a sidelong glance. 'Put a druchii in chains and he'll look for the first chance to escape. Put a druchii in power and he'll fight like a daemon to stay there, regardless of the risk.' He crossed the chamber and picked up the writ. 'This piece of parchment is stronger than any chain ever forged,' he rasped. 'You may think yourself clever, but Malekith can see right through you. You are just another pawn to him. He'll use you as a stalking horse to draw Nagaira to the Black Tower, then once she has been beaten back you'll be nothing but an outlaw once more.'

Malus reached up and took the plaque from Nuarc's hand. 'Then why tell me all this? Aren't you betraying your master's secret designs?'

The warlord let out a harsh, rasping laugh. 'Better for the Witch King that you understand the position you are in, and to know that there is nothing you can do to change it! I've heard reports about your generalship in the latest fighting between the Black Ark and Hag Graef; you did passably well against Isilvar's forces. You're young and headstrong, but you've got a sharp mind underneath all that foolishness. What's more, you can be damned unpredictable, and that's the reason I'm here,' he said. 'I want you to understand how tightly Malekith has boxed you in. Don't try anything stupid; it won't work, and it will likely leave us in an even less tenable position than we're in now. The best chance you have of keeping your head on your neck is to follow orders and enjoy the power you've got while you've got it.'

'Until the danger is past,' Malus said coldly. 'And then you'll tie me to a pole at the crossroads.'

Nuarc met the highborn's gaze unflinchingly. 'Would you rather face your sister's tender mercies instead?'

Malus sighed. 'You've made your point, my lord,' he said, tossing the plaque back onto the mattress. He began working at the lacings of his armour. 'I should be ready to ride within the hour.'

'Very good,' the general said with a curt nod, then turned to leave the room. 'I'll send the servants back in to help you change and bring in a good meal. It'll likely be the only one you'll get for the next few days.'

Nuarc stepped into the corridor outside Malus's chamber, barking orders for the servants. Malus jerked the lacings of his breastplate free with sharp, angry movements, glaring balefully at the Witch King's writ as he worked.

THE DARK STEEDS of the Endless swept over the wooded ridge and thundered down the reverse slope, their lathered flanks heaving and their glossy hooves beating upon the packed cinders of the Spear Road as they came at last to the Plain of Ghrond. A light snow was falling, stirred into stinging gusts by a cold north wind that whispered among the dark pines.

At the top of the ridgeline Malus reined in Spite and surveyed the broad plain, baring his teeth at the biting wind. His cheeks and nose were already chapped from the cold, but the pain kept him awake and alert better than any dose of barvalk could. His exhausted, aching body reeled in the saddle; Nuarc had commanded the Endless to bear him to the Black Tower with all dispatch, and their pace had made the trip down the Slaver's Road seem leisurely by comparison. They stopped only once every few days for a cold meal and a ration of the dwarf liquor, and what little sleep the highborn got was on the move. Malus could no longer say for certain what day it was, but to the best of his reckoning they'd covered the week-and-a-half ride to the Black Tower in just four days. Even the dark steeds seemed to be at the limits of their endurance, something the highborn hadn't thought possible.

Below him the lead riders of the Endless stirred up a cloud of pale grey dust as they galloped along the black ribbon of road that crossed the desolate plain. The ashen expanse stretched to east and west as far as the eye could see, while the horizon to the north was edged with a broken, iron-grey line of mountains that marked the edge of the Chaos Wastes. Perhaps a league to the north, rising out of the pale ash like a sentinel's black spear, rose the Tower of Ghrond.

Each of Naggaroth's six great cities served a purpose for the druchii as a whole: Karond Kar built the sleek black ships that corsair captains used on their slave raids, while Klar Karond was the clearing-house for the flesh trade that the corsairs supplied. Similarly, Har Ganeth forged the weapons and armour that armed the warriors of the state, while the Black Tower could be said to be the forge that made the warriors themselves.

Every unit of troops raised across the Land of Chill was sent to the Black Tower to be trained in the arts of war. Units of spearmen and cavalry took their turn manning the watchtowers along the northern frontier and blooded themselves on cross-border raids into the Wastes, led by sons of prominent highborn families who were there to learn the rudiments of command. The Black Tower was the lynchpin of the northern marches, built during a time when the druchii feared that an invasion from the Wastes was an ever-present threat.

The nauglir reached the base of the steep slope in a few loping strides, grumbling querulously as the highborn spurred the cold one into a ground-eating trot. What little he knew of the Black Tower had come from books in his father's library; Lurhan hadn't thought it necessary to give his bastard son the customary training that his elder sons had received.

Ghrond was a city only in the sense of its population and density of structures; in reality it was a permanent military camp, its buildings devoted solely to martial pursuits. The fortress city had a hexagonal-shaped outer wall more than forty feet high that was wide enough at the top for a troop of knights to ride their nauglir two abreast along its length. Each corner of the hexagon was further fortified into a triangular-shaped redoubt that was a citadel unto itself, with its own barracks, armoury and storerooms. The redoubts extended some ways out from the walls, so that archers and bolt throwers could fire down their length and catch attackers in a withering crossfire. Like the redoubts, the city's two gates were likewise fortified with imposing gatehouses that could rain death upon any attempt to break through their iron-banded doors.

From the southern gatehouse the sentries could see the entire length of the Spear Road, all the way back to the far ridge. As the Endless drew closer the forbidding wail of a horn rose above the battlements and the massive portal slowly swung open. One look at the silver faces of the riders and their black steeds was enough to convince the sentries of their identity.

Within minutes Malus was riding beneath the arch of the southern gate and into a narrow tunnel lit only by a handful of witchlamps. Heavy stone blocks seemed to press in from every side, and the highborn made out narrow murder-holes and arrow slits along both the walls and ceiling of the space. After about ten yards, the highborn was surprised to find the tunnel angle sharply to the right, then dogleg back to the left again. It made a difficult turn for wagons and an impossible one for a battering ram, he noted with approval. An attacker who managed to penetrate the first gate would find himself stuck in the dark confines of the tunnel and ruthlessly slaughtered by the gatehouse's defenders.

After another ten yards the highborn emerged from the inner gate into a small marshalling square lined with low, stone barracks. Foot soldiers were drilling in formation in the square, and the air rang with the clash of hammers from nearby forges as armourers readied the garrison for battle. The commander of the footmen raised his sword in salute as the riders passed, then resumed bellowing orders to his men.

The space between the outer wall and inner wall of the city was close-packed with barracks, stables, storehouses, forges and kitchens, organized into fortified districts that could operate as independent strongpoints in the event the outer wall was breached. An invader would have to spend precious time and thousands of lives clearing these buildings and fighting along the narrow streets before he even reached the inner wall itself. Malus had read somewhere that each building had been further built so that the people inside could collapse it when all hope was lost, further denying its fortifications to their conquerors.

Unlike other druchii cities, the streets of Ghrond were laid out in neat, orderly lines to facilitate the rapid movement of troops. Malus and the Endless made good time riding down the bustling avenues. Ahead of them loomed the black bulk of the fortress's inner wall, its spiked battlements rising sixty feet above the city's fortified districts.

Like the outer wall, the inner wall was built in a hexagonal shape with six small redoubts of its own and a single, solidly built gatehouse. Beyond rose the black tower itself, supported by lesser towers like any drachau's citadel and bristling with spiked turrets fitted with an array of heavy bolt throwers. As the highborn and the Endless were admitted through the inner gatehouse he could not help but shake his head in admiration. All of the power of the watchtowers combined could not equal the strength built into this fortress. A few thousand druchii could hold the Black Tower against a force more than ten times their number. It was an expertly designed death-trap, built solely to ruin an invading army. And he, Malus noted bitterly, was meant to be the bait.

Beyond the inner wall Malus found himself in a small, shadowy courtyard at the feet of the great tower. A troop of Black Guard stood watch at the courtyard's far end, their white faces impassive and their wicked-looking halberds held ready. Attendants in light armour and the livery of the tower's drachau raced from an adjoining stable as the Endless slipped heavily from their saddles. Malus did likewise, pausing only to check the pack containing the daemon's relics and to run a possessive hand over the wrapped hilt of the warpsword. He felt its banked heat through the layers of cloth and was sorely tempted to draw it free and buckle it to his harness. Who here would recognize it, after all? But the memory of the slaughter at Har Ganeth forced him to push the temptation aside. He couldn't afford another mindless slaughter here. With a deep breath the highborn pulled his hand away, removing instead the axe from its loop on the nauglir's saddle and then checking to make certain that the writ was securely tucked into his belt. As he did so there was a clatter of steel as a young highborn dashed from the tower into the courtyard.

The young druchii clearly came from a wealthy family. The hilts of his twin swords were chased with gold and set with small rubies, and his lacquered armour was embossed with silver runes of warding and decorated with gold scrollwork. A hadrilkar of silver encircled his slender neck, worked in the shape of twining serpents. His narrow, pointed face was flushed from his quick sprint, and tendrils of black hair had come loose from the band of gold at the base of his neck. He surveyed the assembled riders quickly and sized up Malus as their obvious leader. The young highborn advanced to a proper hithuan and bowed deeply. 'Welcome to the Black Tower, my lord,' he said. 'I am Shevael, a knight in service to the drachau, Lord Myrchas. How may I assist you?'

Malus could well imagine the thoughts going through the young highborn's mind. His new armour was filigreed with gold and wrought with its own powerful spells of protection, and the heavy gold hadrilkar of the Witch King hung about his neck. Yet he bore no swords to mark his station; instead he clutched the worn hilt of a battle-axe in his had. *The boy probably thinks I'm Malekith's own executioner, come to pay a call on his lord the drachau*, the highborn thought. *And, as it happens, he's not far wrong.*

'Where is Lord Myrchas and his vaulkhar?' Malus said, his voice hoarse from exhaustion.

Shevael's eyes widened. 'I... he... that is, they are in council at present–'

'Excellent,' Malus replied. 'Take me there.'

The young highborn went pale. 'But... that is, perhaps you would care for some refreshment after your long ride?'

'Did I ask for refreshment?' Malus snapped. He let the axe hang loosely from his hands. 'Take me to your master, boy, or would you rather hear the Witch King's decree yourself?'

Shevael took a step back. 'No, of course not, my lord! That is – I mean – please follow me!'

The young druchii turned on his heel and strode swiftly to the tower. Malus followed, grinning wolfishly, and the Endless fell silently into step around him.

Chapter Nine
THE WITCH KING'S VOICE

THE DRACHAU'S COUNCIL chambers lay near the very top of the tower, which did nothing to improve Malus's mood. The climb, up narrow, twisting stairways and down dimly-lit, bustling corridors, seemed to last for hours. By the time the young knight led him and his Endless bodyguards into the council chamber's anteroom he was entirely out of patience. Pulling the writ from his belt he pushed past the startled Shevael and strode purposefully up to the chamber door. The two Black Guard halberdiers assigned to watch the door glanced from Malus to his silver-masked attendants and stepped carefully aside.

Smiling grimly, Malus put his boot against the door and kicked for all he was worth.

The oaken door swung open, rebounding from the stone wall with a thunderous bang. Nobles and retainers in the room beyond leapt to their feet with startled shouts and wrathful curses. Malus rushed within, catching the recoiling door with the flat of his axe and stopping it with a hollow clang.

Across the large, square chamber lay a broad table, covered with maps, parchment notes, wine goblets and pewter plates littered with half-eaten meals. A dozen armoured highborn and their retainers glared fiercely at Malus's intrusion, many with their hands on the hilt of their blades. Four more Black Guardsmen dashed from the shadows, two on either side of the axe-wielding highborn, the spearheads of their halberds aimed for Malus's throat.

Opposite the chamber door, at the far end of the table, sat an older highborn clad in ornate, enchanted armour. Sigils of coiled serpents were worked in gold across his lacquered breastplate, and his right hand was encased in a taloned gauntlet of a type that Malus knew all too well. It was the literal Fist of Night, the magical symbol of a drachau's authority. Lord Myrchas, the drachau of the Black Tower, studied Malus with small, bright black eyes. His long face, accentuated by a narrow, drooping moustache, was marked by dozens of minor scars from the bite of sword and claw. He reminded Malus somewhat of his late father Lurhan, which blackened the highborn's mood even further.

At the drachau's right hand stood a towering, lanky figure in ornate armour, marked with the sigil of a tower engraved upon his breastplate. He was older than Malus, but not so old as the drachau, and his skin was darkened by years of exposure from campaigning in the field. His sword belt and scabbards were studded with gems, doubtless looted on dozens of raids into the Wastes. The lord was bald as a nauglir's egg, and his face and scalp bore the marks of a great many battles. He might have been handsome once, but that changed the day his nose was broken for the fourth time and his right ear was shorn almost completely away by some foeman's blade. His left cheek was scarred and crumpled, lending his angry scowl a horrid, unbalanced cast. 'What is your name, fool?' the scarred druchii roared. 'I want to know whose head I'll be hanging from the spikes atop the inner gate.'

'I am Malus of Hag Graef,' the highborn replied coldly.

Lord Myrchas straightened. 'Malus the kinslayer?' he exclaimed. 'The outlaw?'

Malus smiled. 'No longer.' He raised the writ for the assembled lords to see. 'His dread majesty the Witch King has seen fit to put my notorious talents to good use.'

The drachau held out his taloned hand. 'Let me be the judge of that,' he declared. 'I've heard of your deeds, wretch. For all I know there's nothing in between those metal plates but a fish-wife's tally sheet.'

Malus bowed his head, genuinely amused by the drachau's accusation, and passed the plaque to the nearest lord, who in turn handed it around the table to Lord Myrchas. As the drachau opened the plaque and studied the parchment within, Malus waved a hand at the Endless. 'I suppose these would be the fish-wife's daughters in disguise?'

Lord Myrchas read the parchment, then scrutinized the seal closely. His face turned pale. 'Blessed Mother of Night,' he said softly, raising his eyes to Malus. 'The world has turned upside down.'

'As it is wont to do from time to time,' Malus said darkly. 'Which is why the Witch King requires the services of people like myself.'

The drachau blanched even further, and Malus couldn't help but feel a rush of cruel glee. This was a role he could come to enjoy, he thought. He turned to the tall lord next to Myrchas. 'Now you have me at a disadvantage, my lord. Who might you be?'

The glint of rage in the druchii lord's eye faltered slightly at the sudden change of events. 'I am Lord Kuall Blackhand, Vaulkhar of the Black Tower.'

Malus's smile widened. 'Ah, yes, Lord Kuall. I've come a long way in a very short time to bring you a message from the Witch King himself.'

A stir went through the assembled nobles. Even the drachau leaned back in his chair and stole a bleak look at the vaulkhar. Lord Kuall straightened at the news, the muscles bunching at the sides of his scarred jaws. Whatever his failings, the vaulkhar of the tower was no coward. 'Very well,' he said, his voice tight. 'Let's hear it then.'

Malus nodded formally. 'As you wish. My lord and master has watched your efforts here in the north since the coming of the Chaos horde, Lord Kuall, and he is displeased with what he has seen. *Very* displeased.'

Worried murmurs passed through the assembled lords, and the drachau's eyes narrowed warily. Lord Kuall, however, went white with rage. 'And what would Malekith have me do?' he cried. 'Meet that damned multitude in the field?' He snatched up a pile of parchments and threw them across the table at Malus. 'Has the Witch King read my scouts' reports? The Chaos horde is immense! When it moves it raises so much dust that you can see it from the sentry posts at the top of the tower. You expect me to form lines of battle and try to defeat such a force? We would be completely overrun!' He banged his armoured gauntlet on the heavy table, causing the goblets to jump. 'I've commanded the army of the tower for two hundred years, and I've lead countless raids into the Wastes. In all that time I've never seen a horde such as this. This fortress – ' Kuall pointed a finger at the ceiling – 'was built to break a Chaos horde against its walls. If you had an ounce of sense you could have seen that just riding through the gates. The only sensible course of action is to conserve our forces and prepare for the coming onslaught, where we can bleed the enemy dry against our fortifications.'

The assembled lords listened and nodded, casting uneasy glances between Lord Kuall and Malus. But the highborn was unimpressed.

'So while you cowered in your hole like a rabbit the enemy has systematically destroyed nearly a third of our frontier watchtowers,' he replied coldly, 'not to mention slaughtered hundreds of isolated troops who stood their ground expecting reinforcements that never arrived. Instead you cowered behind these walls to preserve your own skin, and now the kingdom will be vulnerable to Chaos raids for years to come.'

'The Chaos horde must overcome the Black Tower if they hope to press further into Naggaroth!' Kuall shot back. 'They have no choice but to attack us, and here we are in a position of strength.'

'Are you?' Malus said. 'If I recall correctly, slightly more than half your garrison is made up of cavalry. How useful will they be to you in a protracted siege, unless you plan on putting the cavalrymen on the walls and sending their mounts to the kitchens?' He glared hotly at the vaulkhar. 'You have a powerful, and above all, a mobile force at your command, Lord Kuall, and yet you feared to put it to the test against a mass of ignorant savages. Out of timidity you hoped to fight the enemy with half an army while you sat here in your chair and waited for Malekith to come to your rescue. That is not how our people fight, Lord Kuall. That is not how the state responds to animals that trespass on our domain.'

'You dare call me a coward!' Kuall shouted, tearing his sword from its scabbard. The gathered nobles backed hurriedly away from the enraged lord, knocking over chairs and upending cups in their escape.

'I call you nothing,' Malus sneered. 'When I speak it is with the Witch King's own voice, and he calls you nothing less than a failure.' Malus gestured to the Endless. 'Take this wretch and impale him upon the spikes above the inner gate. With luck he'll live long enough to witness the defeat of the horde.'

The masked bodyguards swept forward in a silent rush, swords suddenly appearing in their hands. With a cry of rage, Kuall gave ground, threatening the implacable Endless with the point of his blade. But the warriors scarcely broke stride, advancing fearlessly into reach of the lord's long sword and trapping it with their own. Two more warriors seized Kuall by the arms, and within moments they were dragging the thrashing druchii across the chamber and out the door.

Malus savoured the shocked silence that fell upon Lord Kuall's sudden exit. His black eyes sought out the drachau and he waited for Lord Myrchas to make the next move.

The drachau met the highborn's stare, and Malus could see that Myrchas was weighing his options. For the moment the drachau was untouchable; as one of the Witch King's personal vassals he was beyond Malus's reach, but the reverse was true as well. Finally his expression softened slightly and the highborn knew he'd won.

'What is our dread majesty's command?' the drachau asked.

'The Witch King is assembling the army of Naggaroth and preparing to march here at once,' the highborn replied, feeling a thrill of triumph. 'Until such time as he arrives I will command the forces of the Black Tower.'

Myrchas bristled at the news. 'Malekith cannot name you vaulkhar without the approval of the tower lords!'

The highborn cut off the drachau's protest with a raised hand. 'I did not claim to be the vaulkhar, Lord Myrchas. I said that I will command the army. It is a fine distinction, but an important one, as I'm sure you'll agree.'

'Very well,' the drachau said darkly, realizing that he'd been outmanoeuvred.

'Excellent,' Malus said, then raised his axe and embedded it in the tabletop with a thunderous crash. All of the assembled highborn leapt back with startled oaths, and Malus leaned forward and picked up an empty wine goblet with a fierce grin. 'Now as my first official command I want a bottle of good wine brought out, then you can tell me who you are and report as to the disposition of our forces.'

THE REPORTS LASTED for almost three hours. Malus listened closely to each and every one, forcing himself to stay awake and drinking in every detail he could. His brief time as the lieutenant of Fuerlan's small force had in no way prepared him for the magnitude of commanding the army of the Black Tower.

Malus struggled with the names of the many highborn who came forward to report on one of the many facets of the garrison and the tower's defensive preparations. Lists were presented, detailing the numbers of troops in each regiment, the status of their equipment and their overall readiness, the quantity and quality of their food and the amount of time left in their training period before they were to be sent to their home city. Detailed tallies were given of arrows, crossbow bolts, heavy bolts, spare armour, spare shields, swords, spear-heads, arrowheads, catapult stones, gallons of oil, bundles of torches –

'All right, all right!' Malus interjected, waving his goblet at the pair of highborn who were currently reporting on the status of the kitchens. 'I've heard enough.' The two druchii bowed quickly and returned to their seats, grateful to have escaped Malus's notice with their skins intact. Wincing painfully, the highborn shifted in the uncomfortable council chair and drained the dregs of the goblet in a single gulp.

The highborn did his best to collect his scattered impressions as he held out his goblet to be refilled by a waiting attendant. The Endless had taken up positions by the door, watching the council members from behind their implacable masks.

'It is clear to me that the Black Tower has not squandered its time since the appearance of the horde. Your preparations were misguided, but your dedication and effort are to be commended,' he said. The assembled highborn nodded their heads respectfully. Beside Malus, the drachau's high-backed chair stood empty. Lord Myrchas had taken his leave a couple of hours before.

The highborn focused on a druchii noble across the table who had introduced himself as the commander of the cavalry. He was a whipcord-lean figure in dark armour, swathed in a heavy cloak of glossy bearskin. Malus couldn't remember the druchii's name to save himself. 'Let us get back to basics. How many light cavalry did you say we had, lord...'

'Irhaut, dread lord,' the highborn replied smoothly. Lord Irhaut had a long, hooked nose and three gold earrings that glinted roguishly in his left ear, hinting at a successful former career as a corsair. 'We currently muster six thousand light horse, arrayed in six banners.'

Malus nodded. 'Very good.' He turned to the broad-shouldered highborn sitting beside Irhaut. 'And our infantry, Lord Murmon?'

'Meiron, my lord,' the highborn corrected with a pained expression. He had blunt, craggy features and unusually shaggy brows for a druchii. Malus wondered idly if Lord Meiron's mother hadn't mated with a bear to produce such a child. Lord Meiron consulted his reports and drew himself straight. 'We currently muster fifteen thousand spearmen and a thousand Black Guard in sixteen banners, although four of those banners are scheduled to return home–'

'No one is going home until the horde has been destroyed,' Malus said sternly. Lord Meiron blinked beneath his shaggy brows and nodded hesitantly. The highborn scowled. They've been training troops and leading raids for so long that they can't seem to comprehend anything else, he thought. Well, they'd have a chance to revise their thinking soon enough.

Malus realised his goblet was full and took a deep, appreciative draught. He made a mental note to get a tally of the fortress's wine stores when he had a moment. 'Lord Suheir,' he said, turning to the armoured giant on his right. 'How fare the household knights?'

Lord Suheir turned slightly in his chair to face Malus, appearing a bit surprised that his new commander actually remembered his name. Suheir was head and shoulders taller than any other druchii in the room, and looked strong enough to crack walnuts with his hands. If Lord Meiron's mother had mated with a bear, then Suheir's ill-fated dam had lain with a nauglir. He had a wide face and an almost square chin, an unfortunate combination for a druchii lord. 'The household knights are fifteen hundred strong,' he replied in a booming voice. 'As well as five hundred chariots that haven't been used in a single battle as far as I know.'

Malus rolled the numbers over in his mind as he swirled the wine in his cup. Twenty-four thousand troops! It was easily twice the size of any other garrison in Naggaroth, with the possible exception of Naggarond itself. The notion was far more intoxicating than any vintage he'd ever drunk. The amount of power at his disposal was immense. As he contemplated this his eyes fell to the burnished silver plaque resting on the table before him.

Now he understood Nuarc's words all too well.

The highborn took a deep breath. 'All right. What have we learned about the enemy?'

Heads turned. At the end of the table the oldest druchii present sat up straight in his chair and leaned forward, resting his elbows on the edge of the table. Lord Rasthlan's hair had more grey in it than black, and was pulled back and plaited with plain finger bones and silver wire. Unlike the other highborn he wore only a shirt of close-fitting mail over a kheitan cut in a rustic, almost autarii style. His right cheek was decorated with a swirling tattoo of a snarling hound – a mark of considerable honour among the shades, if Malus's memory served him correctly. Rasthlan certainly looked more at home among the cushions and rugs of an autarii lodge than sitting at a table with civilized folk.

'Our scouts have been tracking the horde since it came together after sacking the majority of the hill forts almost a month ago,' Rasthlan said in a gravelly voice. 'Kuall spoke truly: the army is the largest I have ever seen. Tens of thousands of beastmen, and human tribes besides.'

'Any heavily armoured troops?' Malus asked.

'None that my scouts saw, dread lord,' the scout commander replied. 'But there were giants, and great hill-trolls, and possibly even more terrible things marching along with them in the centre of the host. It appears the horde is led by a very powerful sorcerer or shaman, for the air reeked of dark magic.'

'You may be assured of that,' the highborn replied. 'So, what is your most honest estimate? How large a force are we facing?'

Rasthlan paused, swallowing hard. He looked to the men beside him. 'I could not say for certain, dread lord.'

Malus's dark eyes bored into the older lord. 'Give me your best guess, then. Thirty thousand? Fifty thousand?'

The druchii's gaze fell to the table. 'I wouldn't want to guess...'

'I understand,' Malus said, a hint of steel creeping into his voice. 'So you may take this as an order: tell me, in your best estimate, how large you think the Chaos horde is.'

Lord Rasthlan took a deep breath, then met the highborn's gaze. 'A hundred and twenty thousand, give or take,' he said levelly. 'I've seen them myself. They darken the plains with their numbers. It's like nothing I've ever seen before.'

The rest of the highborn looked uneasily at one another, shock evident in their expressions. Lord Suheir looked at his wide hands. 'Kuall had the right of it,' he said slowly. 'There's no way we can challenge such an army in the field. It would be a massacre.'

Even Malus himself was shocked at such a number, but he kept his face carefully neutral. He studied Rasthlan closely. 'Are you certain of this?' he asked.

The scout commander nodded at once. 'I didn't want to believe it myself, which is why I went and counted their numbers myself.'

Malus nodded slowly, his gaze dropping to the map spread across the table. 'And where are they now?'

Rasthlan rose from his chair and came around the table. 'The horde moves slowly,' he said, 'Less than a dozen miles or so a day. After razing Bhelgaur Keep they turned towards the Black Tower, which means they would be about here.' He pointed to an area of foothills north and west of the Plain of Ghrond, perhaps fifteen leagues distant.

Malus considered the distances and studied the terrain. For the last four days he'd been thinking over all that Nuarc had told him, trying to find a way out of the many snares that had been laid for him. One plan after another had been discarded, until an idea struck him in the early hours of the morning that suggested a possibility of success. Now, looking at the map, he made up his mind. 'Very well. My thanks to you gentlemen. You've given me everything I need to develop a plan of action.' He threw back his head and finished off the contents of the goblet, then set the wine cup carefully on the tabletop. 'It's been a very long day for all of us, I expect. I'm going to find a bed and get a few hours' sleep. We will meet again on the morrow, when I will provide detailed orders for each of the divisions.' Bracing his hands carefully on the arms of his chair, the highborn pushed himself to his feet. 'Until then, you are dismissed. I suggest you all get as much rest as you can. There will be little of it to go around in the next few days.'

The army staff rose to their feet, exchanging bewildered glances as Malus strode purposely towards the door. Finally it was Lord Suheir who summoned up enough courage to speak. 'Dread lord?'

Malus paused, his head swimming with wine and fatigue. 'Yes?'

'Is there something you know that we don't?' he rumbled. 'Lord Rasthlan says that the horde is moving only a dozen miles a day. That means they won't reach the Black Tower for almost a week.'

Malus looked at the captain of knights and gave him a wolfish smile. 'I know. That gives us just enough time to launch our attack.' Then he disappeared from the room, bounded by the swift shadows of the Endless.

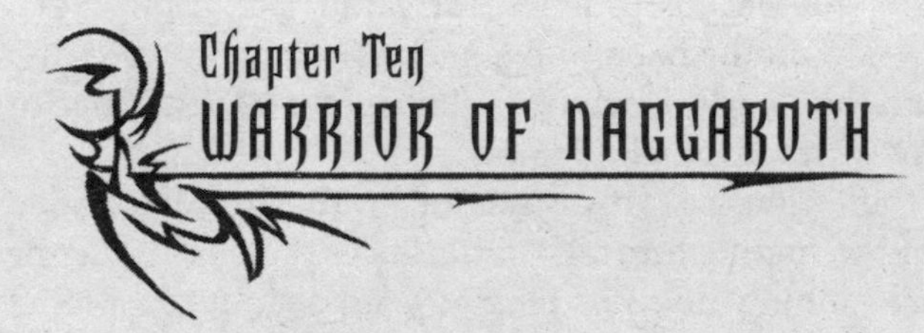

Chapter Ten
WARRIOR OF NAGGAROTH

MALUS DREAMT HE was back in the forest near the City of Executioners, racing through the close-set trees beneath the light of the twin moons. Something was following him; he could hear its ponderous footfalls and the brittle crack of the tree boughs as it forced its way through the woods in his wake. And he knew somehow that if whatever it was managed to catch him it would consume his very soul.

His armour and axe were gone, and the brambles tore at his face and clothes. Like razor-edged claws they shredded his thick kheitan and the robes beneath, and peeled away the skin across his cheeks and forehead. Hot blood coursed down his skin, but he felt no pain. He felt nothing but pure, mortal terror that the thing was going to catch him no matter how hard he ran.

And, sure enough, the heavy footfalls sounded closer, as though his pursuer were a giant, covering leagues with every step. Choking back a cry of fear he ran all the harder, the branches and the briars cutting ever deeper into his skin. He longed to find Spite, but the nauglir was nowhere to be seen. Malus strained to hear the familiar howl of the cold one, thinking it had to be hunting somewhere deep in the wood, but he could hear nothing over the pounding of his heart and the steady *thump* of his pursuer's tread. It sounded as though it was just a few scant yards behind him now; the skin on the back of his neck prickled, but he didn't dare look back, fearful of what might be reaching for him with outstretched talons.

Then without warning he burst into a thickly wooded hollow, finding himself on his knees on a narrow game trail running along its length. With a shudder of relief he realised where he was.

The tree. He had to find the tree. If he could climb back inside his pursuer couldn't find him.

Frantically he leapt to his feet and ran north along the path until he found the bloodstain he remembered on the trail. His heart hammering in his throat he risked a quick glance behind him, and saw that for the moment his pursuer was still just out of sight. Quickly he circled the broad stain and dived deep into the woods on the western side of the path. Thorny vines and brambles cut deep into already bleeding wounds, but he pushed on nonetheless, praying to the Dark Mother that the darkness and the vegetation would conceal him.

Within moments he found himself beside the blasted tree. The old trunk shone softly in the moonlight, like a gift from the goddess. Stifling a cry of relief he forced himself into the dark cleft. Showers of insects and rotten wood rained down on him as he straightened in the darkness, and he took it as a blessing from the goddess.

In his dream the tree was larger inside than without. He turned as the footsteps drew nearer, backing away from the thin slice of moonlight coming through the cleft from outside.

The footfalls were so close now that he could feel the earth tremble with each step. *Thud. Thud. Thud.* He held his breath, his eyes fixed on the thin slant of moonlight before him.

A shadow passed across the cleft. Malus saw a pair of booted feet through the slanted opening, barely a yard away from his hiding place. He took another involuntary step back, deeper into shadow.

The boots shifted left, then right. A voice called out. 'I know you're here little druchii,' Tz'arkan said, his voice slick and deadly as oiled steel. 'It's no use hiding. I can smell you. You're almost close enough to *taste*.'

A shudder passed through Malus at the sound of the daemon's voice. The boots shifted back to the right – then paused. One foot stepped towards the tree.

'Are you in there?' the daemon said. 'Yes, I think you are.'

A scream bubbled up in Malus's throat. He took another step back and fetched up against the uneven bole of the tree. He smelled rot and the wet stink of earthworms. The substance behind him gave slightly beneath his weight, like soft flesh.

Then a hand reached around him and pressed tightly over his mouth and another snaked tight around his waist. Malus smelled the stink of the grave and tasted putrefied flesh on his lips. Worms wriggled from the dead thing's wrist and landed, squirming, on his throat.

'Do not fear, my lord,' a familiar voice breathed in his ear. A cold breath, foul with the stench of rotting meat, lay damply along his cheek. 'The daemon cannot have you. I claimed you first.'

Malus writhed and squirmed in Lhunara's embrace, but her dead limbs held him in an iron embrace. He could smell nothing now but fleshy rot and the bitter smell of grave-dirt. His frantic gaze turned to the shaft of light and he saw the daemon pause outside, suddenly unsure. He tried to scream, to call out the daemon's name. Better to offer up his soul to the daemon's hunger than linger one moment more in Lhunara's foul embrace! But her gelid hand clamped his mouth tightly shut, and he could not get enough air through the reeking miasma that seeped from her decaying skin.

Outside, the boots turned slowly away. 'You can't hide forever, Darkblade,' the daemon called. 'It's only a matter of time before I find you.' Then, to Malus's horror, Tz'arkan walked away. The heavy footsteps receded quickly into the distance.

A cold, slimy tongue traced lightly along the side of Malus's neck. 'You see, I told you I would keep you safe,' Lhunara said, her breath close against his throat. 'No one is going to hurt you but me.'

Then her perfect teeth bit deep into his skin, and for the first time he found the breath to scream.

'MY LORD! MY lord, wake up!'

Malus awoke staring upwards at a starry sky framed by an arch of stone. He lay upon his back, dressed only in a sleeping robe that had somehow tangled around his legs. A cold wind blew against his cheek, tasting of snow. His heart laboured painfully in his chest, hammering like the drumming feet of a charging nauglir.

A dark silhouette hovered over him, backlit by the moonlight. He thrashed violently, still partially in the grip of the nightmare and the figure gripped his arm tightly. 'Be still, my lord! You could throw yourself over the rail!'

The sharp warning penetrated his dulled senses. He blinked away the last vestiges of the dream and realised that he lay on the floor of a narrow balcony, high up on the flank of the Black Tower. Moving slowly and cautiously, he sat upright, helped along by the strong hands of the shadowy attendant. Malus looked out across the white plain, which shimmered faintly in the moonlight. He saw the dark mountains off to the north, limned with the shifting light of the northern aurora. Off to the northwest he could just make out a faint white line of foothills. Beyond them, many leagues north and west, lay Nagaira and the Chaos horde.

'A dream. A terrible dream,' he said to himself, rubbing dazedly at his chin. His body ached and his mouth tasted like a chamber pot. 'I drank too much,' he said absently. 'Never again. Do you hear that Hauclir? Never again, you damned rogue. No matter how much I beg.'

'Hauclir, my lord?' the figure said worriedly. 'It's me, Shevael. The drachau assigned me to serve as your retainer. Don't you remember?'

Malus turned away from the balcony rail and stared closely at the man beside him. 'Ah. Yes. Shevael,' he said in a hollow voice. 'Shevael. Never mind my rambling, lad. It's just wine and memories.'

'Yes, my lord, of course,' the young highborn said, sounding anything but reassured. 'How did you come to be on the balcony in the first place? When I last checked you were sound asleep in your bed.'

Malus rose unsteadily to his feet. The double doors leading from the bedroom to the balcony were wide open; within he could see the banked glow of a pair of braziers, weakly illuminating the wide bed and the tangle of bed sheets that pointed like a trail to where he lay.

'I must have got up in the night,' he said weakly. But he recalled the time in the forest when he'd awoke far from where he'd bedded down. What in the Dark Mother's name is happening to me, he thought? For the first time he found himself missing the constant presence of the Endless. After escorting him safely to the Black Tower and seeing him installed as the commander of the army their duty was done, and they left him to begin the task of preparing a set of chambers for the Witch King's imminent arrival.

The highborn let Shevael lead him back to the bed and pile the sheets and blankets over him. Malus stared at the ceiling. 'What is the hour?'

'It is the hour of the wolf, my lord,' the young highborn answered. 'Dawn will break in another hour and a half. Light comes early this far north.'

'I know, lad, I know,' Malus answered. 'Let me rest here until daybreak, then turn me out. We'll be on the march by midday.'

'Very good, my lord,' the young highborn answered, and retreated from the room. At the door he paused to glance fearfully at the highborn, then slipped out of sight.

Malus paid no heed. He was lost in thought, staring though the open balcony doors at the shifting lights to the north.

THE THUNDER OF three thousand marching feet reverberated down the length of the marshalling square and vibrated against Malus's ribcage. He felt the measured tramp of boots through the heavy stone of the outer gatehouse, and it brought a feral smile of joy to his pallid face.

He had issued his orders scarcely an hour past dawn, and the forces he'd chosen had assembled in good order barely three hours after that. To their credit, his highborn staff hadn't blinked an eye when he'd laid out his plan. Possibly they'd drunk their fears into submission the night before, much as he had.

The scouts, as always, were the first to depart. They'd left almost immediately after meeting with his lieutenants. Lord Rasthlan had left with them, garbed in dark robes and mail just like the autarii themselves. Glancing up at the midday sun, Malus reckoned that the shades were leagues away by now.

Just an hour before a fanfare of horns sounded from the outer gatehouse, and the first three banners of cavalry left as the army's vanguard. The last few squadrons of those horsemen were just departing through the massive gate, and the regiment of Black Guard were crossing the square next. Their captain raised his sword in salute to Malus as they passed beneath the high arch, and he returned the gesture proudly with his upraised axe.

Beyond the Black Guard waited two more regiments of spearmen, then the household knights and the cold one chariots, destined for the battlefield at last. Farther still waited the remaining three banners of the light cavalry to act as the rearguard. The garrison's entire cavalry force and almost a quarter of its infantry – almost half of the entire army, on balance – were being wagered on a single, desperate gamble. The thought chilled him to the marrow, but anything less would have doomed the expedition to certain failure.

Suddenly a loud commotion arose at the far end of the battlements. Malus heard angry shouts over the heavy tramp of feet and glanced along the walkway to see what was happening. The soldiers of the gate watch who were watching the army alongside him suddenly shifted and dodged about as a single figure stormed down the battlements in Malus's direction. The highborn couldn't see who it was, but he had a fairly good idea.

He straightened and made certain his gleaming armour was presentable as the drachau of the Black Tower burst into view. Lord Myrchas was livid, his entire body trembling with rage.

'What do you think you are doing?' the drachau said in a strangled voice. 'Stop this madness at once and return these troops back to their barracks!'

Malus bowed his head regretfully. 'I cannot,' he replied. 'And you have no authority to command me, even if I were your vaulkhar.'

For a moment it looked as though Myrchas would reach for his sword. His hands trembled with fury... and no small amount of fear, the highborn imagined. 'You cannot defeat the horde in pitched battle!' the drachau cried. 'You're sending these men to certain death and leaving the Black Tower defenceless!'

'Defenceless?' the highborn arched an eyebrow. 'Hardly. I've left you with thirteen thousand well-trained spearmen to defend the fortress walls. That should be more than sufficient to hold the Black Tower against ten times their number. And if my plan succeeds, they will not be needed at all.'

The drachau would not be mollified. 'But the horde–'

'My lord, I have no intention of fighting the Chaos army in a pitched battle,' Malus snapped, fixing Myrchas with a fiery stare. 'A horde like that is not held together by training or discipline. It is a clumsy weapon wielded rather tenuously by its war leader. If the leader dies, the army will turn upon itself like a pack of maddened dogs.' Malus pointed a gauntleted finger northward. 'I am taking the most mobile force I can manage and I plan to launch a night attack aimed right at the horde's beating heart. We're going to cut our way to the war leader's tent and I plan on splitting her skull myself.'

'Her?' the drachau said, momentarily confused.

'Never mind, my lord,' Malus said. 'The point of the matter is that a quick, decisive strike could stop this invasion in its tracks. I need the cavalry's mobility and hitting power, and the spearmen will provide a solid rearguard for the squadrons to rally behind.' He leaned close to the drachau. 'Think of the glory when Malekith arrives with his army to find the war leader's head hanging from a gatehouse spike. They'll sing of your heroism the length and breadth of Naggaroth.'

Myrchas thought it over. A faint gleam of avarice shone in his eyes. 'The rewards for such a victory would be great,' he allowed, then frowned worriedly. 'Are you absolutely certain this will work?'

The highborn shook his head. 'Nothing in war is certain, my lord. But believe me when I tell you that while the Chaos war leader is a mighty sorceress, she has no experience whatsoever as a general. She will not expect an attack like this, which gives us a great advantage. At worst we will be able to inflict tremendous losses and sow terrible confusion on the enemy, which will allow us to retire back to the fortress in good order.'

Malus put every ounce of sincerity he possessed into his argument. He believed in the plan; it was the only one he could conceive that would give him a chance of escaping Malekith's clutches, locating the relic and fleeing northward in time. If he could kill Nagaira before the Witch King arrived with his army then he would be able to use his temporary authority to search for the relic in the Black Tower – and the ruins of the Chaos encampment if necessary – without interference. Then he could slip out of the fortress and disappear into the Wastes with no one the wiser.

The highborn struggled to remain patient while the drachau thought it over. Finally, Myrchas nodded. 'I can find no fault with your plan,' he said at last. 'Go with the Dark Mother's blessing and sow fear and loathing among our foes.' He smiled. 'Naturally I regret not being able to accompany you–'

'Say no more, my lord,' Malus assured him. 'Someone must remain behind to command the garrison and await the Witch King's arrival. With luck I should return with the army in about five days.'

The drachau smiled. 'We will be awaiting your return,' he said. 'And now that you mention it, there are a great many matters that I must see to before the Witch King arrives, so I will take my leave.'

'Of course, my lord,' Malus said, bowing deeply. He held the bow as the drachau hurried away, hiding the grim smile of satisfaction on his lips.

THE ARMY MARCHED for the rest of the day and well past nightfall. Malus kept the pace brisk but measured; he'd had enough forced marches in the last two weeks to last a lifetime. Spite seemed to have recovered completely from his exertions on the road with little more than a day's rest and half a ton of horseflesh to renew his strength.

On the following day they marched at a cautious pace through the foothills, awaiting the first reports from the far-ranging scouts. Malus kept the army moving at a walk, both to minimize the amount of telltale dust and to avoid running headlong into the oncoming Chaos army. Timing their approach to the horde would be the trickiest part of the attack.

At midday Lord Rasthlan appeared before the vanguard with a pair of autarii in tow. Malus called a halt and met the scouts beneath the shadow of a copse of fir trees on the reverse slope of a low hill.

'Where are they?' the highborn asked as Shevael passed bread, cheese and wine to the tired-looking scouts.

'About five leagues to the north,' Rasthlan said, drinking deeply from his cup. The shades crouched beneath the trees and ate in silence, gazing inscrutably at Malus. Lord Rasthlan tore off a hunk of bread and stuffed it quickly in his mouth, nearly swallowing it whole. 'They've picked up their pace somewhat, but they shouldn't cover more than two or three leagues before nightfall,' he continued.

Malus nodded thoughtfully. The distance would be just about perfect. 'Do you know for certain where the war leader's tent can be found?'

Rasthlan grimaced and shook his head. 'The Chaos savages are thick as flies along the ground,' he said. 'From the edge of their encampment it is nearly three miles to the centre. Too risky to penetrate, even for these ghosts,' he said, indicating the autarii. 'The war leader's tents will lie in the middle of the camp. They should be easy to find, even in the dark.'

The highborn nodded. 'Will your men be ready by nightfall?'

One of the autarii snorted disdainfully. Rasthlan grinned. 'They are ready now, my lord,' he said. 'We will uphold our end of the plan, never fear.'

'Very well,' Malus replied, feeling the first twinges of anticipation. 'Then we wait here until nightfall.' He turned to Shevael. 'Summon the division commanders to attend a war council in three hours to go over final preparations,' he ordered. As the young highborn rushed off, Malus turned back to the scouts. 'And as for you, I suggest you get some rest. It will likely be a very long night.'

THE LARGER OF the two moons was still low on the horizon when the army rose from their temporary camp and began their march to the enemy encampment. During the day they had wrapped their arms, armour and tack in layers of cloth to muffle any telltale noises while they moved. Each regiment and banner marched with a pair of autarii in the lead, holding small, shuttered witchlamps to signal their fellows and act as pathfinders, guiding the army to its objective.

Solitary flakes of snow drifted from a seemingly clear sky, and Malus's breath sent frosty plumes into the air as he rode alongside the household knights. They travelled in remarkable silence for so huge a force, and the highborn could not help but admire the mettle of the troops under his command. A general with sufficient daring could do much with such an army at his back, he mused, and smiled up at the starry sky.

It took more than two hours to travel two leagues across the foothills, then the pathfinders raised their lanterns and called a halt. As the army slowly ground to a stop, Rasthlan suddenly appeared at Malus's side. 'You may form your lines here, my lord,' he whispered, as though the Chaos troops were just on the other side of the hill instead of nearly a mile away. 'We will go ahead from here and deal with their sentries,' he said. 'Wait for the signal.'

Malus nodded. 'The Dark Mother's fortune be with you, Rasthlan,' he said, and the old druchii vanished like a spectre.

Lantern signals were passed all along the column, and slowly, carefully, the army formed line of battle behind the slope of a long, wooded ridge. Once again, the shades and their shuttered lanterns were invaluable, guiding each regiment and banner into the proper position with a minimum of confusion. Still, it was nearly two hours before the army was properly arrayed. After that there was nothing to do but watch the moons creep across the sky and try not to focus too much on the battle ahead.

The wait seemed to last forever. Each moment Malus strained his senses to detect the slightest sign of alarm, even though he knew intellectually that he was too far away from the enemy camp to hear anything short of war horns. Knights shifted uneasily in their saddles, the creak of leather seemingly sharp as a thunderclap to the highborn's strained nerves. Nauglir grunted and stamped. Tiny bits of harness jingled despite every precaution. After almost an hour Malus discovered that his fingertips had gone numb from holding the reins in a nervous, white-knuckled grip. With a deep breath the forced himself to relax and slowly unclenched his aching hands.

Then came the sign they were waiting for. A hunched figure appeared at the top of the hill and flashed open the cover of his shuttered witchlamp: once, twice, thrice. Other pathfinders were sending the same signal all along the druchii line; the shades had done their deadly work and slain the enemy sentries along a one-mile front. There would be no one to give warning to the beastmen and marauders slumbering in their tents until it was far too late.

Malus looked to the left, just spying the edge of the banners of horse that stretched away to his flank; a similar formation waited at the right end of the knight's battle line, their loose formations stretching for more than a mile to either side. To his immediate right, the bristling line of the household knights checked their reins and stirrups and quietly drew their blades. Behind the knights waited the long line of scythe-armed chariots. A torch burned low in the back of each war machine, ready to light the arrows of the archers who waited alongside the charioteers. Still farther back, the highborn could see the three regiments of spearmen, dressing their lines in long ranks of two. Their spearheads glinted cruelly in the moonlight, though if all went well the footmen would never enter the battle at all. They were a veritable wall of silver and steel that disorganised cavalry units could retreat to and shake off any pursuers so they could rally and return to the fight.

Slowly and deliberately the highborn reached down and unhooked the axe from his saddle. He'd been sorely tempted to carry the warpsword into battle instead, but once again the episode at Har Ganeth gave him pause. What if he succumbed to the killing madness again at a time when he needed to be clear-headed and issue orders to the army? There were no guarantees, he finally admitted, and so he'd left the blade – and the bag with the relics – back at the Black Tower. As much as it worried him to leave the artefacts untended, worse still was the thought of them falling into the hands of his half-sister by some awful mischance. She'd already taken the items from him once before; Malus doubted he'd be so lucky as to retrieve them again.

He turned to the household knights, arrayed in a gleaming line two ranks deep that stretched off into the darkness for more than half a mile, well beyond his line of sight. Closest to the highborn were Lord Suheir, the knight-captain and Malus's retainer Shevael. Both eyed him with a mixture of excitement and wary unease. Every man in the small army knew what they were up against; he'd made certain of it before the troops left the Black Tower. If they won, the Chaos threat would be over. If they lost, few if any of them would return home again. They had to win or die.

Malus leaned over in his saddle and spoke quietly to Suheir and Shevael, certain that his words would be repeated on down the line. 'Remember, we are the spear tip,' he said, his expression fierce. 'Leave the chariots and the light cavalry to do most of the butcher's work. Our only task is to cut our way to the Chaos war leader's tent at the centre of the camp, regardless of the cost. Once we're there, I'll put an end to this invasion once and for all. Clear?'

Both men nodded solemnly. Already he could hear the next men in line whispering his words to the comrade beside him.

Lord Suheir raised his curved sword in salute. 'We are with you, my lord,' he rumbled.

Malus nodded and sat up straight. At that moment he realised that twelve thousand men hung on his next word, awaiting the command to unleash a grim slaughter upon their foes. He smiled to himself, savouring the sensation of power. Suddenly the risks inherent in his plan became meaningless. Could any risk in the wide world be great enough to sour the terrible joy he felt?

The highborn turned his gaze to the summit of the wide hill before him and raised his axe high into the air. 'The household knights will advance,' he said in a low voice, then brought the weapon down in a shining arc. 'Forward!'

Spite lurched forward at a steady walk, head lowering as it sensed that a battle was close to hand. The cold ones of the front rank followed suit, rippling forward like the flick of a long, steel whip. Malus spurred the cold one up the hill slope, eager to crest the summit and see what he could of the vast movement occurring around him.

When he reached the top of the hill he looked immediately ahead and found only more rolling terrain stretching off to the horizon, but to left and right the light horse were surging in a black tide over their own series of foothills, moonlight burning coldly on the tops of their long spears. Behind him came the faint rattle and groan of chariot wheels, growing steadily quieter as the war machines picked up speed.

The druchii army swept across the low hills like storm clouds, low thunder murmuring in the fall of thousands of shining hooves. Malus raised his axe once more at the top of the next hill and swept it downwards. As one, eight thousand knights and cavalrymen spurred their mounts to a trot.

Now the earth shook with the heavy tread of the cavalry, and the iron wheels of the chariots added their own deep-throated rumble as they picked up speed. The barren hills were flashing past now. The nauglir of the household knights were gliding over the rolling terrain like hunting hounds, venomous drool trailing from their dagger-like fangs. As they rode the wind shifted, and in the distance a herd of northern ponies shrieked in terror as they caught the cold ones' scent. Malus could just catch glimpses of dark tent roofs a half-mile ahead, just beyond a trio of low, broken hills.

The highborn swung his axe over his head and put the spurs to Spite's flanks, urging him into a canter.

Spite plunged down the steep slope and bounded swiftly up the opposite hillside, long legs at full extension and a growl rumbling from the cold one's snout as it scented prey just ahead. This time when they streaked over the summit Malus saw that the rolling slopes beyond were carpeted in low, round tents made from crudely sewn hides. The tents of the horde covered everything from horizon to horizon, darkening the hillsides and hollows like a vile disease. The stench of spilled blood and corrupted flesh rolled over him like a cloud, thick enough to hang like a faint haze over the squalid tents of the camp.

The sheer size of the horde struck Malus like an invisible blow. It was one thing to comprehend what a hundred thousand troops represented, but another thing entirely to see it with one's own eyes. *We're like a bucket of water being thrown into a furnace,* he finally realised. *How can we possibly defeat such a foe?*

Despair began to seep like poison into his heart – but just then a tent flap opened almost a dozen yards away and a bewildered beastman staggered out into the night air. Its heavy, horned head swung left and right, taking in the oncoming druchii riders and struggling to make sense of what it saw. Then, in a single moment its expression changed from aggravation to stark panic, and the highborn grinned like a daemon from the Abyss.

One foe at a time, he realised. *We beat them one foe at a time.*

I'm coming for you, dear sister, the highborn thought with savage joy. *Now, after so many months, so many schemes and betrayals, there will finally be a reckoning.*

Fixing the terrified beastman with a predatory glare Malus raised his axe and screamed to the heavens.

'Warriors of Naggaroth! CHARGE!'

Chapter Eleven
NIGHT AND FIRE

SHEVAEL RAISED A long, curving horn to his lips at Malus's command and blew a wild, howling note that was answered up and down the druchii line. The household knights roared their bloodlust to the heavens and broke into the Chaos camp in a storm of steel and red ruin.

Malus screamed like a tormented shade, his face alight with daemonic wrath as he drove Spite down a narrow, filth-strewn lane between leaning rawhide tents. Tent ropes parted like threads and poles crackled like kindling as the heavy cold ones smashed headlong through the closely-packed tents. Shouts and screams echoed from within as the nauglir crushed trapped beastmen underfoot or snapped at flailing shapes struggling to escape their collapsed shelters. Geysers of red sparks shot skyward as fires were scattered or stomped by rushing, scaly feet, and orange flames flared brightly where coals landed on brittle hides or oily bedding.

A dark, hulking shape burst from a tent just ahead and to Malus's right. He dropped his reins and raised his axe in a two-handed grip, striking the beastman in the side of the head in a vicious, underhanded swing that shattered the monster's skull. Another beastman erupted from the shadows of his tent ahead and to the left, brandishing a long, rusty sword. The horned fiend swung at Spite's toothy snout, but the nauglir ducked its bony head and bit off the attacker's left leg just above the knee. The beastman's wail of agony swept over the onrushing highborn and was quickly lost behind him as Malus drove ever deeper into the enemy encampment.

Sounds of battle and the thunder of hooves mingled into an echoing roar like the grinding fury of an avalanche. Pandemonium reigned inside the Chaos camp; some beastmen ran for their lives while others lashed out at anything that moved. Swarms of fiery motes traced glowing arcs overhead as the druchii charioteers shot flaming arrows deeper into the camp. Horns blew, horses screamed and marauders shouted hoarse, blasphemous curses to the sky.

Ahead, the reeking path abruptly jogged to the right around a tent festooned with skulls and bloody scraps of freshly skinned druchii hides. Snarling, Malus put his spurs to Spite's flanks and ran right over the rawhide shelter. Something wailed and gibbered within, its cries cut short by one of the nauglir's stamping feet. On the opposite side of the tent a dark shape stumbled out into the open, clutching a curling staff of grey wood. Malus caught a brief glimpse of the bray shaman whirling on its cloven hooves and raising a clawed hand to cast some terrible spell before Spite lunged at the beastman and bit its head off.

The highborn leaned back in the saddle as his mount leapt clear of the collapsed tent. Malus looked frantically to the right, trying to keep track of his knights, but saw only the reeling sides of half-collapsed tents and glimpses of helmeted heads and hacking, red-stained swords rising above the low shelters. Where had his trumpeter gone? 'Shevael!' he shouted, his voice instantly swept away in the maelstrom of battle.

'Here, my lord!' came a faint reply, just on the other side of the tents to Malus's right. One of the shelters burst apart in a cloud of tattered hides and flailing ropes as the young highborn rode his nauglir through it. The knight's pale face was streaked with blood and his eyes shone with battle-lust. 'We have them on the run!' he said, shouting to be heard even though he and Malus were only a few yards apart. 'I've never seen such a slaughter!'

'Stick close to me, lad!' Malus shouted back. 'Sound the signal for the knights to rally! We're getting scattered by these damned tents!' The highborn knew that time was not on their side. For now they had the advantage of surprise, but once the shock wore off the Chaos horde could overwhelm the druchii attackers by sheer force of numbers.

Shevael, wrestling with the reins of his agitated cold one, stared quizzically at Malus. 'What was that about the tents?' he shouted. Then suddenly his eyes went wide. 'Look out, my lord!'

Malus whirled, but Spite had seen the onrushing beastmen first. The cold one spun to the left, nearly throwing Malus out of the saddle, and the axe blow aimed for Malus's neck glanced off his left pauldron instead. The highborn cursed, fighting for balance, and threw a wild swing at the beastman's upturned snout that hacked off part of the misshapen beast's left horn.

Four of the goat-headed monstrosities had rushed out of the darkness at Malus, and now they swarmed around the flank of the cold one, aiming blows at both Spite and Malus alike. One of the beastmen thrust a spear at the cold one's snout, gouging a deep furrow just above the warbeast's upper fangs, while another slashed at Spite's neck with a heavy, broad bladed cleaver. The axe-wielder brayed a blasphemous oath and swung again at Malus's chest. Malus anticipated the blow and tried to lean back out of the weapon's reach – but the fourth beastman leapt up and grabbed the highborn's left arm, trying to drag him from the saddle.

Whether by accident or design, Malus was pulled full into the axe's path and the weapon struck him in the chest, just over his heart. A mundane steel breastplate would have crumpled under the savage blow, but the sigils of protection woven into the armour held fast and turned the blade aside with a discordant clang and a shower of blue sparks. Before the beastman could recover and strike another blow Malus shouted a curse and brought down his axe on the warrior's head, striking the beastman right between the eyes. The warrior fell, spilling blood and brains from the cleft in his skull, and the highborn planted a heel in Spite's right side before the creature holding his arm could pull him to the ground. On command the warbeast pivoted right, slashing its powerful tail in an arc to the left. It struck the unwary beastman full in the back with bone-crushing force, tearing the warrior free from Malus and sending its broken body hurtling through the air.

Foam dripping from its fanged snout, the beastman with the cleaver switched targets and charged at Malus, but Spite lunged forward and caught the running warrior in its teeth, shaking the creature like a dog shakes a rabbit. Bones crackled and snapped, and the cleaver spun out of the beastman's lifeless hands. The nauglir took a quick, convulsive bite and the warrior fell in two bloody pieces. That left the lone spearman who turned and ran for its life, bleating in terror as it headed deeper into the camp.

Malus settled himself back in the saddle and grabbed the reins in his left fist. 'Sound the call for the knights to rally and follow me!' he shouted at Shevael, and kicked Spite into a run.

The sky above the Chaos camp glowed a dull orange from the fires of burning tents. Sounds of battle echoed from every side; he wondered how the cavalry was faring to either side of his knights but there was no way to tell from where he was sitting. He cut the straightest path through the camp he could manage, driving Spite over and through any tent in his path. Behind him he heard Shevael sound his war-horn and then distant shouts and thudding feet as the household knights responded.

Trusting that the knights were right behind him, Malus plunged ahead, searching desperately for any signs he was nearing Nagaira's tent. How far into the camp was he? A mile, a mile and a half? There was no way to be sure. The scouts said three miles to the centre of camp, he thought grimly, watching hunched-over beastmen scramble out of the path of the charging cold one. One of the creatures stumbled on a rope, and before it could recover he hacked off its head as he swept by, splashing dark blood against the side of a nearby tent.

Without warning Spite burst into a large, cleared area surrounded by tents. Malus quickly stole a look behind him to see if Shevael and the knights were back there, and the lapse of attention very nearly cost him his life.

Suddenly the air rang with the shrill scream of horses and the bitter oaths of men. Two small objects struck Malus in quick succession, one bouncing off his breastplate and the other ricocheting from his pauldron and scoring a bloody line across his cheek. Startled, the highborn brought his head around just as another hand axe spun by, missing his nose by inches.

He'd ridden right into an improvised picket line where a band of marauders had tied up their horses for the night. The small, grassy space was packed with a dozen screaming, rearing horses and their men, who now turned on the highborn and attacked him with whatever weapons were to hand.

Spite, smelling horseflesh, bellowed hungrily and leapt for the nearest animal. The horse shrieked and reared, slashing at the air with its hooves as its rider shouted vile oaths and struggled to keep his seat. Malus was in a similar predicament, shouting and cursing at the warbeast as it clamped its jaws around the horse's neck and pushed forward on its powerful hind legs, trying to bear the animal to the ground.

Another axe hissed past Malus's head. Shouting, tattooed warriors rushed at him from left and right, brandishing swords and short spears. The highborn jerked at the reins, trying to get Spite to release the squealing horse, but the nauglir refused to give up its prey. The nauglir surged forward, driving the animal over onto its side. Its rider leapt clear, but Malus, caught unawares by the sudden movement was catapulted from the saddle. He flew over Spite's bloodied head and landed just on the other side of the thrashing, dying horse – a few scant feet from its enraged owner.

The marauder was on him in an instant, bellowing a war cry in his barbarian tongue. A rough hand seized the highborn's dark hair and pulled his head up, exposing his throat to the marauder's upraised blade. Malus caught the downward-sweeping sword against the side of his axe, and then drove the end of its haft into the marauder's leg just above the knee. The blunt haft rebounded from the human's thick muscles, but the painful blow staggered him for a moment. Malus jabbed him again, this time in the groin, and the marauder's grip on his hair loosened. The highborn tore himself free and rolled quickly away, scrambling to his feet beside the dying horse to receive the barbarian's charge – and a hurled axe flew out of the darkness and hit Malus in the side of the head.

The axe had been poorly thrown, and struck Malus with the top edge instead of the blade. But the world dissolved in a flash of searing pain, and he dimly felt the impact as his body hit the ground once more. Sounds came and went, and though he could still see, his mind couldn't quite make sense of what was happening. He felt, distinctly, a rivulet of ichor make its way slowly down the side of his head and begin to pool in the hollow of his throat.

He felt the ground shake beneath him, and an awful, low moaning reverberate through the air. The world seemed to grow dark, and for a moment an icy rage galvanized him at the thought that he was about to die.

At that moment, everything snapped back into place – and he saw that the darkness was the shadow of the howling marauder, looming over him with sword upraised.

With a shout Malus tried to roll further away but fetched up against the twitching corpse of the marauder's horse. The sword swept down in a blurring arc and the highborn caught the blow on the haft of his axe. More blows rained down amid a stream of burning curses, several slipping past his guard and ringing off his enchanted armour. Gritting his teeth, Malus threw up his left arm and caught the next blow on his vambrace, then chopped one-handed at the human's right knee. He felt the keen blade split the kneecap and the man fell onto the highborn's lower body, bellowing in rage and pain.

Quick to follow up on his success, Malus sat up and swung hard for the marauder's shaggy head – but the man caught the haft of the axe in his left hand and stopped it cold. Glaring balefully from beneath craggy brows, the marauder let out a lunatic chuckle and flexed his powerful shoulders and arms, forcing the weapon back. Malus cursed and spat, the axe quivering in his hands, but the human's fearsome strength was far greater than his own. Slowly but surely the highborn was pushed backwards and the Chaos warrior dragged himself up the highborn's body, drawing a long, serrated dagger from a sheath at his belt.

Malus's axe was forced past his head and the curved blade driven into the blood-soaked ground. The marauder loomed over him, his scarred lips pulling back to reveal crudely filed teeth. Hot, foetid breath blew in the highborn's face. The marauder whispered something in his bestial tongue and raised his dagger to strike.

Suddenly the highborn's body spasmed and searing ice flowed through his veins. He cried out in shock as needles of pain wracked his eyes. The marauder, seeing what was etched in them, recoiled from Malus with a shriek of wordless terror that ended in a bone-jarring crunch as Spite lunged over the horse's ravaged body and bit the man cleanly in half. Malus was deluged in a shower of blood and spilled entrails as the marauder's lower torso emptied itself onto his chest.

'Mother of Night!' Malus cursed furiously, shoving the steaming remains away and climbing to his feet. Spite had returned to feasting on the horse's innards, and the highborn swatted the nauglir across its bloody snout with the flat of his axe. 'Stop thinking with your damned stomach, you great lump of scales!' he shouted hoarsely. The nauglir flinched from the blow, shaking its gore-stained snout like a large dog, and lowered obediently onto its haunches.

Druchii knights swarmed through the cleared area, and the mangled bodies of horses and marauders lay in bloody heaps all around. Malus staggered over to the nauglir and rested his pounding head against the saddle for a moment before putting his foot in the stirrup and levering himself back into his seat.

'My lord!' Shevael cried from the other side of the cleared area. He hauled on his reins and trotted quickly to his master's side, his bloodstained sword resting against his shoulder. 'I saw you go down, and then the marauders came at me, and – Blessed Murderer! You're wounded!'

The highborn rubbed at the sticky mess covering his face and neck. 'Most of this isn't mine,' he growled, scanning the area quickly. He counted close to fifty knights milling about the picket area, their armour splashed with streaks of gore. Overhead the sky glowed a fierce orange, and the stink of burning hair hung like a pall over the battlefield. There were faint shouts off to the north and the east, but the sounds of fighting had all but tapered away. 'Where are the chariots?' he demanded, spitting bits of human flesh out of his mouth.

Shevael gave Malus a blank look. 'I… don't know,' he said sheepishly. 'We lost sight of them right after I sounded the call to rally. We must have got separated in the confusion.'

Malus cursed under his breath. He had been depending on the chariots to support their withdrawal after they killed Nagaira. The highborn stood as straight in the saddle as he could and tried to see over the leaning tops of wrecked tents, but with the darkness and the columns of smoke rising from nearly every direction it was impossible to see where his troops were. The sea of rough tents was acting against the druchii now, channelling the riders into a dark, twisting maze that worked to separate the banners from one another. 'It's too quiet,' he said uneasily.

'It's been like that for several minutes,' Shevael said. 'The Chaos horde is in full flight. The attack has filled them with panic!' he said excitedly.

But the highborn shook his head worriedly. 'Something's not right,' he said. 'We've got to get moving, Shevael. Where is Lord Suheir?'

Shevael pointed to the north. 'He continued on with most of the knights a few moments ago,' the young highborn replied. 'He said that he caught sight of a cluster of tents on a nearby hill that might be the war leader's pavilion.'

Malus gathered up Spite's reins. 'That's where we need to be,' he snapped. 'Household knights!' he cried, raising his gory axe. 'With me!'

Lord Suheir's knights had blazed broad trails through the jumble of tents, trampling everything in their path as they drove relentlessly north. Malus picked the centre path and led the knights along at a brisk trot, searching the twisting side lanes for enemy activity as they rode. Could the enemy have panicked so completely? If so, would Nagaira still be in her tents? He tried to guess how long it had been since the attack began: five minutes, perhaps? Ten? It was hard to be sure. Time became elastic in the heat of battle, seeming to rush by in some moments and slow to a crawl in others.

They rushed forward into darkness, hearing the roaring of the flames swell around and ahead of them. Fires had leapt out of control among the filthy tents, and the night sky was thickening with stinking smoke. His eyes strained to make out the nearby hill that Shevael spoke of, but he could see nothing in the shifting murk. Worry started to eat at his nerves; his army was no longer under his control, which meant that he had almost no way of pulling them back if something went disastrously wrong. In case they were separated, all of the banner and regimental officers knew a series of locations to retreat to along the route back to the Black Tower, but would they turn back in time? A moment's indecision could cost thousands of lives. For a moment he was tempted to order Shevael to sound a general retreat, then lead the household knights himself on to find Nagaira's tent. But the Chaos horde would hear the horn as well, and once they saw the druchii forces breaking away they would rush in pursuit, leaving Malus and his men advancing right into their teeth. He beat his armoured gauntlet on the cantle of his saddle in frustration. There were no good options that he could determine.

Suddenly a wild shout and the clash of arms echoed through the murk in the near distance. As if on cue, the wind shifted, drawing back the veil of smoke and revealing a roughly circular cluster of low, indigo-hued tents covering a broad hill less than a quarter mile ahead. A fierce melee had erupted at the base of the hill; Malus could see Lord Suheir's knights hacking away at a large force of beastmen, who fought with ferocious zeal against their better-armed foes. Suheir's larger force was moving quickly to surround the base of the hill completely, cutting it off from the rest of the camp. Clearly the knight-captain believed that he'd found their objective, and looking up at the cluster of tents, Malus agreed.

'This is it!' he cried to the knights following in his wake. 'Forward up the hill – kill everything that gets in your way!' With a shout, the knights of the Black Tower spurred their mounts forward, forming into a wedge formation as compact and powerful as a spearhead. 'Shevael, sound the charge!'

The young highborn let out a long, howling note from his horn and like a bolt shot from a crossbow the wedge of knights hurtled towards the hill. Lord Suheir's knights heard the horn and saw Malus's approach, and riders scrambled to open a gap in their lines for the wedge to pass through. Howling, roaring beastmen swarmed into the gap, oblivious to the doom bearing down on them.

At the point of the wedge, Malus raised his axe above his head and gave his foes a savage, red-toothed grin. Horned heads turned at the thunder of the knights' approach. Braying calls rang out from the knot of beastmen, and the huge creatures hefted clubs, mattocks and axes to receive the highborn's charge.

The highborn gauged the distance carefully, glaring balefully at the snarling mob of beastmen. At the last moment, just before Spite crashed into their ranks, he planted his heels in the nauglir's flanks and hauled back on the reins. 'Up, Spite!' he cried. 'Up!'

With a thunderous roar the cold one bent low – and leapt into the mass of enemy troops. The one-ton war-beast smashed into the enemy like a hammer, scattering and trampling the beastmen with bone-crushing force. Malus chopped at upturned snouts and chests, alternating blows to his left and his right, inflicting horrific wounds on his stunned foes. Thick, bitter blood burst from ruptured arteries and shattered skulls.

But the rear ranks of the beastmen refused to give way – if anything they redoubled their attack in the face of Malus's charge. A howling beast rushed at the highborn from the right, smashing his club into Malus's hip. His armour turned aside much of the blow, but he roared out in pain and buried his axe deep in the beastman's shoulder. Spite lunged forward and bit off another beastman's head, its skull and horns crunching between the nauglir's jaws like brittle wood. An axe blow glanced from the highborn's left leg. Malus yanked his weapon free from his victim's shoulder and brought it down on the head of his foe to the left. Brains spattered against the highborn's face. Then a surge of armoured figures swept up on Malus's flanks as the rest of the knights cut their way to his side.

'Again, Spite! Up!' he shouted, kicking his heels. The nauglir obeyed, gathering itself and leaping up and through the thin line of beastmen blocking their way. As they landed, Malus pivoted the nauglir hard to the right, using its powerful tail to smash aside a pair of beastmen that had escaped the cold one's rush. Their numbers scattered by the brute force of Malus's manoeuvre, the beastmen became easy prey to the knights following in his wake, and the remaining warriors fighting against Lord Suheir's troops began a fighting withdrawal up the hill. Malus turned to his men and pointed at the beastmen with his axe. 'At them! Into their flanks!' He put his spurs to Spite's flanks and led the knights up the hill at a shallow angle, intercepting the retreating beastmen. Pressed hard from behind and now attacked from the flank, the beastman rearguard collapsed.

Malus kept Spite moving steadily uphill, riding down a fleeing beastman and burying his axe into the warrior's back. Spite lunged forward and caught another in its jaws, biting through its abdomen and letting legs and torso roll bloodily downhill. The nauglir's lashing tail accounted for another foe, breaking its legs with a vicious sweep and leaving the beastman to be trampled by the oncoming knights.

Ahead, a single surviving beastman disappeared inside the shadowy opening of the first tent. Malus reined in Spite outside the enclosure and leapt to the ground, axe at the ready. Within moments he was surrounded by a half-dozen more knights, including Shevael and Lord Suheir. 'Well done, Suheir,' Malus said, saluting the knight-captain, then he addressed the assembled druchii. 'Remember, we're after a potent sorceress. She's no doubt defended by all manner of magical traps and summoned beasts. When we reach her, hold our line of retreat open and let me deal with her.'

Suheir and the knights nodded their helmeted heads, saving their breath for the hard fighting ahead. Malus adjusted his grip on the blood-slick axe haft. You'll not escape me this time sister, the highborn thought grimly. You should have fled while you had the chance.

'All right,' he said. 'Let's go.'

Weapons ready, the druchii entered the gloomy confines of the first tent. The enclosure was dimly lit by a few guttering oil lamps, and the air was thick with a musky incense. Within lay piles of metal that glittered dully in the weak light: fine swords and battered armour, many still marked with dried blood and bits of flesh, as well as silver plates, goblets and other bits of valuable plunder looted from the razed watchtowers. Lord Suheir eyed the piles with some bemusement. 'A funny place for a treasure trove,' he murmured.

'They are offerings to the sorceress,' Malus replied. 'The beastmen and the marauders give her their best plunder as a sign of subservience. It's a statement of power, not greed.'

'It sounds as though you know this sorceress well,' Suheir mused.

'More than I'd like,' the highborn replied, edging across the enclosure.

At the far end of the wide tent lay a heavy hanging of red-dyed canvas. Malus paused before the hanging, uncertain of what lay beyond. Suheir shouldered his way through the group, hefting his shield. 'I'll go first,' he said quietly, stepping carefully up to the covered opening. He studied the cloth and its borders carefully, and finding no strange markings, he slashed his sword across the hanging, revealing the beastman waiting in ambush on the other side.

With a braying roar the horned warrior lunged at Suheir, chopping at the knight's helmeted head. Suheir absorbed the blow against the face of his shield and stabbed low with his sword, catching the beastman in the belly. The warrior staggered, bellowing in rage and pain, and the knight-captain slashed his sword across the creature's abdomen, spilling its guts onto the grassy floor. The beastman collapsed with a groan and Suheir knocked it aside with his shield, then advanced warily into the space beyond with Malus close behind.

The second enclosure was even darker and smokier than the previous one. Huddled shapes knelt in groups of eight in each corner of the space, their heads bowed in supplication as they faced four pathways through the square space. Each pathway led to another cloth hanging, including the one the druchii entered through. Suheir started upon seeing the silhouetted figures, then bent close and prodded one with the point of his sword. 'Dead,' he grunted. 'Looks like mummified beastmen. The incense covers the stink, I suppose.'

Malus nodded silently, gooseflesh racing down his spine as he remembered a similar chamber in the daemon's temple far to the north. 'We're in the right place,' he whispered. 'Head through the opening on the other side of the tent.'

Suheir stepped warily among the mummified corpses and cut down the hanging on the opposite end of the tent. Beyond lay a long, rectangular tent, lit at the far end with two small witchlamps. Along the length of the tent treble rows of kneeling figures lined both sides of a narrow aisle. 'Blessed Murderer,' Suheir cursed softly, studying the mummified attendants.

They were not beastmen this time, but druchii highborn, clad in battered armour and ragged, bloodstained kheitans. Some had limbs and heads crudely stitched back into place. Their helmets had been removed, revealing gaping head wounds here and there, and showing the looks of fear and agony frozen on their pallid features.

'More tribute for the war leader,' Malus growled. 'We're close now. Press on.'

Suheir took a deep breath and nodded gravely, then edged his way down the long aisle. At the far end lay a pair of hangings this time, their indigo panels stitched with arcane sigils in gold and silver thread. An invisible nimbus of magic hung about the portal, setting Malus's hair on end.

The highborn turned to the men behind him. 'Wait here,' he said. 'Suheir and Shevael, come with me.'

Steeling himself, he shouldered past the knight-captain and pushed his way past the heavy cloth panels. Everything about this felt wrong. Where were the attendants? The guards? He feared that the pavilion had been abandoned when the attack began, and their bold assault had been for nothing.

Malus stepped past the hangings into a spacious tent set with tables, small bookshelves and chairs, all of which were piled with books, papers and yellowed scrolls. Candles burned on several tables, and a pair of braziers near the centre filled the space with reddish light.

At the far end of the enclosure, on a small dais set with a low-backed chair, sat a solitary figure in a dark, hooded robe.

For a moment Malus was too stunned to react. He could feel the intensity of the figure's gaze smouldering hatefully from the shadows of the wide hood.

'It's a trap,' he declared, and knew with an awful certainty that his intuition was true. He couldn't imagine how Nagaira could have anticipated his attack, but she'd waited here in her tent, knowing that he would come for her.

Grabbing his axe tightly, Malus charged across the room. 'Hear me, Tz'arkan!' he hissed. 'Grant me your gifts!' It was the one and only advantage he possessed, and he'd planned to use it when he came face-to-face with his sister. Now he prayed that if he struck swiftly enough he could forestall whatever ambuscade she'd devised.

Black corruption seethed in Malus's veins, spreading like a cold fire beneath his skin. He crossed the room in an eye blink propelled by a daemonic wind. With a savage curse burning on his lips he struck at the hooded figure with all his strength.

The axe blurred through the air, straight for the figure's head. Quicker than the eye could follow, a pair of long blades swept up from beneath the robes and blocked the highborn's downward stroke with a flare of sparks and a ringing clash of steel. The loose robe fell away and the figure rose, effortlessly pushing Malus backward off the dais.

Instead of Nagaira, Malus found himself face-to-face with an armoured Chaos knight, clad in armour similar to a druchii knight but covered in patterns of blasphemous runes painted in blood. Red light seeped sullenly from gaps in the sorcerous armour, and shone from the oculars of the champion's ornate, horned helmet. Twin druchii longswords held Malus's axe at bay with fearsome strength. Around the champion's neck rested a heavy, red-gold torc.

The Amulet of Vaurog! Tz'arkan hissed, roiling inside Malus's chest.

And with that, the trap was sprung.

Chapter Twelve
SHIELDS AND SPEARS

A SECOND CHAMPION, Malus realised with a sense of ominous dread. Suddenly the tremendous size of the Chaos horde made terrible sense. Nagaira hadn't raised the horde alone, but had allied herself with a powerful warlord and won him to her cause.

There was a tremor in the air of Nagaira's tent, like the movement of unseen spirits, and suddenly a chorus of screams and the clash of steel rang out in the antechamber behind the druchii. Then in the far distance Malus heard a roaring, skirling sound that cried out from all along the invisible horizon – it was the wailing of hundreds of war horns, loosing the Chaos horde at last.

With a shriek of rage Malus drew back his axe and hammered the Chaos champion with a storm of vicious strokes at head, neck, chest and arms. Sparks flew and tempered steel sang, but the champion blocked the furious blows with superhuman speed. A return stroke slipped easily past Malus's guard and rang off his pauldron; another struck like an adder and glanced off his right wrist. The champion's twin swords clashed and whirled in a graceful, deadly dance, driving the highborn inexorably backwards in spite of Tz'arkan's potent gifts.

Malus blocked a lightning thrust to his stomach with the haft of his axe and thrust upwards, hoping to catch the champion beneath the chin with the weapon's curved upper edge, but the armoured warrior checked his advance at the last moment and let the axe slide harmlessly by. Without stopping the highborn pivoted smoothly on his heel and swung around and down, aiming for the warrior's right knee, but the champion anticipated the blow and his right-hand sword parried the stroke with ease. At the same time his left-hand blade blurred at Malus's head, and only the daemon's inhuman reflexes drew him back in time. Even so, the sword drew a shallow cut across the highborn's forehead, sending thick streams of ichor down the side of his face.

He'd heard tales of the phenomenal power and skill of warriors chosen by the Chaos gods, but the reality was far more terrifying than he'd imagined. Even the zealots of the cult of Khaine, who worshipped the art of killing, could not compare with the champion's implacable skill. Thinking quickly, Malus retreated from the armoured warrior, desperately looking for some way to turn the battle to his advantage.

The momentary distraction was nearly enough to seal his fate. A sword leapt like lighting at the highborn's face; Malus twisted at the last moment, dodging the blow with a hiss of surprise, but realised, too late, that the attack was a feint. The champion's second sword swung down in a vicious arc and caught his left leg, just above the side of the knee. Fiery pain shot up Malus's leg and it gave way beneath him, toppling him to the matted earth. He fetched up next to an oak table plundered from one of the fallen watchtowers as the champion pressed his advantage and loomed over the highborn like a swooping hawk.

Malus threw a frantic swing at the warrior's midsection, hoping to spoil his attack, but the swing was off-balance and only served to leave him more exposed than before. The champion's right-hand blade rose above his helmeted head and chopped down in a backhanded blow that struck the haft of Malus's axe above his right hand and sheared through it like a sapling. The warrior's left-hand sword plummeted like a thunderbolt, and the highborn raised the severed length of axe-haft and caught the fearsome blow on the seasoned oak between his white-knuckled fists. The keen blade split the haft once again and the sword struck the highborn's breastplate hard enough to drive the air from his lungs.

Then Malus heard a roar like an angry bull and an onrushing shadow swept over him from behind. There was a crash of steel against iron and a shower of fiery orange coals seemed to drift lazily through the air as Lord Suheir smashed aside one of the braziers in a headlong charge at the Chaos champion. The powerfully built knight-captain swung a fearsome stroke at the champion's helm, but the warrior swayed backwards with serpentine grace and let the blade pass harmlessly by, then lashed out with his right-hand sword in a backhanded stroke that struck Suheir's vambrace a glancing blow. Malus saw a spray of blood burst from the point of impact, then watched as the champion thrust with his left-hand sword and stab its reinforced point into the knight-captain's side. The sword punched cleanly through Suheir's breastplate and sank an inch deep, just above the waist. Suheir staggered for just a moment, then lashed out with a backhanded stroke of his own that knocked the champion's stabbing blade aside before rushing the armoured warrior with his steel-rimmed shield held before him. For the first time the champion seemed taken by surprise, and back-pedalled furiously in the face of Suheir's bull-like charge.

Hands grabbed at Malus's shoulders, trying to pull him upright. The highborn looked up to see Shevael's pale, terrified face. The young knight's movements seemed clumsy and slow to the highborn's daemonic reflexes. 'How do we kill him?' Shevael moaned.

The Chaos champion's retreat was swift, but not swift enough. With a roar, Suheir struck the warrior's breastplate with the edge of his shield and set the champion crashing backwards through a small bookcase. Malus grabbed Shevael's arm and staggered upright, biting back a savage curse at the pain in his damaged leg.

Just a few feet away Suheir pressed his attack, hammering at the champion with one fearsome blow after another that tried to batter aside the warrior's defences. The champion blocked each stroke with nimble movements of his left-hand sword. Then, just as Suheir drew back for another punishing stroke, the champion lashed out at the knight-captain's shield arm, knocking it wide so that he could lunge forward with his right-hand sword and strike the side of Suheir's left knee. The knight-captain's armour didn't carry the same enchantments as Malus's did; steel pins snapped, lames and poleyn shattered and the champion's sword carved deep into the knee-joint. The druchii fell onto his good knee with a bellow of pain, covering his wounded leg with his shield as the Chaos warrior sprang to his feet like a hill-cat and levelled his weapons at Suheir's head.

The Chaos warrior was so intent on finishing the knight-captain that he didn't see the table Malus hurled at him until it was far too late. With no time to duck or dodge the solid oaken tabletop the champion could only raise his swords and smash the hurtling furniture to bits with his twin swords.

Above the splintering crash of the thick wood rose a furious roar and the ringing clash of steel on steel. The Chaos champion staggered back half a step – and slowly lowered his head to the length of druchii steel jutting from his midsection. Suheir's fearsome strength had driven his blade clean through the champion's torso, emerging more than a foot from the warrior's steel backplate.

And yet the champion did not fall. For an appalling instant the two warriors were transfixed, each staring at the wound Suheir's sword had made. A line of thick, black ichor flowed heavily down the back of the silver steel blade. Then with a guttural growl the champion's swords flashed and Suheir's head bounced across the matted earth. The knight-captain's body toppled onto its side, pouring a freshet of blood onto the ground, while the champion drove his right-hand sword into the dirt and used his free hand to reach for Suheir's sword, still jutting from his abdomen.

Shevael let out a panicked wail and Malus pushed him away, gritting his teeth at the pain as he limped quickly across the chamber. Flames were climbing the back wall of the tent and licking at several of the bookshelves, kindled by the scattered coals from the upended brazier.

The young highborn staggered, his face a pale mask of terror and rage. With a trembling hand he drew his second sword, and with a deep breath a sense of eerie calm stole across his features. 'Make your escape, my lord,' the young highborn shouted. 'I'll cover your retreat.'

Shevael's grim tone brought Malus up short. 'No, you young fool!' he cried. 'You don't stand a chance–'

But the young highborn wasn't listening. With a furious shout he charged at the struggling champion, his twin swords describing a deadly figure-eight pattern. The Chaos champion lurched backwards in the wake of the sudden attack, stumbling on a pile of spilled books, and Shevael's swords struck the warrior multiple times in the head, chest and leg. But the young highborn's blows were hasty and poorly aimed, and could not penetrate the champion's heavy armour. The Chaos warrior righted himself and with a convulsive motion wrenched Suheir's ichor-stained sword from his body. Still shouting curses at the champion, Shevael pressed his attack, but he underestimated the Chaos warrior's skill. As the young highborn rushed in the champion backhanded Shevael across the face with the pommel of Suheir's dripping blade and in the same motion extended his left arm and stabbed the young knight in the throat. Bright, red blood burst from the awful wound and Shevael collapsed to the ground, gasping and choking for air.

Cursing bitterly, Malus reached his objective. His armoured fingers closed about the iron grillwork of the second brazier, the drying blood on his armoured fingers hissing on contact. Using his daemonically-infused strength he lifted the red-hot container and hurled it at the champion, catching the Chaos warrior full in the chest. The warrior fell with a resounding clang and a hiss of scorched flesh, his body covered in searing coals and ash. More embers scattered across the enclosure, burning holes in the tent wall and starting more fires among the shredded papers.

Malus leapt to Shevael's side, but already the blood flow from this torn throat was ebbing and his eyes were glassy and unfocused. The highborn shook the young druchii roughly. 'Don't die on me you damned fool!' the highborn snarled, but it was already far too late. Shevael's eyes rolled back in his head and his body went limp.

Cursing bitterly, the highborn pulled the horn from around Shevael's neck and with a grim look in his eye he pulled off the young highborn's sword belt and buckled it about his waist. The tent by this point was blazing on every side, and waves of heat and choking smoke surrounded him. Coughing furiously, he snatched up the young highborn's swords just as the Chaos champion regained his senses and kicked his way clear of the burning brazier.

Malus fought a tide of black rage as the champion struggled to his feet. He wanted nothing more than to avenge himself upon the foul warrior, but this was not the time. The Chaos fiends had sprung their ambush, and if he didn't get his troops out of the camp they were going to be slaughtered. He'd sooner see his soul lost to Tz'arkan for all time than suffer such a black stain to his honour. With a last, hateful look at the Chaos champion, Malus turned and raced back the way he'd come.

As he pulled back the double hangings however, he was brought up short by a nightmarish scene of carnage. The long, rectangular tent swarmed with the pale figures of the living dead. The druchii corpses that had knelt in supplication along the narrow aisle had sprung to grisly life at some invisible command and attacked the knights Malus had left behind as a rearguard. Many of the stitched-together revenants had been hacked apart, but the rest now hunched over the ruptured bodies of the tower knights, their chalk-white hands slick with blood and torn meat. Several slack-jawed faces turned in Malus's direction as he stood upon the threshold, and the highborn recoiled from the charnel scene with a blasphemous curse.

Behind him the champion lurched to his feet and gathered up his swords. Malus looked quickly about, seeing nothing but flames to left and right, and came to a decision. Taking a deep breath, he raised Shevael's blades and dived headlong through the blazing canvas to his left.

Heat and smoke washed over him for a searing instant, and then he was stumbling through the darkened confines of an adjoining tent, piled high with cushions and sleeping furs. Malus staggered headlong across the tent and slashed at the far wall with both swords. A draught of cool air washed over the highborn's face and he leapt through the shredded cloth, emerging into the night air. Screams and wild howls echoed through the flame-shot darkness all around the hill as the Chaos horde charged out of their hidden positions outside the camp and rushed at the druchii raiders. Knowing that every second counted for the isolated bands of cavalry and footmen, the highborn put Shevael's horn to his lips and blew the general retreat as loudly as he could. He sounded the call three more times, pointing the horn to the east, north and west, then let the instrument fall to his side and headed back to the waiting knights as quickly as he could. As Nagaira's pavilion burned, Malus cut his way through two more tents that lay between him and the mounted warriors, kicking aside piles of skulls and golden plunder as he went.

At last he emerged, bloodied and smoke-stained, before the nervous household knights. They were facing outwards in a large circle, listening to the echoing cries of the enemy and waiting for the onslaught to begin. Even the nauglir sensed the peril approaching, pawing the earth and lowering their heads threateningly.

'Here, Spite!' Malus called as he staggered up to the circle. The knights started at the ghastly apparition of the highborn. 'My lord!' one of the druchii cried out. 'We feared the worst–'

'And you were right to do so,' the highborn said grimly, sheathing his left-hand sword. 'I've led us straight into an ambush.' Without waiting for Spite to sink to his haunches the highborn took a deep breath and hauled himself into the saddle. For good measure he drew the war-horn and sounded the retreat one last time, eliciting a chorus of savage howls from the darkness close by. 'That's it,' he shouted. 'Close order formation! We're falling back to the spearmen and we're not stopping for anyone or anything.' He raised the sword in his right hand.

'Household knights! Forward!' Malus said, and kicked Spite into a run just as the first mobs of beastmen came howling out of the burning night.

MALUS AND THE knights came thundering down out of the charred outskirts of the Chaos encampment with a screaming horde at their heels. True to his word, they'd smashed through or trampled over everything that stood in their path. The highborn's sword streamed thick ropes of blood into the ashen wind, and the nauglirs' snouts glistened with the vital fluids of beastmen and marauders who had been caught before the avalanche of steel and scale.

More than a dozen riderless cold ones loped in the formation's wake, following along with the rest of the pack now that no rider lived to guide them. Knights had been pulled from the saddle by leaping horrors, or felled by flung axes or spears. Each loss was a blow to Malus's pride, a mark of failure that burned worse than any blade and added its weight to the disaster unfolding around him.

As they burst from the smoking confines of the camp Malus looked to the brim of the low hill ahead and his spirits rose as he saw the long lines of spearmen, their shields and spear tips gleaming against the firelight. If they could hold long enough...

Malus pointed his sword to the left and the household knights responded, pivoting smartly and thundering past the spear wall's right flank. The highborn saw the wide-eyed faces of the front ranks as they galloped by, and sensed the fear gripping the young spearmen. No one had told them what was going on, but they knew something wasn't right.

The highborn led the knights down the reverse slope of the hill and called a halt. Off to the right, some fifty yards away, stood a knot of some two hundred cavalrymen. One banner of horse out of six; Malus glanced quickly about and bit back a curse when he could find no more. He turned back to the knights. 'Who is the senior knight now that Lord Suheir is dead?'

Searching glances passed between the assembled warriors. Finally a gruff-looking older knight raised his hand. 'I am, my lord. Dachvar of Klar Karond.'

'Very well, Dachvar. You're in command now,' Malus said. 'Rest your men and see to your mounts. I expect to have need of you again shortly.' Without waiting for a reply he turned Spite about and headed up behind the spear regiments at a run.

The three units stood in close formation, nearly shield-to-shield about a quarter of the way down the hill-slope. Each spearman carried not only his spear, shield and short sword, but also a heavy repeating crossbow and a quiver of black bolts. These were now being loaded by the rear two ranks of each company as the highborn reached the crest of the hill and found Lord Meiron and Lord Rasthlan studying the howling, roaring mob of Chaos troops massing on the far hill-side some two hundred yards distant. A short distance down the reverse slope he saw Rasthlan's autarii scouts crouched together in a small group, smoking pipes and speaking to one another in low tones.

Malus reined in beside the two commanders and hastily returned their salutes.

'My compliments on your deployment, Lord Meiron,' the highborn said, using the advantage of height to study the disposition of the spear regiments. 'I'd hoped we wouldn't have need of your spears, but now it appears you'll anchor our rearguard. Has there been any sign of our chariots or the rest of our cavalry?'

'None, my lord,' Meiron replied gravely. 'It's possible the chariots were caught in the fires that swept through the enemy camp – we haven't heard the rumble of their wheels for some time.' He gave the highborn a shrug. 'As to the cavalry, they may be half a dozen leagues away by now. Most of those young bravos are like wolf cubs – they'll chase anything that moves.'

'Lord Irhaut thinks like a hill bandit, my lord,' Rasthlan interjected. 'He has trained his banner leaders to retreat in the face of a superior foe and lead pursuers away from the rest of the army. What Lord Meiron means is that the light horse could be miles away to east and west, drawing off as many of the Chaos forces as possible.'

From the look on Meiron's face it was clear he meant to say no such thing – he was a dyed-in-the-wool infantry commander with nothing but disdain for cavalrymen – but Malus accepted Rasthlan's explanation with a knowing nod. 'Then let us pray to the Dark Mother that he and his men are successful,' the highborn said, his expression grim. 'Because it looks like we have all we can handle right here.'

A cacophonous roar filled the air at the edge of the Chaos encampment. Beastmen threw back their heads and brayed to the smoke-shrouded moon and tattooed humans beat their swords against their shields and howled the names of their blasphemous gods. They swelled in number with every passing moment, spilling like a black tide down the slopes of the far hill. Malus couldn't guess at the size of the mob, but it was certain that the druchii were heavily outnumbered. The noise washed over the spear formations and murmurs of fear could be heard from among the state regiments. The Black Guard, holding the centre of the line, were silent and still as statues, waiting simply for the battle to begin.

Lord Meiron turned to the spearmen and bellowed in a leathery voice that sawed through the raucous din. 'Stand fast, you whoresons!' he snarled. 'Shields up and eyes front! Those degenerate bastards are working up the courage to charge up this hill and throw away their lives! If I were a holy man I would fall to the ground and thank Khaine almighty for foes as stupid as these!'

Cheers and hisses of laughter went up from the ranks, and the spearmen shook their weapons at the swelling horde. Lord Meiron turned back to Malus and smiled proudly. 'Fear not, my lord,' he said. 'We'll see to these animals.'

'I'll hold you to that, Lord Meiron,' Malus said with a nod, then wheeled Spite about and rode downhill to the group of cavalrymen. The light horsemen were stragglers from a number of different banners and were clearly exhausted, their faces and armour stained with layers of smoke and blood. As the highborn approached, the riders sat straighter in the saddle and chivvied their mounts into something resembling a formation. Malus pulled quickly into shouting distance and cried, 'Secure the spears' left flank! The household knights will take the right.' The banner leader acknowledged the order with a salute and began shouting orders to his men, and the highborn turned Spite about and raced back to the waiting knights.

By the time he reached Dachvar the Chaos warriors were on the move. They seethed down the long slope in a ragged, bloodthirsty mass, running, shambling and loping with twisted and slithering strides. They waved crude weapons above their misshapen heads and screamed for the blood of their foes. To Malus's eyes there looked to be more than ten thousand of them, a sight that filled even his black heart with dread. It never should have come to this, he thought bitterly. How had Nagaira anticipated him?

The ground shook to the thunder of thousands of pounding feet. Horned heads and upraised swords stood out blackly against the hellish backdrop of the burning Chaos encampment.

When the first of the enemy warriors were a third of the way from the bottom of the far hill, Malus heard the rough voice of Lord Meiron cry out, 'Sa'an'ishar!' Instantly a rustle ran through the spear regiments as warriors readied their shields and levelled their long spear. Then: 'Rear ranks! Ready crossbows!'

A ripple of armoured forms ran the length of the battle line as druchii warriors raised their repeating crossbows to their shoulders and angled the weapons skyward. Lord Meiron raised his sword. 'Ready... ready... fire!'

Fifteen hundred crossbows thrummed, and a rain of black bolts hissed through the air. Not a one could fail to find a mark as they plunged into the mass of enemy troops, and howls of rage turned to agonized shrieks as the bolts tore through the poorly armoured warriors. Hundreds of humans and beastmen fell, their bodies trampled by their fellows as the rest of the mob ran on.

The charging Chaos troops had reached the bottom of the hill. An oiled rattle echoed up and down the line as the druchii quickly reloaded their weapons. 'Ready!' Lord Meiron cried. 'Fire!'

Another hissing storm of bolts plunged into the Chaos ranks. Hundreds more were wounded or slain, their bodies piling up at the base of the slope. Savage beastmen clambered over riddled corpses or knocked their injured mates aside, some crawling on all fours as they tried to reach the druchii line.

Once again the repeater crossbows rattled, readying another volley. The front ranks of the foemen were less than fifty yards away. 'First two ranks kneel!' Lord Meiron cried, and the spearmen dropped obediently to one knee. 'Rear ranks, fire!'

Black death scythed through the attackers, the powerful bolts punching completely through the closest enemy troops. The first three ranks of the Chaos warriors toppled like threshed wheat, and even Malus shook his head in awe at the scale of the slaughter. In less than a minute the hill slopes had become a killing field, carpeted with the bodies of the dead.

Yet still the Chaos horde came on.

They struck the line of spearmen with a great, rending crash of steel on wood that echoed from the hillsides. Axes, clubs, swords and claws battered against shield and helm, and the druchii line staggered beneath the weight of the enemy assault. It bent backwards a slow step at a time... then stopped. Malus could hear the rough voice of Lord Meiron spitting savage oaths at the troops, and the Black Guard responded with a collective roar. Spears flickered and stabbed into the press of foes, and howls of rage turned to screams of agony as the druchii warriors put their training and discipline to lethal effect.

But would it be enough? Beastmen and marauders were dying by the score, but from Malus's vantage point he could see spearmen pulled from the ranks and torn apart, or dashed to the ground by terrible blows. The flanking regiments were taking the worst of the punishment, their rear ranks rippling like wheat as wounded men were pulled from the line and new men rotated to take their place. The Chaos attack showed no signs of faltering, and more troops were streaming from the camp every minute to add their weight to the battle. If just one of the regiments broke and ran, the other two would be overwhelmed in moments.

They couldn't remain on the defensive for long, Malus saw. Their only option was to attack.

He drew his bloodstained sword and turned to Dachvar. 'We've got to take the pressure off the spearmen,' he said. 'The household knights will form line and we'll charge the Chaos bastards in the flank.'

'Aye, my lord,' Dachvar replied with a nod, then wheeled his nauglir about and trotted the length of the formation. 'Form line and prepare to charge!' he cried, and the knights readied themselves for battle.

Taking the lead, Malus angled Spite to the east and led the formation of knights around the side of the hill, where they could sweep around the slope and strike the Chaos warriors from the left flank. Long minutes passed while the large formation repositioned itself. Malus listened intently to the battle raging on the hilltop, knowing that every passing minute pushed the spearmen closer to the breaking point. Finally, Dachvar signalled at the far end of the line that all was in readiness, and Malus raised his sword. 'Sa'an'ishar! The household knights will advance at the charge!' Then he lowered his blade and the knights let out an exultant roar, kicking their mounts into a run.

There was neither the time nor the distance to work the formation up into a proper charge; the knights swept around the slope like a huge pack of wolves, plunging into the flank of the enemy with a bone-crushing impact of claws, teeth and steel. Spite trampled two beastmen beneath his broad feet and bit the head off another; Malus stabbed a stunned beastman in the back and slashed his sword across a leaping marauder's neck. The mob recoiled at the sudden shock, and the knights forced their way deeper into the mass, their red swords rising and falling and their cold ones flinging mangled bodies high into the air. Meiron's spearmen cheered and redoubled their efforts, reclaiming the few yards of ground they'd lost and pushing the enemy back down the slope.

Axes and clubs battered at Malus's armoured legs. A beastman tried to climb onto Spite's neck, swinging a cleaver-like sword at the highborn's chest. Malus caught the creature's sword-arm with a blow to the wrist that severed its hand, then stabbed the howling fiend in the chest. Its body left a gleaming trail of blood as it slid from the cold one back into the seething mob below, but another beastman literally leapt to take its place. Malus cursed, trading blows with the creature even as he felt another pair of hands to his left trying to pull him from the saddle. The charge had inflicted considerable damage but the mob continued to hold its ground, bolstered by its reinforcements and motivated by fear of its terrible leaders. Now that the knights were stuck in they'd lost their most crucial asset: mobility. Soon the greater numbers of the enemy would tell against them.

Malus feinted a cut at the beastman in front of him, inviting a response. When the creature lunged at him with its sword he was ready, stabbing it in the throat. The beast fell to the ground, coughing blood, and the highborn turned his attention to the braying monster pulling at his left leg. Distantly, he heard an ominous rumble of thunder roll from the depths of the Chaos encampment. What new threat was Nagaira sending his way?

A quick look uphill showed that the spear regiments had ceased their advance, fighting from their original positions at the brow of the hill. To his immediate left, one of the spear units had no foes to contend with at all thanks to the arrival of the knights. Still the enemy mob fought on, surrounding the hard-pressed knights and tearing at them in a frenzy of hate. No sooner had

Malus despatched the beastman on his left than a heavy blow smashed into his hip on the right. Desperation began to take hold, and he considered calling a retreat.

Then suddenly the roll of thunder swelled in volume and Malus heard a titanic crash off to his right. Screams and howls of fear rent the air, and it seemed as though the entire enemy mob recoiled like a living thing. Malus heard the spearmen to his left start to cheer, and then he saw that the Chaos warriors were *retreating*, scattering into the darkness to the northwest. The household knights spurred their cold ones in pursuit, cutting down the fleeing foes, until shouted commands from Dachvar brought them to a halt.

A rattling rumble echoed up the slope behind Malus; he turned and saw it was one of the war chariots that had accompanied them from the Black Tower. Standing up in his stirrups, he could see more of the chariots milling about at the base of the hill, their wheels and fearsome scythe blades dripping with blood.

The charioteer behind the highborn reined in his paired cold ones, and the knight standing beside him dismounted and hurried over to Malus. 'My apologies for losing you during the advance, my lord,' the knight said gravely. 'We were forced to stick to those damned, twisting paths, and once we diverged it seemed that we never could head back in the right direction again.'

Malus leaned back in his saddle, breathing heavily and watching the last of the beastmen disappear into the smoke. 'The loss was sorely felt,' the highborn said. 'But your return more than made up for it. Gather your chariots, commander. You are now the rearguard. The spears must fall back to the next rally point with all haste, while we still have a little breathing room.'

The commander of the chariots saluted and headed quickly back to his mount. Malus reached behind him for his war horn, trying to remember how to sound a proper recall and withdrawal. By the grace of the goddess he'd won a momentary reprieve, but he still had to get the remainder of his army back to the tower before they were overrun.

Chapter Thirteen
THE LONG, BLOODY ROAD

'HERE THEY COME again!' one of the spearmen cried, his voice cracking with exhaustion and strain.

The marauder horsemen were pouring back over the ashen ridge, the hooves of their lean-limbed horses kicking up plumes of chalky dust that clung to the bare arms and faces of their riders. Ululating howls rose from the horsemen as they picked up speed down the shallow slope and thundered directly towards the ragged lines of the retreating druchii force.

Spears and shields rattled awkwardly as the exhausted soldiers readied themselves for yet another attack. Lord Meiron took a quick swig of watered wine from a leather flask at his hip and barked out hoarsely. 'No one shoots this time! Conserve your bolts until ordered to fire. Front ranks keep your damned shields up this time!'

Malus leaned back against his saddle and tried to rub the grit and exhaustion from his eyes. The band of horsemen was larger this time – yet another knot of marauders had caught up with the limping druchii raiders. The hit-and-run attacks were getting larger and more frequent. For the thousandth time since dawn he turned in the saddle and looked to the south. They had reached the Plain of Ghrond just at first light, and the sight of the distant tower had renewed their spirits somewhat, but for the last four hours they had only managed half-a-dozen miles. Chaos horsemen had been harassing them constantly, nipping at their heels like packs of wolves. The attacks had grown so numerous that the spearmen were forced to march in battle formation, limping along in a ragged line six hundred yards across.

They had marched all through the night, probed constantly by hunting parties of Chaos horsemen who struck at the rear columns of the retreating army and faded back into the darkness. For most of the night the surviving banner of light horse had fought hard to keep the enemy cavalry at bay, but now the horses were exhausted. Malus had realised belatedly that this was part of the marauders' strategy, but now it was too late. As the marauders swept down on the waiting spearmen the druchii cavalry could only watch helplessly from their staggering mounts, well behind the lines.

Lord Irhaut and the bulk of the light horse had never reappeared over the course of the night. Malus had kept the retreating force as long as he could at each of the rendezvous points, but there had been no sign of the lost horsemen. Finally, at the last rendezvous, the highborn had been forced to make a difficult decision. He'd summoned Lord Rasthlan and ordered him and his autarii scouts to break off and try to locate the scattered cavalry and link them up with the main body of the force. Rasthlan had accepted the order stoically, though it was clear from his manner that he didn't expect to find anyone still alive. That was the last Malus saw of him and his scouts.

Now he was out of ideas. For the last five hours the only horsemen who'd come riding over the ashen ridges had been painted in crude tattoos and crying for druchii blood.

The marauder horsemen fanned out into a thundering line as they charged at the druchii spearmen. Wild, tattooed faces screamed the names of blasphemous northern gods, and sunlight flashed on the tips of their short spears. The druchii had learned from experience that the marauders would play at pressing home a charge, then launch their spears at nearly point-blank range and wheel away, retreating back up the ridge to prepare for another attack. For the first few attacks the druchii had punished the marauders severely, meeting them with volleys of crossbow bolts that cut down riders and mounts alike. But now their store of bolts was running low. They'd emptied the chariots of all their remaining ammunition, but even so they only had enough for a few volleys left.

The chariots had long since been given over to carrying the wounded. As for the nauglir, they were fearsome shock weapons, but Malus knew better than to pit them in a pursuit against the nimble marauder horses. Like the light cavalry, the knights and the surviving chariots could only sit and watch as the Chaos attack thundered home.

The marauders thundered closer, screaming like tormented shades and wreathed in clouds of ashen dust. At twenty yards the line of druchii spearmen crouched as one, raising their battered shields to cover their exposed faces.

With a furious shout the marauders let fly, hurling a cloud of black spears in a long arc onto the druchii soldiers. They struck the upraised shields with a staccato rattle; some glanced from curved helms or caught on mailed shoulders. Here and there a warrior screamed and fell, clutching at the spear driven deep into his body.

As the last of the spears struck home Malus felt himself relaxing. He could see the spearmen do the same, straightening slightly and lowering their shields a bit as they waited for the horsemen to turn and head back for the ridge.

This time, however, they didn't. In half a second the marauders were past the point where they always turned about, and Malus saw that something was wrong. By the time his exhausted mind realised what was happening it was already too late.

The marauders let out another roaring shout, plucking swords and axes from their belts and crashed full-tilt into the druchii line. By luck or by design the marauders struck one of the battered state regiments, and the spearmen reeled from the impact. Unprepared for the sudden charge, the front ranks of the regiment fell screaming beneath the blows of the howling Chaos warriors. The rear ranks, overcome with shock, began to break away and flee for the illusory safety of the nearby chariots.

'Goddess curse them!' Malus snarled. He turned to his knights. 'Dachvar! We're going in!'

Dachvar wearily drew his sword. 'The household knights are ready, my lord,' he said gravely. The side of his face and neck were black with dried blood from a spear attack during the night. Already, shouted cries were spreading among the surviving knights as they readied themselves for battle. After a night of running they were eager to spill more of the enemy's blood.

The broken spearmen were in full flight now, dropping their weapons and running in terror from the raging marauders. Malus welcomed the black rage that swelled up from his heart and filled his limbs with hateful strength. 'Sa'an'ishar!' he snarled. 'Charge!'

Spite leapt forward with a growl, eager at the prospect of horseflesh. The marauders had possessed enough sense to attack the far end of the battle-line, away from the weary knights, but the charging cold ones covered the few hundred yards in less than ten seconds. The marauders were heedless of their doom, lost in their orgy of slaughter until it was far too late.

Malus gave Spite its head, drawing both of his long blades as the nauglir leapt upon the lead marauder horse. The mangy equine was borne over with a hideous scream, its spine severed by the cold one's snapping jaws. Its rider leapt clear with a savage curse, only to have his skull split as Dachvar thundered past.

'On, Spite! On!' the highborn cried, driving the cold one forward with spurs and knees. Roaring hungrily, the cold one lunged for another nimble horse, catching one out-flung foreleg and biting it off in a spray of bitter blood. The animal fell end-for-end, shrieking and writhing, and the nauglir landed right on top of it, biting and snapping at its back and hindquarters.

The beat of rushing hooves brought Malus's head around – a marauder was racing at him from behind and to the left. The highborn seized the reins with the fingers of his left hand and hauled for all he was worth, pulling the nauglir free of its prey and turning the beast to face the oncoming threat. He only managed it halfway, turning the cold one perpendicular to the charging horseman. The marauder had to choose between swinging wide of the cold one's jaws and passing out of range of Malus, or turning in the opposite direction and risking the cold one's deadly tail for a chance of exchanging blows with its rider. Grinning like a fiend, the marauder chose the latter.

Malus met the oncoming rider with a furious scream, slashing left-handed at the horse's reins and following up with a furious right-handed thrust for the barbarian's eyes. The reins parted like a snapped thread, but the horsemen turned aside the highborn's second blade with the steel rim of his round shield. Laughing, the horseman lashed out with his axe, and Malus felt the blade strike home just above his collarbone. The iron axe head rebounded from his enchanted armour; another six inches higher and the weapon would have slashed his throat open to the spine.

Spite roared and turned in place, snapping at the horse's hindquarters, but the marauder forced his mount tight against the cold one's flank and kept hammering away at Malus's guard. The axe arced down again, aiming for Malus's head, but this time the highborn caught the curving beard of the weapon against the back of his left-hand sword and tried to pull it towards him. But his exhausted limbs were weaker than he imagined, and the marauder seemed to have arms of spring steel. Still laughing, the barbarian snarled something in his bestial tongue and pulled his axe back, neatly dragging Malus from his saddle. The next thing the highborn saw was the scratched iron boss of the horseman's shield as he smashed it into Malus's face. He screamed in rage and pain, blinded by the blow, and swung his right-hand sword in a wild stroke that connected with the horse's ribs and the marauder's leg.

Both beasts let out a pained yell, but the marauder continued to pull on the highborn's sword with his axe.

Malus couldn't breathe, his mouth filling with ichor from his broken nose. Blinking away tears of pain, he looked up to see the horseman raising his ichor-stained shield and taking aim at the highborn's outstretched neck. With a shout Malus twisted painfully at the waist and stabbed upwards with his free blade. The point of the sword sank into the marauder's side, just beneath the edge of his broad leather belt. The horseman stiffened, his laughter stilled at last. Red blood ran thickly down the side of the druchii's dark blade; Malus clenched his fist and twisted the sword in the wound. With a convulsive wrench he tore the blade free and the horseman slid lifelessly from the saddle.

As the riderless horse bolted away, Malus levered himself back into his seat and rubbed the back of his left gauntlet over his stinging face. The battle was already over; a bare handful of marauders were racing back to the safety of the ridgeline and the household knights were sitting on their mounts amid a field thick with the bodies of humans and savaged horses. A weary cheer went up from the ranks of the Black Guard, but the sound was lost in the roll and rumble of thunder to the north.

Frowning, Malus looked to the ridgeline and saw that the sky overhead was a roiling mass of black and purple clouds. Streaks of pale lightning crackled in their midst, and a cold wind tasting of old blood stirred the dust and brushed at the faces of the battered druchii host.

Now the purpose of the steady attacks became clear. The marauders had slowed the retreating army to a crawl so that the rest of the horde could press on and catch them.

Lord Meiron was shouting savage curses at the survivors of the broken regiment, chivvying them back into ranks. The household knights turned their mounts back towards the rear of the battle line, casting uneasy glances at the ridge to the north. Malus sat in place for a moment, weighing the odds. He looked to the south, at the distant image of the tower. So close. So damned close.

Lost in his bleak reverie, Malus was startled by the sound of Lord Meiron's voice. 'My apologies, my lord,' he said gruffly. 'The captain of the regiment was one of the first men slain in the charge. I've taken command of the unit personally, and I assure you they won't turn their backs on the enemy again.'

The highborn turned his gaze to the ridgeline. 'There's a storm about to break, Lord Meiron.'

'So I see, my lord,' Meiron answered calmly.

'We don't have much time,' Malus said. 'I reckon we're still a good five miles from the tower. How fast can your men run?'

'Run, my lord?' the infantry commander said. 'We've done all the running we're going to. No, this is where we'll make our stand.'

Malus met Lord Meiron's eyes. 'We can't,' he said. 'We'll be cut to bits. That's the main body of the horde over there.'

'I know, my lord. That's why there's no point running. They've got us. If we run their horsemen will just ride us down.' Lord Meiron drew himself up to his full height. 'And I have never run from a foe in all my life, least of all these animals. I'll not start now.'

Malus narrowed his black eyes. 'I could order you.'

Meiron stiffened. 'Then you'd make me a mutineer, my lord,' he said. 'You'd best get the nauglir and those dandy horsemen moving. I don't expect we have much time now.'

A look of understanding passed between the two druchii. Malus nodded. 'Very well, Lord Meiron,' he said darkly. 'I will not forget this, and I swear to you, neither will the enemy.'

The druchii lord nodded solemnly. 'I'll hold you to that, Malus of Hag Graef. In this life and the next.' Without another word the infantry commander turned on his heel and marched back to his men.

Malus watched him go, his heart bitter. 'In this life and the next,' he said to himself, and drew upon the reins. He kicked Spite to a trot and headed for the waiting knights. With enough of a head start the mounted troops could reach the tower safely, and it shamed him to think that a part of him was glad to be escaping Nagaira's trap.

You will pay for this, sister, he thought. By the Dark Mother I swear it. You will suffer a hundredfold for every man of mine you slay.

He reached Dachvar and the knights and spoke a few, quiet orders, then turned about and rode to the light horse. The cavalry he ordered to move at once, then as they started for the tower he went to the chariots and got them moving as well. The last to go were the knights, and behind them all rode Malus himself.

The black clouds were past the ridgeline now, heading inexorably south towards the tower. Lighting lashed across the sky and smote the backs of the mounted men with blows of thunder.

The last sight Malus had of the battered ranks of spearmen was a line of straight backs and a thicket of spears, aimed towards the storm rolling from the north. He caught sight of Meiron's square-shouldered form standing in the front rank of his regiment, eyes forward, awaiting the coming of the foe.

Along the rear ranks of the spear regiments, young druchii stole quick glances over their shoulder at the retreating cavalry and knights, their faces pale and uncomprehending.

THE STORM CLOUDS paced the dispirited riders all the way back to the tower, dogging their heels with flashes of pale lighting and imprecations of thunder. It took them nearly an hour to reach the high, black walls, and the entire time Malus would catch himself looking back over his shoulder, wondering if Meiron and his men still fought on.

Sombre faces lined the outer walls as the riders made their way to the tower gate. As they came near the gatehouse Malus saw four banners flying from the battlements, their heavy fabrics shifting listlessly in the faint wind. He saw a black crag on a white field surmounted by a silver circlet, and a blue banner with three black masts. Between them was a grey banner with a rearing, dark green nauglir, and above all rose the cloth-of-gold banner of lost Nagarythe, bearing the sign of the dragon and the crown.

Malekith had arrived with his army, and the armies of Clar Karond, Hag Graef and the Black Ark of Naggor rode with him.

On the long ride northward he'd imagined returning to the tower at the head of a victorious army, listening to a fanfare of trumpets from the walls as he bore the head of his sister before him. Now he returned in defeat, with but a broken remnant of the warriors he once led. He felt the weight of each soldier's stare as he led Spite aside and watched the survivors of his army make their way inside the fortress. As the last of his knights disappeared inside the walls, a mournful chorus of horns rose from the gatehouse. The highborn turned in the saddle to see the white plain behind him awash with a black tide of marching troops. Nagaira's horde had reached the Black Tower at last.

With a creak of great hinges the gates of the fortress began to grind shut. Malus took a last look northward before spurring his nauglir inside.

The remainder of his troops waited in the marshalling square beyond the gate, arrayed in parade ranks to either side of the centre path. A single druchii waited in the centre of the square, sitting astride a huge black destrier. Malus approached the old general wearily. Even Spite was too tired to more than sniff in the horse's direction.

Nuarc crossed his hands over the cantle of his saddle and gave the highborn an appraising stare. 'You look like someone dragged you through a butcher's shop,' he said without preamble.

'A *burning* butcher's shop,' Malus corrected, glaring back at the general.

To the highborn's surprise, Nuarc nodded sombrely. 'I know the place,' he said quietly. His expression turned businesslike. 'Malekith wishes to hear your report.'

'Yes, I expect he does,' Malus answered with a sigh. A bitter smile played across his bloodstained face.

Nuarc frowned. 'Something amuses you?'

'I was thinking that a thousand brave druchii just gave their lives so I could safely make it to my execution,' he said. 'Lead on, Nuarc. Let's not keep the Witch King waiting.'

* * *

NUARC OFFERED TO give Malus time to clean up, but he declined with a mirthless smile. Better that the Witch King and the assembled lords see what the future held for them, he thought.

The general led the weary highborn through the inner gate and into the high tower. Malus's gait was as unsteady as a babe's. Belatedly he realised that he'd been in the saddle for two days straight. It was a wonder his legs worked at all.

He did notice that he felt no pain from his wounds. Some experimental prodding along his scalp and his knee hinted that the injuries were healing very quickly indeed, thanks to the daemon's black corruption. The highborn wondered perversely how many strokes a headsman would need to take off his head. Would his body keep wriggling for hours afterward, like a snake?

Nuarc cast a curious look over his shoulder at the highborn. Had he laughed aloud? He couldn't recall.

The general led him to a pair of tall doors etched with the tower sigil of Ghrond. A score of black-robed Endless watched Malus impassively as the doors swung open and he was admitted inside.

Malekith studied him with burning eyes from an iron throne no less impressive than the one he presided from at Naggarond. The throne room was larger than the Court of Dragons, built to admit several hundred nobles and their retinues. At the foot of the dais were four ornate chairs, arranged in a semicircle. Four druchii nobles, clad in martial finery, bolted to their feet as Malus and Nuarc made the long walk across the echoing chamber. Malus felt their hot glares like irons against his skin, but the heat made little impression upon him after all the fire he'd recently endured.

He recognized Lord Myrchas at once. The Drachau of the Black Tower was pale with rage, but a glitter of fear shone in his black eyes as Malus was brought before the assembled lords. No doubt he remembers our conversation at the tower, the highborn thought, and he fears that I shall pull him down with me. A not unreasonable assumption.

Then Malus recognized the druchii standing beside Myrchas and felt his heart skip a beat. For a moment he fancied that the vengeful shade of his father Lurhan had risen from the Abyss to torment him. He recognized his father's ornate armour and the great sword Slachyr, the ancient blade of Hag Graef's vaulkhar, but the face of the man wearing the armour looked strange to him. The last time he'd seen his half-brother Isilvar's face it was a pallid green, soft and paunchy from decades of fleshy decadence. Now all that soft skin had melted away, leaving sharp bones and deeply sunken eyes that glittered with almost feral hate. His black hair, still bound in wires with hidden barbs and hooks, was held back with a golden circlet, and his ropy neck was bound by the thick gold hadrilkar of the Witch King's retinue. Malus noted that Isilvar wore his collar of service on the outside of a high collar of supple suede. No doubt to keep the heavy gold from chafing his delicate skin, the highborn thought sarcastically.

Next to Isilvar stood a lanky druchii clad in vivid blue robes and polished silver armour, and of all the nobles in the room only he looked at Malus with something other than anger or hate. Malus supposed he was the drachau of Clar Karond, the one ruler of the six cities he hadn't managed to mortally offend in the last year. The drachau regarded the highborn bemusedly, as if uncertain what all the fuss was about. It took him a moment to realise that the ruler of Clar Karond was somewhat drunk.

On the opposite side of Lord Myrchas stood a tall, narrow-shouldered figure in ornate armour chased with silver and gold. He had a long face and a small, square chin – a handsome man that reminded Malus at once of his mother Eldire. But there was nothing welcoming in Balneth Bale's eyes, only a black gulf of endless hate.

If the assembled lords expected him to quail before their withering stares they were disappointed. He spared them only the briefest of glances, focusing the majority of his attention on the armoured figure upon the throne. When he reached the foot of the dais – surrounded by the circle of hateful lords – he sank slowly to one knee. 'I come at your command, dread majesty,' he said simply.

'Have you done my bidding, Malus of Hag Graef?' Malekith asked, his voice seething from his ornate helm like air from a banked forge.

'I live to serve, dread majesty.'

'Then tell me of all you have done.'

And so he did, relating his arrival at the Black Tower and his failed attack on Nagaira's camp. He left out no particular – even, to his surprise relating the heroism and self-sacrifice of Lord Meiron and his spearmen. 'It was because of their courage that I stand here to relate these facts, dread majesty,' Malus said. 'I am ashamed that I led so many of your finest warriors to their deaths.'

'There, you see, he freely damns himself!' Lord Myrchas declared, levelling an accusing finger at the highborn. Once it became clear that Malus wasn't going to scapegoat him for the loss of the battle, the drachau's demeanour had reverted to type. 'He deserves the same fate that Lord Kuall suffered! At least Kuall didn't throw away ten thousand of our best men!'

'For all we know, he led those men to their deaths as part of a plan he's worked out with Nagaira herself,' said the new Vaulkhar of Hag Graef. Isilvar's voice, once silken and refined, was now a guttural ruin, worse even than the hoarse growl of Nuarc. The sound brought a smile to Malus's face, though he was careful to keep his face turned to the floor. 'He and my sister have engaged in conspiracies for years, dread majesty. It was she who wrought such ruin in my home city last spring, and it was he who so disfigured our drachau that he remains convalescing to this day. It is clear to me that they were working together to destroy Hag Graef, and I believe they now conspire to destroy the Black Tower and perhaps supplant you as well. He should be slain at once!'

'If he is to die, dread majesty, let it be by my hand!' swore Balneth Bale. The self-styled Witch Lord of the Black Ark stepped beside Malus, his hands clenched into fists. 'He led my son and his army to ruin before the walls of Hag Graef. This is a matter of blood feud!'

'Let Balneth Bale strike him down dread majesty!' Isilvar declared. 'Let him avenge his son and the feud between our cities will end as well!'

But Malekith seemed not to hear the pleas of his own vassals. '*What of this second Chaos champion?*' he asked.

Malus shrugged. 'I do not know, dread majesty. His appearance in Nagaira's tent was a surprise to me. But he is mighty; he bears tokens of favour from the Ruinous Powers, and his body cannot be harmed by mundane weapons. I suspect that he is the real power behind the horde. The warriors serve him, while he in turn serves Nagaira.'

'*And how large is the host that is arrayed against us?*'

Malus paused. Now he knew how Rasthlan had felt when he'd put the man to the question days earlier. 'I would say that the enemy still numbers around a hundred thousand warriors, dread majesty.'

The number shocked even Isilvar into silence. Malus could clearly hear the scrape of steel against steel as the Witch King turned his head to regard Nuarc. *'How does our own army fare?'*

'We were able to muster forty-four thousand troops, dread majesty: eighteen thousand from Naggarond, two thousand from the Black Ark, and ten thousand each from Hag Graef and Clar Karond, plus two thousand mercenaries scraped from the harbour leavings at the City of Ships. Taking Malus's losses into account that puts the garrison here at around fourteen thousand. So we can muster fifty-eight thousand effectives against Nagaira's host – more than enough to bleed her army dry against these walls. When our additional forces from Karond Kar and Har Ganeth arrive we will be in position to pin the enemy against the walls of the fortress and destroy them.'

'Providing Nagaira employs none of her sorcery,' Isilvar said darkly. 'Or we face treachery from within.'

Malus could take no more. He was battered and torn, physically exhausted and now his knees were beginning to ache. With painful effort he struggled to his feet. 'If it please your dread majesty to slay me then let us be done with it,' he said. 'I acknowledge my failure in the field. What is your decision?'

For a moment no one spoke. Even Malekith seemed taken aback by the highborn's weary frankness. *'I see no failure here,'* the Witch King said at length. *'You drew Nagaira to the Black Tower as I commanded.'*

'But, dread majesty,' Myrchas exclaimed. 'He lost half the army–'

'Lost?' the Witch King said. *'No. He spent them as a warlord must to achieve his aims, fighting an enemy that has invaded our kingdom. Something none of you have done.'*

'But... you can't intend to install him as Ghrond's vaulkhar!' Myrchas cried. 'I won't have it, not with all the offences he has perpetrated against my fellow lords.'

'No. He will not be Vaulkhar of the Black Tower,' Malekith said. *'He will no longer command armies in the field.'* The Witch King leaned forward on his throne and stretched out a claw-like hand to Malus. *'Instead, I name him my champion, to confront the enemies of the state and slay them on my behalf.'*

'You can't mean that,' Malus heard someone say. It took a moment to realise it was him.

'It is my decree, Malus of Hag Graef, that you will be named my champion, and will bear the three golden skulls of Tyran upon your armour so that both friend and foe know that you fight in my name. The honour of the kingdom rests upon your shoulders. Do not forsake it, or the wrath of the Dark Mother shall be upon you.'

'I... I hear and obey, dread majesty,' Malus replied, bowing before the throne. This wasn't a true reward, he knew, but another facet of Malekith's game. He was just too tired to see what the Witch King's stratagem was. Regardless, it wasn't as though he could refuse.

'How can this be?' said Isilvar, his ruined voice charged with genuine outrage. 'He has committed grave crimes against the kingdom, and against you personally, dread majesty. How is it he not only continues to live, but is deemed worthy of such an honour.'

'He lives because it serves the Witch King's purposes that he do so,' said an iron voice from across the hall. Morathi slid silently out of the shadows, her eyes glittering with cold menace and authority. 'It is a lesson that all of you would do well to learn.'

'*What of my brides, Morathi?*' Malekith asked, referring to the witches cloistered in the Black Tower's convent.

'They are foolish, weak-willed girls,' Morathi replied disdainfully. 'But we may yet get some decent work out of them before the siege is finished. There are gaps in their training I must take steps to rectify.'

'*Make it so,*' the Witch King said, then regarded his vassal lords once more. '*Go now, and prepare for the coming assault. Nagaira's warriors encircle the city even as we speak. Serve me well, and your rewards will be great.*'

None of the assembled lords had any question what the alternative would be.

Chapter Fourteen
THE TEMPLE OF TZ'ARKAN

The Chaos Wastes, first week of winter

BEYOND THE SHADOWY portal of the great temple an inky darkness awaited, pulsing with blasphemous power. It swirled and eddied about Malus as he staggered along the narrow processional, recoiling from the possessed druchii as if in supplication to the daemon that rode within him.

The temple was much changed since he'd last been inside. No, it was *changing* – potent energies coursed through the ponderous stones and prickled invisibly across his icy skin. Tz'arkan swelled painfully within the highborn's tortured frame, and the forces at work within the great building responded, ordering themselves according to the daemon's will.

Malus's body moved of its own volition, driving him forward like one of the risen dead. At the far end of the processional he reached the temple antechamber. More than a hundred figures dressed in ceremonial robes lined the narrow aisle that ran through the large hall. The ancient forms had knelt in obeisance for so long that the bodies within had long since crumbled to dust, leaving behind only petrified shells of leather garments and rune-carved bone. He remembered the first time he'd seen these wretched figures, and how he'd wondered what sort of awful terror could have inspired the temple slaves to press their foreheads to the stone floor until they finally died.

Now he knew all too well.

His boot heels echoed forlornly along the dusty marble floor as he walked among the ranks of the damned. Suddenly he heard a rustling sound, like the crumbling of ancient parchment and the crackle of ruined leather, and his heart went cold as he saw the ranks of the temple servants slowly, jerkily straighten. Dust swirled within the depths of their drooping hoods, coalescing in the ghostly shapes of skeletal faces. Green globes of bale-light shone eerily from their shadowy eye sockets and their spectral mouths moved in silent adoration of their returning overlord. Ethereal hands brushed against his boots and the hem of his robes, and Tz'arkan's cruel will measured his every step, basking in the horrid worship of those agonized souls. At the far end of the chamber corroded steel creaked wearily as the armoured shells standing guard over the chamber raised their rusting blades in salute. Green fires burned within the oculars of the guards' helmets, and the runes worked into their Chaos armour crawled with sorcerous energies.

Do you see, Darkblade? This is but a glimpse of the glories to come. The dead will rise to do my bidding even as the living give their souls to sate my glorious appetites. These are but the smallest tastes of the wonders that could have been yours had you simply chosen to serve me.

On he went, past the tormented ghosts and into another large hall containing the altars of the four gods of the north. Behind each altar rose a horrific idol dedicated to one of the Ruinous Powers; Tz'arkan led Malus to the idol of Slaanesh and forced the highborn to his knees before the abominable figure. His hands made twisting signs in the air and his lips formed debased words that no mortal was even meant to speak. Ichor bubbled from his throat and trickled down his pallid cheeks as the daemon forced him to participate in the horrid worship of the Great Devourer. On and on the ritual went, until he feared his teeth would splinter and his lips run like tallow, and his tortured mind screamed for release.

The next sound he recognized was the daemon's laughter, cruel and cold, echoing in his brain. *You are weak, Darkblade. So weak. This is the so-called hero of Ghrond? Your mind could not even fathom a simple acolyte's benediction. And to think I once saw such potential in you.*

Tz'arkan dragged Malus to his feet and forced him onward, into the great, cavernous space where the bridge of fire waited.

Blistering heat smote the highborn's pallid face; the reek of sulphur stung his nose and caked his aching throat. The earth itself roared angrily in the vast open space, stirred to wrath by the unnatural being trapped in the chamber above. At the far end of the long plaza, some fifty yards away, stood the statue of a winged daemon, crouching on its talons and limned by the sullen, red glow of the lake of fire at its back. The sight of the muscular, human-shaped daemon with its snarling animal face seemed almost comical now after the horrors he had witnessed during the siege of the Black Tower.

With each step the heat beating against his skin increased, and with each step the fearful energies of the daemon seemed to grow as well. Tz'arkan's power radiated from his body; he could feel it seeping from his pores like venom, soaking into the dark, stone walls and tainting them from within.

There was an angry crash, and a plume of molten stone burst from the great chasm that lay beyond the waiting daemon. Malus dimly recalled the last time he'd travelled the floating stair the river of burning stone had lain hundreds of feet below the level of the plaza. Now, it surged and roiled just a few dozen feet from the edge of the square. The heat was unbearable. Malus could feel his skin baking and his lungs ached fiercely with each shallow breath. He tried to close his eyes against the burning air, but the daemon held him in a merciless grip, forcing him onward towards the fire.

Before long he couldn't breathe. Wisps of smoke rose from his tattered robes, and he feared his eyes would burst. He fought against the daemon's control, his efforts growing more and more frantic as he was pressed ever closer to the inferno.

Tz'arkan hissed with delight. *Your fear is sweet. There is nothing so delicious as a mortal's death throes! But I will not permit you to die Malus, not yet.*

There was a furious hiss and an eruption of steam from the edge of the precipice. Huge boulders rose in serried ranks from the boiling rock, their faceted surfaces glowing with incandescent heat and dripping streams of liquid fire onto the roiling sea below. They formed a floating stairway to a spur of rock that hung from the ceiling of the great cavern. Beyond, Malus knew, lay the chambers of the temple sorcerers and then, the tribute chamber and prison of the daemon itself.

His skin was burning. He could smell his hair singeing in the heat. His lungs clenched, aching for a taste of cool air, and his eyes felt as dry as leather. Yet he was helpless to resist the daemon's iron control.

He seeks to break you, Malus thought. Here, at the very last, he wants to ensure his control over you. Even now he fears you may be able to circumvent his plans. Malus focused on that notion, taking hope from it even as his body was wracked with burning pain and forced to do the bidding of an inhuman will.

The highborn mounted the steps concealed in the daemon statue's flanks, noting the molten glow of heat along the trailing edges of its stone wings. His mind reeled for lack of air, but his body worked like a wood puppet, leaping heavily from one floating stone to the next.

Beyond the rocks curved a stone staircase, intricately carved with dozens of naked figures writhing in eternal torment. He vaguely remembered a body that lay sprawled along the stairs, its forearms slit from wrist to elbow. How he wished he'd taken heed of the corpse's silent warning!

Slowly and painfully the daemon drove him onward, up the stairs and into the charnel house of the sorcerers' sanctums. Here the five Chaos champions had built chambers for themselves and their servants. Those same servants had turned upon one another in the end, their minds broken by the daemon's manipulations as they waited in vain for the return of their masters until they slew one another in an orgy of cannibalism and murder.

Looking back, it amazed him how blind he'd been to the dire portents laid right before his eyes. He'd been such a fool – and what ruin had been borne from it!

The daemon drove him past the lifeless, blood-streaked apartments, strewn with crumbling debris from the brutal fights that had raged there. After a few minutes he frowned, his gaze sweeping the floors of the rooms he passed and peering along the dimly lit corridors. Where had all the bodies gone? Had they finally crumbled to dust once the daemon invoked its hideous curse?

Finally he came to the great ramp, worked with hundreds of runes and leering alabaster skulls, and the tall double doors made from solid gold. A nameless dread seized Malus's throat at the sight of them, like a condemned man catching sight of the impaling stake. Beyond those doors lay the entrance to the daemon's chamber and the end of his terrible quest.

And so it comes down to this, he thought bleakly. I've walked alone out of the Chaos Wastes, fought daemon cultists and Chaos-tainted pirates, commanded armies and fleets and fought grim battles for the fate of entire cities. Not long ago a whole kingdom rested in my hands. But this is how it ends, walking like a lamb to slaughter. It was enough to make the fiercest druchii weep tears of rage.

He had nothing left now. Desperately he wracked his brain for some trick, some stratagem to turn the tables on the daemon before it was too late. But how could he fight a creature when he couldn't even master his own wretched body?

Up the ramp the daemon drove him. The golden doors, balanced on perfect hinges, swung open at the touch of invisible hands.

Beyond, Malus heard the skeletal rustle of ancient fabrics and the creak of dried skin. It was the bodies, he realised. The bodies of the dead scholars and servants.

See? The dead rise and serve the worthy.

Tz'arkan forced him across the threshold before a bowing assembly of mutilated corpses, worn and withered by time. Heads rose to behold their immortal master, their dried lips smeared against their faces in unctuous, lunatic grins. Skeletal fingers clenched into claws and hollow eye sockets gaped at infernal wonders beyond the ken of mortals.

Here are your servants, Darkblade, the daemon declared mockingly. *They will aid you in what must be done, for there is little time left.*

The undead servants scraped and rustled as the highborn moved stiffly among them. They shambled ahead on the stumps of ruined feet, driven by the same implacable will as he, across the gleaming marble floor and the curving lines of the sorcerous wards that had kept the daemon imprisoned for thousands of years. Their frail robes fluttered in the waves of invisible power that reverberated through the air. They paused before the great, basalt doors, flanked by massive statues of winged daemons, and waited for his approach. In the shadows to either side of the waiting slaves swirled figures of brown dust. They cringed and genuflected to Malus, and he remembered the hideous mummies who'd lain in a torturous half-life before those selfsame doors, unable to find release in death thanks to the powers of the binding spells laid like a trap beneath them.

As Malus crossed the first of the arcing silver lines he felt a tremor pass through him. As cold as he'd been before, now he felt as though he were frozen in ice, his spirit wreathed in powers he could barely comprehend. He wondered if he would linger here, trapped within these terrible wards once the daemon feasted upon his soul.

Deep within the bleak despair gripping his brain, the tiny spark of an idea flickered to life. He scarcely dared consider it, half-afraid the daemon would read his thoughts. Malus frowned. Could it be possible? Did he dare?

Did he have any choice?

The undying servants pushed the black doors aside and ushered Malus into the cold radiance of the tribute chamber. The vast hall contained the wealth of dozens of plundered kingdoms now lost to time: coin and gems, plate and graven statues – more wealth than any man could spend in a thousand lifetimes. Even now, despite his dire straits, the sight of the treasure chamber kindled his avaricious heart.

But of all the wonders piled high in the tribute chamber, none could match the enormous crystal that dominated the centre of the room. It was roughly faceted and larger than a man, set in a low tripod of iron. The enormous stone glowed with a softly pulsing blue light, a strangely alluring colour considering the black evil that lay within.

His gaze drifted to the small, unassuming pedestal just a few yards inside the room. It had lain empty for a year now, he thought grimly. Hands trembling, he pulled off his gauntlets and gazed bleakly at the red stone planted on his finger. If he'd had any real courage he would have tried sawing it off rather than leave this place wearing it!

The servants shuffled amid the gleaming splendour, searching for the tools that the daemon desired. Malus's body spasmed as the daemon reasserted its fearsome control. *The relics, little druchii,* Tz'arkan commanded. *Lay them out and prepare yourself for the ritual.*

His heart sinking, Malus could only watch as his body obeyed the daemon's commands like a dog. He laid his saddlebag carefully on the stone floor and drew out four of the relics, each one wrapped in dirty cloth. First the Octagon of Praan, then the Idol of Kolkuth and the Dagger of Torxus. Finally he pulled free the Amulet of Vaurog, and his heart went cold at the ordeal he'd gone through to get it. Of all he'd endured to gain Tz'arkan his relics, the price he'd paid for the damned amulet would haunt him for all time. Last of all, he reached for the warpsword at his belt.

No, the daemon commanded, forcefully enough to send ichor running from the highborn's eyes and ears. *The servants will see to the blade.*

Two of the shambling corpses knelt beside Malus and slid the long, black sword from its scabbard. Wisps of smoke rose from their withered hands as they handled the burning blade.

Malus watched the servants lay the blade beside the other relics, while another pair of servants approached from deeper within the chamber. One carried an urn made from gold and etched with spirals of sorcerous runes. The other held a tablet of ancient, weathered stone, carved with dense lines of blasphemous script.

Take the urn, the daemon said. *Remove the cover, and I will show you what must be done.*

He tried to fight it, like the condemned man fights against the grip of his executioners. But for the first time his indomitable will failed him. Malus watched helplessly as his hands took the heavy urn from the corpse's hands and pulled free the lid. Inside was a grey powder that reeked of the crypt.

The highborn could feel the daemon's joy as the urn was opened. *The bones of my tormentors,* it said. *Gathered from the far corners of the world. All five of the champions who trapped me were ground up to fill that bowl. All but that scheming fool Ehrenlish – in the end I got all but his skull, but that will be enough.*

Tz'arkan turned Malus bodily and marched him to the crystal. *Use the dust to lay out the sigil precisely as I command,* the daemon said. *You must do this alone, Dark-blade. I cannot force you. Follow my instructions in every particular. Your soul depends on it.*

All at once he felt the grip of the daemon loosen – the change was so sudden Malus swayed on his feet, stopping his fall only by effort of will. His gaze drifted to the black blade, lying on the stone just a few feet away.

Do not attempt it, the daemon said. *I will stop you before you take a single step, then I will make you suffer in ways you never dreamt possible. Remember the chamber of the altars? That was a gentle kiss compared to what I could do if I were truly displeased. And in the end you would have even less time to save your eternal spirit. Now, begin.*

The instructions flowed like icy filth into the highborn's brain. He gasped at the hideous images flowing through his mind and reached into the urn for a handful of dust.

Chapter Fifteen
THE CORPSE-HANDLERS

The Black Tower of Ghrond, four weeks before

THE CRASH OF thunder smote the walls of the fortress like a hammer blow, causing many of the defenders on the wall to duck their heads and cry out in fear. The earth-shaking roar all but drowned out the high, skirling wail of the horns, crying their shrill warnings from the redoubts. Malus rose to his feet from the base of the battlements and peered out at the lightning-shot blackness. A savage, reeking wind roared in his face and tangled the loose strands of his sweat-streaked hair.

All was darkness upon the ashen plain. He counted the seconds, waiting for a flash of pale lightning. There! A bolt of fire burnt across the heavens, revealing a rushing tide of monstrosities charging for the walls.

'Sa'an'ishar!' he shouted to the spearmen crouching against the battlements beside him. 'On your feet! Here they come!'

Now the roaring of the advancing army could be heard above the raging tempest, and the strobe and flicker of the lightning increased overhead, pushing back the clinging shadows and revealing the oncoming attackers less than twenty yards from the base of the wall. Already the ground there was carpeted with the bodies of marauders and beastmen, and as Malus watched, a black rain of crossbow bolts began to fall upon the screaming horde from the sloping redoubts to the left and right. Horned, half naked beastmen screamed and stumbled, pierced through by the deadly bolts. Some ran on, while others fell to the blood-soaked earth and died. Still the seething mob charged forward, undaunted by the deadly hail. Long ladders bobbed above lines of grim-faced barbarians; when one of the ladder-men was struck down another marauder ran to take his place. Some men kept going with two or three bolts jutting from their bodies, driven forward by unholy battle-lust and the blessings of their fearful northern gods.

Malus drew his swords and set his jaw in a grim line as the attackers drew closer. Already his armour was splashed with dried blood and stinking ichor, and his arms felt leaden from all the killing he'd done. He couldn't recall if this was the third assault or the fourth. At this point he didn't even know if it was day or night. The clouds that had rolled in before the advancing horde had tightened about the Black Tower like a shroud, blocking out the pale northern sunlight. Once the fighting began, time lost all meaning.

With groans and bitter curses the druchii company assigned to hold this stretch of wall clambered slowly to their feet. They were state troops from Clar Karond, evidenced by their blue robes and the short, lightweight kheitans favoured by druchii corsairs. When the first attack had begun the troops were in high spirits, but now their faces were tired and grim, stained with grime and other men's blood. They looped their arms through battered shields and took up their weapons – one warrior in three hefted a repeater crossbow, while the rest drew their short, stabbing swords. They tested their footing amid the pools of drying blood that stained the paving stones and watched the oncoming mob to see where the ladders would likely land. A young druchii ran down the line, scattering sawdust from a wooden bucket. It would soak up some of the blood once the fighting started in earnest, but there was never quite enough.

Malus leaned back and peered down the length of the wall, checking to make sure all the troops were standing to. He saw a pair of legs still stretched out across the paving stones and jogged down to take a look. 'On your feet, spearman,' the highborn growled, kneeling before the warrior. The warrior was a young woman, called up to fight with the regiment in the wake of Malekith's proclamation of war. There wasn't a mark on her that Malus could see, but her face was white as chalk and her lips were blue. Most likely the blow of a hammer or club had ruptured something beneath the skin and she'd bled to death in her sleep. Taking hold of her mail shirt, Malus dragged her over to the inner side of the wall and rolled her over the edge. Already there were deep drifts of corpses piled on the flagstones forty feet below. Men were stripping the bodies of armour and weapons and dragging the corpses to the furnaces. Even in these cold climes, the dead could carry pestilence that could decimate the fortress city's defenders.

The rest of the line looked ready, as far as he could see. Each of the eight sections of wall was held by a single regiment, stretching for more than two and a half miles between the hulking redoubts. The regimental commander anchored the far end, while Malus's end had been anchored by the second-in-command. That fellow's brains had been splashed against the side of the embrasure just a few yards to Malus's right. He'd happened to be nearby when the officer died, and without thinking had stepped in to take his place. That had been during the second assault, and he'd remained ever since.

Malekith had given him no orders after declaring him champion. With no troops to command – not even a retinue to call his own – it was as though he'd been swept aside in the haste and confusion of the impending attack. He'd found his way to his chambers, found servants to fill a bath and bring him food, and watched as a pair of smiths from the fortress armoury affixed a set of three golden skulls to the breastplate of his armour. The skulls marked him as the Witch King's champion: Athlan na Dyr, the Taker of Heads. As far as Malus was concerned, they made him a tempting target for every bull-head and barbarian that came over the walls.

Nevertheless, when the horns began to wail he had buckled on his harness and headed for the wall.

He'd hoped that when the attack began it would be led by Nagaira's champion. The warrior, aided by the Amulet of Vaurog, would be a literal engine of destruction atop the city walls, but Malus hoped that with enough spearmen behind him the champion could be pulled down long enough for him to pull the artefact from around his thin neck. After that they could hack the bastard to pieces and hang his helmeted head from the battlements, and Malus would find a way to slip out of the fortress and make his way into the Wastes.

But nothing had gone according to plan so far. The champion had yet to show himself among the screaming throngs, and most of the warriors on the wall regarded Malus with open resentment and hostility. The spearmen of the Black Tower had heard the stories of his disastrous expedition to the north, and blamed him for the loss of their mates and of their commander, Lord Meiron. But they were far from the worst – as Malus walked the battlements he came upon warriors from Hag Graef and the Black Ark, both of whom saw him as the blackest of villains after the ill-fated events of the previous spring. They were just as likely to stab him in the back or throw him from the walls in the middle of an attack, Witch King's champion or no. He'd stayed so long with the regiment from Clar Karond simply because he was just another officer to them.

The crossbows along the battlements were firing now, and Malus could hear the screams of the dying, forty feet below. 'Ladders coming up!' one of the warriors shouted, and the highborn rushed up to the battlements to see how many had landed nearby.

There were only two: one was very close to the redoubt at his right, while the other was almost ten yards to his left. Others going up farther down the line were someone else's problem. Swift-footed barbarians were already scrambling up the long ladders, many with a throwing-axe gripped in their teeth. More barbarians at the base of the wall were flinging axes up at the defenders, but the druchii paid them little heed.

'Crossbows cover the ladders!' the highborn yelled, although there was little need. The men on this part of the wall knew the routine well by now. Bolts from their crossbows and from the firing slits of the nearby redoubt raked along the line of men climbing hard for the wall. The marauders advanced fearlessly into the storm of black-fletched bolts, pressing on even after being shot multiple times. When they could climb no more they hurled themselves clear of the ladder, screaming or laughing like madmen the whole way to the ground, and those below would redouble their efforts to reach the top.

And reach the top they would. They always did, despite the appalling losses they suffered. The crossbows could only fire so fast, and the Chaos warriors had no fear of death. Slowly but surely the line of warriors inched closer to the battlements.

'Four men on each ladder!' Malus roared, rushing forward to welcome the first foe who came over the battlements. Obediently the troops crowded close around the end of each ladder, ready to strike the attackers from multiple directions at once. This wasn't duelling or elegant swordplay – this was pure butchery, killing men as quickly and efficiently as possible. So long as they kept the enemy warriors from gaining a foothold on the battlements they could almost slaughter the oncoming attackers at will.

Suddenly the air hummed with half-a-dozen thrown axes, burning through the air in short, glittering arcs as the warriors closest to the top let fly. There was a clash of steel and a warrior beside Malus toppled without a sound; a hurled axe had cleft the spearman's helmet and buried itself in his forehead. 'Shields up, damn you!' the highborn shouted. 'Mind their axes!' He himself reached up and checked the strap on his new helmet. Malus hated wearing the thing, but it was far better than the alternative.

A face appeared at the top of the ladder, grinning like a daemon. Malus leapt at him with a shout, and just missed having a hurled axe embedded in his face. His sudden move threw the man's aim off, sending the spinning projectile blurring past his ear, and before the warrior could drag out his sword Malus stabbed him through the throat. Blood poured in a flood down the barbarian's tattooed chest, but the warrior kept coming, forcing his way up the ladder and onto the battlements. Spearmen dashed in from both sides, stabbing and hacking at the man, and Malus tucked his shoulder in and crashed into the reeling man's bloody midsection, sending him flying out into space.

But the warrior's last seconds bought more time for the man behind him. A sword thrust slid off Malus's armoured belly, and then the screaming beastman lowered his horned head and butted the highborn in the chest. The force of the impact hurled him back a few feet, and the bellowing warrior leapt quickly onto the battlements. Druchii warriors pressed in on either side of the foe, stabbing and slashing with their short blades. Roaring in fury, Malus leapt back into the fray as well, catching the warrior in the middle of a turn and hacking through the side of his neck. Hot blood sprayed across the spearman as the horned warrior staggered beneath the blow. One of the spearmen rushed at the warrior, intent on finishing the creature off, but the beastman was far from finished. With a braying shout it lowered its broad sword and caught the onrushing spearman with a thrust to his right thigh that tore clean through the muscle and cut a major artery. The druchii fell with a scream, clutching at the mortal wound, while his companions plunged their blades into the beastman's back.

A barbarian reached the battlements next and leapt over the dying beastman straight at Malus, his face twisted with madness and his arms outstretched in a deadly embrace. Snarling in disdain the highborn ducked clear of the warrior's foolhardy attack, then rushed after the madman's tumbling body and kicked it off the edge of the inner wall. The dying druchii was trying to drag his way clear of the melee, leaving a thick trail of blood through the newly lain sawdust.

Another druchii fell to the paving stones, grappling with a dagger-wielding barbarian. Malus rushed over, planted a foot between the marauder's shoulders and split his skull with a downward sweep of his sword. Two more Chaos warriors had made their way onto the battlements, and a third waited at the top of the ladder, looking for a space to clamber across. Cursing lustily, the highborn dived back into the fray, using his longer swords to telling effect.

One beastman went down, his neck carved to the spine while he traded blows with a nearby spearman, while the marauder to the beastman's left collapsed with the point of the highborn's left-hand sword buried in his kidney. The warrior on the ladder leapt to take their place, but Malus was ready for him. He rushed in as the barbarian jumped, effectively moving in beneath the hulking warrior and stabbing upwards into the man's unprotected belly. The barbarian screamed, bringing his axe down on the highborn's back, but his enchanted plates turned aside the powerful blow. Gritting his teeth, Malus staggered beneath the weight of the dying warrior, but he summoned up his hate and pushed forwards with all his might, unloading the limp form onto the next man scrambling up the ladder.

Taken by surprise, both marauders plummeted, screaming, to the ground.

The next warrior up the ladder never reached the top before a crossbow bolt buried itself in the side of his head. For the space of a few seconds the defenders had some precious breathing room. 'Close up ranks!' Malus shouted. He pointed to the limp form of the mortally wounded druchii. 'Someone drag him out of the way. Quickly now!'

A quick check of the other ladder showed that the druchii there had things well in hand; so far none of the attackers had even reached the battlements before dying underneath the defenders' blades.

More spearmen rushed over to surround the ladder next to Malus. Breathing heavily, the highborn stepped back to let the fresh warriors take their turn. He rubbed a gauntleted hand across his mouth, inadvertently smearing his lips with a foeman's blood. Mother of Night, I could use a drink, he thought.

Just then he heard a shrill note sounding from the redoubt to his right. He frowned, trying to puzzle out his meaning – then he heard the guttural roars and agonized screams coming from the next wall over. Spitting a blasphemous curse, Malus turned and ran for the redoubt's iron door, just a few yards to his right. He pounded on the portal with the hilt of his sword shouting imprecations to the druchii on the other side. Within moments the bolts were drawn back and the heavy door opened to admit him.

The highborn brushed past the sentry at the door and ran down the long, narrow passageway that connected to the next wall over. Shouts and commands echoed up and down the corridor from the crossbow and bolt thrower teams firing from inside the fortification, calling out targets and shouting for more ammunition. He passed barrels of water that held long, heavy bolts tipped with glass orbs that glowed a baleful green: they were dangerous and volatile dragonsfire bolts, held in reserve in case the enemy horde sent giants or other huge creatures against the walls.

The passage ran on for almost fifty yards, then angled sharply right. Another fifty yards later and the highborn reached another iron door, watched over by a pair of nervous sentries. Hands and sword hilts were pounding frantically on the other side of the door. The sentries saw Malus coming and snapped to attention. 'The enemy has reached the wall,' one of the warriors began.

'I heard the horn,' Malus snapped. 'Open the door and let me through.'

The two men hesitated – then saw the fearsome look on the highborn's face. As one, the warriors turned to the door and drew back the heavy bolts.

Almost at once there were panicked warriors pushing the door open from the outside. Snarling with rage, Malus drew the iron portal open and roared at the men on the other side. 'Stand to, you worthless dogs!' he said, blocking the doorway with his bloodstained form.

The white-faced spearmen recoiled at the wrathful figure standing before them, and Malus quickly stepped into the space they vacated. Behind him the iron door slammed shut again and the bolts shot home. 'Where do you bastards think you're going?' the highborn raged. 'You're here to defend this wall or die in the attempt. Those were the orders the Witch King gave you!'

But Malus saw at once that the situation was very grave indeed. The battlements near the redoubt were littered with dead and dying spearmen, and marauders were pouring over the battlements. There were fifty spearmen between Malus and the raging battle, all crammed tightly against the side of the redoubt. As far as he could tell the enemy was also pushing hard in the other direction, trying to reach one of the ramps that led down into the city proper. If that happened there might well be no stopping them.

There was a ramp just to Malus's right, and the marauders were fighting hard to reach it. Only the sheer press of the panicked spearmen were holding them momentarily at bay. 'Move forward, damn your eyes!' the highborn commanded. 'There's no safety back here! If the foemen don't kill you I surely will!'

The men wavered, weighing their options. One look at Malus showed that the highborn was deadly serious and perfectly capable of carrying out his threat. One of the spearmen, a senior warrior, exclaimed 'Our commander is dead, highborn, and we don't have enough soldiers to drive the enemy back!'

Malus considered calling for reinforcements from the redoubt, but quickly cast the notion aside. Jostling a pair of spearmen aside, he checked the avenue at the base of the ramp and saw no less than two hundred druchii poring through the piled bodies at the base of the wall. 'Who are they?' he demanded, pointing at the corpse-handlers with his sword.

The exasperated trooper glanced down at the druchii band. Despite his panic, his lip curled in distaste. 'Mercenaries,' he replied. 'Harbour scum hired by the drachau of Clar Karond. Captain Thurlayr refused to have them on the wall. Said gulls like them were only fit for picking over the dead.'

Malus shook his head in disbelief. 'That kind of thinking is what got Thurlayr killed, soldier,' he snapped. He grabbed the front of the trooper's mail shirt and pulled him close. 'What's your name?'

The warrior looked into the highborn's black eyes and went pale. 'Euthen, my lord.'

'Well, now you're *Captain* Euthen,' Malus hissed. 'Take charge of these fools and get them back in the battle by the time I return or I'm throwing you off the wall myself. Do you understand?'

'Y... yes sir. Clear sir.'

'Then get to it, Captain,' Malus shouted, pushing the man away. Without waiting for a reply he shoved past another spearman and raced down the long ramp towards the mercenaries.

The harbour rats had the look of corsairs, from what Malus could see at a distance. Tattered robes of different hues, lightweight kheitans and blackened mail were common, and the warriors carried a wild assortment of weapons, including a profusion of daggers and looted throwing axes. Approximately half the mercenaries were poring over the bodies at the base of the wall, stripping them not only of weapons and armour but valuables as well. As he watched, one of the druchii took a dagger to the ring finger of a druchii officer, popping the digit loose with a practiced motion – and then losing it among the pile of corpses beneath him. The rest of the mercenaries sat on the paving stones of the avenue and played at dice or dragon's teeth, seemingly oblivious to the desperate battle being waged on the battlements above.

'Form up!' Malus shouted at the cutthroats. 'The enemy is on the battlements, and it's time you earned your keep!'

The corsairs looked up at the distant figure of the highborn as though he were speaking in a foreign tongue. The looter who'd been groping among the corpses for the officer's severed finger frowned up at Malus. 'We're not allowed,' he shouted back in a bemused voice. 'This one here – ' he pointed at the officer's corpse – 'said we weren't fit to stand 'mongst real soldiers.'

'Besides,' chuckled a female, scooping up her dice, 'it's a good deal safer down here.'

'It won't be for long once the enemy reaches the ramps!' Malus snapped. 'And you can't spend your ill-gotten coin if you're hanging from some beastman's banner-pole! Now get off your arses and get up here!'

The cutthroats looked to one another, considering their options. Malus didn't wait for them to reply – arguing with them would only weaken his already shaky authority, so it was better to act as though he expected them to obey. He turned and ran back up the ramp, and within moments was gratified to hear someone down below start barking orders in a surprisingly professional tone. At least someone down there knows what he's doing, Malus thought.

On the battlements, things looked grim indeed. The Chaos foothold was already more than fifteen yards wide and expanding steadily. Euthen had managed to bully the panicked spearmen back into the fight, but their numbers were too few to accomplish much more than keeping the enemy away from the near ramp.

Malus shoved his way into the crowd. 'Form a wedge!' he shouted, elbowing cursing spearmen into a rough semblance of the formation. 'Wider! All the way to the edges of the parapet!'

Trusting that the soldiers would follow his command, the highborn worked his way to where the tip of the wedge would begin. He found Euthen the erstwhile captain there, fighting valiantly against a leering Chaos marauder wielding twin axes in his knotty hands. As Malus approached, he watched the marauder carefully, looking for a sign that he was about to strike. Euthen lunged in, attempting a half-hearted swipe at the marauder's leg, and the barbarian tore into the spearman with a terrible howl, hacking into the druchii's left shoulder with one axe while the other sent the captain's short sword spinning off the edge of the parapet. But while the warrior was savaging the hapless Euthen, Malus rushed in and stabbed the barbarian cleanly through the heart.

The warrior sank to the stones with a curse on his lips. Meanwhile, Malus took the injured Euthen by the collar and gave him a gentle shove in the direction of the ramp. 'Warriors of Clar Karond!' he cried, raising his sword. 'Form wedge on me!'

No sooner had he said this than a red-haired barbarian rushed at Malus with a savage yell, his greatsword swinging in a wide arc for the highborn's head. Malus saw the move and hissed disdainfully, ducking and stepping into the stroke so that the wild blow passed harmlessly overhead, then stabbing the warrior in the groin with both of his blades. The man fell with a terrible scream, and Malus quickly stepped past him, deeper into the press of foes. 'Advance!' he ordered.

Miraculously, the spearmen did. Now Malus had foes on three sides, but the men to the left and right aimed their blows at the soldiers in front of them. The warrior before Malus snarled and chopped at him with his axe; the highborn blocked the blow with his left-hand sword and then slashed open the thigh of the warrior to his right. The injured marauder faltered and the spearman in front of him finished the man with a thrust to the neck. When the axe-wielding barbarian attacked again, Malus blocked with his right-hand sword and stabbed his other blade into the marauder on the left. Then he devoted his sole attention to the warrior in front of him, trapping the warrior's axe with a sweep of his left sword and stabbing the marauder in the eye with the blade in his right.

And so the slaughter began. Coldly, methodically, the druchii began to reduce the Chaos foothold. Malus knew that if they could at least fight their way to the enemy ladders then they could cut off their foes' reinforcements, then eventually sheer numbers would eliminate the rest of the marauders that had made it to the walls.

Working together the spearmen made steady progress. Soldiers were struck down to either side of the highborn, only to be replaced by the next spearmen in line. After almost ten yards there were no spearmen left, but Malus saw that the corpse-pickers had taken their place. The mercenaries were clearly in their element in this style of fighting, accustomed as they were to the tight quarters and close sword-work of boarding actions aboard ship. They struck down barbarians with underhanded cuts to their legs, or knives flung into their throats. Sometimes Malus would strike at a man to his flank and then look back to see the foe in front of him collapsing with a throwing axe buried in his skull.

Finally they'd cut off all of the enemy ladders and had cut the marauders down to less than a dozen warriors – and that was when things became truly dangerous. The surviving marauders realised they were trapped, and as one they decided to take as many of their hated foes with them as they could.

A warrior came screaming at Malus with a bloodstained sword in his right hand and a battered shield in his left. Eyes wild and foam flying from the corners of his mouth, he unleashed a flurry of blows that the highborn had to devote all his energy to deflect. He tried to knock the man off his stride with a lightning stroke to his eyes, but the marauder simply caught the blow on the edge of his shield and barrelled on, hammering away at Malus's guard.

So intent was the highborn on this frenzied warrior that he failed to notice when the man on his left slipped in a pool of blood and went to one knee. His opponent crowed in triumph and brought down his heavy warhammer – against the side of Malus's head.

The shock was all-powerful. One moment Malus was locked in a deadly battle with the man in front of him and the next he was hurtling to the ground. He bounced off the paving stones face-first, his brain unable to grasp how he'd got there.

There was a roaring in his ears, like a raging surf that ebbed and flowed just above his head. Everything blurred; the only thing he felt with perfect clarity was a thin trickle of ichor leaking down his cheek.

I'm bleeding, he thought stupidly, and realised that he was likely about to die.

But instead of seeing a sword or hammer descend on his skull, he saw a druchii boot heel come down just inches from his face. The roaring continued, and the boot moved on, to be replaced by another.

He lay there watching boots stamp and slide past him for what seemed like a very long time, and it wasn't until the roaring in his ears tapered away that he realised he hadn't been killed after all.

The next thing he knew there were rough hands pulling at him, trying to roll him over. 'That was the damnedest thing I've ever seen, if you don't mind me saying so, captain,' said a voice. 'Reminds me of this damn-fool highborn I used to know–'

The hands rolled him over, and Malus found himself looking up into a dark-eyed, grinning face. He recognized the scarred features at once, and let out a bemused grunt.

'There you are, Hauclir, you damned rogue,' he said. 'Where is that wine I asked for?' And with that the world went utterly dark.

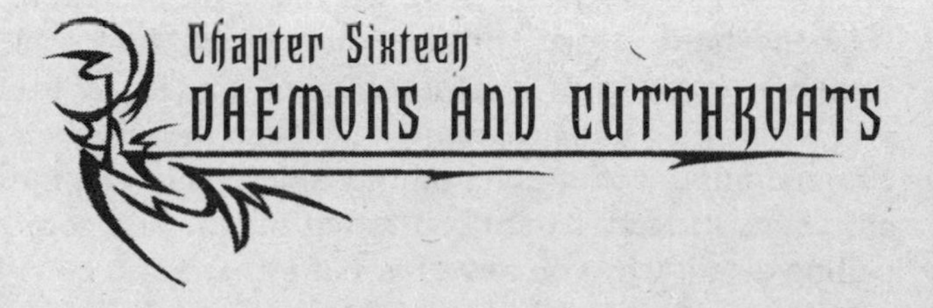

Chapter Sixteen
DAEMONS AND CUTTHROATS

COLD WATER SPLASHED Malus in the face. He came to, sputtering and coughing, propped up against the hard stone of the battlements. Pools of blood and body parts littered the paving stones around him.

A figure knelt in front of the highborn, holding an upended water bottle. 'Sorry to wake you, my lord,' Hauclir said calmly, 'but it looks like we're about to be attacked again, so I don't have the luxury of allowing you to sleep off that little knock you got on the head. You and I have a bit of talking to do while we're both still able to do it.'

Malus tried to rub the water out of his rheumy eyes. When his vision returned, he found Hauclir to be studying him intently, paying especial attention to his face and neck. The former guard captain was dressed much like the rest of the mercenaries, though the cut of his robes were finer and better kept, and his kheitan was thick, sturdy dwarf-hide. He wore his customary mail hauberk, and his short sword sat in its oiled scabbard. A long, knotted oak cudgel dangled loosely from his right hand.

The highborn shook his head bemusedly. 'I thought I was dreaming,' he muttered thickly. With tentative fingers he reached up and prodded at the side of his head.

'I had much the same reaction,' Hauclir said dryly. His lips twisted in a sarcastic grin, but his dark eyes were cold and hard. 'Now, I'm not going to ask how you somehow went from a closely-hunted outlaw to the Witch King's personal champion; I've seen the way your damned mind works, and nothing you do surprises me any more. Instead, I want you to tell me, in very compelling detail, why you saw fit to betray each and every man in your service after we left you at Karond Kar.'

Malus's own expression hardened. His former retainer's impertinent tone caused the highborn to bristle. 'You were my damned vassal!' he snapped. 'Your life was mine to use as I pleased! I owe you no explanation.'

But Hauclir was far from cowed by the highborn's imperious tone. A slow, dangerous smile spread across his scarred, angular face. 'Look around you, my lord. Do you fancy you're reclining in your high tower back at the Hag? No. You're sitting on a battlefield, surrounded by blood and spilled guts, and the nearest nobleman for two miles is lying at the bottom of the wall with the rest of the rubbish. Right at the moment I own this part of the fortress wall, so you're going to play things by my rules. So let's hear your story, my lord, and it better be a good one, or else I'll chuck you over this damned wall myself.'

The former retainer's tone was light, even cheerful, but Malus looked in his eyes and saw the anger burning there. He had absolutely no doubt that Hauclir meant every word he said. So he shrugged, and told the former guardsman everything.

Or at least he tried to. He hadn't got much past receiving Tz'arkan's curse when the next wave of attackers came howling at the walls. Malus was forced to wait while Hauclir and his men drove off the assault. His weapons had been taken from him, and he wasn't sure he could stand up yet, anyway.

They were interrupted twice more by enemy assaults before Malus finally got Hauclir to the moment their paths crossed once again. The former retainer sat wearily against the battlements beside Malus, picking dried bits of blood from his haggard face. For a long time he didn't speak at all. 'So. A daemon, you say?'

Malus nodded. 'A daemon.'

Hauclir grunted. 'Well, that explains your eyes. And the fact that your head wasn't splattered across the flagstones by that damned hammer.'

The highborn sighed. 'I don't deny there are certain advantages to the situation.'

'And you had no idea it was your father who was at Vaelgor Keep?' the former guardsman asked. 'Who else did you think it could be?'

'It could have been anyone, Hauclir. Lurhan wasn't flying his banner outside the keep, after all. At the time it made more sense that it was Isilvar, working in conjunction with my sister.'

Hauclir grudgingly nodded. 'Yes. I suppose you're right.' He looked sidelong at his former master. 'But you realise that now I have an even more compelling reason to throw you over the wall.'

Malus spread his hands. 'You wanted the truth, Hauclir. Can I have my swords back now?'

'Certainly not. You're a damned daemonhost!'

'For the Dark Mother's sake, Hauclir!' Malus snapped. 'I had a daemon inside me from the moment I returned from the north. Did I ever once try to kill you? No. In fact, I made you a very rich man.'

'Before you broke one of the cardinal laws of the land and I had it all stripped away from me.'

The highborn folded his arms tightly about his chest. 'Shall I beg your pardon, then? What do you want from me, Hauclir? I did what I had to do. Do you think you could have done any better in my place?'

'Gods Below, my lord. I have no idea,' the former guardsman said. He sighed. 'To be honest, it didn't hit me as hard as some of the others. Your man Silar took it the worst, him and Arleth Vann. Dolthaic, he was just angry about losing all the gold.'

Malus nodded thoughtfully. 'Arleth Vann thought that all of you had gone to sea after the battle outside Hag Graef.'

The former retainer shrugged. 'That was Silar and Dolthaic's idea. I just followed along. Couldn't stay in Hag Graef any more, so why not? The two of them put to sea a day after we got there. Looked up the master of the *Shadowblade*; Dolthaic said he knew the captain from a raiding cruise the summer before. They asked if I wanted to go, but I've seen all the ocean I ever want to see. So, I stayed on around the dockyards, picking up the odd work here and there. And then I fell in with these rats,' he said, indicating the mercenaries sitting a discreet distance away. 'We were shaking down bridge travellers for tolls when Malekith's call to arms reached the city. The drachau scooped a lot of the gangs up after that. I'm sure he hopes none of us survive to go back and dirty up his precious city.'

Malus nodded. He reached down and picked up his dented helmet. 'So, it appears I owe you my life.'

'Again.'

The highborn grinned. 'Yes. Again.'

'You don't expect me to serve you again, do you?' Hauclir asked. 'I'm not your man any more, my lord. Not after all that's happened.'

Malus shook his head. 'I'm still technically an outlaw, despite all the finery. I couldn't hold you to your oath if I wanted to.'

'But you still need my help,' Hauclir said.

'Do I?'

'Oh, yes, my lord, you do. And you damned well know it.'

The highborn spread his hands. 'Nothing escapes you, it seems. All right. Name your price.'

Hauclir made a show of thinking things over. 'That Chaos champion has the amulet you need, correct?'

'Correct.'

'And your sister's tent was chock full of loot, correct?'

'Before I burnt it to the ground, yes.'

The former guardsman nodded. 'Well, I expect your path is going to take you back into her vicinity before all is said and done,' he said thoughtfully. 'Me and mine get all the loot we can carry, and we're yours for the asking.'

The highborn looked at Hauclir bemusedly. 'You're a fool. You realise that, I trust?'

'So my mother told me,' he answered. 'Do we have a deal, or not?'

Malus nodded. 'Done.'

'All right then,' Hauclir said, rising to his feet. 'I'll go and explain things to the troops.'

The highborn watched his former retainer go, shaking his head in amazement. For the life of him, he couldn't be certain who was getting the better end of the deal, but all of a sudden he felt much better about his chances of getting the amulet and getting out of the Black Tower alive.

Sometime later Hauclir remembered to return Malus his swords. The rubies in both pommels had been carefully pried away.

IT WAS NOT long after the twelfth assault that the roiling darkness suddenly receded, leaving the fortress's defenders blinking wearily in the pale light of early morning. Cheers went up from within the city, as the soldiers took the sunlight as a sign the siege had been lifted, but the exhausted warriors holding the battlements saw the enemy encampment for the first time and knew that their ordeal was perhaps only just beginning.

The Chaos horde was camped in a broad band that completely surrounded the fortress city. Cook fires by the hundreds sent thin tendrils of smoke into the sky, and herds of northern horses mingled in great corrals around the camp's circular perimeter. The dusty ground seethed with motion, the dark figures moving about on their errands like a multitude of ravening ants. Malus looked out over the part of the encampment opposite his part of the wall and shook his head in awe. Was there no end to the damned beasts?

If he stood at the far left end of the wall and leaned out far enough to see past the rightward redoubt he could glimpse a pavilion of indigo-dyed tents, just like the ones he'd burned a few days ago. There was a strange distortion in the air above and around the tent, similar to the haze of hot air over a forge. That was where Nagaira and her champion would be found.

His eyes ached and his stomach rumbled, and he hadn't been clean since the Dark Mother alone knew when. Most of the mercenaries were sound asleep, stretched out on the filthy paving stones with their weapons across their chests. Over the last two days he'd got to know many of the sell-swords in the company. None of them had names; only nicknames, to make it harder for the city watch or anyone else to track them down using sorcery. He met a professional killer named Cutter, an unlucky cutpurse named Ten-thumbs, a gambler named Pockets and too many others to count. The highborn learned at length that Hauclir's nickname was Knock-knock, which privately amused Malus.

There were nearly a hundred of the cutthroats to begin with, but after throwing back no less than seven attacks their numbers had dwindled to sixty-five. Almost half that number was wounded to a greater or lesser degree; supposedly there were aid stations and orderlies to patrol the walls and remove injured soldiers, but they'd seen nothing like that since taking charge of their stretch of wall. They had long since run out of bolts for their crossbows as well. Malus had tried to use his authority to get more from the closest redoubt, but the captain in charge had flatly refused, claiming that only Lord Myrchas could authorise such a transfer. The highborn hadn't pursued the matter further. The less he had to deal with that den of snakes in the citadel the better.

He did send some of his more talented foragers into the city in search of food and drink, once it became clear that no one was going to send them anything to eat. In this, the mercenaries were singularly successful, returning to the wall with roast fowl, boiled eggs, fresh bread and cheese and several bottles of decent wine.

Malus didn't ask any questions, and the foragers were happy to not give any answers.

Three hours into the morning, Malus was sipping from one such bottle when the iron door of the far redoubt swung open and a ramrod-straight figure in gleaming armour strode into the sunlight. Nuarc made his way slowly but purposefully down the length of the wall, eyeing the snoring mercenaries with a look that was somewhere between outrage and bemusement. The few cutthroats still awake returned the general's gaze with the flat stare of hungry wolves.

When the general reached Malus's reclining form his expression of shock only deepened. 'By the Dark Mother!' he exclaimed. 'We were starting to think you'd been killed. No one's seen you at your apartments for days.' Nuarc jerked his head in the direction of the mercenaries. 'What in the Blessed Murderer's name are you doing with this rabble?' he asked. Then his face turned deadly serious and he leaned close to the highborn. 'They aren't holding you for some sort of ransom, are they?'

The notion gave Malus the first real laugh he'd had in a very long time. 'No, my lord. They know very well that I'm not worth the trouble.' He cocked his head at the general. 'Out for a stroll in the sunshine, general?'

Nuarc glowered at the grinning highborn. 'Out to see what the enemy is up to, and to check on things along the wall,' he said darkly. 'And to get away from those caterwauling fools back at the citadel, truth be told.'

Malus held up the pilfered bottle. 'Can I interest you in some wine, general?' Much to the highborn's surprise, Nuarc accepted the offer and took a deep draught before handing it back. The gesture sobered Malus at once.

'How bad is our situation, my lord?'

On reflex, the general glanced at the mercenaries some feet away to make certain they were out of likely earshot. 'Things could be better,' he admitted. 'We've held the walls for almost three days now, but the regiments have taken a bad beating. The hardest hit units have been rotated off the walls, but our reserves are being stretched thin.'

'Rotated?' Malus exclaimed. 'We've been up here for two days! No one's brought us food or ammunition, and no one's sent orderlies for our wounded.'

'That's because no one knows you're here,' the general answered grimly. 'None of the mercenary companies are part of the army's muster list, and no one back at the citadel is capable of thinking past their own damned agendas.'

The thought shocked Malus. 'You mean to tell me no one is in command?'

Nuarc shook his head. 'Each drachau thinks of nothing but his own honour and prestige. They intrigue against one another constantly, and no one will cooperate towards the city's defence. They've staked out which walls belong to each drachau, and they spare no thought for the others.'

'But... but that's absurd!' Malus cried. 'What does the Witch King say about this?'

The general shrugged. 'He watches and waits to see which lord will assert himself. It's his way. But Myrchas is too timid, Isilvar is too inexperienced, Balneth Bale is too weak and Jhedir of Clar Karond is too drunk. About the only consensus Myrchas, Isilvar and Bale have reached is that you have to be put to death at the first available opportunity. Fortunately for you, they can't decide what manner of execution to use.'

Malus shook his head in stupefied wonder. 'What about our reinforcements, then?'

Nuarc took a deep breath. 'Any forces from Karond Kar would have a long way to travel, even if they commandeered every available boat and sailed them to the western shore of the Sea of Malice,' he said. 'They aren't expected for a week or more. Troops from Har Ganeth, on the other hand, should have been here by now. No one knows what could have caused their delay.'

Malus could venture a guess, but thought it wiser not to say. He took a long draught from the bottle and rolled it around his tongue. 'I regret that I cost the army a further ten thousand troops,' he said bitterly.

'Nonsense,' the old general barked. 'I might have done the same thing. It was a good plan, but you assumed too much.'

The highborn considered this, and nodded. 'All right. What do you think we should do now?'

'Me?' Nuarc replied, a bit surprised at the question. He looked out at the enemy encampment for a moment before replying. 'I would pull the army back to the inner wall.'

Malus blinked. 'But then we'd be trapped.'

'We're trapped *now*, boy,' the general shot back. 'The inner wall is higher, and there's less ground to have to defend. We could rotate units more often and still make the enemy pay a steep price every time they tested us. We're very well supplied, so Nagaira can't starve us out, and ultimately time is not on her side. Our warriors at sea are returning home even now, and within a month she would be facing a powerful army of highborn marching up from the south.' The general shrugged. 'But no one has asked my thoughts on the matter.'

The highborn took another drink and turned his face to the sky. 'Well, at least the sun is shining.'

'I know. That's what worries me the most,' the general said.

'And how is that, my lord?' Malus asked.

'Because up until now your sister has put a great deal of effort into keeping the city locked in darkness. According to Morathi, the cost of such effort is considerable, especially in the face of opposition from her and the city's convent.'

'Morathi has been fighting against Nagaira? I hadn't noticed.'

'Did you imagine all that lightning was your sister's doing?' Nuarc asked. 'It doesn't make much sense when one is spending all that energy to keep things dark, now does it?'

'No, I suppose not,' Malus replied peevishly.

'So there you are. She pits her strength against Morathi and the witches for three days – and now this.' Nuarc raised his head slightly, almost as though he were sniffing the air. 'Something's up, boy. She's changing tactics.'

That was when they heard the sound. Malus had no words for it; it was a horrible, wailing, tearing noise that seemed to reverberate through the air and yet not be a part of it. One thing Malus was certain of – it came from the direction of Nagaira's tent.

Tz'arkan reacted immediately, its daemonic energies rippling along Malus's skin. *Your sister's gifts are potent indeed,* it hissed. *She has opened a great doorway between the worlds.*

'Between the worlds?' Malus muttered. Then he understood. 'Chaos,' he said to Nuarc. 'Nagaira is calling upon the storms of Chaos. She's summoning monsters to send against the walls!'

At that same moment the alarm horns howled from the redoubts. The mercenaries were awake at once, scrambling warily to their feet. 'We need crossbow bolts,' the highborn said. 'Quickly!'

The old general nodded. 'I'll see to it,' he said, and hurried back to the nearby redoubt.

Malus drew his swords. 'Stand to, you wolves!' he called to the cutthroats. 'The bastards are going to try their luck again!'

Hauclir came striding swiftly down the line, barking commands to his men. 'What's going on now?' he asked, his sword and cudgel ready.

The highborn gave him a bleak look. 'Remember the Isle of Morhaut?'

'Oh, damnation,' Hauclir said, his face turning pale.

At the far end of the line the redoubt door opened and a pair of soldiers were all but hurled out onto the parapet by Nuarc, each one carrying a barrel full of crossbow bolts. 'Load the crossbows! Quickly now!' Malus yelled. 'We haven't much time.'

And indeed, he was right. No sooner had he spoken than he heard the heavy *bang* of the redoubt's bolt throwers, and something not of the mortal world screamed and gibbered just out of sight around the redoubt's sloping flank. Everyone on the parapet turned in the direction of the sound, their faces full of dread.

Chapter Seventeen
MOVE AND COUNTERMOVE

THE SLITHERING THING that lurched into view from around the corner of the redoubt was a hideous knot of roiling muscle and misshapen bone as large as a nauglir. Mouths that were little more than muscular tubes lined with dagger-like teeth writhed and gaped like serpents above the fleshy mass, and great, scythe-bladed arms lashed and stabbed at the air, reaching madly for prey. The abomination had been pierced by a bolt from one of the redoubt's bolt throwers, and its body was wreathed in seething green sorcerous flame. It lurched a few more steps towards the wall, shrieking an agonizing, lunatic wail, then collapsed into a shrivelling, burning mass.

The cutthroats' cheer of relief was short-lived however, as it became clear the otherworldly creature was far from alone.

A huge pack of smaller creatures came racing around the end of the redoubt, loping, slithering, bounding and scuttling with hideous, predatory grace. They flowed past the burning Chaos creature and charged straight for the fortress wall, throwing back their bald heads and screeching hungrily at the defenders above. Behind them lurched three more of the larger, more powerful monstrosities, bellowing angrily as they dragged their bulk across the ashen ground.

Hard-bitten cutthroats screamed like frightened children as the seething pack of Chaos beasts reached the wall and began to scuttle up its sheer height like spiders. 'Stand to, you dogs!' Malus roared. 'Crossbows! Don't just stand there! Open fire!'

Galvanized by the steely tone in Malus's voice the handful of crossbowmen stepped to the battlements and leaned over the edge and fired at the monsters rushing up the fortress wall. Two bolts struck home, dislodging a pair of the screeching fiends and sending them plummeting to the ground, where they struck hard and curled in upon themselves like dead insects. Reassured by the knowledge that the monsters could die like any other living thing, the mercenaries regained some of their lost courage and readied their weapons as the beasts drew nearer.

The heavy bolt throwers in the redoubt banged once more, and twin streaks of green fire plunged down at the shambling behemoths still crawling towards the wall. One of the dragon's fire bolts missed, splashing a pool of searing fire along the ground, but the other struck home. The blazing monster continued to shamble forwards even as it died, its wails adding to the cacophony of noise assaulting the defenders' senses.

More war horns blared, and cries of battle echoed all across the northern quadrant of the fortress. Cursing under his breath, Malus dashed to the inner edge of the parapet and leaned out as far as he dared, peering at the section of wall on the other side of the redoubt to his right. The next wall over was the scene of a desperate battle as the spearmen there grappled with a furious pack of Chaos beasts. On the other side of these spearmen lay the north gatehouse. Malus had no doubt that was where the monsters would go. If the gatehouse fell then the whole outer wall was lost.

Screeching and roaring, the first of the Chaos beasts came scrambling over the battlements and threw themselves at the waiting mercenaries. A druchii went down with a multi-legged monster wrapped around his torso, his sword driven clean through the beast's midsection. Another creature crouched on the battlements and lashed at two of the cutthroats with whip-like tentacles lined with tiny, fanged mouths. Malus saw Hauclir block a lunging beast's charge with his heavy cudgel and hack the thing open with his short sword. Ten-thumbs levelled his crossbow and shot another point-blank, the heavy bolt punching clean through the monster's body. Another mercenary shrieked in agony as a monster drove its blade-like forelegs into his eyes.

More and more of the creatures were swarming over the wall every moment. Blood and ichor stained the parapet in equal measure. Malus saw Nuarc standing by the redoubt's open door, slicing a charging monster neatly in half with his rune-marked sword. 'We need reinforcements!' the highborn yelled over the din. 'We can't keep this up for long!'

But Nuarc shook his head. 'They'll never get here in time,' he cried, rushing forward and stabbing another beast that had fastened onto a mercenary's throat. 'We hold the wall with what we have or not at all!'

Damn those fools in the citadel, Malus thought! Their petty intrigues were doing Nagaira's work for her.

Just then a fierce wind rushed over the top of the redoubt and buffeted Malus's face. He smelled brimstone and old blood, and heard a vast rushing of wings. Instinct spurred Malus into motion even before the wave of flapping figures burst overhead. 'Get down!' he yelled at Nuarc, crashing into the older druchii and driving him back against the redoubt wall just as a swarm of winged monsters came roaring down the length of the parapet. The creatures lashed at the struggling druchii with their long, saw-bladed tails; a few snatched up unsuspecting mercenaries in their talons and flung them screaming from the wall. Under assault now from two sides, the defender's courage began to waver, and they started to give ground to the snarling beasts.

Malus pushed away from Nuarc with an angry snarl. 'Not another step back!' he roared at his men. 'You can stand and fight or run and die! Kill these bastards before they kill you!' To the terrified crossbowmen he yelled, 'Shoot those damned flying beasts out of the air!'

Once again the defenders redoubled their efforts under the lash of Darkblade's tongue, but Malus knew that he couldn't keep things going for long. Another major reversal and the battle could turn into a rout.

A long, lean shape with six legs and a gaping, tooth-lined orifice in place of a head clawed its way up the body of the mercenary nearest Malus and then launched itself at the highborn. Roaring an oath, he caught the monstrosity on the point of his blade and threw it screaming over the battlements. The winged creatures came rushing in again, but this time several tumbled from the sky with crossbow bolts buried in their pale bodies. Malus sliced off another's wing as it shot past, sending it careening full-tilt into the side of the redoubt. Another of the mercenaries was plucked from the parapet, but this time both druchii and monster went tumbling to the ground with the cutthroat's dagger buried in the creature's chest.

Malus sensed that the tide of battle was starting to turn in the defenders' favour. No more of the swift creatures were appearing over the battlements, at least, and the mercenaries were rallying themselves and ganging up on the monsters that remained.

Then he heard the wailing cry from the other side of the wall and his heart lurched in his chest. He'd forgotten about the two behemoths.

Malus dashed to the battlements and peered over – then ducked his head back just as quickly. One of the monsters was almost within arm's reach, trailing a slick of yellow slime as it slithered its way up the wall. The second creature had flattened against the wall of the redoubt to avoid the punishing fire of the bolt throwers and was nearly to the top of the wall as well. Malus pounded on the edge of the battlements in frustration. He couldn't imagine anything less than a dragon's fire bolt being able to destroy the huge creatures.

His gaze drifted to the open redoubt door. Maybe he didn't need the bolt throwers at all.

Malus dashed inside the redoubt. The two sentries who normally stood watch at the door had evidently fled, or perhaps been killed out on the parapet when the Chaos beasts first attacked. He ran down the long corridor for another few yards, until he came to a water barrel holding a pair of the long, glass-tipped dragon's breath bolts. He pulled the long, spear-like bolts from the water, taking great care not to knock them together, then turned and hurried back the way he came.

Nuarc was waiting for him just as he emerged from the doorway. The general recoiled from the highborn with a startled hiss. 'What in the name of the Murderer are you doing with those!' he exclaimed.

'Taking care of some pests,' Malus replied, just as the first of the behemoths appeared at the edge of the battlements with a wailing roar.

'Get back!' Malus yelled at the mercenaries nearby – who were already falling over one another trying to escape the monster's thrashing limbs. Then he hefted one of the long bolts like a javelin, took two quick steps and hurled it at the monster's side.

The bolt wobbled in the air as it flew the short distance to the target. Faster than Malus thought possible, the beast saw the projectile coming and smashed it out of the air with the sweep of a scythe-like arm, breaking the glass globe at the bolt's tip and showering itself with liquid flame. Shrieking and flailing in agony, the monster sizzled like fat dropped in a fire, then fell away from the battlements and tumbled like a comet to the ground.

Even as the first monster was plummeting to earth Malus took up his second bolt and peered cautiously over the battlements. Instantly a pair of scythe-arms lashed at him, missing his face by scant inches. The behemoth was only perhaps a dozen feet below, clashing its multiple jaws and undulating inexorably upwards. With a cruel grin the highborn held his ground and took deliberate aim. All he really had to do was drop the bolt onto the creature, and within moments it too was burning in a greasy heap at the base of the wall.

The last of the smaller Chaos beasts took another of the mercenaries with it when it died – farther down the wall one of the druchii fell from the battlements with a scream, still stabbing at the beast that was burrowing its way into his chest. Malus watched beast and victim fall to their deaths and said a silent thanks to the Dark Mother that it was the last of them.

Leaning against the battlements, Malus took in the scene of carnage that stretched the entire length of the long wall before him. Bodies and pieces of bodies lay strewn everywhere, amid puddles of congealing blood and stinking ichor. The mercenaries were pulling their wounded comrades to their feet, but there were too few of them. Not three minutes ago there had been sixty-five mercenaries fighting alongside him, and now he was hard-pressed to count more than thirty that were still breathing. He scanned the battered cutthroats for a glimpse of Hauclir, and found the former guard captain at the far end of the line, working hard to get the mercenaries ready in case of another attack.

Nuarc stood just a few feet away with his back to the redoubt wall, wiping dark fluid from the length of his blade with a coarse piece of cloth. 'A near run thing,' the general said, 'That was an inspired piece of lunacy, fetching those dragon's breath bolts. Never seen that done before.'

Malus grinned tiredly and was about to reply when a warhorn wailed a shrill, insistent note from the gatehouse. Nuarc stiffened, and Malus saw the briefest flicker of fear in his dark eyes. 'What is it?' he asked.

Cursing under his breath, Nuarc dropped his cleaning cloth and dashed a few yards down the wall. Malus joined him, following the warlord's gaze to the scene of slaughter unfolding along the neighbouring wall.

Chaos beasts were swarming over the battlements in a glistening flood, racing over the torn corpses of the defenders and pouring down the long ramps into the city beyond. At the far end of the wall where it met the gatehouse, two of the huge Chaos monsters were hammering and prying at the iron door leading into the gatehouse proper.

Behind the monsters, bloodstained swords in hand, stood Nagaira's Chaos champion.

The armoured figure was surrounded by lesser Chaos beasts, which circled his heels like hunting hounds. Worse still, more than a dozen armoured Chaos warriors stood ready on the battlements behind the champion, waiting for the door to come down. As Malus watched, a half-dozen of the winged nightmares flapped heavily up from the base of the wall, each one clutching another armoured warrior in its talons.

Malus's heart sank. The attack on their wall had just been a feint, aimed at keeping them occupied so that they couldn't come to the gatehouse's defence. They'd outsmarted him again! 'Hauclir!' he barked. 'Form up your wolves! Now! We've got to get to the gatehouse–'

'There's no damn time,' Nuarc said, his voice tight with anger. 'Your men are spent and the enemy has a secure foothold. You'd be pulled apart before you even got close to the gatehouse.'

'I can get more of the dragon's breath–'

'And do what? Throw it at the enemy and then advance into the flames? Use some sense, boy!' Nuarc snapped. 'Remember what I said about the inner wall being easier to defend? We have to fall back now, before those bastards get the outer gate open, or we'll never make it at all. Come on!'

Without waiting for a reply, Nuarc broke away and hurried down the length of the wall, calling for the mercenaries to follow. The harbour rats, already at the limits of their endurance, were all too eager to escape. Malus took a moment to glare hatefully at the enemy champion, who wore the one thing the highborn needed to reclaim his soul and seemed capable of thwarting him at every turn.

As he glared at the armoured fiend, the champion straightened, and as though he were able to read the highborn's thoughts, the helmeted head turned and looked his way.

Malus raised his sword and levelled it at the champion. 'This isn't over yet,' he said to the baleful warrior, then he swallowed his bitter fury and turned to follow quickly in Nuarc's wake.

'First he costs us ten thousand men, and now he's cost us the fortress's outer wall!' Isilvar shouted, pointing an accusing finger at Malus. 'I tell you, he's in league with Nagaira, somehow. How else can one explain such incompetence?'

The vaulkhar and the three drachau were seated in high-backed chairs with velvet cushions, in a lesser audience chamber than the grand court chamber at the base of the Black Tower. A large, marble topped table before them was set with the remains of a sumptuous lunch, now all but forgotten in the wake of the day's disaster. Lord Myrchas studied Malus coldly, rolling a Tilean grape between his pale fingers. The Witch Lord, Balneth Bale, made a show of studying the parchment map of the inner fortress laid out on the table, but how much of it he could see amid the platters, goblets and bits of food was open to discussion. Lord Jhedir of Clar

Karond chuckled at Isilvar's tirade and took another sip of wine.

Sitting in the shadows behind the four lords sat Malekith himself, fingers steepled and red light seeping from the oculars of his horned helm. The Witch King hadn't said a single word since Malus had been called to make his report. The highborn stood defiantly beyond the end of the long table, with Nuarc standing close behind him. Retainers and servants shuffled quietly about the room's perimeter; on the north end of the chamber stood a high, arched entryway that opened onto a narrow balcony which looked down over the inner wall and the city beyond. Hauclir stood by the open archway, idly cleaning his nails with a small knife and dividing his attention between events without and within.

'I wasn't aware that I'd been placed in personal command of the outer wall defences,' Malus hissed. Unlike the richly attired nobles, he'd come to the audience chamber after finding a place in the citadel for the surviving mercenaries. He was still clothed primarily in steel, blood and black ichor. 'Perhaps that explains why no one along the outer wall had the faintest idea what was happening, nor were they given any leadership or direction once the north gate fell. It would certainly explain why my section of the wall received no food, ammunition or medical orderlies in the entire two days I and my men stood guard there. Why, if only I'd known, dear brother. Perhaps I could have saved the wall and the Dark Mother only knows how many of our men!'

The retreat to the inner wall had begun well enough; the Black Tower's garrison was familiar with the plans for such a manoeuvre, as laid down by Lord Kuall, the previous vaulkhar, and they had even drilled for it regularly. But once the gate fell and the Chaos horde came swarming into the city, confusion and panic quickly took hold. With no clear chain of command there was no one to organize a rearguard to hold the attackers at bay so the rest could get to safety. Worse, the regiments from Malekith's army had to deal with their own set of conflicting orders from their individual drachau, commanding them to think of themselves first and everyone else second, if at all. The retreat quickly became a free-for-all. Regiments from the same city stuck together and left their rivals behind. Entire regiments were isolated in the city and wiped out, while there were rumours that there were at least three instances of druchii regiments fighting one another for the chance to escape the enemy.

Nuarc and Malus had done what they could, gathering up stray units and forming an ad hoc rearguard that managed to hold the central avenue outside the inner gate for some three hours before finally being forced to retreat. At this point Malus had no idea whether they'd done any good or not. Now night was drawing in, and the highborn found it hard to believe he'd been standing on the outer wall just eight hours before. He was more tired than he'd ever been in his life, and at that moment he wanted nothing in the world so much as the chance to reach over and tear out his brother's throat with his bare hands.

Isilvar met Malus's burning gaze without flinching. 'The fact remains that you were on the wall – in fact, according to your own report, you were adjacent to the main enemy attack all along. Yet you did nothing to stop it, interestingly enough.'

'I was in the middle of a *battle*,' Malus shot back. 'Where were you? In the bath? Having your teeth filed?

You're the damned Vaulkhar of Hag Graef, the most powerful warlord of the most powerful city in Naggaroth. Do you even know how to use that sword you're carrying?'

Isilvar leapt to his feet, his dark eyes glittering. 'I could show you if you like.'

'You had your chance to show me in the cult chamber beneath Nagaira's tower,' Malus replied with an evil grin. 'But you ran like a frightened deer, then. Did you tell yourself you were escaping for the sake of Slaanesh and her cult, or did you save the self-serving excuses for later?' He leaned over the edge of the table. 'I should think that if anyone here is familiar with conspiring with Nagaira, it would be you.'

The vaulkar went pale – with rage or fear Malus wasn't entirely sure. 'You... you have no proof of such a thing!' he rasped, his hand rising unconsciously to his throat.

'Care to put that to the test, dear brother?' Malus said, a cruel smile playing at the corners of his mouth. He noticed Myrchas, Bale and even Jhedir casting long looks at the trembling figure of the vaulkhar.

Across the marble-floored chamber, Hauclir cleared his throat. When Malus didn't respond, he tried again, louder this time.

The highborn turned to regard Hauclir. 'Are you well?' he said icily.

'Well enough, my lord,' he said, straightening. The former guard captain gestured to the balcony with his knife. 'I think there's something out here you might want to see.'

'Do I look busy to you, Hauclir?' Malus snapped, indicating the assembled nobles with a sharp sweep of his hand.

'Of course, my lord, but–'

'Can it wait?'

Hauclir frowned. 'Well, I suppose it can,' he said.

'Then trouble me with it later!' the highborn said with a look of exasperation.

The former guardsman folded his arms, glowering at his one-time master, then shrugged. 'As you wish,' he said, turning back to the open archway.

Malus turned back to Isilvar, trying to recapture his train of thought. Isilvar still glared at him from across the table, his hand in the hilt of his blade. His face seemed a bit calmer now, the highborn noted with a frown.

But before he could continue there was a thunderous boom that rolled through the open archway beside Hauclir. Everyone except Malekith jumped at the sound.

Malus glanced worriedly at Hauclir. 'What in the Outer Darkness is that?' he cried.

The former guardsman gave the highborn a sardonic glare. 'Evidently nothing of any import,' he said peevishly.

Snarling, Malus rushed to the archway with Nuarc in tow. Even Isilvar and the drachau rose from their chairs and made their way warily across the room.

With a passing glare at his impertinent former retainer, Malus stepped onto the balcony and looked down from a dizzying height at the top of the inner wall and the glittering ranks of the troops massed to defend it. Beyond lay the corpse-choked streets and the smouldering buildings of the outer city, teeming with looting bands of beastmen and drunken marauders.

In a wide square a few hundred yards from the inner gate however was a sight that made Malus's heart skip a beat. Long lines of straining beastmen were pulling a pair of enormous catapults down the long avenue and into firing positions alongside a third siege engine whose throwing arm was already being winched back for another shot. A pall of stone dust hung in the air above the gatehouse, indicating the catapult's intended target.

Beside Malus, Nuarc let out a low curse. 'They must have been assembling them under cover of that damned darkness,' he muttered. 'Your sister is more resourceful than I imagined.'

'She lacks martial experience, but she's well read,' Malus said grimly. 'Do you think they can knock down the gatehouse with those things?'

The warlord grunted. 'Of course they can. All they need is time and ammunition, something they seem to have in abundance.'

Malus fought down a swell of frustration. Nagaira wasn't giving him a chance to catch his breath for a single moment. He didn't have to consider the situation very long before he realised what must be done. Turning on his heel he strode back into the chamber. Isilvar and the drachau retreated as he swept inside, as though he carried some kind of plague.

The highborn turned to Lord Myrchas. 'Is there a tunnel?'

'Tunnel? What do you mean?'

'Is there a tunnel leading from the citadel into the outer city?' Malus snapped. 'Surely there must be some way to launch raids in the event the outer wall is breached.'

The drachau of the Black Tower started to speak, then paused. He frowned in bemusement.

'For the Dark Mother's sake, Myrchas! Don't you know?'

Before the drachau could embarrass himself further, Nuarc spoke up. 'There is such a tunnel. I saw it once when I was studying the plans of the citadel.'

The highborn nodded curtly. 'All right then. Lead on, my lord,' he said to Nuarc, then gestured at Hauclir. 'Let's go and get the men.'

But an armoured figure stepped into Malus's path. Isilvar stood nearly nose-to-nose with his half-brother. 'And where do you think you're going?' he said, hand on the hilt of his sword.

Furious, Malus stepped forward, catching Isilvar's sword arm and the wrist with one hand and shoving him hard with the other. The vaulkhar fell in an undignified heap, his scabbarded sword tangled beneath him.

'While the rest of you sit here peeling grapes and squabbling like children I'm going to take care of those catapults,' he snarled. 'No doubt by the time I return you'll have invented some other set of excuses to explain away your clean hands and faint hearts.'

Isilvar's face turned white with fury, but he made no reply. Malus gave his half-brother a mocking salute, then, glaring angrily at the assembled drachau, he motioned for Nuarc to take the lead and followed him from the room.

Meanwhile, in the shadows, the Witch King watched Malus go and kept his own silent counsel.

Chapter Eighteen
THE DRAGON'S BREATH

'OH, FOR THE Dark Mother's sake!' Hauclir hissed in exasperation, holding open the small burlap bag so the mercenaries could see the clinking contents within. 'Which one of you halfwits thought it was a good idea to let Ten-thumbs carry the incendiaries?'

The cutthroats exchanged sheepish looks. In the light of the single witchlamp in Malus's hand, the three mercenaries looked like mischievous shades. Pockets smirked at the former guard captain. 'Ten-thumbs only drops stuff he's trying to steal,' she said, her voice pitched just loudly enough to carry down the line of waiting troops. 'Besides, we figured if he went up in flames no one would miss him.'

Thin hisses of laughter echoed up and down the line. Even Malus found it hard not to grin. They were twenty feet underground, at the far end of a mile-long tunnel that ran from the citadel into the outer city, right in the midst of the bloodthirsty Chaos horde. The tunnel seemed well-made, its square stones slick with dark patches of moss and dripping slime, but everyone eyed the tarred black cross-beams holding up the low ceiling with evident worry. Even weak attempts at humour were welcome.

'Easy for you to say, Pockets. He doesn't owe you any coin,' Hauclir replied. Working carefully, he reached into the bag and pulled out the globes of dragon's breath one at a time. Each glass sphere was wrapped in thick wads of rough cotton to conceal the distinctive green glow and keep the volatile contents safe. He parcelled out the incendiaries among the group, handing one to Pockets, one to Cutter, one to Malus and keeping one for himself, then – with a look of pure trepidation – handing one back to Ten-thumbs. The young cutpurse accepted the deadly orb with as much aggrieved dignity as he could manage.

'I'll take the extra one,' Malus said, holding out his hand. 'And never mind what I may or may not owe you.'

'Very good, my lord,' Hauclir said, handing the orb over. The highborn set the incendiaries carefully at the bottom of a carry-bag tied to his belt, then looked over the raiding party one last time. There were only seven mercenaries, counting Hauclir; Malus felt that a smaller group had a better chance of getting close enough to the siege engines to hit them with the orbs and then slip away again in the confusion. Three of the cutthroats carried crossbows, and Malus had managed to appropriate one for himself from the citadel armoury. Hauclir had further assured him that both Cutter and Pockets were light on their feet and good with their knives.

'All right,' the highborn said, turning and raising the witchlamp to illuminate the narrow shaft at the end of the tunnel. Rusting iron staples had been hammered into the packed earth, providing a ladder to reach the surface. 'According to Nuarc, this opens into a warehouse in the armourer's district. Once we're on the surface, no lights or unnecessary talking.'

Pockets gave Malus a slow wink and a feline smile. Her alabaster skin and sharp features reminded the highborn of a maelithii. The black eyes and filed teeth didn't help. 'No worries, my lord,' she said in her rough harbour accent. 'We've a bit of experience in this sort of thing.'

'Except usually we're breaking into the warehouses instead of breaking out of them,' Ten-thumbs said. He was the youngest of the mercenaries, with a long, lean face and large, nervous eyes.

'Let's get on with this,' growled Cutter, flexing his gloved hands. The assassin was shorter than the average druchii, and slightly darker of skin, giving him an exotic appearance. His face was scarred by a pox he'd had as a child, and his right ear looked like it had been chewed by rats. As near as Malus could tell he was also unarmed; he couldn't see a knife anywhere on the druchii's body.

Malus took a deep breath and nodded. 'Cutter, Pockets, you first. See what's up there and report back.'

Cutter went right for the rungs and climbed swiftly up the shaft. Pockets moved with a bit more caution, following slowly in the assassin's wake. As the two cutthroats climbed the shaft, Malus snuffed out the witchlamp and set it carefully on the tunnel floor. He turned his head in Hauclir's direction. 'Now we just hope that there isn't a crate of iron bars sitting atop the trap door,' he muttered.

They waited in silence and utter darkness, breathing softly and listening for the slightest sound. Above them,

Malus thought he heard the faint scrape of a door, and distant, muffled noises – voices, perhaps? He held his breath. Were there Chaos warriors in the warehouse?

The tiny noises faded, leaving only silence.

As the darkness and silence enfolded him like a shroud, Malus was left with only his thoughts – and the presence of the daemon.

Devoid of sensory distractions, the highborn was hyper-aware of his physical form. All at once he felt the weight of fatigue bearing down upon his shoulders and blurring his mind. He felt hunger, and pain from a half-dozen minor wounds, but as sensations they were cold and somehow distant, as though sensed from the other side of a wall of stone.

He flexed his hands, feeling them brush against the insides of his armoured gauntlets, but again, the sensation was diffused. Alarmed, he reached up and touched his face, feeling the cold steel fingertips of the gauntlet as a dull pressure against his cheek. His heart quickened fearfully, and he felt the daemon shift slightly in response. This time, however, it wasn't a sensation of snakes coiling in his chest – he felt the daemon move through his entire body, like a leviathan sliding beneath his skin.

It wasn't a barrier that separated Malus from his own body – it was Tz'arkan itself. The daemon's hold upon him was more complete than he'd dared imagine. It was as if their roles had been reversed, and now he was the dispossessed spirit lurking in a form not his own.

Immediately the daemon's presence subsided, like a predator pausing warily in mid-stride. Gritting his teeth, Malus forced himself to calm down, to slow the ragged beating of his heart. Tz'arkan was paying close attention to his reactions. Clearly the daemon did not want him to know the extent of its control. But why?

The answer suggested itself immediately. The warpsword. It had the power to counter the daemon's influence. No doubt Tz'arkan feared that if he knew how much control the daemon truly had over him, it would drive him to take up the burning blade again. So long as the warpsword remained in its scabbard on Spite's back the daemon had the upper hand – and, the highborn realised with growing horror, more freedom of action than it would have otherwise.

The nightmares, he thought. What if I wasn't stumbling about in my sleep? What if it was the daemon, moving me about like a puppet?

Suddenly there was a muffled shout from above, and the sound of running feet. Malus heard a choking cry that sounded almost directly overhead – then something metal came rattling and clanging all the way down the twenty-foot shaft, striking sparks from the iron rungs as it fell. Malus and the cutthroats spat muted curses as the object struck the floor of the tunnel next to the highborn's boot with a muted thud.

Malus bent down and groped around for the object. His armoured fingertips rang faintly on metal, then his hand found the hilt of a sword.

Faint movement sounded overhead. 'All clear,' Pockets whispered.

The highborn frowned up into the darkness. 'Is there any point whispering now?' he asked in a normal voice.

'I don't know. Maybe.' The gambler sounded defensive. 'Can't be too careful, right?'

'Evidently not,' Malus growled back. 'We're coming up. Try not to drop anything on our heads in the meantime.'

The highborn took the lead, reaching for the first of the iron rungs and then slowly working his way upwards in the cave-like darkness. His hands seemed to find the rungs effortlessly, and he wondered now if the daemon was subtly guiding his hand, using senses beyond the highborn's ken.

As he neared the top, Malus found the darkness lessened somewhat by a faint, orange glow that etched hard lines and black silhouettes out of the greater gloom. He found the top edge of the shaft and levered himself up out of the hole, finding the dark shape of Pockets waiting for him a few feet away. Large crates, many filled with what looked like metal bars or sheet stock, stood in orderly rows around the hidden trapdoor. Next to Pockets sprawled the body of a marauder, his scarred hand seemingly outstretched towards the open shaft.

'We found a group of these animals cooking meat over a small fire on the other side of these crates,' the druchii cutthroat whispered. 'Cutter and I got the lot of 'em, but this one must have been off taking a piss somewhere. It was his sword went down the shaft.'

Malus straightened and looked about. They were near the front of the building, and the orange glow he'd seen earlier came from the marauder's small fire and the shifting light of much larger fires streaming in through the building's large, open doorways. The highborn moved quietly across the cluttered space and peered warily outside. As night had fallen the Chaos horde had started fires all across the outer city, and pillars of flame and smoke billowed into the air from the warehouses scattered across the city's districts. A warm, hungry wind whispered through the eaves of the warehouse, stirred to life by the churning columns of fire, and Malus thought he could hear the faint cries of the horde borne aloft on the hot air as they celebrated their victory.

For the moment the nearby streets appeared to be empty. Malus breathed a sigh of relief. He glanced back at Pockets. 'How many marauders were there?'

'Five, counting this one,' she said.

The highborn nodded. 'Strip them of their cloaks and furs. We'll need them.'

As Pockets went to work the first of the mercenaries began appearing from the shaft. Malus kept watch in the meantime, going over his battle plan one last time and looking for possible weak points. After the debacle in the north he was determined not to tarnish his honour with yet another costly defeat.

Within minutes Hauclir was standing beside him. 'We're ready, my lord,' he said quietly.

Malus nodded and went back to join the assembled troops. He reached down and picked up the first set of stained furs atop the pile that Cutter and Pockets had gathered. 'Hauclir, you and the crossbowmen put these on,' he said, wrapping the stinking hide around his shoulders. 'Pockets, Cutter and Ten-thumbs will stay in the middle of the group.'

Hauclir's lip curled in disgust, but he obediently bent down and picked up a bloodstained cloak. 'This isn't going to fool anyone.'

'If we keep our distance it should suffice,' Malus said. 'We just have to look similar enough in the darkness that we don't raise any suspicions until we reach the square.'

Once Hauclir and the crossbowmen were wrapped in marauder attire the raiding party set off, creeping stealthily down the dark, corpse-laden streets. The exit point of the tunnel was to the south of the citadel, so they were forced to spend almost three hours in a circuitous route around the inner city until they could come within striking distance of the siege engines.

The Chaos horde had completely surrounded the inner fortress, filling the outer city like a swarm of maddened locusts. Fires burned out of control in parts of the city, and howling bands of beastmen and marauders rampaged through the once-orderly districts, looting and destroying everything in their path. Screams of terror and pain rent the night; the enemy had taken hundreds of prisoners after the outer wall had fallen, and now they sated their bestial appetites on their captives in every horrific manner possible. The small raiding party went all but unnoticed amid such pandemonium; only once did a band of marauders come close enough to get a good look at the shadowy group, and they were shot dead before they could shout an alarm. Pockets, Cutter and Ten-thumbs took their furs and the raiding party continued on.

Finally, just past midnight, the raiders found themselves north of the broad square containing the siege engines. The massive catapults had been firing without pause for hours; each siege engine was the size of a town house, resting on massive, ironbound wheels and held together with iron pins as thick as shinbones. Almost a hundred slaves per engine were used to crack the massive arms into firing position, and another fifty more were put to work loading the siege engine with boulders or hunks of masonry weighing hundreds of pounds. Already the thick walls of the inner gatehouse and the tall gates themselves were showing signs of damage. Nuarc had been right; given enough time the Chaos engines would dash the fortifications to the ground.

Unfortunately for them, Malus thought with a vicious smile, their time was nearly up.

The raiding party had gone to ground in a looted barracks some two blocks north of the square, close enough to hear the crack of the taskmasters' whips and the bang of the catapults as they fired. One last time Malus considered the final stages of his plan. Everything seemed to be in place. It's all going according to plan, the highborn thought. Obviously there's something I'm missing. After a moment's thought he motioned Cutter over.

'My lord?' the cutthroat said, settling quietly into a crouch beside the highborn.

'I want you to scout around the square,' Malus said. 'We've had good fortune so far, but I'm starting to wonder how much of it we have left. Go and see if there's anything out of the ordinary.'

'Right you are, my lord,' Cutter growled, and vanished into the darkness. In the meantime the raiders settled down in the shadows and did what they could to rest.

Another hour and a half went by. The night grew steadily colder as the night passed into early morning, and the paving stones outside glittered with a thin layer of frost. Malus was reminded of the passing of the seasons and the last few grains of sand remaining in the daemon's hourglass. Was he fighting the wrong battle, he wondered? Here he was risking his life for the defenders of the fortress when he needed to be finding a way to get the Amulet of Vaurog and escape to the north. As it was, he only had a few days left before he began cutting into the time necessary to reach Tz'arkan's distant temple.

For the moment, his plight and the fortress's plight was one and the same. So long as Nagaira and her champion were surrounded by an army they were safe. That was going to have to change.

Hauclir and several of the cutthroats were sleeping in their filthy cloaks when Cutter finally returned. He settled down beside Malus. 'It's an ambush,' the pox-marked druchii said. 'There's a hundred marauders waiting in a barracks to the west of the square, with lookouts posted on the roof.'

Startled murmurs passed among the cutthroats. Suddenly Hauclir was wide-awake. 'They expect us to hit the catapults?'

'Of course they would,' Malus said, nodding to himself. 'They know we can't afford to let them pound us at their leisure.' It's possible that they even expect me to lead the raid, Malus suddenly realised. It is, obviously, the sort of thing I would do. He rubbed his pointed chin thoughtfully. 'We still hold the advantage, though.'

'Because now we know where the ambushers are,' Hauclir said.

'Exactly,' the highborn replied. He glanced back at Cutter. 'All of the ambushers are in a single building?'

The assassin nodded. 'If it hadn't been for their lookouts I'd have never known they were there. No lights, no fires – they're a clever bunch of animals.'

Malus thought it over. A crucial decision had to be made. 'All right,' he said at length. 'Hauclir, take Cutter and the crossbowmen and circle around to the west. When you're in position, kill the lookouts and then hit the ambushers with your dragon's breath. That will be our signal to attack the siege engines.'

'*Our* signal?' Pockets said, looking to Ten-thumbs. 'What, the three of us?'

'A hundred marauders cooking alive should provide an ample distraction,' Malus replied coolly. 'Enough for us to get into the square and employ our own orbs. Then we break away in the confusion and return to the tunnel.'

The female druchii shook her head in horror. 'There's no way. It's suicide.'

But Malus smiled. 'Not at all. If there's one thing I know well, it's that you can get farther on pure audacity than anything else. Just do what I do, and we'll get through.' Without waiting for any further protests, he nodded to Hauclir. 'Get your men and get moving,' he said. 'We'll give you half an hour to get into position.'

Without a word, Hauclir rose to his feet and motioned to the crossbowmen. Within minutes Malus watched them disappear across the narrow street and down a shadowy alley to the west.

Pockets and Ten-thumbs gathered their weapons and met Malus at the doorway. 'He's as mad as you are, my lord,' she said, nodding in the direction Hauclir had gone.

Malus grinned ruefully. 'He served a highborn once who was fond of foolish risks. A complete madman. I suppose it left its mark on him.'

The female druchii frowned. 'Really? I should have guessed. What a liar!'

Malus gave her a bemused look. 'What are you talking about?'

She shrugged. 'He told us his old master was a hero, as vicious and clever as they came.'

The highborn's grin faded. 'He couldn't have been more wrong,' he said, suddenly uncomfortable. 'Come on. We've got to get closer to the square.'

Keeping to the shadows, the three druchii sidled down the long avenue towards the siege engines. Lines of slave workers came and went, dragging wagons loaded with boulders to feed the great catapults. Marauders on horseback lashed at the slaves and urged them on with savage curses. Whenever one of the riders drew close Malus led the cutthroats inside the closest building until the horseman passed.

It took nearly twenty minutes to work their way down the two blocks to the edge of the square. A small band of marauders waited there, ostensibly guarding the avenue entrance, but they were passing looted wineskins back and forth and grunting to one another in their bestial tongue. The highborn led the two mercenaries into the deep shadow of a nearby alley. 'We wait here,' he whispered. 'Get your orbs ready. When the commotion starts, I'll take the catapult to the left. Ten-thumbs, you take the one in the middle, and Pockets will go to the one on the right. Aim for the winding drums; even if they have some sorcerous means of dousing the flame, it should burn through the ropes quickly enough to knock the catapults out. We'll meet on the other side of the square and head for the tunnel.'

As it happened, they didn't have long to wait. Off to their right they heard a great *whoosh*, and a chorus of wild screams, and suddenly the marauder horsemen were racing past, heading for the square as fast as their mounts would take them. 'Now!' Malus hissed, and he dashed into the street, running along behind the horsemen. He could see a shifting green glow to the west, in the direction of the sounds, and knew that Hauclir and his men had been brutally successful.

The marauders guarding the entrance to the square were swaying on their feet and howling like the angry dead, torn between their orders and their instinct to race to the fight. They paid no attention to the horsemen or the small band of warriors trailing in their wake. The slave crews for the siege engines had been driven into three groups by their furious taskmasters and herded to the back of the square, away from the waiting siege engines. Malus turned and nodded to the cutthroats and headed straight for the catapult on his left, fishing one of his orbs of his carry-bag.

As he loped past one of the slave-gangs a whip-wielding taskmaster turned to look at him as he sped past and shouted a question in his barking tongue. Malus continued on, picking up speed. Green light shone between the fingers of his right hand.

The taskmaster yelled again, his tone sharper this time. Malus bared his teeth in a snarl. Just a dozen more yards to go.

As fast as he was, Pockets was faster. At the far end of the square bedlam erupted as the first of the catapults burst into flame. Angry cries of alarm echoed back and forth among the marauders. Throwing caution to the wind, Malus ran for his target as fast as he could.

A furious shout sounded behind the highborn, and he heard the thunder of hobnailed boots pounding after him. He reached the rear of the catapult and kept going, running for the huge winding mechanism in front. Off to the right, the second catapult was bathed in a sheet of hissing flame.

Just as he reached the far end of the catapult a chaos marauder leapt around the corner into his path, two short axes held ready. He shot the snarling man in the face with his crossbow, then half-spun on his heel and threw the green orb at the cable-wound drum looming above him.

The glass shattered and the liquid inside ignited with a roar and a dazzling green flash. Air rushed past Malus like a giant's indrawn breath, and for a terrifying moment he felt himself pulled *towards* the blaze. He staggered, then regained his footing and raced for the far end of the square as fast as his feet would carry him.

By now the entire square blazed with green light. A thrown axe whirred past his head, and he worked the reloading lever on his crossbow as quickly as he could. The shadows beckoned to him from twenty yards away. At the moment it felt like twenty miles.

Hoof beats clattered across the paving stones to the highborn's right. A horseman was spurring his wild-eyed mount right at him, a short spear held ready to throw. The crossbow's bolt racked home in the firing trough with a loud *clack*, and Malus stopped just long enough to raise his weapon and shoot the marauder high in the chest. The Chaos warrior threw his spear at the same moment, and the weapon struck Malus in the right shoulder, glancing off his enchanted armour. The blow hit hard enough to spin the highborn half-around, and he found himself stumbling backwards and facing almost a score of screaming marauders, closing fast with the burning catapults blazing at their backs.

At the sight of his face the two men in the lead drew back their axes and let fly. The first one went wide, but the second smashed into the highborn's left arm with enough force to knock the crossbow from his hand. Malus shouted a curse and tried to fumble in his bag for the second orb, but gave up in a moment and simply hurled bag and all at the oncoming enemies.

The bag sailed through the air and landed at the lead marauder's feet but swathed in cotton and the thick burlap, the orb refused to break! Malus cursed and groped for his sword – just as the lead marauder tried to knock the bag aside with a savage kick.

Whump. The marauder band disappeared in a fierce explosion, sucking away even their screams in a rushing torrent of air. Teeth bared in a feral grin, Malus turned about and all but dove into the deep shadows of an alley beyond the square.

Swallowed up by the welcoming darkness, Malus listened to the furious shouts of the enemy echo all around him. Sword and axes clashed as warriors of the horde turned on one another in confusion. The sound was sweet to the highborn's ears.

Above the sound of the enemy's disarray rose another noise, high and sharp like the whistle of a razor-edged blade. The warriors of the Black Tower were cheering.

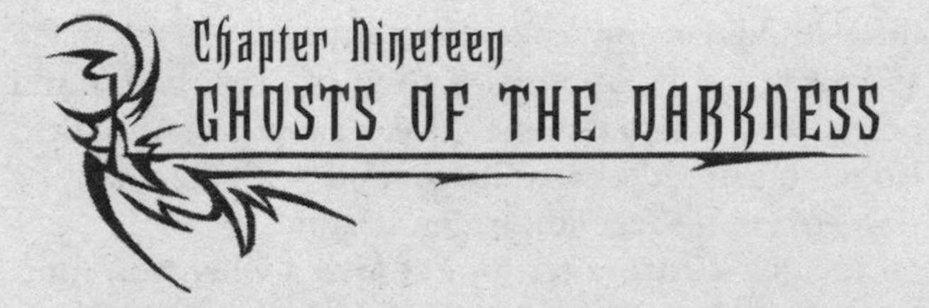

Chapter Nineteen
GHOSTS OF THE DARKNESS

MALUS DREAMT HE was falling into darkness. Cold wind, damp and mouldy as a tomb, blew against the back of his neck and tangled his black hair as he plummeted downwards. From moment to moment his toes and fingertips would brush the packed earthen walls of the narrow shaft. Every so often he felt gnarled roots slip past his fingers, but never in enough time to snatch at them and save himself.

Slow, daemonic laughter echoed in his ears as he plunged into the Abyss.

The impact, when it came, startled him. It reverberated like thunder in the noisome blackness, and it felt as though every bone in his body shattered like glass. And yet there was no pain; just a creeping coldness, spreading through him like oil.

He could not guess how long he lay there. Malus could feel cold ichor seeping from his shattered skull and spreading across the earth beneath him. He lay there, waiting to die, but his body refused to submit to its injuries.

Then another wind brushed his face – this time from above. It reeked of blood and sickness and bodily vice, of every depravity Malus could imagine and more. And then he heard the laughter once more, and realised what was coming for him.

He rolled onto his knees, feeling bones cutting through his insides like jagged glass. His stomach spasmed, and he vomited a soup of black liquid and pulverized organs onto the unseen earth. The wind tickled at his neck like a lover, and with a groan he staggered to his feet and began to run.

Laughter echoed after him. 'I love it when you run!' the daemon's voice said behind him. 'Look over your shoulder, Malus! I'm right here behind you!'

But he didn't dare look. If he turned around, even for an instant, he knew Tz'arkan would catch him. As long as he ran, he was free.

Malus lurched and stumbled blindly down a long corridor, hands flung out before him. He crashed left and right into walls of packed earth as hard as stone and smelling of the grave. Splinters of bone pressed against the insides of his skin, burst through and then fell away in spurts of black fluid. Yet still he ran on, his body wired together by nothing more than galvanic fear and icy madness.

Then without warning he reached the end of the line, crashing headlong into an unyielding wall of earth. Malus was hurled to the ground by the impact, but the laughter of the daemon drove him back to his feet in an instant. He beat at the wall with his ragged fists; he clawed at the stone-like earth until the flesh of his fingertips was torn away. The laughter grew louder in his ears, and the air grew cold around him – and then his flailing hand closed around something hard and metallic jutting from the earthen wall.

An iron rung. He recognized it at once, and feverishly began to climb upwards, reaching frantically for the next iron staple and grabbing it with an almost hysterical wave of relief. Was he in the tunnel beneath the Black Tower? He had to be! The knowledge sped his climb even further, until it seemed that the laughter behind him was starting to fade. Tz'arkan, it seemed, didn't know how to climb. A lunatic giggle escaped his stained lips.

The trapdoor was exactly where he reckoned it would be. Malus pushed against it and it flew open, allowing a flood of warm, orange light to spill down from the space above. Now it was his turn to laugh as he struggled upwards, desperate for the glow of an honest fire.

That was when the hand closed about his ankle. 'You and I are not finished yet, Darkblade,' the daemon hissed. 'You have given yourself to the darkness, remember?'

He cried out, kicking and pulling at his leg, but the daemon was far stronger. Slowly, inexorably, he was pulled back down into the shadows.

Until he felt a strong pair of arms circle his chest and pull him upwards as though he were a child. Tz'arkan held on for a moment, struggling vainly, then the iron grip about his ankle gave way. It might have taken his foot with it, but at that moment Malus didn't care.

Strong hands hauled him upwards into the light. He hung there like a babe, laughing and weeping with relief. A shadowy figure stepped towards him, limned with fire. A cold hand caressed his cheek, tracing lines through the thick sludge coating his skin.

'There you are, beloved,' Nagaira croaked. She smiled, and rivulets of filth oozed over her ruined lips as she bent close to him. Her pale skin was marbled with pulsing, black veins, and there was only blackness where her eyes ought to be. Malus looked into their depths and realised that there were *things* living there, beings older and vaster than time. He screamed and tried to struggle, but the Chaos champion held him from behind, his armoured hands tightening around Malus's arms until black ooze ran from between his steel-clad fingers.

'We've come a very long way to find you,' Nagaira said. Her breath was cold and putrid, like air escaping from a corpse. The icy nothingness in her eyes pulled at him. 'There's so much I want to show you. So much that you need to see.'

Then her lips covered his, and he tasted icy, squirming rot against his tongue as the ancient things behind Nagaira's eyes took notice of him for the first time and the world exploded in pain.

WHEN MALUS OPENED his eyes he was lying on a cold, stone floor and his kidneys were aching like they'd been kicked.

'I apologize for that, my lord,' he heard Hauclir say. 'But you gave me little choice.'

He tried to move, and found himself tangled in something heavy and voluminous. With a groan he rolled onto his back and found himself wrapped in a bed sheet and blanket. Hauclir stood over him with a grim look on his face, holding his cudgel in his scarred hands. Five livid scratches ran down the right side of his face.

'Do you know who I am this time?' the former guardsman said. 'Or do I have to jog your memory again?'

'Jog my organs is more like,' Malus said with a grimace. 'Help me up, you damned rogue.'

With a grunt, Hauclir bent and pulled the highborn awkwardly to his feet. Malus looked about and realised he was standing in the hallway outside his quarters. He hissed a bitter curse. 'Again,' he muttered.

'You mean this isn't the first time you've walked in your sleep and assaulted people?' Hauclir grumbled.

'No. Not the first time,' Malus replied, entirely oblivious to Hauclir's impertinent tone. 'What in the Dark Mother's name is happening to me?'

'If I didn't know you, I'd say you were going mad,' Hauclir replied. 'Unfortunately, I *do* know you.' He glanced about quickly, ensuring that they were alone. 'Is it the daemon?' he whispered.

Malus frowned. 'I don't know. It's possible. I've lately wondered the same thing myself.' He pulled irritably at the sheets wound around his legs. 'Let's get out of this corridor before someone sees me like this. What is the hour?'

'A bit past midmorning, my lord,' Hauclir answered, setting aside his cudgel and bending to help unwind the highborn. 'Lord Nuarc told us that we were to stand down and get some rest while we could. Do you remember?'

Malus stepped out of the sweat-stained sheets and tried to focus his thoughts. 'The last thing I remember clearly is crawling across the floor of my room and climbing into bed.' He registered a familiar taste in his mouth and winced. 'There was wine involved, wasn't there?'

'Just a bit,' Hauclir agreed.

'I think I could stand some more,' Malus said, and staggered back through the open door into his apartments.

The doors to the balcony were open again, letting in a long rectangle of pale sunlight that stretched halfway across the room. His shuffling feet sent dark bottles clinking and spinning across the floor. 'Gods Below, Hauclir,' the highborn cursed, looking over the array of empty bottles. 'How much did we drink?'

'*We*, my lord?'

There wasn't a single bottle left with so much as a drop of useful liquid inside it. Growling irritably, the highborn staggered towards the balcony. A terrible disquiet lurked at the back of his mind, and he couldn't quite say why.

Or perhaps better to say I'm having a hard time being specific, the highborn thought ruefully. The Dark Mother knows I have more than enough to vex me at the moment.

Malus shaded his eyes with his left hand and squinted into the morning light. A muted clamour rose from the inner wall, and from his high vantage point he could see that the Chaos horde was assaulting the inner fortress. The sight filled him with apprehension, for reasons he couldn't explain.

'How long has the attack been going on?' Malus asked.

'Started right at dawn,' Hauclir replied, joining Malus at the balcony. 'They've been at it ever since.' He eyed the highborn. 'Good thing we're up here resting and drinking wine instead of down there fighting,' he said pointedly 'Isn't that right, my lord?'

'Wine,' the highborn said thoughtfully. 'Right. Fetch another bottle will you? And something to eat. Bread, cheese – whatever you can find. I've got to get into my armour.'

The former guardsman opened his mouth to protest, but gave it up for a lost cause. 'As you wish, my lord,' he grumbled.

MALUS FOUND LORD Nuarc giving orders by the inner gatehouse, directing three regiments of spearmen against seemingly endless waves of Chaos warriors. A battering ram still burned fitfully a few yards short of the gate, surrounded by the charred bodies of its operators, and warriors continued to repel long siege ladders cast up by swarms of enemy troops. Crossbow bolts filled the air like swarms of flies, surrounding the ladders nearest the gatehouse with dark clouds of death. A steady rain of bodies fell on either side of the high wall as marauders and beastmen were slain upon the battlements or shot through as they clung to the sixty-foot ladders.

Heads turned as the highborn reached the battlements. Spearmen from Hag Graef and the Black Ark raised their weapons in salute as he passed, and a ragged cheer followed Malus and Hauclir all the way to the gatehouse itself. The daring raid on the catapults – now just a trio of charred hulks in the square to the north – had turned Malus and the cutthroats into heroes overnight. It was a small victory, in the grand scheme of things, but it was the first of its kind for the weary defenders, and they celebrated it as only desperate soldiers can.

Even Nuarc's customary glare was tempered with a modicum of respect as the highborn joined him above the gatehouse. 'I thought I told you to get some sleep,' the warlord shouted over the din.

'I tried, but you're making too much noise down here,' the highborn shouted back. 'I don't suppose you could keep it down a bit?'

The general laughed. 'I can't help it if the bastards won't die quietly,' he replied.

Shaking his head, Malus studied the battle raging along the walls. 'How bad is it?' he asked.

'We're actually doing well so far,' Nuarc replied. 'We've got twice as much manpower here than we had at the outer wall, and it's a higher and more difficult climb. Also, the enemy attacks are fierce, but uncoordinated this time. I think you must have stirred something up when you destroyed those siege engines last night.'

'Stirred something up,' the highborn echoed thoughtfully, looking out at the wreckage in the square. 'Has there been no sign of Nagaira or her champion?'

'None,' the general said. 'I don't know why, but I've learned long ago not to question good fortune when it comes my way.'

But the more Malus thought about it, the more troubled he became.

'Something wrong, my lord?' Hauclir inquired.

'I don't know,' Malus answered. 'Wait – no. Something's not right. I just can't figure out what it is.'

Hauclir surveyed the activity on the walls and shrugged. 'Everything looks in order from up here.'

'That's part of the problem,' Malus said. 'Nuarc thinks we stirred something up last night when we attacked the catapults, but I don't think so. They were expecting a raid, and had troops waiting to ambush us.'

The former guard captain thought it over. 'They laid their trap and we blew it up in their faces. That would be enough to stir anyone up, don't you think?'

A spark of realization struck Malus. 'The catapults were bait,' he said, a look of dread dawning on his face.

Hauclir's frown deepened. 'I suppose so,' he said. 'But we foiled the trap.'

'No!' Malus cried. 'That's not the point. They knew we would have no choice but to attack those catapults. In fact, they counted upon it!'

'To what purpose?'

'What else? Now they know we have another way out of the castle.'

Hauclir's jaw dropped. 'And if we can get out, they can get *in*. Gods Below, my lord. Could they be that clever?'

'This is Nagaira we're talking about. Of course they can be that clever,' Malus growled. Suddenly his dream took on an awful clarity that sent a chill down his spine. 'Let's go.'

'Go where?' Hauclir asked, though the tone in his voice suggested he already knew the answer.

'To gather your cutthroats and see how clever my sister truly is,' the highborn replied.

THE ENTRANCE TO the long tunnel lay in the bowels of the Black Tower itself, on the same level as the fortress's vast cisterns. Holding aloft a half-dozen witchlamps on long, slender poles, Malus, Hauclir and all thirty mercenaries rushed though the cavernous, arched chambers, passing broad, stone-capped basins that held the tower's water supplies. Their weapons were ready and they cast wary glances into every shadowy corner they passed. Malus led the way, fearful that they were already too late.

'Even supposing your theory is correct,' Hauclir said breathlessly, 'the beasts would still have to find the entrance to the tunnel, and I know for a fact we weren't followed.'

'They don't need to see us to be able to track us,' Malus said grimly. 'They could set hounds on our scent; they could set *beastmen* on our scent, for that matter. We're just fortunate they haven't found their way into the fortress yet.'

Pockets, jogging along behind the two druchii, piped up. 'I don't suppose either of you brought some more of those terrible little orbs with you?'

Malus shook his head. 'We've few enough left as it is, and if we tried to use one in the tunnel it would eat through the wooden supports and bring the thing down on our heads. And I don't want to cut off our only escape route unless it's absolutely necessary.'

The druchii loped along to a dark alcove at the far end of the cistern network. There, some ways off from the rest of the storage containers, lay a circular, wooden cover similar to the ones that sealed the tower's real cisterns. At Malus's direction two of the cutthroats pulled the cover aside to reveal a spiral staircase winding down into darkness.

'Crossbows up front,' Hauclir ordered, then the former guard captain turned to Ten-thumbs. 'You stay up here,' he said. 'If you hear fighting, you head upstairs as fast as you can and get reinforcements. I don't care who they are.'

'Yes, Captain,' the young thief said, his eyes wide and fearful.

Malus plucked a crossbow from a nearby cutthroat's hands and quickly loaded it. Cutter cleared his throat and spoke. 'We should douse the lights,' he said.

The mercenaries shared anxious looks. Pockets frowned. 'You want us to go down there blind?'

'Better to go in dark than lit up like daybreak,' the assassin replied. 'If those animals have found their way in, they're likely carrying torches, which gives us easy targets.'

The highborn saw the wisdom of it at once. 'Do as he says,' he commanded. When all of the lights had been extinguished, the small band of warriors were swallowed by absolute darkness. 'The two men with lamps farthest back will bring theirs along,' he said. 'The rest, leave yours aside. When I call for light, you ignite your lamps. Understood?'

Murmurs of assent rose from the back of the party. Malus nodded, feeling his heart hammering in his chest. 'All right, let's go.'

They descended the winding staircase totally blind, shuffling along one shallow step at a time. Men stumbled against one another, whispering curses, and occasionally a scabbard or sword tip would clink against the stone. The air turned chill and dank by slow degrees. Malus held his crossbow levelled, listening for the slightest sound of footsteps coming up to meet him.

At length, Malus felt his boot scrape against earth. A wisp of cold air caressed his cheek and he shuddered at the memory of the dream he'd had, little more than an hour before. Men shuffled into place on either side of him. 'Hst!' he whispered, just loud enough for keen druchii ears to hear. 'We'll walk forward slowly for a few yards and stop. Listen for my signal.' Quiet grunts to either side and behind him acknowledged the order.

They edged forward down the long tunnel, careful to make as little noise as possible. The blackness was total; infinite. The mercenaries could hear nothing but the sound of their own breath, hissing between clenched teeth. Finally, after Malus reasoned that nearly all of the troops had reached the bottom of the stairs, he whispered, 'Halt. Front rank, kneel.'

He and the two men beside him sank slowly to one knee, clutching their crossbows tightly. They peered into Abyssal blackness and listened for the slightest sound on an oncoming foe.

Minutes passed. Malus saw no hint of light in the darkness or heard any sounds of movement. There was an unmistakeable tension in the air, but his own troops could easily account for that.

Time dragged slowly on. Warriors shifted uncomfortably, drawing hissed warnings from Hauclir. Malus bared his teeth. They were out there. He was certain of it.

The warrior immediately behind Malus bent low and whispered in the highborn's ear. 'Message from Hauclir. He wants to know if we should advance down the tunnel.'

'No,' the highborn whispered. 'The enemy will have to come to us, and we're better situated here–'

He froze. Was that a faint scuff of a foot somewhere ahead? Malus listened, not daring to breathe. Another sound – perhaps the tiny rattle of a buckle or chain. Or it could be his imagination, stoked by tension and absolute blackness.

Malus thought the situation over and reached a decision. He raised his crossbow to his shoulder, aimed at waist height, and fired.

The thump of the crossbow was loud enough to startle the warriors behind Malus – but nothing like the agonized scream that rent the darkness farther down the tunnel.

'Both ranks, open fire!' Malus ordered, quickly reloading his crossbow. More bowstrings thumped, and heavy bolts thudded into shields or glanced from steel armour with glints of bright blue sparks. Some of the bolts sank into flesh, drawing more bloodcurdling screams, and then the tunnel echoed with the thunder of running feet as the Chaos troops began their charge.

The close confines of the tunnel rang with frenzied shouts and blasphemous war cries. It sounded like a thousand warriors were bearing down on Malus and his meagre force. There was no real way to tell how close they were in the bedlam of shouts and screams echoing all around him. 'Keep shooting!' he shouted into the din. 'Aim low. They can't get to us if we block the tunnel with their bodies!'

Fire. Reload. Fire. For almost a minute Malus's arms worked in deadly rhythm, working the loading lever of his repeater crossbow and firing into the darkness. Marauders screamed and stumbled with a clatter of mail and steel-rimmed shields. The sharp smell of blood and voided bowels thickened the subterranean air.

Malus fired again, and this time his victim's agonized scream sounded almost directly in front of him. 'Front rank, pass your crossbows back and draw steel!' he roared. He shoved his own weapon back to the warriors behind him and yelled back at the mercenaries as he drew his twin blades. 'Lights!' he called.

The order came just barely in time. Cold, green light flooded the narrow tunnel and revealed an axe-wielding barbarian not three feet from Malus. The human's face was twisted in a rictus of rage and pain, and a crossbow bolt was buried to the fletchings in his muscular left shoulder. The sudden glare from the witchlamps blinded the warrior for an instant, and the highborn lunged forward and thrust his right-hand blade through the muscles of the marauder's upper thigh. A fountain of arterial blood poured from the wound, and the warrior staggered, howling in pain. But before he could recover he was dashed against the side of the tunnel by the warrior behind him as his frenzied tribe-mate rushed to come to grips with his foes.

'Stay on your knees!' Malus ordered the men to either side of him. The howling barbarian came right at the highborn, his shield held low. Malus feinted with his right-hand sword and blocked a sweeping axe-stroke with his left – and then the druchii behind Malus shot the warrior point-blank in the face. The steel bolt punched clean through the warrior's skull and struck the marauder behind him in the throat.

Yet no sooner had both men collapsed than their tribe-mates were clambering over them to hack at the hard-pressed druchii line. Malus and the men in the front rank fought like rats, stabbing at exposed knees, feet, thighs and groin. They slit men's bellies where they could, and where the enemy's guard was too strong they held the barbarian off long enough for a druchii crossbow to fell him.

And yet there seemed to be no end to the bastards. Bodies began to pile so high in front of the druchii that the marauders had to drag them aside in order to reach their foes. Malus's knee was sodden with spilled blood. He soon lost count of the number of men who died trying to force their way down the tunnel, and his arms began to burn with exhaustion from near-constant battle.

The fight seemed to rage for hours, but Malus knew that it was most likely only a handful of minutes. The druchii exhausted their ammunition before long, and the second rank drew their own blades and joined in the swordplay. The marauders were able to press them more closely after that, but they still faced the difficult task of fighting two swordsmen at once.

Exhaustion began to take its toll. The druchii to Malus's right faltered for only a moment and a barbarian axe dashed out his brains. Instantly another warrior leapt forward and knelt in his place as Malus cut the barbarian's hamstring with a quick flick of his wrist. Other druchii died behind him, struck down by flung axes or the thrust of saw-edged blades. Their formation contracted slightly, falling back a few feet towards the stairs. Malus began to wonder when the reinforcements were going to arrive.

And then suddenly a horn wailed down the tunnel from out of the darkness, and the marauders fell back at once. They dragged away as many of the dead as they could, something Malus had never known the marauders to do before. A ragged cheer went up from the surviving druchii, but Malus cut them off with a sharp wave of his hand. Something wasn't right.

Then he heard it. The heavy tread of armoured feet, rolling like thunder towards the battered druchii warriors. Suddenly he realised that the enemy had used the barbarians to wear them down and soak up their ammunition, preparing them for the hammer blow.

'Mother of Night,' he cursed. 'On your feet!' he called to the men beside him. 'Get ready!'

But by then it was already too late.

The figure that loomed before them in the witchlight had once been a man. In some sense he still was, but now his body was swollen with corruption. Muscles as thick as a nauglir's threatened to burst from the warrior's taut skin, and his eyes shone like embers from behind a massive, horned helmet of dark iron. The Chaos warrior was clad in heavy armour from head to toe, adorned with jagged spikes and curling horns, heavy chains and cruel hooks festooned with shrivelled heads. His massive hands gripped a pair of hand axes that looked too large for a sane man to wield, and yet wield them the warrior did, tearing into the surprised druchii with a bloodcurdling roar.

The mercenary to Malus's left died without a sound, the front of his head shorn away by a flickering sweep of an axe. The druchii to Malus's right leapt forward with a shout, thrusting at a gap in the warrior's armour just above his thigh. But the blade missed the gap and skated harmlessly off polished iron, and the warrior punched the haft of his left-hand axe through the mercenary's skull.

Seeing an opening, the highborn lunged forward, chopping down on the warrior's left wrist and half-severing it in a spray of blood. To Malus's horror, the warrior laughed and smashed his right-hand axe into the highborn's side. It was only the enchantments woven into his armour that saved the highborn from the fearful blow; as it was, the impact knocked him from his feet and smashed him against the side of the tunnel wall.

Screaming a wild war cry, Pockets charged at the towering Chaos warrior, clutching a sword and dagger in her small hands. The warrior snarled contemptuously and swatted at her with his axe. But the nimble druchii ducked beneath the blurring sweep of the blade and then leapt onto the warrior's massive chest. Before the surprised warrior could react she howled like a mountain cat and buried her dagger to the hilt in the warrior's right eye.

With a gurgling cry the warrior fell to his knees, and Pockets sprang clear barely an instant before a heavy axe crashed into the warrior's neck and hacked away his head in a spray of hot gore. The warrior behind the headless corpse kicked the body over with a booming curse and leapt for the girl's retreating form, his axes blurring and moaning in the reeking air.

Druchii leapt at the monster from three sides, and were mown down like wheat. The charging mercenary to the warrior's right was flung back against the wall in two pieces. Dead ahead a cutthroat rushed forward, trying to cover Pockets as she retreated, and got his head struck off for his trouble. Malus ducked beneath the warrior's deadly swing and lunged in from the right. His right-hand sword crashed against the side of the warrior's armoured knee and his left-hand blade snaked upwards, catching the warrior beneath the chin and driving upwards into his fevered brain.

But the resolve of the cutthroats had collapsed before the onrushing Chosen, and a terrified flight began. Malus pulled his sword clear of the toppling warrior just as the witchlamps wobbled crazily and then abruptly dwindled as the retreating troops bore the two men back around the turn of the staircase.

More Chaos warriors howled for blood in the sudden darkness. Swearing lustily, Malus raced for the staircase after his men. The climb upwards was a frantic pursuit of crazily swinging light; the lamp men always seemed just at the verge of the turn in the stair, so the highborn could only catch wild glimpses in the shifting glow before it vanished once more. He saw terrified faces and wide, dark eyes, fearful glimpses thrown past narrow shoulders and stumbling forms practically crawling up the stairs as fast as their hands and feet could carry them. Behind Malus the darkness echoed with wild, bestial shouts as the Chosen warriors gave chase.

Then, without warning the close confines of the staircase opened up into the arched space of the cistern vaults, and the panicked retreat came to an abrupt halt. Witchlights bobbed and swung in the open space above, shedding narrow streams of pale light. All Malus could see were the backs of four or five struggling druchii trying to get off the stairs, but he clearly heard Hauclir's voice, rolling over the mercenaries like thunder. 'Any one of you takes another step forward I will split your skull myself!' he roared. 'Stand your ground! The enemy will advance no further into the citadel! We have to hold at all costs until reinforcements arrive!'

The reinforcements aren't here yet, Malus thought? Blessed Mother of Night!

He didn't know whether to thank Hauclir or kill him. On the one hand, he's stopped the rout in its tracks, but on the other hand the highborn was now trapped on the staircase at the tail end of the line with a howling Chaos horde heading his way!

Vicious oaths and bloodthirsty cries echoed crazily up the staircase. Malus turned about, levelling his swords. 'Turn and face the enemy!' he cried to the men behind him. 'They can only come at us one at a time on the stair. We can hold here for a long while if we keep our nerve!'

Thankfully the men listened. He felt them shuffling about, and blades appeared above his head. He steeled himself and crouched low, waiting for the inevitable assault.

He heard the onrushing warriors climbing the staircase, their shouts growing louder and louder. It was all but impossible to see more than a few feet down the staircase – the damned witchlamps kept swinging as though caught in a gale, creating wild patterns of light and shadow along the stairs.

Then, just as it appeared that the warriors were almost at the next turn of the staircase, the howling stopped. Silence fell like a shroud. Malus heard mercenaries gasping for breath above him. Someone moaned fearfully. He bared his teeth and tightened his grip on his blades.

There was the faint scratch of a boot heel on the stone stairs below Malus. A faint ring of harness. Then the shifting light picked out the gleaming tip of a rust-stained druchii sword. The highborn caught the scent of rot and wet earth, like a recently opened grave.

Slowly, gracefully, the Chaos champion rose into the wavering light, his helmet upturned to Malus and the Amulet of Vaurog glinting at his neck.

Chapter Twenty
MIDNIGHT ALLIANCES

THE CHAOS CHAMPION fixed Malus with a gaze like a viper, filling his veins with dread. The armoured warrior seemed to float up the stairs towards Malus, swords outstretched like a lover's waiting arms.

'Mother of Night,' Malus cursed desperately, raising his own twin blades. 'Daemon!' he hissed. 'Attend me! Lend me your strength!'

The daemon stirred, shifting disconcertingly beneath the highborn's skin – but the customary rush of icy power did not come. Malus had barely enough time to register Tz'arkan's treachery before the champion struck.

Silver steel blades darted and slashed at the highborn's legs and abdomen, striking sparks where the keen blades slipped past Malus's guard and glanced from his enchanted armour. He parried furiously, roaring with anger at the daemon's betrayal, because he knew that, even without the terrible power of the Amulet at the champion's disposal, he was no match for the warrior's Chaos-fuelled abilities.

He took a glancing blow to the side of his knee and barely parried a swift thrust at his groin. The champion was not only skilled but well versed in the art of sariya fencing. His technique matched Malus's almost perfectly, and the realization only enraged the highborn further. Malus channelled all his hatred and fury into his blows, allowing certain attacks through his guard in order to strike back at his foe. Powerful blows rained down on his breastplate and fauld, turned aside time and again by the potent sorceries of the armourers of Naggarond. In return he struck at the champion's arms and neck, hoping to sever a sword-hand, or better yet strike off the warrior's helmeted head. But the champion's speed was such that most often Malus's blows cut through empty air or struck a glancing blow on the champion's armour. It was as though the warrior could anticipate his every move.

There was a furious commotion among the mercenaries behind Malus, but he couldn't spare even a momentary glance over his shoulder to see what was going on. Then a dagger whirred past his head and struck the champion with such force that it penetrated his breastplate just beneath the collarbone. A normal warrior would have been staggered by the blow, but the champion scarcely noticed. It did cause the warrior to hesitate a fraction of an instant, giving Malus the chance to sweep aside the champion's left-hand sword and stab his foe through the throat. Dark blood coursed down the flat of the highborn's blade, but the warrior pulled himself off the tip of the sword as a man recoils from the prick of a thorn, and then immediately renewed his attack.

A figure brushed past Malus, charging down the staircase towards the champion. Hauclir caught the champion's right-hand sword against the side of his scarred cudgel and hacked at the warrior's wrist with his short, heavy sword, but the blade could not penetrate the champion's iron armour. Quick as a snake, the champion pivoted and lunged at Hauclir with his left-hand blade, and it was all Malus could do to knock it off-track with a blow from his own sword.

Moments later Cutter joined in the fight as well, throwing another dagger that rang off the champion's armoured leg. The Chaos warrior responded with a lightning-quick cut at the assassin's neck, but the druchii evaded the blow with astonishing speed. Seeing his opportunity, Hauclir lunged in and smashed his cudgel against the champion's right arm. The blow would have broken the bones of a lesser man, but the champion simply staggered slightly and forced the former guardsman back with a lunge at his throat.

Now, with three skilled opponents pressuring him from different angles, the Chaos champion was forced onto the defensive. Malus pressed his attack, raining blows on the warrior's left arm and shoulder. Sparks flew and fragments of iron armour were hewn away by the force of the highborn's blows, but the champion held his ground, countering each attacker in turn with swift parries and deadly feints. Malus was starting to think that they were gaining the upper hand – and then Hauclir stepped in on the champion's left, smashing his cudgel against the warrior's right knee and then reversing the blow to swing at the champion's head. The Chaos champion appeared caught off guard, thrusting his blade at Cutter's neck, but the attack was only a feint. Like a thunderbolt the champion's sword plunged down, slicing through Hauclir's right thigh. The former guard captain fell with a curse, and Cutter lunged forward with a yell, thrusting for the champion's eyes – only to have the Chaos warrior's left-hand sword bury itself deep in his right shoulder.

Seeing both druchii fall in the space of a single second filled Malus with terror and rage. Unleashing a terrible war-scream he put all of his strength and speed into a single cut that smashed into the champion's temple. Sparks flew, and the force of the blow whipped the champion's head around. Still shrieking his rage, the highborn followed up with a backhand blow that smashed into the warrior's helm right at eye level. Iron snapped with a discordant clang, and the champion's helmet burst asunder.

The warrior's head snapped back from the force of the blow. Black hair, matted with filth and old blood fell loosely to the champion's shoulders. Pallid skin, gleaming with sickness and shot through with pulsing black veins, shone greenish-white in the witchlight. A single, black eye fixed Malus with a glare of implacable hate. The other eye was sightless and glowed with grave-mould. A terrible sword wound cleft the warrior's skull above that ruined eye, its ragged edges black with corruption and squirming with parasitic life.

Malus looked into Lhunara's face and cried out in terror and anguish. 'Gods... oh Gods Below!' he cried. 'You can't be...'

Lhunara's black lips pulled back in a lunatic grin. Unlike his dreams, her teeth were still perfect and white. Her muscular body trembled, and a terrible, bubbling sound rose from her throat. It was the foulest, most vile laughter Malus had ever heard.

'With hate... all things are possible,' she croaked, drawing back her dripping blades. 'With hate... and the Dark Gods' blessing.'

She took a step towards him, and Malus looked in her ruined eyes and knew he was about to die.

He was saved by a thin, reedy voice that echoed from the top of the staircase. 'Dragon's breath!' Ten-thumbs shouted. 'Stand clear!'

Malus turned and saw the young thief standing less than ten yards away, holding a glowing green orb in his upraised hand. Hauclir shouted up at the boy through gritted teeth, 'No, you fool! You'll kill us all!'

'Throw it, boy!' Malus shouted. 'Do it now!'

But Lhunara was already gone, dashing fleet as a deer down the staircase until she was lost in darkness. Malus cursed bitterly and slumped onto the stairs, the vision of her hateful face lingering like a ghost before his eyes.

Mercenaries rushed down the stairs to grab Hauclir and Cutter and pull them clear. Hauclir glared up at Ten-thumbs. 'Who in the Dark Mother's name gave you that orb?' he snarled.

Ten-thumbs grinned. 'What? This?' he tossed the glowing ball above his head – to the horrified shouts of everyone nearby – and snatched it deftly out of the air. 'I've had this for quite a while. It's my little ace in the hole.' He tossed the orb from hand to hand.

And missed.

Ten-thumbs let out a horrified squawk and lunged for the glowing orb. The slick glass bounced through his fumbling fingers and plunged towards Malus, Hauclir and the horrified mercenaries. Dozens of hands grabbed for the orb, slapping the glowing ball this way and that, until finally it bounced free and smashed against the wall about four feet above Malus's head.

Cutthroats scrambled in every direction, screaming in terror.

The small witchlamp burst with a sharp *pop* and a smell like a lightning storm. Small fragments of glass rained down on Malus's head.

'Oh, damn,' Ten-thumbs groaned. 'My mother gave me that light. I've had it since I was a child.'

Silence hung heavy in the air. The cutthroats, who moments before had been convinced they were about to burn alive, reeled like drunkards, overcome with relief. Hauclir leaned back against the outer wall of the staircase and glared up at the morose thief. 'By the Dark Mother, I don't know whether to kiss you or skin you alive.'

Nervous chuckles broke out among the cutthroats, quickly turning into gales of loud, hysterical laughter as they came to grips with their unexpected salvation. A pair of mercenaries helped Hauclir and Cutter up the staircase. Hands reached for Malus, but he pushed them away. Slowly, awkwardly, he staggered upright. His limbs felt like cold lead, and his head was cased in bitter ice.

He was the last to climb the curving stair into the cold shadows of the cistern vault. By the time he made it to the top the echoing space was full of angry warriors. Lord Isilvar stood at their head, his expression pale with fury. The cutthroats had drawn together in a tight knot around their wounded leader, glaring balefully at the sneering faces of Hag Graef's spearmen

'What is going on here?' Isilvar grated.

'A battle, dear brother. What else?' Malus shot back. He hadn't expected Ten-thumbs to be quite so successful at drumming up reinforcements. In the back of his mind he realised that they were sorely outnumbered and far from any reliable witnesses should Isilvar suddenly decide to murder the lot of them. The knowledge did nothing to blunt his impertinent tongue. 'I realise you don't see much of these, what with your duties as vaulkhar.' Before Isilvar could reply, Malus plunged onward. 'The Chaos forces have discovered the tunnel. We managed to hold them off until you arrived, but they could be massing for another assault even as we speak.' The highborn grinned mockingly. 'I yield the honour of repelling the next wave to you, as is only fitting to your rank.'

Muscles bunched furiously at the corners of Isilvar's jaws. 'We will have to fire the tunnel and collapse it,' he said. 'The Chaos horde has redoubled its assault on the walls, and every available man is needed at the parapet.'

'Then if you will excuse me, brother, I must hasten to my duty,' Malus replied. Without waiting for Isilvar's leave, he motioned to his men and made to depart. For a brief moment it looked as though the ranks of Hag Graef spearmen would refuse to let them pass, but Malus met the gaze of an older spearman who nodded curtly and stepped aside. The druchii behind the spearman followed suit, and suddenly there was a long, clear path through the spear company leading across the cistern vault. Helmeted heads, both veteran and conscript, nodded respectfully to Malus and his troops as they limped past.

Hauclir, shored up by Pockets on one side and Cutter on the other, came up alongside the highborn. 'That Chaos champion,' he began, 'she looked as though she knew you. Who is she?'

'A nightmare,' Malus said in a dead voice.

* * *

At first, all he could hear were voices. They were muffled and echoed strangely, as though heard from beneath the surface of a deep, dark lake.

'My time runs short,' Nagaira said. The sound of her voice was powerful, vibrant and utterly wrong, full of discordant tones like shattered glass. 'I have obligations to fulfil, mighty one. Obligations that will not be denied.'

'Do not speak to me of time,' Tz'arkan hissed. 'Mine runs short as well. But he knows the way, now. He knows what must be done.'

'But will he act? That is the question.' There was the faint chime of finely hammered silver, and the sound of a knife cutting through meat.

'Who can say?' the daemon growled. 'Nothing you mortals do makes any sense to me.'

The blackness began to fade. Shapes formed to either side of him. He was lying on his back, tangled in sheets. Cold air caressed his bare chest. Nagaira and the daemon spoke above his prone form like adults talking over a sleeping child.

'I fail to see why all this is necessary,' Nagaira said. 'Your scheme is overly complicated to my mind.'

'As complicated as your revenge at Hag Graef?' the daemon retorted.

'Point taken,' she said with a sigh. There was another faint ringing of metal, and this time Malus watched the blurry form of his sister lift a goblet to her lips and drink. 'Yet couldn't you simply deliver Malus to me yourself?'

Suddenly Malus was very alert. The shapes resolved further. He could see Nagaira clearly now. She was sitting in a chair, tucked close to a banquet table, turning a silver goblet in her black-veined hands. Her touch left lines of black tarnish across the gleaming curve of the metal. A knife and fork rested at the edges of the plate set before her, which was piled with steaming cuts of bloody meat. She took no notice of Malus at all, fixing the black emptiness of her gaze upon the being sitting opposite her.

'It is not so simple as that,' the daemon replied. Malus turned his head to look upon the daemon, but its shape was concealed in deep shadow. A plate of bloody meat sat untouched before it. 'You are thinking in such immediate terms, my child. Consider the implications of my plan in their full measure, and what it will mean for you once we have returned from the north.'

'Then he must be persuaded to act,' the druchii witch said. She carefully set the goblet on the table before her.

'Of course,' Tz'arkan replied. 'Do as you think best.'

Malus tried to move, but the sheets pulled tight, trapping him fast. Nagaira looked down at him, reaching to touch his cheek with a long, claw-like nail. 'How much of my brother will remain, after all is said and done?'

'Enough,' the daemon said at length. The shadowy figure reached forward and dipped a clawed hand into Malus's chest. The highborn glanced down, past his chin, to see Tz'arkan lift his still-beating heart from the gaping cavity of his chest. 'You see? It is still quite strong. So is his mind. He should satisfy your appetites for some time to come.' The daemon leaned back in his chair and gestured expansively at the highborn's ravaged body. 'Will you take any more for your plate, child?'

Nagaira leaned forward, peering thoughtfully at Malus's face. 'I should like his eyes,' she said. 'I've always loved them, you know.'

A strong hand clamped down on Malus's forehead, pressing it to the table. Another figure entered his field of vision, looming over him from above. Lhunara bent over him, her ravaged face lit with a lover's smile. Wriggling maggots fell onto his cheek from the gaping wound in her head.

She pressed a cracked thumbnail to the corner of his eye and he began to scream.

HANDS WERE PRESSING him down onto the bed. Malus kicked and thrashed, screaming in rage and fear. He heard low voices cursing above him, and for a dizzying instant he wasn't sure if he was waking or still trapped in the dream. With a wild effort he tore his arms and shoulders free, shoving away the shadowy figures looming over his bed, and rolled to its edge just in time to vomit a large quantity of rancid wine onto the stone floor.

'I told you those last two bottles were mostly vinegar,' Hauclir said from across the room. 'But you wouldn't listen. Of course, you might have been too drunk to hear me at that point, but I thought it was worth a try.'

Early morning light filtered in through the bedchamber's open window. Hauclir sat in a chair near the balcony entrance, his wounded leg propped up on a low table dragged over for just that purpose. Vague figures moved quietly about in the darkened chamber, patching armour or sharpening their weapons. Pockets and Ten-thumbs were roasting meat over a brazier near the foot of the bed, whispering to one another in low voices.

Malus writhed his way out of the sodden bed sheets and staggered onto his feet. His mind swam from the after effects of wine and shock. The dream still hung in his mind with dreadful clarity. Was it real? Was the daemon consorting with Nagaira now? How could he know for certain? He looked to Hauclir, but what could he say that the daemon wouldn't also hear? 'What is the hour?' he asked blearily.

'Early morning,' Hauclir said. 'Too early, in fact. And thank you for asking about my wound. It's not nearly as bad as I feared.'

'We have to get to the nauglir pens,' the highborn interjected. 'Now.'

Hauclir studied Malus carefully. 'You're still drunk, my lord.'

'Since when has that ever made a difference? Help me get into my armour,' the highborn replied, tugging at his stained nightshirt.

BUTCHERS' CLEAVERS ROSE and fell outside the nauglir pens within the citadel's expansive inner compound, and vast lakes of blood glittered in the early morning sun. As Malus and Hauclir approached the low stone structure a group of young servants were pulling the bodies of beastmen and marauders from the back of a wagon and lining them up for the cutters to inspect. Several hundred nauglir consumed a great deal of meat in a given day, and the druchii saw no reason to waste anything that came their way.

The roar of battle from the inner wall, less than half a mile distant, had continued unabated since the day before. Chaos warriors were hurling themselves in endless waves against the high walls. Hauclir said that soon they wouldn't need ladders at all, but could scale the walls over the piles of their own dead.

The former guard captain was limping painfully along beside Malus, using an improvised crutch made from a pair of spear hafts. 'Why the sudden rush to visit your cold one?' he asked, a glint of suspicion showing in his dark eyes. 'If you're planning on a quick ride into the country I don't think you're going to get very far.'

'I need to get something from my saddlebags,' the highborn said curtly. His mind was still churning over the implications of his dream. In retrospect, he should have expected this, he thought angrily. Now that he'd enlisted the aid of his mother Eldire and then bound himself to the warpsword, Tz'arkan was bound to try and find ways to outmanoeuvre him and retain the upper hand. He had no idea that the daemon could speak to Nagaira through his dreams. Was it also responsible for his many nightmares about Lhunara? The thought both terrified and enraged him.

He'd been a fool to put the warpsword away, risk or no risk. That was going to change.

Malus rushed past the bloodstained butchers and down the ramp into the pens. The chamber was dark and the air dank and acrid with the scent of scores of the huge warbeasts. Each nauglir had its own pen, not unlike a horse's stall, but made of dressed stone rather than wood and secured by a stout gate of iron.

It took several minutes before the highborn found the pen where Spite was kept. The nauglir was dozing on the sandy floor, snout tucked behind its curved tail. The warbeast stirred as Malus quickly unshackled the gate and slipped inside the pen. Hauclir, his clothes still stained with fresh blood, wisely chose not to follow.

'There you are, beast of the deep earth,' Malus said. At the sound of its master's voice the cold one rose quickly to its feet. Force of habit led the highborn to check the cold one's claws, teeth and hide for signs of illness. 'It looks as though these imbeciles are treating you well,' he muttered, eyeing the bloodstained sand nearby. 'And your appetite is good.'

Malus moved his inspection to his saddle and tack, then to the saddlebags still strapped to the cold one's back. The bag containing the relics was still safely secured, and next to it lay the long, wrapped bundle of the warpsword. He fancied he could already feel the heat of the burning blade, like a brazier of banked embers waiting to be stirred to life. Taking a deep breath, the highborn reached for the sword.

Instantly a spasm of burning pain shot through Malus's body. He doubled over with an agonised groan, his hands clenching into trembling claws. Spite started at the sound, glancing back at Malus with a warning growl.

The daemon shifted and tensed beneath the highborn's skin. *Oh, no, little druchii,* Tz'arkan purred. *I don't think so.*

'My lord?' Hauclir cried. 'Are you all right?'

But the highborn couldn't speak; indeed, he could scarcely breathe for the pain that wracked his chest and arms. He dimly saw Spite slinking slowly away from him, and his experienced eye immediately recognized that he was in dire trouble. Beyond the roaring in his ears he heard the cold one rumble deep in its throat.

He forced every iota of his will into forcing words past his gritted teeth. 'Re... lease me,' he grated.

Oh, I shall, little druchii, the daemon said. *But first, perhaps I'll let this beast of yours bite off your sword arm. I can make you stick your hand in its mouth if I wish. Would you like to see?*

A violent tremor wracked the highborn's body... and his right arm slowly, haltingly, began to rise.

'My lord!' Hauclir cried. 'What in the name of the Outer Darkness are you doing?'

Across the pen, Spite let out an angry bellow. Immediately the other nauglir in the pens took up the roar, shaking the air with their thunderous cries.

Such weak, crude flesh you have, Darkblade, the daemon said. *It's no great loss if a part of it is torn away. In fact, I'm entirely happy to let your stinking beast bite both of your arms off, if that's what I must do to keep you away from that sword. I have new allies now, you see. They can finish the job you started and give me what I want.*

A thin, despairing wail rose from Malus's lips as he watched his right arm fully extend. His body moved like a children's doll, turning jerkily towards the cold one. Spite's head was lowered, its powerful tail lashing tensely across the sandy floor. The cold one was about to strike.

Suddenly a robed form lurched across the sand and knocked Malus to the floor just as the nauglir struck. Its blocky jaws clashed shut, scattering sprays of venomous drool right where Malus had been standing moments before.

'Back, you damned lump of scales!' Hauclir roared, lashing at the beast's face with his crutch in one hand and trying to drag Malus clear with the other. Spite snapped at the offending stick and ground it to splinters, but it bought Hauclir enough time to drag Malus halfway across the pen. The highborn's legs flailed at the sandy floor, trying to help push them along. The cold one let out another furious bellow, its talons digging furrows in the sand, but before it could gather itself to charge, Hauclir pulled the highborn through the gate and slammed the iron barrier closed.

'Gods Below, my lord, what was that all about?' Hauclir demanded, his breath coming in ragged gasps. Fresh blood spotted the bandage wrapping his thigh.

Before Malus could speak, the daemon whispered warningly in his ear. *Be very careful what you say, Darkblade,* he warned. *Or the next time you wake you'll find every one of your precious servants with their throats cut.*

The highborn gritted his teeth. 'I... was just checking on my belongings,' he said. 'The damned beast just didn't care for my scent. Too much wine, as you said.'

The former guard captain frowned. 'Are you certain that's all?' he said, his dark eyes scrutinizing his former master.

'What else could it be?' Malus snapped, his voice bitter. Before Hauclir could reply he cut the druchii off with a wave of his hand. 'No more questions. I want to go to the wall and check on the state of the siege. I've got a terrible suspicion that something big is about to happen.'

Chapter Twenty-One
BETWEEN THE LIVING AND THE DEAD

COLUMNS OF GREASY, black smoke rose from behind the inner wall of the fortress, and the air was thick with the smell of roasting flesh. Every half-mile along the avenue behind the wall rose a pyre for the druchii dead, each one tended by a score of exhausted servants and a couple of hollow-eyed officers who noted down each soldier given over to the flames. The orderly removal of corpses to the funerary furnaces had been abandoned days ago. The dead were piling up far faster than the removal crews could handle, and most of the men had been pressed into service on the battlements besides.

The piles of the enemy dead were vaster still, rising in stinking heaps more than twelve feet high in places and running the entire perimeter of the wall. Malus was awed by the sheer scope of the slaughter and more than a little disturbed at the Chaos horde's near-suicidal zeal. They will bury us in their own dead if they must, he realised with a mixture of worry and admiration. All that matters to them is victory and ruin, and they will keep coming at us until their leaders are dead or the last barbarian has been cast from the walls.

He caught himself wondering what sorts of things he might accomplish with such an army at his back and ruthlessly forced such thoughts aside.

With Hauclir limping along in his wake he made his way up the long, bloodstained ramp to the battlements alongside the northern gatehouse. Bodies and bits of armour plunged past the two druchii in a grisly hail-storm as the troops on the parapet cleared away the detritus of the latest assault. The most recent attack had been seen off as the highborn had crossed the inner compound from the nauglir pens, and the sudden silence along the battlements was eerily disturbing after what seemed like hours of screams and bloodshed.

The highborn was appalled at the scene of carnage atop the wall. The dark stone parapet was mottled with a thick layer of blood, sawdust and viscera, and druchii spearmen sat or slept amid the filth, too exhausted and numbed to even notice. Broken weapons, bits of armour and pieces of flesh littered the entire length of the wall. Great ravens hopped and croaked at one another as they sought for choice morsels among the motionless bodies of the living. Even Malus, who had recently walked the blood-soaked streets of Har Ganeth, was stunned by what he saw. He glanced back at Hauclir and saw that the former guard captain's face was pale and grim.

Beyond the walls the outer city was a wasteland of burnt buildings and rude tents. Exhausted Chaos war-riors sprawled like packs of wild dogs along the filth-strewn avenues, and hundreds upon hundreds of dead bodies carpeted the killing ground before the inner wall as far as Malus's eyes could see. Howls and gibbering cries rose and fell among the ruins, barking curses in a language none of the defenders could understand, but whose meaning was utterly clear. Soon, all too soon, the killing would begin once more.

There was a commotion ahead as Malus neared the door to the gatehouse. A trio of spearmen were struggling with a fourth warrior, who was shouting and struggling wildly in their grip. 'They won't stop! They won't stop coming!' he cried, his dark eyes wide in a face covered in dried blood and grime. 'We can't stay here! We can't!' The warriors struggling with the panicked druchii exchanged frightened glances. One of the soldiers drew his stabbing sword.

'What's all this?' Malus snapped, the sharp tone in his voice surprising even himself. The struggling warriors started at the barked command, and even the panicked druchii subsided in their arms.

The troops looked to one another, and the most senior man cleared his throat and replied. 'It's nothing, dread lord. We're just taking this man off the wall. He's unwell.'

'There's nothing wrong with this soldier,' Malus snarled, stepping forward and pushing his way into the knot of spearmen. He grabbed the panicked druchii by the scruff of the neck and forced him to stand. 'You've got both your eyes and all of your limbs,' he snapped. 'So what's wrong with you?'

The spearman trembled in the highborn's grip. 'We can't stay here, dread lord,' he moaned. 'It's been days, and they just keep coming–'

Malus shook the man like a rat. 'Of course they keep coming, you damned fool,' he growled. 'They're *animals*.

It's all they know how to do.' He shoved the man against the battlements, forcing his body in the direction of the enemy camp. 'Listen to them! What do you hear?'

'Howls! Black curses!' the druchii shouted angrily. 'They never let up! It goes on and on for hours!'

'Of course it does!' Malus shot back. 'Every single one of those beasts are sitting out there in the muck and cursing your name loud enough that all the Dark Gods can hear it! Do you know why? Because they want nothing more than to get past these walls and slaughter every living thing they can reach, but *you won't let them*. They're the biggest damned army that's ever marched against Naggaroth, and you are standing up here on the wall with your spear and keeping them from the one thing they desire.'

The highborn dropped the man onto the filth-encrusted parapet. 'It's ridiculous! Absurd! They rise from their stinking tents each day and caper like fools before their twisted altars, working themselves into a blood-soaked frenzy that nothing on earth could stand against – and every day they slink back to their tents with their tails between their legs and lick their wounds in the shadow of these black walls. Of course they curse your name! The very thought of you burns like a coal in their guts because you've beaten them every time they've come against you. Every damned time.' He pointed out at the enemy camp. 'You should savour those sounds, soldier, because they are a lament. They're the sounds of fear and desperation. And it's all because of you.'

The spearman stared at Malus in shock. The highborn looked down at him and smiled. 'Victory is in your grasp, soldier. Are you going to let it slip away now, or will you beat these bastards once and for all?'

'You can count on us, dread lord! We'll kill every last one of the beasts!' cried a spearman just a few yards away. Malus was startled by the outcry; looking over, he realised that most of the warriors had risen to their feet while he spoke, and now they hung on his every word. Their dirty, bloodied faces beamed with fierce pride.

The panicked spearman rose shakily to his feet. He swallowed hard and looked Malus in the eye. 'Let them come, dread lord,' he said. 'I'll be waiting for them.'

A cheer went up from the assembled troops. Malus grinned, a little uncomfortably, and waved to the survivors of the regiment. 'Get some rest,' he shouted, and waved in the direction of the enemy camp. 'Enjoy the music while you can.' The warriors laughed, and Malus turned away, striding swiftly for the gatehouse.

Nuarc was waiting for him at the entrance to the fortification. The general's face was as filthy as any common soldier, its lines deepened by exhaustion and hunger. Nevertheless, he gave Malus an admiring grin. 'That was well done, boy,' he said quietly. 'I probably would have just let his file mates take care of the problem.'

The highborn shook his head. 'Then we'd just be doing the enemy's work for them,' he said. 'I'm spiteful enough to want to make those beasts work for every single one of us they kill.'

Nuarc chuckled. 'Well said.' He motioned to the highborn. 'Come inside. You look like you could stand to eat something.'

He led Malus and Hauclir into the gloomy corridors of the gatehouse, passing through deserted rooms and corridors lined with barrels of heavy bolts, until they reached a long room pierced with firing slits that looked out onto the killing ground before the gate.

Perhaps a dozen weary-looking druchii soldiers, male and female alike, looked out over the corpse-strewn approach with their crossbows close to hand. A brazier in the centre of the low-ceilinged chamber provided a modicum of warmth, and upon a nearby table sat a couple of loaves of bread, some hunks of cheese and dried fish, along with a half-dozen leather jacks and several bottles of wine.

'Help yourself,' Nuarc said, waving at the contents of the table. The troops on watch cast predatory glances at the two interlopers who had been welcomed into their midst, like a pack of dogs suddenly forced to share their meat. Malus's stomach roiled at the sight of food, but Hauclir nodded his head respectfully to the warlord and helped himself to the food.

Nuarc poured some wine into one of the jacks and took a small sip. 'Word of your exploits has been spreading among the men. First the raid on the siege engines, and now the battle in the tunnel. You're fast becoming the hero of the hour.'

Malus let out a disdainful snort. 'Never mind the fact that the battle in the tunnel wouldn't have happened if I hadn't fallen for Nagaira's stratagem,' he growled. 'If those poor fools think me a hero, then things are desperate indeed.'

Hauclir chuckled around a mouthful of dried fish, but Nuarc stared into the depths of his wine jack and frowned. Malus caught the gesture and sobered at once. 'How bad is it?'

'We're barely holding on at this point,' Nuarc said gravely. 'As best we can tell, we lost just over a third of our troops in the debacle at the outer wall, and the rest are worn out. We don't lack for food or weapons, but the constant attacks have taken their toll. If we have another day of attacks like yesterday we could lose the inner wall by mid-afternoon.'

The revelation stunned Malus. 'What about the reinforcements from Har Ganeth and Karond Kar?'

Nuarc shook his head, his expression grave. 'There's been no word. At this point I doubt they will arrive in time, if at all.'

'And what of those damned lords in the Black Tower?' the highborn snarled. He began pacing the long room like a caged wolf. 'Have they any bold plans to save us from disaster?'

Nuarc reached for the wine bottle once more. 'I've heard rumours,' he said. 'Are you sure you won't take some wine?'

'Gods, no, general,' Malus said. 'I've had enough of that vinegar to last me a while.'

The warlord poured himself a healthy draught. 'There are indications that your brother the vaulkhar is contemplating a plan that will end the siege in a single stroke.'

Malus chuckled bitterly. 'He plans to lead the garrison against the Chaos horde?'

Nuarc shook his head. 'He intends to turn you over to Nagaira.'

The highborn's weak humour faded. 'You can't be serious.'

'I wish I wasn't,' Nuarc admitted. 'But you embarrassed Isilvar and the other nobles in front of the Witch King – and what's worse, your exploits are winning the admiration of the troops. That makes you very dangerous, as far as they are concerned.'

'Malekith would never allow such a thing!'

The warlord shrugged. 'I've served Malekith for more than three hundred years, boy, and I can't say what he will or won't allow. It's clear to me that he's testing Isilvar and the other lords, but to what end I can't begin to guess. The thing is, they are beginning to realise this as well, and it's making them nervous. They want the siege to end, and giving Nagaira what she wants is the quickest and easiest way to do it.'

'If Isilvar actually believes that, he's an even bigger fool than I imagined,' Malus said, torn between murderous rage and cold panic. 'If Nagaira believes that she can take the Black Tower – and humble the Witch King in the bargain – she won't hesitate to do so.'

Nuarc grimaced. 'I was afraid you were going to say something like that,' he replied. 'Then we'd best figure out another way of ending this siege before Isilvar and the other lords decide to take matters into their own hands.'

Malus bared his teeth in frustration. 'I believe I'll have a bit of that wine after all,' he said.

At that moment an earth-shaking rumble swelled up from the north, causing the oaken table to rattle and the wine bottles to wobble and clink against one another. A strange peal of thunder rent the air, like the sound of a hammer on glass. The druchii at the firing slits were suddenly alert. One of them turned to Nuarc with a frightened look on her face. 'You'd better come see this, my lord,' she said. 'Whatever it is, it can't be good.'

Nuarc and Malus rushed to the firing slits, shouldering aside wide-eyed druchii warriors. The old warlord's expression turned grim. 'Damnation,' he hissed.

Outside, beyond the far curve of the outer wall, a huge column of swirling smoke rose into the cold, clear sky. Green threads of lightning pulsed and rippled through the roiling murk, and even from almost six miles away Malus could feel the winds of sorcery tingling in waves across his skin. As they watched, the column of dark magic rose more than a thousand feet into the air and poured out its energies across the sky. Blackness spread outwards from the column in an inky, turbulent pool, casting a dreadful pall across the war-torn land beneath. More tortured thunder squealed beneath the tainted sky, and a sudden gust of cold, dank wind beat against the face of the inner wall.

'Damnation is right,' Malus said. 'I don't like the looks of this at all.'

Nuarc turned to one of the warriors. 'Sound the call to stand to,' he ordered. 'Unless I miss my guess, the enemy is about to hit us hard.' The warrior nodded, his face white with fear, and dashed from the room.

The wind picked up, skirling eerily through the narrow firing slits and filling the druchii's nostrils with the smell of damp earth. Green lightning strobed through the black sky overhead, glinting on the swords and shields of beastmen and marauders who were starting to trickle down the narrow lanes towards the killing ground before the inner fortress. Thunder keened overhead, and fat, greasy drops of rain began to spatter against the battlements. Above them, on the roof of the gatehouse, horns began to wail, their cries all but lost in the rising wind.

Within seconds the rain became a drenching downpour, tinged green by constant flashes of lightning. Cold air billowed through the firing slits; the druchii warriors recoiled with a curse, gagging on an overpowering stench of corruption. Malus cursed as well, but for a different reason entirely. A moment before he could clearly see the Chaos army massing for another assault, but now they were hidden completely by sheets of oily rain. They could be halfway across the killing ground by now.

The highborn turned to Nuarc. 'Will Morathi and her witches intercede against this awful rain? This could cost us the inner wall if we can't see the enemy until they're standing on the battlements!'

Nuarc shook his head helplessly. 'She is even harder to predict than her son. If Malekith orders her to do so, then perhaps she will.'

'Then you've got to get back to the citadel and speak to the Witch King!' The highborn turned to Hauclir, who was busy stuffing parcels of food and a bottle of wine into the sleeves of his robe. 'Hauclir! Put that down and escort Nuarc back to the Black Tower. Quickly!'

The former guard captain hurriedly folded his arms, causing the pilfered food and wine to disappear. 'As you wish, my lord,' Hauclir grumbled.

Nuarc snapped off a series of commands to the warriors, naming a half-dozen who would accompany him back to the citadel. Malus took the opportunity to join Hauclir and lead him towards the chamber doorway, out of earshot. 'When you've got Nuarc back to the citadel, round up the harbour rats and get back here as quick as you can,' he said quietly. 'We may have to do something drastic in the next few hours if we're both going to get what we want from Nagaira.'

'Drastic? Like what?' Hauclir whispered.

'Honestly? I haven't the faintest idea,' Malus replied, managing a roguish grin. 'Just like old times, eh?'

Hauclir winced. 'Old times? The ones where we nearly got drowned, or burnt up, or eaten by daemons?'

Malus glared at his former retainer. 'Now see here – what about all the good times?'

'Those *were* the good times.'

The highborn bit back a retort as Nuarc and his escorts approached. 'Just get back here as quick as you can, you damned rogue,' he said quietly.

Malus followed the small party to the rear of the gatehouse and left them at a spiral staircase that would deposit them at an iron door set beside the inner gate. Then he drew his twin blades and made his way to the outer wall.

Moments later he reached the exit leading out onto the battlements and saw the heavy oaken door rattling in its frame, buffeted by a howling wind. Shouts and screams echoed faintly from the other side. Gathering his courage, the highborn pulled open the rattling door – and found himself standing upon the brink of hell.

Druchii warriors reeled beneath the lash of reeking wind and noisome rain, many crouching and pressing the tops of their helmets against the battlements to get some relief from the hideous storm. Forks of green lightning rent the skies overhead, seemingly close enough to touch. Malus saw pale faces lit with absolute terror and heard cries of fear all up and down the struggling line of spearmen. To the highborn's horror he saw almost a dozen ladders already rising above the edge of the wall, their wooden rails quivering with the tread of hundreds of feet.

Less than twenty yards away half a dozen warriors were struggling with a thrashing figure lying on the paving stones. Malus heard shouts of anger and fury and saw a long dagger plunge again and again into the prone figure. A black rage boiled up from his heart.

'Stand and face the enemy!' he roared into the howling wind. Swords in hand, he strode out onto the parapet, heedless of the sheets of stinking water that blew into his face and into the crevices of his armour.

'The warriors of Naggaroth do not cower in the face of the storm! They fight or they die! Make your choice!'

Heads turned to Malus as he passed by. Lightning flared, lending his face a daemonic cast. Slowly but surely the spearmen of the regiment gripped their weapons and rose to the feet. Whether they did it out of honour, or shame, or fear of what he might do to them, Malus neither knew nor cared.

The brawl was still raging when Malus reached it, and with a furious shout he took to kicking the spearmen who were punching and stabbing at their victim. Fearful shouts rose in response to his angry blows. One knife-wielder even turned on Malus for a brief instant, his bloodstained knife ready, until he realised who he faced and recoiled with a frightened shout.

Now Malus could see the thrashing, snarling warrior at the bottom of the pile. Each flicker of lightning revealed ghastly wounds to the druchii's chest, belly and legs – horrible rents torn by knife, sword and axe. The warrior had his pale hands around the neck of another spearman, and was trying to pull his struggling victim within reach of his torn lips and broken, bloodstained teeth.

Malus realised how little blood there was around the snarling warrior, and then a cold knot of realization turned his guts to ice.

The druchii was dead. He'd been dead for hours.

With a horrified shout, Malus slashed down with his blades, severing the revenant's right arm at the elbow and then shearing half its skull away. The creature recoiled and his screaming victim pulled himself free – but the revenant tried to lunge for the warrior yet again, even as his brains spilled out onto the paving stones. The highborn stepped in quickly and with a backhand swing he severed the creature's head from its shoulders. Only then did the wretched thing flop lifelessly onto the stone.

Thunder roared close to Malus's ear. Warriors cried out in terror. One of the spearmen looked up at Malus, bleeding freely from a line of deep scratches carved into his face and neck. The highborn recognized him as the panicked soldier he'd spoken to only minutes before.

'It's the rain, dread lord!' he shouted over the wind. 'It got onto Turhan's face and it brought him back to life!'

'Blessed Mother of Night,' Malus whispered, suddenly realizing Nagaira's plan. He strode quickly to the inner edge of the parapet and looked down into the deep shadows at the foot of the wall.

Lightning burnt through the air overhead and Malus glimpsed the heaving mounds of rent and smashed corpses – hundreds, perhaps thousands of them – clawing their way free of the tangled piles that lined the inner avenue and staggering towards the long ramp leading to the top of the wall.

The scene was the same as far as Malus could see, all along the sections of the inner wall. His sister's infernal sorceries had trapped the defenders between two armies: one living and the other dead. *And I just sent Hauclir and Nuarc down into the midst of that nightmare,* he thought.

Horns began to wail all along the wall. Whether it was a cry of warning or a call to retreat, Malus could not tell. He couldn't begin to guess how such a plague of revenants could be stopped in time – all he could do was hold his part of the wall with the troops and the resources he had at his command.

Thinking quickly, Malus turned to the bleeding warrior. 'You! What's your name, spearman?'

'Anuric, dread lord,' the soldier stammered.

'You're Sergeant Anuric now,' Malus snapped. He swept his stained sword in an arc, indicating the druchii who'd struggled with the revenant. 'Take these men and get to the gatehouse as fast as you can. Grab all the dragon's breath bolts you can find and hurl them onto the ramp! Do you understand?'

The warrior nodded. 'Understood, dread lord!'

'Then why are you still sitting there? Go!' He shouted, and the warriors scrambled to obey. Shouts and screams of battle were already sounding up and down the line as the first of the Chaos attackers reached the top of the wall. As the spearmen ran back for the gatehouse Malus turned and dashed in the opposite direction, racing the shambling corpses to the top of the steep ramp.

The eight segments of the inner wall were each about three-quarters of a mile in length, but now it seemed to stretch for leagues in the flickering, chaotic darkness. Malus slipped and staggered across the oily paving stones, dodging frantic battles between screaming spearmen and howling Chaos marauders and buffeted by fierce winds that threatened to hurl him from the parapet and plunge him into the mass of shambling revenants below. Frenetic glimpses of desperate fights came and went as the highborn ran past. A spearman went down with a beastman tearing at his throat, blood bursting from the druchii's mouth even as he drove his sword again and again into his attacker's muscular chest. Another spearman crawled blindly across the paving stones, bawling like a babe from the ruined pulp that had once been his face. A pair of spearmen dragged a flailing marauder off the battlements by his braided hair and threw him face-first onto the parapet, where one of them reached down and expertly slit his throat from ear to ear. The flood of steaming blood lapped at Malus's feet as he raced past.

He was twenty yards from the end of the ramp and he could see that he was going to lose the race. The first of the revenants were almost at the top, and none of the warriors at that end of the line had any idea what was coming up behind them.

'End of the line! Look to your backs!' Malus shouted at the top of his lungs, but his words were all but lost in the roaring storm and the maelstrom of battle. Snarling in frustration, Malus started to shout again – but a snarling figure tackled him from behind, driving him face-first into the paving stones.

Malus heard a beastman's snarl just above his head and felt its hot, foetid breath against the back of his neck. Then a sharp blow and a searing pain lanced down the length of his right jaw, and he felt hot, thick ichor splash against his cheek. Roaring like a beast himself, the highborn tried to twist beneath his attacker, driving his armoured elbow into the side of the Chaos warrior's bony snout. The beastman roared and tried to stab Malus again with his jagged knife, but the blade glanced off the highborn's backplate. Driven by pure instinct, Malus twisted back fully prone and reversed his grip on his right-hand sword with a quick flick of his wrist, then brought the sword around behind him with all the strength he could muster. The blade sank deep into the beastman's side, and Malus continued to roll, forcing the stunned and bleeding warrior off the inner edge of the parapet.

Breathing heavily, Malus clambered to one knee and saw a pair of revenants rushing towards him with grimy hands outstretched.

The undead monsters had reached the top of the wall, and already the druchii at the end of the line were being overwhelmed. Malus saw two spearmen attacked from behind and dragged down beneath a mob of tearing hands and clashing jaws. The rest were retreating with horrified screams, yielding still more of the parapet to the shambling fiends.

Malus leapt at the oncoming revenants with a fierce war-scream, his twin blades weaving a whistling pattern of dismemberment and death. Two quick swipes and the monsters' hands were chopped to jagged stumps; then the highborn darted a step to the left and with two quick blows chopped off an arm and the leftmost revenant's head. Before the body had even hit the paving stones Malus reversed his stance and lashed out at the creature to his right, decapitating it cleanly with a single, blurring sword-stroke. 'Aim for their heads!' he shouted at the reeling warriors. 'Follow me!' And laughing like a madman, he threw himself into the press.

The undead warriors knew neither pain nor fear, but their only weapons were claws and teeth and unnatural vigour. Fuelled by rage and spiteful hate, Malus carved a fearsome swath through the oncoming revenants. He knew that if he could reach the top of the ramp and stem the tide of creatures that reached the parapet then they could still hold the top of the wall. He sliced away fingers and parts of hands, lopped off arms and hacked away skulls. Marauders, beastmen and druchii all fell before his flickering blades.

He fought his way along twenty yards of blood-soaked parapet, felling everything that rose before him. The battle seemed go on for hours, until the slaughter became a kind of terrible dance. Malus heard the furious shouts of the warriors behind him as they followed in his wake, and howled like a wolf loose amid the sheep. For the first time since the march on Hag Graef, many months past, he felt truly alive.

When he reached the far end of the wall it took the highborn by surprise. A pair of headless revenants slumped to the paving stones and his blades struck sparks against the wall of the far redoubt just behind them. More of the undead were trying to force their way onto the parapet, but now a solid knot of druchii spearmen at Malus's back had reached the top of the ramp and were hacking at the monsters with murderous efficiency. The highborn fetched up against the wall of the redoubt and tried to shake off the battle-madness as best he could.

Just then there was a crackling *whoosh*, and a sheet of green flame shot skyward along the back of the inner wall. Cheers went up among the druchii as the dragon's breath ignited among the shambling horde. Malus turned and saw Anuric staggering towards him, a look of weary relief plain on the young druchii's face. The spearman raised his hand in salute, then his eyes rolled back in his head and he collapsed face-first onto the parapet. A pair of marauder throwing axes jutted from the spearman's back.

Beyond the spearman's prone form the druchii line was a seething mass of fierce battles as waves of Chaos warriors poured over the battlements and leapt at the defenders. The druchii were holding on by their teeth, but there seemed to be no end to the furious assault.

Leaving the spearmen to hold the ramp, Malus advanced on the wavering line. As he passed Anuric's body he paused, then after a moment's consideration he knelt and rolled the young druchii's body off the edge of the wall, giving him over to the ravening flames as befitted a son of Naggaroth. Then he opened himself once more to the battle-madness and leapt howling into the fray.

Chapter Twenty-Two
THE BLOOD OF HEROES

THERE SEEMED NO end to the killing.

As the corrupting rain fell and the wind howled its fury Malus stalked like a mountain cat along the length of the embattled druchii line, falling like a thunderbolt on the Chaos attackers and then passing on to the next desperate battle, leaving hewn limbs and twitching bodies in his wake. Always he struck the enemy from an unexpected angle, sliding a quick thrust into an unsuspecting warrior's ribs or slicing his hamstrings as he focused on the druchii in front of him. His deadly efforts had nothing to do with honour or glory; it was cold, calculated slaughter, repeated again and again all along the length of the blood-soaked wall.

The druchii fought back like the cornered animals they were. With the seething green fires raging at their backs, the spearmen knew there was nowhere to run, and so the harder they were pressed the more vicious they became. Marauders and beastmen were seized and thrown bodily into the hungry flames that raged along the ramp, or set upon from every angle like a deer beset by a pack of wolves. The druchii fought on despite grievous wounds, falling only after the last of their blood had been spilled onto the paving stones. It was as if Malus's battle-madness had infected them as well, and little by little the tide began to turn back in their favour. The knots of struggling Chaos warriors dwindled, driven further and further back towards their rain-slick ladders, then before long the defenders were standing at the ladders themselves and raining blows down on the heads of anyone who tried to scale them.

Malus could not say how long they fought. The storm raged on and on, showing no signs of slacking, and time lost all meaning, measured in lunatic flashes of green light. Again and again he caught himself searching among the struggling warriors, looking for a glimpse of Lhunara. Strangely, Nagaira's champion made no appearance during the desperate battle.

When the final wave broke against the battlements he was back at the far end of the line beside the gatehouse, standing behind a trio of roaring, blood-drenched spearmen who were crouched like snakes beneath the battlements opposite the last of the scaling ladders. For a long time they'd lurked there and ambushed each warrior that had come over the wall, stabbing upwards into the man's legs, belly and groin and then throwing the screaming victim into the fire. They had slain so many men this way that it had become a kind of routine, and so when a massive, bull-headed beastman came roaring up out of the darkness the spearmen were caught completely off-guard.

With a furious bellow the minotaur leapt over the battlements in a single bound, landing amongst the startled spearmen and laying about with a pair of enormous hand axes. One druchii was cleft in twain from shoulder to hip with a single blow; another took a splintering blow to the chest that hurled her broken body end-for-end over the inner side of the wall. The third druchii, still consumed with bloodlust, leapt at the towering beast with a fierce shout, burying his stabbing sword in the minotaur's side. But the blade penetrated barely a finger length in the monster's thick hide, and the minotaur struck the spearman a desultory blow with the back of one axe that tore the druchii's head from his body. Malus bared his teeth at the monster before him and rushed in with both swords flashing.

His first stroke slashed across the monster's enormous, muscular thigh, drawing a pained roar and the whistling stroke of a bloodstained axe. Malus tried to twist out of the way of the blow, but the weapon still caught the trailing edge of his right pauldron and the impact hurled him back against the gatehouse wall as though he'd been kicked by a nauglir. The impact knocked the breath out of him and his head struck the stones with a resounding crack that left him momentarily blind. His hearing, however, worked just fine, and he could hear the minotaur's furious bellow as it rounded on Malus and moved in to finish the highborn off.

Acting on pure instinct, Malus threw himself forward, rolling between the minotaur's legs as the beast's twin axes carved furrows in the gatehouse's stone wall. Still blinking stars from his eyes, the highborn rose to his feet and slashed his swords across the cable-like tendons behind the minotaur's knees. The crippled beast collapsed with an agonized roar, and Malus brought his swords down in a scissor-like motion that sliced open both sides of the creature's thick neck almost to the spine. Red blood sprayed in steaming arcs across the stone wall of the gatehouse, and Malus spun on his heel in search of more foes.

And that was his mistake. He'd finished with the minotaur, but the minotaur wasn't finished with him.

The highborn heard a furious bellow at his back, then a tremendous impact smashed into his left shoulder and hurled him to the paving stones. Fiery pain spread in a red wave down the left side of his back, but Malus had little time to appreciate the extent of his injury. Still roaring, the minotaur launched itself at Malus, half-leaping, half-dragging its huge bulk after him.

Cursing in pain, Malus rolled onto his back as the bull-headed monstrosity loomed over him. A heavy axe smashed into his breastplate; Malus cried out as ribs cracked beneath the ensorcelled steel, but the axe-head glanced aside from the curved plate. The minotaur drew back its weapon for another strike, but Malus lashed out like a viper, severing the creature's hand with a deft stroke of his right-hand blade. Roaring, maddened by blood loss, the monster smashed the jagged stump of its wrist into Malus's face. Splintered bone gouged the highborn's cheek and hot blood poured thickly into his eyes.

Screaming in rage, Malus lashed out blindly with his sword and connected with something as resilient as a young sapling. He struck again and sheared through – and the minotaur's head fell free, smashing the high-born in the face.

Then the heavy body, still spurting blood, collapsed on top of him.

Hot liquid flowed over the highborn's face and neck, filling his nostrils and pouring into his gasping mouth. I'm going to drown on a castle parapet in the middle of a plain of ash, he thought wildly. Coughing and sputtering, he tried to push the minotaur's heavy body aside, but the dead weight refused to budge.

After what felt like hours, the flood of gore tapered away. Dimly, Malus heard pounding foot steps and muffled shouts. The body of the minotaur shifted slightly, then suddenly rolled free. Cold rain lashed at the highborn's face – not the foetid corpse-rain of before, but honest, clean water. Malus gaped like a fish, greedily drinking it in. He rubbed thick ooze out of his eyes and blinked at the stormy sky. Green lightning still raged overhead, but the darkness had thinned somewhat, paling to an iron-grey.

Hands pulled at the highborn's arms. Silhouettes crowded at the corners of his vision. Lightning flashed, and he made out the thin, worried face of Ten-thumbs and Hauclir's cynical grin. 'I can't leave you alone for a minute without you getting into some kind of mischief, can I, my lord?' the former guard captain said.

Malus flopped about in their arms like a drunkard, wincing in pain no matter which way he turned. 'Perhaps if you'd actually been here for the battle this might not have been necessary,' the highborn snarled.

'Well, we'd have been here sooner – mind the leg, my lord! – but some fool set fire to the ramp.'

Malus found himself on his knees, using Hauclir like a ladder to haul himself upright. A black handprint stood out prominently on his bandaged thigh. Peering past Hauclir's shoulder, Malus saw the spearmen rolling the last of the enemy dead off the forward edge of the battlements. The dragon's breath had finally exhausted itself, having run out of fuel to burn. The survivors of the spear regiment staggered about in a weary daze, their bloodstained faces slack with shock and exhaustion. Malus was stunned at how few of them were left. He counted less than three score where just a short while ago there had been almost a thousand.

No one cheered. There were no celebrations of victory. The few survivors were glad enough to still be alive. That was all the glory that mattered to them.

Malus pushed himself away from his former retainer. Already the pain was subsiding, and an icy knot in the side of his chest spoke of the daemon's power knitting his broken bones back together. He looked about at the dozen cutthroats that had followed Hauclir back from the citadel. Cutter and Pockets were busy looting the enemy dead; the wounded assassin had a bloodstained bandage plastered to his shoulder and was busy pointing out places for Pockets to search. Ten-thumbs was chasing a bouncing gold earring along the parapet, his young face a mask of exasperated determination.

Malus shook his head wearily. 'Did Nuarc make it back to the citadel?'

Hauclir nodded. 'We got out just before those damned revenants started to stir and made damned good time getting back to the tower,' he said. 'Getting back here was a different story. There are packs of those revenants all over the inner compound now.'

'Did we hold the rest of the wall?'

The former guard captain nodded. 'Khaine alone knows how, but we did. For now, at least.'

Malus frowned. 'What's that mean?'

Hauclir looked back over his shoulder at the exhausted troops, then nodded his head at the gatehouse. 'Let's talk inside,' he said quietly.

A sense of foreboding crept over the highborn. Nodding wordlessly, he led the cutthroats into the gatehouse. Out of the rain, however, the stink of spilt blood and the oily residue of Nagaira's sorcerous rain rose like a cloud around the highborn, half-choking him. 'Upstairs,' he gasped. 'We'll talk on the roof.'

They found the spiral staircase leading to the top of the gatehouse and emerged once again into the howling wind and rain. Cloaked druchii huddled together around the four large bolt throwers mounted along the battlements, paying little heed to the small band of warriors at the far end of the broad, flat space.

Malus pulled off his armoured gauntlets and tried to clean them in a large puddle of rainwater. 'All right, what's going on?' he said quietly.

Hauclir knelt beside the highborn. 'Nuarc ordered me to remain once we'd reached the citadel in case he needed to relay any messages back to you. He was in talking to the Witch King for quite a while, and when he came out he wasn't alone. Your half-brother left first, looking like he'd been made to swallow a live coal, and then came a whole flock of messengers. Nuarc came out last of all, and had some interesting news.'

Malus splashed water on his face and rubbed it through his matted hair. 'Well, what did he say?'

'He said that the Witch King is getting ready to make his move,' Hauclir replied. 'Malekith is pulling the best regiments from the inner wall and bringing them inside the citadel even as we speak, as well as all the nauglir from the pens.'

Malus thought the news over. 'So we're letting the Chaos horde take the inner wall?'

Hauclir shrugged. 'At this point I'm not certain we could stop them if we wanted to. The Witch King's leaving behind enough of a rearguard to slow down the next assault, but no more.'

All at once Malus felt wearier than he'd ever felt in his life. He glanced down at the layers of blood and ichor coating the scarred surface of his armour and shook his head in frustration. 'And what does Nuarc and the Witch King ask of me?'

'Well, that's the interesting thing,' Hauclir replied. 'I'm to return you to the citadel at once.'

Malus frowned. 'And did Nuarc say why?'

'Not in so many words,' the former guard captain said. 'All Nuarc told me was that he thought Isilvar had failed the Witch King's test... and that put you in an interesting position.'

The highborn let Nuarc's words sink in for a moment. 'Are... are you telling me that Nuarc thinks the Witch King is going to name me Vaulkhar of Hag Graef over Isilvar?'

'Frankly I have no idea what I'm telling you,' Hauclir replied. 'Nothing you highborn do makes any sense to me. I'm just relating to you what Nuarc said.'

Malus nodded to himself. Would Malekith do such a thing? Why not? He'd already made Malus his champion – was it so far a leap to hand him the rank of vaulkhar? The thought of it quickened his pulse. How sweet a victory that would be: to humble Isilvar before the assembled lords and see him humiliated in the court of Hag Graef!

Only Tz'arkan stood in his way. The highborn's hands clenched into fists. Was there a way to claim his due from Malekith and still ride into the north to put an end to the daemon's infernal curse?

Perhaps, he thought. If he saw to it that the siege was broken and Nagaira destroyed.

Malus said, rising swiftly to his feet. 'I'll go straightaway to the citadel, but I want you and your warriors to get to the nauglir pens and make certain that Spite is brought into the tower.'

Hauclir chuckled. 'I'm sure the beast can take care of itself, my lord.'

'It's not Spite I'm worried about so much as the gear on its back,' the highborn said. 'There are... relics amid my saddlebags that must not fall into Nagaira's hands. Do you understand?'

The former guard captain gave Malus a searching look. 'Yes, my lord,' he said carefully. 'I understand clearly.'

'Then get moving. I don't want to keep Nuarc waiting.'

But just as the highborn and his cutthroats headed for the gatehouse stairs the air reverberated with the sullen rumble of drums.

The sound came from the broad square at the edge of the outer city. Malus hesitated, torn between a desire for haste and the need to know what the enemy was up to. Finally he turned and shouldered his way through the mercenaries, cursing under his breath as he strode swiftly to the gatehouse battlements.

His keen eyes saw a throng of bare-chested beastmen filling the square, their chests and arms painted in blood. They brandished bloody axes and bundles of severed druchii heads, still streaming trails of fresh gore. Malus could just make out the sound of a guttural chant weaving in and out of the rhythm of the great drums.

Behind the beastmen came a long line of stumbling, naked figures, spurred on by the barbed lashes of a dozen marauder overseers. Each of the druchii prisoners had suffered brutal tortures at the hands of their captors, their bodies marked with crude strokes of knife and iron.

Hauclir joined Malus's side and sneered disdainfully at the procession. 'If they think to break our will with a little torture they've come to the wrong place.'

'No,' Malus said warily. 'This is something else.'

The prisoners were herded into groups of eight and made to kneel at specific points in a rough circle at the centre of the square. Then came a band of beastmen wearing brass tokens and necklaces of skulls, each carrying a wide brass bowl and a longhaired brush. Filling the air with savage yells and barking cries, the beastmen dipped their brushes in the gleaming bowls and began to trace a complicated symbol across the stones of the square.

As they worked, Malus saw a figure clad in a dark robe and gleaming armour plate approach the edge of the square. It was no beastman or hulking marauder; Malus recognized the commanding stride of his half-sister at once.

He turned to the druchii gunners nearby. 'Can you hit those bastards from here?'

One of the warriors shook his head. 'Not a chance.'

'What if you used dragon's breath?'

The gunner let out a disgusted snort. 'We're out. Some damned officer came and took them all during that last attack.'

Nagaira walked gracefully into the centre of the expanding sigil, accompanied by a pair of hulking minotaurs who carried another druchii prisoner between them. The wretched figure had suffered the attentions of Nagaira's torturers far more than any of the other prisoners. His pale skin was covered with deep scars or fresh brands that stretched over almost every inch of his exposed skin, and his arms were bound in chains of brass. The prisoner's head rose at the sound of the drums, and even from so great a distance Malus recognized the druchii's face.

'Mother of Night!' he exclaimed. 'That's Lord Meiron!'

With a crash of drums the sigil was completed. A thousand beastmen threw back their horned heads and roared at the raging sky. Nagaira spread her arms and cried out a series of guttural words in a foul tongue that caused the assembled prisoners to writhe in fear and pain. Invisible waves of power radiated from the witch, distorting the air around her.

Something in her incantations disturbed Tz'arkan, causing the daemon to tense threateningly beneath Malus's skin. *The little bitch has forgotten where her true allegiance lies,* the daemon hissed.

Before Malus could wonder what Tz'arkan meant, Nagaira's chant reached a crescendo. Lightning flared and a peal of thunder split the sky like the fist of an angry god. As one the beastmen raised their axes with a furious shout and turned upon the helpless prisoners, hacking them to pieces in an orgy of slaughter.

Fiery light burst from the bloody lines etched upon the stone. Lord Meiron stiffened, then screamed. The air around the druchii blurred, and his ravaged body started to swell. Malus felt his blood turn cold. 'Blessed Mother of Night,' he whispered, his voice full of dread.

Hauclir turned to Malus, his expression fearful. 'What would you have us do, my lord?' he asked.

'Run,' the highborn said. 'Run!'

Out in the square, Meiron's body continued to expand. The highborn's back was arched in agony and his muscles bulged until the skin split like an overcooked sausage, revealing the gleaming meat within. Meiron's face fell away from the dripping, shrieking skull, and a long pair of new limbs rose like blades from the highborn's back. As Malus watched, those limbs unfurled into a pair of gleaming, leathery wings.

The daemon continued to grow, wreathed in the boiling blood of the hundreds of sacrificial victims murdered in the square. Light and heat coalesced around the infernal creature's hands, taking the shape of a long, gleaming axe and a fearsome, barbed scourge.

Towering over the howling beastmen in the square, the bloodstained daemon raised its distended skull and roared a challenge at the defenders of the Black Tower.

The druchii manning the bolt throwers screamed in terror and several of the warriors ran for the stairs, hot on the heels of the fleeing mercenaries. Malus watched Hauclir and the cutthroats begin descending the spiral stair and knew that they would never reach the ground alive unless something was done to hold the daemon at bay.

He turned back to the towering fiend and met the daemon's brass eyes, raising his twin blades in challenge. Tz'arkan recoiled inside Malus's chest, sending a spasm of pain through the highborn's heart. *What are you doing, Darkblade?* the daemon snarled.

'Do you not want Nagaira to see the error of her ways?' Malus declared.

The blood-soaked daemon spread its wings and leapt into the sky with a bloodthirsty roar. Malus threw back his head and laughed like one of the damned, and Tz'arkan's black vigour coursed through his veins.

Frantic commands echoed around Malus as the druchii still manning the bolt throwers wrestled their heavy weapons around to aim at the winged terror. The daemon seemed to fill the sky before them, its brass eyes and curved tusks gleaming in the dim light. Heavy cables banged, and four bolts streaked skyward. One missed the plunging daemon's head by less than a yard; another punched a neat hole through the creature's right wing. The last two bolts smashed full into the daemon's broad chest, their iron heads digging deep through iron-like layers of muscle and bone.

The twin impacts staggered the daemon in mid-flight. Bellowing in rage, it crashed against the edge of the gatehouse battlements, shattering the stone merlons to bits and sending a web-work of cracks along the building's thick roof. Malus was hurled backwards by the impact, throwing him beyond the sweeping arc of the daemon's fearsome axe. The blow meant for him hissed through the air and smashed a bolt thrower to splinters instead; blood and body parts of the three crew scattered in a wide arc from the impact. Snarling, the daemon lashed out at a bolt thrower to its left with its barbed scourge, wrapping it and two of its crew in a net of woven cables. Wood crackled and metal groaned as the daemon used the scourge to pull its massive bulk the rest of the way onto the battlement. The screams of the bound crewmembers turned to liquid shrieks as the barbed tendrils pulled taut and ground them into pulped flesh and bone.

Uttering a bestial roar of his own, Malus leapt back onto his feet and flew like an arrow at the axe-wielding daemon. With Tz'arkan's power burning in his limbs, the highborn was a blur of black armour and sharpened steel. He crossed the groaning roof in an eye blink, darting within the reach of the daemon's weapons and slashing fiercely at its axe arm. The keen blades rang from iron-hard muscle and bone, and then Malus felt the daemon's hot, foetid breath against his face as it snapped at him with its powerful jaws.

Malus sensed the daemon's lunge and tried to twist out of the way at the last moment, so instead of biting off his right arm the daemon's jaws closed on his armoured shoulder instead. Its fangs could not penetrate his enchanted plate but the highborn let out an agonized shriek as the metal plates compressed, twisting his arm from its socket and snapping his collarbone like a dry twig. The daemon lifted him off the ground and bit down hard once again, grinding broken bones together in Malus's chest, then it tossed him aside like a hound would a dead rat. He hit the stone roof hard, shrieking in pain once more, and skidded more than a dozen feet until he stopped near one of the last two bolt throwers at the far edge of the gatehouse roof.

Even as he ground to a halt the daemon was moving within him. Muscles spasmed and twisted of their own accord, dragging his mangled arm back into position with a crackling of sinew and bone. Malus screamed and thrashed, his eyes wild with pain, but Tz'arkan's terrible will prevented him from losing consciousness. The highborn's lunatic gaze fell upon the two bolt thrower crewmen just a few yards away, cowering in terror behind their weapon. '*Shoot... it!*' he snarled at them past ichor-flecked lips. The wide-eyed druchii took one look at Malus and leapt back into action, feverishly working at the twin cranks that drew back the weapon's steel bow.

The daemon rose to its full height, yanking its bloodied scourge loose from the mangled bolt thrower in a shower of splintered wood and steel. At the far end of the gatehouse the other surviving bolt thrower team lost their courage and ran for their lives, but their screams caught the winged fiend's attention. It lunged for the fleeing druchii, slicing one in half with a sweep of its axe and trapping the other in the barbed tails of its scourge. The daemon whirled towards Malus, swinging the scourge in an arc that sent the trapped crewman tumbling and screaming through the air. The flailing druchii missed the last bolt thrower by just a few feet before plunging into the darkness beyond the gatehouse.

With a loud *click-clack* the bolt thrower's cable locked into firing position. The crew scrambled to load another bolt in the firing channel just as the gatehouse roof trembled beneath the daemon's thundering footfalls. Malus gritted his teeth and once more surged to his feet, working the life back into his right sword hand, then rushed to meet the charging fiend.

He anticipated the lash of the daemon's scourge and ducked beneath its whistling tails, then cut to his right and drove the points of both his blades into the monster's left thigh. The weapons bit deep, drawing tendrils of black smoke from the daemon's bloodstained flesh. Roaring angrily, the winged fiend checked its pace and spun, slashing out at Malus with its axe. As fast as the highborn was, he could not move fast enough to avoid a glancing blow to the chest that broke ribs and smashed him aside like a child's toy.

As Malus tumbled once again along the gatehouse roof the last bolt thrower fired, and another iron-headed bolt punched into the daemon's abdomen. The monster staggered beneath the blow, then lashed at weapon and crew with its scourge. Both of the druchii weapon handlers were shredded in the passage of the barbed tails, and the bolt thrower itself was torn from its mount.

Baring its teeth in a feral grin, the daemon turned back to Malus, but the highborn was already on his feet again, fuelled by rage and pain as his shattered ribs were drawn back into place by Tz'arkan's will.

Malus ducked a sweeping blow of the daemon's axe, then stabbed out with his sword and raked a long, ragged gash along the length of the fiend's muscular arm. Snarling like a wolf, he nimbly dodged the fiend's backhanded swipe – and then the barbed tails of its scourge wrapped tightly around his legs.

He was pulled off his feet and dashed hard against the unyielding stone. It was Tz'arkan's power alone that allowed him to roll aside just as the daemon's axe smashed down beside him. Stone splintered, and a huge section of the gatehouse's roof collapsed in a shower of dust and debris, plunging Malus and the daemon into the space below.

Malus hit the tumbled stones hard and rolled against the side of the daemon's chest. Before the fiend could react he raised his left-hand blade and drove it with all his might into the daemon's shoulder, burying the weapon to the hilt. Roaring with rage, the daemon tried to pull Malus away with its scourge, but the highborn held on for dear life and drove his other blade into the fiend's muscular throat.

With a furious roar the daemon unfurled its wings – and suddenly more black smoke poured in a flood from its many wounds. Heat radiated from the fiend's body like a banked forge. Screaming in thwarted rage the daemon leapt skyward, and exploded in a clap of thunder and a blast of light.

Malus was hurled end-for-end through the air, striking the broken edge of the roof and bouncing along its length. The highborn fetched up hard against the line of battlements that looked over the citadel's inner compound, his skin scorched and his ears ringing from the blast. His swords were gone, lost when the daemon was banished. Gathering up his courage and trusting in Tz'arkan's power he rose to his feet and leapt over the battlements, plunging like a stooping hawk to the pavement sixty feet below. He hit the ground hard enough to crack the paving stones, but his body absorbed the blow with supernatural resilience.

It was hard not to smile. Terrible as Tz'arkan's gifts were, they could be exhilarating at times.

Guttural howls shook the air along the battlements of the inner wall. Nagaira's daemon might have lost its challenge, but it had put the druchii defenders to flight, and now the Chaos horde had seized the inner wall at last. Already, shadowy figures were racing down the long ramps into the inner courtyard itself, hard on the heels of the retreating druchii spearmen. Snarling like a wolf, Malus rose to his feet and raced off into the darkness. The siege was quickly coming to a head, and within the Black Tower the Witch King was preparing to make his move.

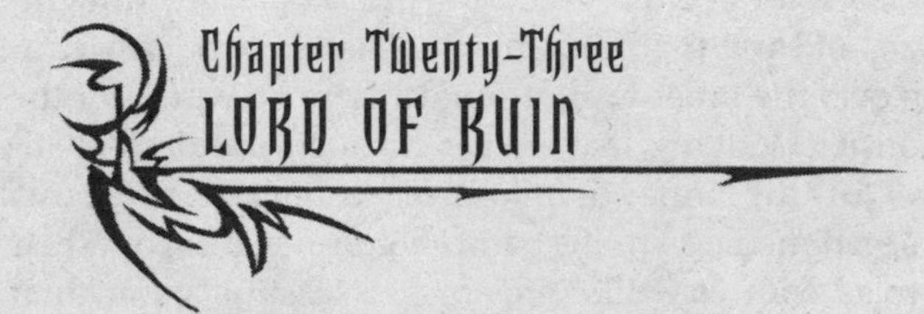

Chapter Twenty-Three
LORD OF RUIN

WITHIN THE WALLS of the inner keep the air reverberated with screams of terror and the guttural howls of the dead. The courtyards were full of panicked druchii racing for the safety of the Black Tower. Empty-handed soldiers, their spears cast aside, clambered over one another and stumbled along the cobblestones, fleeing for their lives. Craftsmen, apprentices, servants and slaves fled along with them. Like fear-maddened animals they turned upon one another in their frenzy to escape. Malus saw soldiers drawing their stabbing swords and lashing out at anyone in their path. A druchii wearing a blacksmith's apron fell with a scream, groping at the bloody wound in his back; his apprentice whirled and dashed out a spearman's brains with a heavy mallet, spattering his mates with a spray of gore. The highborn came upon a regimental officer facedown on the paving stones, a pool of dark blood spreading from his slashed throat. A sword with a jewelled pommel rested in his lifeless hand and a puddle of gold coins spilled beneath him from his torn coin-purse. It was more wealth than most low-born druchii saw in a lifetime, but no one spared it a second glance.

White faces etched with fear glimmered in the unnatural darkness, swirling like a cloud of panicked birds around Malus. Most of the panicked troops were looking back the way they'd come, listening to the exultant roars and wailing horns of the Chaos warriors swarming over the inner walls. It made them easy prey for the monsters stalking like wolves through the deep shadows of the inner compound. Nagaira's revenants dragged men down like panicked deer, tearing out their throats with claw-like fingers and feasting upon their steaming entrails. More than once Malus was forced to race past a screaming druchii buried beneath a knot of snarling, clawing monsters.

Once, a pair of pale, withered arms reached for him out the shadows of a nearby doorway. The revenant had once been a druchii spearman, his face half shorn away by the blow of a northman's axe. Cracked nails clawed at his throat; with a snarl Malus grabbed the hissing creature by the neck and tore its head from its shoulders. By the time the headless body clattered to the ground the highborn was long gone, running as fast as he could down the long avenue towards the citadel.

His body still felt cold and swollen. Muscles slid like steel cables beneath his skin, coated in thick, oily corruption. The daemon's gifts he'd summoned at the gatehouse had not ebbed, a realization that both comforted and disturbed him at the same time.

With the daemon's unnatural speed he slipped like a ghost through the chaos of the rout. Caught between the Chaos horde and the waiting revenants, Malus feared that not one man in five among the fleeing druchii would reach the safety of the Black Tower. Malekith had been wise to pull his best troops from the walls in advance of Nagaira's attack.

He could guess the Witch King's intentions. The Chaos horde would be scattered and disorganized after the bloody pursuit, drunk with slaughter after destroying the exhausted remnants of the routing spear regiments, and Nagaira's sorceries would be depleted as well. When Malekith launched his counterattack, bolstered by the magical prowess of Morathi and the witches of the Black Tower's convent, the tables would well and truly turn. More than half of the enemy army would find itself trapped within the confines of the inner courtyard, facing fresh, disciplined infantry and the Witch King's battle-hungry knights. The slaughter would be awesome to behold, Malus reckoned, worth even the hundreds of druchii being sacrificed around him.

If Nuarc was correct about the Witch King's intentions, then it could be he who led the charge, as befit the Vaulkhar of Hag Graef. Malus smiled hungrily at the thought. After he finished massacring the troops within the inner compound he would rally the army and lead them into the outer city and beyond. They wouldn't stop until Nagaira's head dangled from one of Spite's trophy hooks.

Another of his half-sister's revenants lurched out of the shadows towards him, arms outstretched. Malus grabbed the creature's shoulder and the side of its neck and tore it down the middle like a sheet of wet parchment. He flung the dripping pieces aside and laughed lustily at the dark sky, anticipating the glories to come.

A few moments later he reached another wide courtyard that lay at the foot of the tower itself. Green fire flickered balefully from two large pyres to either side of the highborn, casting a riot of reaching shadows across the cobblestones and limning the polished helms of the two spear regiments formed up outside the doors of the great citadel. Bodies littered the broad square: revenants shot through the skull by sharp-eyed crossbowmen and a few unlucky druchii who'd been caught in the crossfire.

Malus slowed his pace somewhat as he loped into the square, showing his open hands as he approached the twin regiments. To his surprise, a ragged cheer went up from the spearmen as he strode forward. The sound quickened what little blood remained in his shrivelled veins, and he acknowledged the accolades with a raised fist and a wolfish grin.

He passed down the narrow gap between the two regiments and found a mounted officer waiting for him on the other side. The highborn raised his sword in salute. 'It is good to see you, dread lord,' the officer shouted over the thunderous din. 'The Witch King commanded me to watch for you, and bid you to attend him at his war council without delay.'

Malus's grin widened. 'I'll not keep his Dread Majesty waiting,' he shouted back. 'Has a group of infantry passed through here in the last quarter-hour with a cold one in tow? I sent my retainers to the pits to fetch my mount just before the gatehouse was attacked.'

The officer shook his head. 'We've only had a handful of troops pass through so far,' he cried. 'None of them with a nauglir.'

Malus's smile soured. He looked back the way he'd come, gauging the distance between the citadel and the nauglir pits. Where in the Dark Mother's name were they?

Something had gone wrong, he thought. They might have run afoul of a pack of revenants or been overtaken by a band of panicked troops. He fought against a tide of despair. Hauclir would get them back in time, he told himself. The insolent rogue is no end of trouble sometimes, but he's never failed me when it mattered. The highborn turned to the officer. 'Keep an eye out for them, and make certain they get inside,' he shouted. There was nothing more he could do. The officer nodded and turned his horse about, heading back to his waiting troops. Malus spared a final look at the tumult raging beyond the fires, and ran on to the tower.

Beyond the battle-line the black doors of the citadel yawned wide, ready to receive the lucky few who survived the flight from the inner wall. The green glow of witchlamps held back the darkness in the cavernous halls within, and the air rang with a different sort of clangour. Formations of spearmen stood ready, their scarred faces set in masks of concentration as they checked weapons and harness, while knights and their squires tended their wargear and the needs of their scaly mounts. The air was taut with coiled tension, like a crossbow ready to fire. Malekith had drawn back his mailed fist and now merely waited for the proper moment to strike.

Malus paused just inside the doorway, momentarily uncertain of where to proceed. Would the Witch King hold his council in the throne room, or the less formal chambers near the top of the tower? Just as he'd resolved to find a page or tower servant to ask, one appeared at his elbow.

'If you would follow me, dread lord,' the page said, bowing low. 'I am to conduct you to the council chambers.'

The highborn nodded curtly. 'Lead on, then,' he said absently, his mind awhirl. Malus fell into step behind the page, his mind immersed in drawing up hasty battle-plans for the Witch King's small army.

He followed the page upstairs, climbing the tall tower to the upper council rooms. Malus scarcely noticed the climb, buoyed by the daemon's cold strength and thoughts of the glory that awaited him. *We'll have one last reunion, dear sister,* the highborn thought grimly. *And then I'll send you screaming into the Abyss where you belong.*

Two guardsmen stood with bared blades outside the door to the council chamber. They saluted as Malus approached, and the page retreated with another deep bow. At the door, the highborn paused, suddenly realizing how filthy he was. Every inch of his enamelled plate armour was coated with dust, grime and blood, and his face only slightly less so. Then he shrugged, allowing himself a grim smile. *The Witch King wanted a warrior to lead his armies,* he thought. *A warrior he shall have.* He laid his gauntleted hand on the door and pushed it wide, striding swiftly within.

The small room was dimly lit, bathed in the sullen glow of a pair of banked braziers. Maps and parchments were scattered across the broad table, just as Malus had last seen it. Retainers moved quietly among the shadows, attending upon the seated lords who watched the highborn approach. Balneth Bale glared coldly at Malus from his right, while Lord Myrchas scowled at him from the left. Lord Jhedir was conspicuously absent, Malus noted at once. Likely facedown in a puddle of wine somewhere, the highborn thought disdainfully.

As he stopped before the table the retainers retreated back to the far walls of the room, and Malus realised with a frown that none of the silver-masked Endless were present either.

His gaze fell upon the shadowy figure reclining at the far end of the table and his heart went cold.

'All hail the conquering hero,' Isilvar sneered, his ruined voice dripping with hate. He straightened in his chair and leaned towards Malus, until the red glow of the braziers painted his cheeks the dull colour of dried blood. 'You see, my lords? I told you he would reach the citadel safely. My half-brother has a talent for escaping the disasters he creates.'

'Where is Malekith?' Malus demanded, fighting a slowly rising tide of panic.

Isilvar smiled cruelly. 'Below, in the audience chamber. He is calling a council of war. Didn't you hear?'

Malus bared his teeth in a wolfish snarl, angry at having been outwitted so easily. 'I heard. He has commanded me to attend upon him.' The highborn coldly surveyed Isilvar and his allies. 'I suppose Jhedir is there as well. Interesting that the Witch King values the counsel of a drunkard over the likes of you, don't you think?'

He turned on his heel – and saw four of Isilvar's men barring his path to the door. Steel glimmered in their hands. Suddenly Malus was acutely aware of the empty scabbards at his hip.

'We have little need of councils, brother,' Isilvar replied. 'Our plan has already been set into motion. This siege begins and ends with you, Darkblade. As much as I would love to see you dragged back to the

Hag in chains and taken apart one piece at a time, the needs of the moment demand that I give you to our dear sister instead.' The vaulkar's smile widened. 'I'm certain she has something very special in mind for you.'

Malus's mind raced as he tried to think of a way out of his half-brother's trap. He looked to Lord Myrchas and Balneth Bale and wondered how strong their alliance truly was. 'You thrice-damned fool,' he said to Isilvar. 'I'm the Witch King's champion. Do you think you can just march me out through the citadel's doors and hand me to Nagaira?'

Isilvar chuckled. 'Certainly not. Thanks to you, however, we won't need to.' He beckoned to the shadows with one long-fingered hand.

A hooded figure glided silently into the crimson light, dressed in druchii robes and a worn kheitan of dwarf hide. Grave mould glowed faintly from the depths of the hood where one of the figure's eyes should have been.

Malus turned and threw himself at the druchii guarding the door. Fuelled by the daemon's power he crossed the distance between them in an instant. In a blur of motion he snatched the sword from one of the stunned warriors and smashed the druchii to the floor with an open-handed blow to his chest. The sword flickered in Malus's hand and another of the guards fell back, clutching at the gushing wound in his throat.

The highborn reached for the iron ring of the chamber door – and his entire body convulsed with a wave of icy pain. Gritting his teeth, Malus forced his hand to close about the ring, but his muscles rebelled. Tremors wracked his armoured frame as he bent every iota of will towards his escape, but it was as though flesh and bone had been transformed into solid ice.

A groan slipped past his thin lips. Inside, the daemon chuckled maliciously.

Your sister is waiting, little druchii, Tz'arkan said. *We wouldn't want to disappoint her, would we?*

Slowly, achingly, his body turned away from the door. The stolen sword fell from his hand. Across the room, Isilvar watched Malus's body betray him with a mix of cruel delight and bemused wonder. He turned to Lhunara. 'I trust my sister understands the nature of the exchange?'

The hooded figure nodded. *'You will have your victory, Isilvar,'* she said, her voice bubbling up from dead lungs. *'Slay all within the inner wall, and the rest will retreat to the north. Harry the rearguard as long as you wish. We will slip away when night falls.'*

Isilvar nodded. 'Excellent.' He smiled to his fellow lords. 'By nightfall we shall all be heroes, and the Witch King will reward us well.' The vaulkhar glanced at Malus, who still trembled with thwarted rage. 'By tomorrow the Witch King will have forgotten all about my lost brother.' He gestured dismissively to Lhunara. 'Take him down the hidden stair to the cistern tunnel,' he said. 'We are late for the Witch King's war council.'

Lhunara bowed stiffly to Isilvar, then stretched out her hand to Malus. The daemon within him stirred, and to the highborn's horror his legs began to move. Slowly at first, then with gathering strength, he crossed the room like an obedient dog and fell in beside his former lieutenant.

The lords rose from their seats and filed past Malus. Balneth Bale fixed the highborn with a hateful stare and spat full in his face. 'My only regret is that I cannot slay you myself,' he growled. 'I will pray tonight that this sister of yours prolongs your suffering for a great many days.'

Lord Myrchas came next. He eyed Malus up and down, shaking his head in frightened wonder. 'You are an even greater fool than I imagined,' he said, then walked away.

Isilvar was last. He leaned close to Malus's immobile face. 'I wish you could have seen the look on your face when you walked into this room,' he said, his voice sweet poison. 'Did you honestly think I would sit meekly by and let you take my title from me? I won't see you die, brother, but I did watch your dreams turn to ash in a single instant. I will savour that moment for centuries to come.'

And then he was gone. The door swung shut, and attendants busied themselves with removing the body of the druchii Malus had killed. Lhunara turned to her former lord. Her cold breath stank of mould and corruption. She raised a gloved hand and traced a fingertip along Malus's jaw.

'Mine at last,' the revenant said, and her body trembled with terrible, bubbling laughter.

Chapter Twenty-Four
THE AMULET OF VAUROG

THERE WAS A hidden stair at the far end of the council chamber that wound its way down the length of the tower and into the lower levels. Malus followed his former retainer as obediently as a hound, raging inwardly as Tz'arkan manipulated his limbs like a master puppeteer. From time to time the highborn heard voices and shouted orders emanating from the other side of spy-holes and hidden doors along the stairwell. At one point he could have sworn that they passed within a scant few yards of Malekith's war council itself. Malus fought every step of the way, praying to every god and goddess he knew for someone to hear their passage or stumble onto their escape. But Lhunara's luck held out, and Tz'arkan's iron grip kept Malus helpless as a babe.

Before long a chill settled against Malus's skin, and he knew that they had descended below ground. A few minutes later Lhunara led him through a narrow door and into the cistern vaults. They walked through utter darkness, picking their way past the deep wells with unnatural ease. Malus found himself wishing with every step that the daemon would put a foot wrong and send them plunging into cold, brackish water. With all his armour he would sink like a stone. A watery death was preferable to remaining a slave in his own skin!

Isilvar had never set fire to the secret tunnel as he'd claimed. In the heat of battle it had never occurred to Malus that his half-brother would try to use it for other purposes. In retrospect, however, he was probably the one person in the tower who could treat with Nagaira effectively, owing to their ties to the Cult of Slaanesh.

They emerged into the wasteland of the outer city, now all but deserted with the bulk of the horde howling at the foot of the Black Tower. Lhunara led him down the corpse-choked lanes, past burnt-out buildings covered in obscene sigils and squares filled with victims of sacrifice and debased revelry. Ghrond had been transformed into a city of the dead; the carnage beggared anything Malus had seen in the bloody streets of Har Ganeth. The Black Tower had been transformed by the terrible siege into a city of ghosts, and there was still more hard fighting yet to come.

Beyond the outer gate waited the rude tents of the Chaos encampment. No sentries challenged Lhunara as she led Malus across the ashen plain; camp followers and wretched slaves clad in tattered rags peered warily from behind tent flaps or scattered like rats down the twisting lanes as the Chaos champion led the highborn to the pavilion of indigo-dyed tents that Malus had first spied days before. The air still roiled and seethed about the seat of Nagaira's power; the closer Malus got to her tents the more he felt a curious pressure building behind his eyes, as though something unseen was pressing insistently against the inside of his skull. Tz'arkan reacted to it as well, swelling painfully within the highborn's chest until Malus felt he was about to burst.

Huge, horned figures stood guard outside Nagaira's tent: more than a score of minotaurs, clad in crude iron armour and hefting fearsome double-bladed axes. They bellowed a challenge at Lhunara as she approached, until the Chaos champion pulled back her hood and showed them her face. At the sight of her terrible visage the monsters bent their ponderous heads as one, their nostrils twitching as Malus marched stiffly past.

The pavilion of indigo tents wasn't the elaborate, interlinked affair that Nagaira's previous abode had been. Rather, Malus counted nine smaller tents, festooned with arcane sigils and constructs of freshly cleaned druchii bones, arrayed around a larger, central enclosure. The highborn reckoned the smaller tents were given over to Nagaira's personal retainers; he wondered which one was Lhunara's. Did a creature such as she even feel the need for sleep, or to take refuge from the elements?

As they approached the central tent Malus could feel the air roiling about him, churned by otherworldly energies emanating from within. The heavy hide flaps covering the entrance billowed open at their approach, crackling like whips in an invisible wind. Faint screams and cries of terror rose and fell within.

Lhunara and the daemon led Malus inside. He could no longer tell who was leading whom, for Tz'arkan seemed to gain strength and urgency from the obscene energies seething about the tent. Beyond the entrance the large enclosure was subdivided by heavy canvas hangings, reminding the highborn of his sister's tent during the march on Hag Graef. In this case, however, the chambers were arranged in a crude spiral, leading them along a labyrinth of sorts around the circumference of the witch's tent. Along the way they passed through a succession of dimly lit spaces, each one marked with complex sigils formed of powdered gold, silver and crushed bone. The powders were the only signs of material wealth Malus could see. So much for Hauclir's visions of plunder, Malus thought bleakly.

Before long Malus could not say whether he walked in the mortal world or trod upon the threshold of another, far more terrible realm. The darkness about him stirred like ink, sliding over his skin like smoke, and strange whispers of horror and madness echoed in his ears.

Behold your future, Malus heard an unreal voice whisper to him. Whether it came from Lhunara, or Tz'arkan, or himself, he could not rightly say.

The chambers narrowed as they went. Canvas hangings pressed in about Malus, thick with oily darkness and sorcerous energies. Fear built within him, but his limbs were no longer his to command. The daemon bore him onwards through the suffocating blackness, until they rounded a final turn and the highborn found himself at the heart of Nagaira's sanctum.

There was no light. Instead, the air itself seemed leeched of shadow, creating a grey sort of gloom that hurt the eye to look upon. Malus saw no walls, or roof. A horrid, atonal chanting filled the tortured air, uttered from the twisted throats of nine beastmen shamans. They knelt in a broad circle, their horned heads thrown back and the muscles of their necks etched in taut relief in the strange half-light. Within the circle formed by the warped figures of the beastmen lay nearly a dozen shrivelled corpses, sprawled in an untidy heap before a figure that left Malus's tormented mind reeling in terror.

It was formed of inky layers of darkness and hues of smoke and shadow, swirling in the silhouette of a druchii-like figure standing with arms outstretched as though beckoning like a lover to the wailing victim floating helplessly before it. The victim was an autarii, his naked body unblemished save for dozens of ritual tattoos snaking across his muscular arms and shoulders. His body was stretched as though upon an invisible rack; each muscle tensed and twisted like ropes beneath his skin.

As Malus watched, wisps of steam began to rise from each of the autarii's tattoos, glittering like melting frost and swirling in thin tendrils about the Shade's agony-wracked form. The wisps of sorcerous power flowed towards the shadowy figure, as though drawn in by a hungry inhalation; the surface of the figure's body shifted, and Malus saw scores of horrific faces take shape along the being's limbs and torso. The obscene visages drank in the Shade's magical bindings, until the mist began to turn a pale shade of pink, then bright crimson. The autarii's body began to shrivel, his muscles softening like wax and his skin growing ashen. His screams bubbled and his eyes burst, and his tongue split apart. Within moments it was over. Another smoking, shrivelled husk clattered to the floor beside its fellows, and the beastmen's horrid chanting devolved into a chorus of joyous, barking cries.

The beckoning figure was swathed in crimson mist, swirling and mingling with the shifting currents of darkness until it smoothed into a patina of dusky skin that Malus knew all too well. The body shifted slightly, taking on beguiling curves and long, black hair.

Between one heartbeat and the next the monster took the shape of his half-sister, naked and perfect.

Nagaira did not have the hollow eyes Malus saw in his dreams. They were dark orbs of jet, just like his. Her thin lips curved into a cruel smile. When she spoke, however, her voice was the same whispering chorus from his worst nightmares.

'The autarii are a bestial breed, but they understand the nature of spirits and how to bind them,' she said. 'Their souls are strong and sweet, like wine. Even that highborn fool who led them held enough power to make him savoury.' Her catlike smile widened. 'They were a fine gift, brother. I have saved them until last.' She beckoned to him with a taloned finger. 'Now you're here, and the final moves of the game are at hand.'

Within the confines of his mind, Malus snarled like a trapped wolf, but his body moved to the daemon's bidding. He and Lhunara stepped within the circle, and the beastmen bowed deeply, pressing their horned heads to the floor. Tz'arkan made no attempt to step over the piled bodies of the Black Tower's scouts. Bones snapped like twigs and grey skin turned to ash beneath Malus's boots.

The very air constricted about Malus like a fist. The air he breathed was hot and curdled, searing his lungs. When Nagaira moved towards him, the awful pressure only increased. Her vortex of power didn't emanate from her sorcerous circle, but from Nagaira herself; it seeped like acid from her skin, etching itself onto the fabric of reality around her. To the highborn's surprise, even Tz'arkan subsided as she approached, and Malus thought of the scores of unnatural voices intermingled with her own. How many pacts had she sealed with the Ruinous Powers for the strength she now possessed, and how could he hope to overcome it?

Nagaira stepped close, her eyes glittering like a serpent's. 'Have you no kiss for me, dear brother?' she said in her unearthly voice. She leaned in to him, her power rippling through his armour and sending waves of pain through his flesh. Her lips pressed lightly against the side of his neck and his heart skipped a beat at the touch. When she stepped away her lips glistened with black ichor.

Malus's jaw worked, but it was the daemon who spoke. '*Have a care, witch,*' Tz'arkan said. '*This is my body now, not your brother's! I have invested too much in it for the likes of your caresses.*'

Nagaira inclined her head. 'I forgot myself, oh Drinker of Worlds. It has been some time since my brother and I were together. There is much I wish to share with him.' She turned to Lhunara. 'Where are the relics?' she snapped, as though speaking to a slave.

The demand caught Lhunara unawares. She was staring intently at Malus, as though she were mapping the course of each black vein woven beneath his sickly skin. Her ruined face turned to Nagaira, blinking away her reverie. '*Relics?*' she said, a momentary frown of consternation twisting her festering brow. '*Relics? There were no relics, witch. Only him.*'

Nagaira struck the revenant with the back of her hand, swifter than a serpent. The blow echoed through the unearthly space, hard enough to break the neck of a living druchii. The witch snarled, 'Fool! Without the relics we cannot proceed! Have the maggots eaten so much of your brain that you cannot understand this?' She pointed to Malus. 'Until the great Tz'arkan has been freed, Malus is *his*. Do you understand? We must find these relics, or you will never have the vengeance you seek.'

Lhunara rocked back on her heels from the force of the blow. Her one eye was bright with fury. *'I searched his quarters and found nothing,'* she hissed.

For a moment, Malus dared to hope. Here was an opening he might exploit. But then his lips moved, and the daemon answered them. *'He keeps the four relics on the back of his cold one,'* Tz'arkan said. *'He sent his retainers to fetch it from the nauglir pits near the citadel, but they never returned.'*

Lhunara's cold fists clenched at the sound of the daemon's voice. *'Then we shall find these trinkets among the dead once we've completed the destruction of the Black Tower,'* she said contemptuously.

'Prepare yourself, then,' Nagaira replied coldly. 'The Witch King is stirring in his tower, and the true battle for the city will soon begin. Do not fail again, revenant. The eyes of the Dark Gods are upon you.'

If Nagaira meant to unnerve the revenant with her threats, they came to nothing. Lhunara bowed curtly, and with a possessive glance towards Malus, she turned on her heel and strode swiftly from the chamber.

Nagaira watched her go with narrowed eyes. 'You made a grave mistake when you betrayed that one,' she said to Malus. 'She is as fierce and as implacable as a winter gale. Who knows how long she lay in the shadow of Tz'arkan's temple with that terrible wound in her head? Yet she refused to die. She lay there and prayed to the darkness with every last shred of her will, until the Gods Who Wait finally answered as she drew her last breath. They would have given her anything she asked, but she wanted one thing, and one thing only. Not wealth, nor power, nor even a whole skin. No, she wanted nothing more than pure, bloody-minded revenge.' Nagaira smiled in grudging admiration. 'By the time I found her she had already raised a sizeable army from the beastmen and the human dregs that surrounded the mountain. Once I realised how much she wanted you, it was easy enough to forge an alliance and place the Amulet of Vaurog around her neck.' She laughed coldly. 'I think the fool must have loved you, brother. Is that not rich? What else could have birthed such terrible hate?' The witch smiled at her brother. 'Sometimes, when she thinks she is alone, she whispers to herself all the terrible things she dreams of doing to you. So gloriously vicious and single-minded,' Nagaira said with a terrible sigh. 'It makes her easy to control, much like you once were. Who knows? If she serves me well in the battle to come I might even give you to her as a reward. If we triumph here I can afford to be magnanimous.'

'So you intend to betray Isilvar,' Tz'arkan said.

The witch snorted derisively. 'Betray? That implies we had an agreement in the first place,' she said. 'He came crawling to me, looking for a way out of the trap he'd fallen into. I knew from the moment the siege began that he'd try something like this. All I had to do was apply pressure and wait.'

'And the Witch King?'

Nagaira shrugged. 'Malekith grew more predictable as the siege wore on. He would never abandon the Black Tower without a fight, and once we were past the outer wall it made a counterattack inevitable. By now, Morathi's colossal arrogance has led her to believe that I have exhausted my energies during that last attack, so now is the time to strike. Do you imagine I could pass up such an opportunity?'

The daemon chuckled. *'I imagine you have little choice. You have your own masters to serve, witch. Such power does not come without fearsome promises of repayment.'*

Nagaira's expression froze. 'There were... agreements... that were made,' she allowed. 'Malekith and his mother will make fine gifts for the Gods Who Wait, and they have never been as vulnerable as they are now. I should think you would be pleased,' she said haughtily. 'An ally upon the Iron Throne would make your plans much easier, I should think.'

'Plans?' the daemon said.

'You are the Scourge,' she said simply. 'The prophecy was written by you in aeons past to pave the way for your rise to power. You mean to use the druchii as the agents of your ambition in this universe.'

'And you?' the daemon asked.

The witch smiled faintly and bowed. 'I live to serve the Prince of Pleasure,' she said in her unearthly voice.

Tz'arkan smiled. *'You amuse me, witch,'* it said. *'But there is little time for battle. My time grows very short. Malus will have to ride that nauglir of his to death in order to reach the temple as it is.'*

'Ride? Great Tz'arkan, once I've offered the Witch King and Morathi to the Dark Gods and seized the Iron Throne, we will fly to your temple on dragon wings,' she said. 'There is time enough for the vengeance I seek.' She cocked her head, as though listening to some faint sound. 'I must take my leave of you, dread lord. Already the winds of magic are stirring. Morathi and her pitiful novices are readying themselves for the attack.' She made to leave, then paused, looking thoughtfully at Malus. The witch stared intently into his eyes, as though trying to find the highborn amid the darkness that was the daemon. 'Are you so attached to this body?' she asked, touching Malus's breastplate with a curved talon. 'Once you are freed you may take any form you like.'

'That is so,' the daemon allowed, *'but the prophecy has attached itself to his name. I must continue to be Malus for a time, once I have been set free.'* Inwardly, Malus could feel the daemon's amusement. *'Of course, if you could ensure that the real Darkblade were to vanish from sight...'*

Nagaira laughed. 'Be assured, dread lord. That would be no trouble whatsoever.'

'Then we will speak of this again at the temple in the north,' Tz'arkan replied. *'Go and claim your vengeance, witch. I will wait here until you return, and savour your brother's despair.'*

Nagaira bowed again, and stepped from the circle. As one, the beastmen rose and followed her into the darkness.

Outside, a warhorn wailed. Malus sensed movement about the Chaos encampment, as the last reserves of the horde were called to battle. Did Nagaira truly have the power to trap and destroy the Witch King himself? After what he'd seen, the highborn thought it possible.

Still as a statue, the highborn was left to wonder as the kingdom of the druchii teetered on the edge of ruin. Despair threatened to overwhelm him.

Curled like a serpent in the darkness, Tz'arkan drank deep from the well of Malus's pain.

MALUS SOON LOST all track of time. Few sounds penetrated the chambers of Nagaira's tent, and once she was gone there was no relief from the darkness. He might have lingered for mere minutes, or hours, or even days. Each moment was more agonizing than the next, as Nagaira's stratagem inched towards completion.

He didn't notice the sounds at first. They slowly impinged on his awareness as a kind of faint scratching, like rats scampering in the walls.

Malus focused his attentions on the noise. It came and went, but always from the same general direction, off to the highborn's left.

After a time, the scratching became faint, raspy sawing. Then he heard a harsh whisper.

'How many damned compartments can one tent have?'

'Shut up and keep sawing,' hissed a familiar voice. 'We've got to be close to the centre now,' Hauclir said

'You said that the last two times,' the first voice shot back. Malus thought it sounded like Pockets.

Within Malus, the daemon stirred. He felt Tz'arkan's cold, cruel smile. *The Dark Gods are generous,* the daemon murmured. *We shall have pleasant diversions to occupy us while we await your sister's return.*

Tz'arkan turned Malus about and stalked across the inner chamber. His hands reached out and found the canvas wall. Moments later something sharp poked the fabric from the other side.

Malus's lips worked. 'Hauclir?' the daemon whispered, using the highborn's voice.

'My lord?' the former retainer responded. 'It's good to hear your voice! Are you bound, or injured?'

'No, I'm well,' the daemon replied. 'But Nagaira's sealed this chamber with some spell. I can't get out.'

'We'll see to that, my lord,' Hauclir answered. The object poked hard against the canvas. After a moment the needle tip of a dagger poked through.

'Gods Below,' Pockets hissed. 'This is like cutting through stone.'

'Keep at it,' Hauclir ordered. As Pockets continued to work her knife through the ensorcelled fabric, the former retainer whispered to Malus. 'We'll have you out in just a moment, my lord.'

The daemon smiled. 'What about the relics?'

'We have them as well,' Hauclir replied. 'Spite is close by.'

'That's excellent news,' Tz'arkan said. Malus could only watch in horror as his hand slid down to the dagger at his belt. Slowly, quietly, the daemon drew the weapon free.

Pockets drove her knife through the canvas wall and began sawing downward. After a few moments she'd cut a slit large enough for a man to wriggle through. The daemon raised Malus's dagger. 'Come inside,' he said. 'There are statues of gold and silver in here. It's time you got your reward.'

Malus raged helplessly within the confines of his own body, trying to regain control of his own limbs, but the daemon's grip was stronger than iron. He could see the slaughter that was about to unfold the moment Hauclir poked his head inside the chamber.

'That's the best news I've heard all day,' the former retainer answered. 'Give me your hand.'

'Of course,' the daemon replied, shifting the knife to Malus's left hand and extending the right one through the torn fragment. He reached for Hauclir blindly, groping about with Malus's armoured fingers.

Then all at once his hand found something and closed around it. Malus felt the smooth hilt of a sword – and a torrential rush of heat that poured through his hand and set his veins afire.

The daemon let out a furious shout as the Warpsword of Khaine took Malus in its burning grip. Tz'arkan tried to let go of the blade, but the highborn's fingers would no longer obey. Hungry fire seared Malus from head to foot, and he cried out in agony and triumph as the daemon's hold was broken.

After a moment Malus realised that Hauclir was hissing urgently at him. He forced himself to take a deep breath and answer. 'What is it?'

'I said, could you possibly scream a little louder? I'm pretty sure there are a few scattered tribes on the other side of the Chaos Wastes that didn't hear you.'

Malus laughed quietly, flexing his fingers around the hilt of the blade. 'Step away, you damned rogue,' he said, and sliced carefully at the tent wall. The canvas peeled back with a hiss of burnt fabric.

Hauclir, Pockets and Cutter rushed into the chamber, holding small witchlamps in their hands. The former retainer looked about the space and frowned. 'I don't see any gold or silver,' he said.

'No,' Malus replied breathlessly, holding the sword aloft. 'That was an utter lie.'

'I should have known,' Hauclir said with a sigh.

The highborn looked at the cutthroats in wonder. 'What in the Dark Mother's name are you doing here?'

Hauclir shrugged. 'Blame it on your cold one, my lord,' he said. 'It took us forever to fight our way to the nauglir pens. There were packs of those damned revenants lurking in every doorway, it seemed. Once we finally got there and let Spite loose, the damned thing sniffed at the air and just went loping off. We couldn't stop it, so we decided to follow the beast and see where it was going,' he said. 'It led us out through the south gate, then outside the city itself. We thought for sure someone would challenge us, but the camp is deserted. Nagaira's called all her troops into the city. At any rate, after a bit we worked out that the nauglir was hunting for something, and we figured it might be you.'

Malus nodded. 'But this?' he asked, showing Hauclir the sword.

'Oh. That was easy,' he replied. 'It was obvious you were trying to get it from Spite back in the nauglir pits, and the daemon managed to stop you. I figured that if you were to be found out here then the daemon must have had a hand in it, so I thought that bringing the sword along was a wise move. Was I right?'

'You have no idea,' Malus answered. 'In fact, you may have saved Naggaroth.' He quickly told the cutthroats about Nagaira's plans. 'She believes she has the power to bring down Malekith and Morathi both,' he said at last.

The cutthroats looked to one another fearfully. 'Can she?' Hauclir asked.

'After all I've seen... yes. I think she can.'

'Then I think we need to get your mount and run for our lives,' Hauclir replied.

But Malus shook his head. 'No. Malekith may be vulnerable, but so is Nagaira. She might have enough strength to master the Witch King and Morathi, but not all three of us at once,' he said. 'And she has to be destroyed.'

'For the sake of the kingdom?'

'Don't be stupid,' Malus snapped. 'For my sake. The witch knows too much.'

'Ah, of course. Your pardon, my lord,' Hauclir said dryly. 'Well, then. What would you have of us?'

Malus's hand tightened on the burning blade. He could feel its hunger now, seething like coals in his gut. 'Follow me,' he said to the cutthroats. 'And when the killing starts, stay out of my way.'

THEY WERE JUST emerging from the Chaos encampment when the Witch King launched his attack.

War horns screamed from the tall tower, and Malus watched as a dark form raised its serpentine neck atop the citadel and roared a challenge at the sky. With a powerful sweep of leathery wings, Malekith's dragon Seraphon launched into the dark sky. At the same moment, green lightnings smote the darkness, rending it and driving it back. In the searing flashes of light, the highborn spied an armoured figure on the dragon's back, brandishing a glowing sword at the Chaos horde.

The sword swept down and Seraphon dove with a thunderous roar, filling the inner compound with a hissing stream of dragon flame. Shouts and screams rose from the dying warriors, and the final battle was joined.

Malus, Hauclir and the cutthroats came to a halt a quarter mile from the open city gates. Spite paced alongside the small band, sniffing the air warily. The former retainer turned to the highborn. 'We're going in there?' he said, pointing to the city. Pillars of fire and smoke were already wreathing the Black Tower, and the clash of swords and armour could be heard from where they stood.

'Only so far as the square outside the inner gate,' Malus replied. 'That's where we'll find Nagaira, I expect.'

'And how do you plan on stopping her?'

'Don't worry,' Malus said. 'I have a plan.'

'Do I want to know what the plan is?' Hauclir asked.

The highborn shook his head.

'You're probably right,' Hauclir agreed. 'Lead on.'

With Malus in the lead, the small band raced through the ruins of the outer city. Forks of green lightning lashed down from the boiling skies, plunging like knives again and again onto the square outside the inner gate. Seraphon continued to swoop low over the inner compound, scouring the area with ravening bursts of fire as the outnumbered druchii army fought their way from the citadel. Somewhere ahead, in the thick of the fight, Lhunara would be wreaking bloody havoc on the Witch King's troops.

Malus expected that the Chaos horde would fall back, drawing the druchii host out past the inner gate and up to the great square. That's when Malekith would take the battle directly to Nagaira, and she would spring her trap.

They got to within less than a hundred yards of the square before their path was blocked by a herd of waiting beastmen. For the moment their attention was focused solely on the sorcerous battle being waged nearby.

Malus led the group into the shadow of a burnt-out barracks. 'Here is where we part ways,' he said. 'I must face Nagaira alone.'

'What do you want us to do?' Hauclir said.

The highborn looked his former retainer in the eye and drew a deep breath. 'I want you to circle around the square and wait,' he replied. 'When I attack Nagaira it's only a matter of time before Lhunara comes running. You will have to hold her off long enough for me to deal with my sister.'

'Blessed Murderer,' Cutter said. 'She nearly killed me the last time.'

'And me as well,' Hauclir replied.

Malus nodded. 'How is your leg?' he asked.

'Fine, oddly enough,' the former retainer said. He reached down and pulled his stained bandages aside. Only a dull, black scar showed where Lhunara's blade pierced his leg. 'I can't explain it.'

Malus noted the ichor stains darkening the bandages. It was the daemon's energies, he thought. I bled onto your bandages, and it seeped into the wound. He set his jaw. 'That's fortunate,' he said. 'Because you'll need all the luck you can get. Just hold her off long enough for me to deal with Nagaira. That's all I ask.'

The cutthroats looked to one another. Hauclir shrugged. 'We've come this far,' he said. 'We'll see this through.'

Malus nodded, clapping Hauclir on the shoulder. 'Go, then. I'll see you all shortly,' he said, hoping that it would be true.

The cutthroats moved off to the east. Malus laid a hand on Spite's snout. 'Stand,' he said, rubbing the nauglir's scales appreciatively. 'Wait until I call, beast of the deep earth. You've done enough for me already.'

Then, sword in hand, he stepped into the street and started to run.

The herd of Chaos warriors filling the street outside the square was unaware of the danger bearing down on them until it was far too late. Distracted by the pillars of lightning and deafened by the thunderous explosions, they did not notice the dark blur racing down the debris-strewn avenue until he was upon them. Half a dozen beastmen fell dead, glowing wounds smoking in their chests, before the enemy could even react.

Malus tore into the enemy with a savage howl, the warpsword carving through the tight-packed ranks like a scythe. Weapons snapped and armour melted at the blade's touch; arms and legs tumbled across the cobblestones and heads were shorn away. The highborn grew stronger with every blow, and the movements of his enemies seemed to slow, until they appeared to be standing still. He slipped past their feeble blows and slaughtered them by the score, until finally the enemy could take no more and melted away in every direction. Those who tried to run through the square itself were cut apart by the angry slashes of lightning that raged within.

Covered in steaming gore, Malus staggered drunkenly to the edge of the open space. In the centre of the square shone a hemisphere of green light more than sixty paces across. Lightning flared and rebounded from this sorcerous shield, maintained by Nagaira's shamans, who sat in their customary circle and chanted arcane phrases skyward. Within the circle, Nagaira floated a few feet off the ground. Once again she was no more that the black shadow-shape that he'd seen in the tent, surrounded by curling tendrils of black smoke that wove about her like a net of serpents.

Beyond, Malus could see fighting atop the inner wall. Malekith's counterattack had pushed the besiegers almost to the inner gate itself. Very soon the Witch King would reach the square and fall into Nagaira's clutches. Malus was running out of time.

Brandishing the burning blade, Malus charged at the shamans' glowing sphere. Lightning seemed to drip lazily from the air, splashing against the ward and playing about the square. He struck the glowing ward with the warpsword, and a web of red cracks spread across its surface. Instantly the beastmen were aware of him, shouting magical chants and pointing fetishes of bone at the damage to the sphere. The cracks faded as he drew back his blade, but he struck the surface again and again. Slowly but surely, the damage spread.

More lightning arced down, as though Morathi sensed the change in the nature of the ward and had redoubled her efforts. The green glow began to dim as its energies were strained to the utmost. Across the square, Malus saw huge figures approaching the ward at a dead run – they were Nagaira's minotaur bodyguard.

Undaunted, the highborn continued his punishing assault.

Within the hemisphere, Nagaira slowly turned to face him. Her night-haunted face was devoid of expression, but he could feel the cold pressure of her furious stare.

Another barrage of lightning bolts hammered at the ward. Malus timed his strokes with the thunderclaps, adding to Morathi's assault. Then, without warning, the shield collapsed, shattering like glass beneath a hammer blow. There was a flare of light, and several of the beastmen collapsed, blood streaming from their ears. Several more were immolated in bolts of green lightning, leaving charred husks sprawled across the paving stones. A bolt of lightning even struck Nagaira herself, momentarily staggering her.

With the shield broken, the minotaurs charged across the intervening space at Malus, axes held ready. The highborn rushed at them with a ferocious cry, and the burning blade sang through the air. One of the huge warriors swung wide and was cut in half as the highborn raced past. Another lunged at the highborn with a sweeping cut and had both hands sliced away.

An axe crashed into Malus's pauldron; the highborn spun and drove his sword through the minotaur's abdomen, boiling its guts. Another axe struck him full in the breastplate. Laughing, Malus tore his sword free and cut the legs out from under the enemy champion.

Lightning raged among the howling minotaurs, blasting warriors to the ground. A bolt struck Malus and flung him skyward, dropping him in a heap several yards away. Still smoking, he lunged back onto his feet and returned to the fray. Only three of the huge champions were left, stunned and shaken by the blast. Malus cut them down.

Then a strange buzzing filled the air, like a swarm of angry hornets, and Nagaira struck him with a bolt of pure darkness.

It passed through his armour as though it wasn't there, and he felt his organs melt at its touch. A spear of pure agony lanced through Malus's chest, and he spat sizzling ichor onto the stones. His sister loomed above him almost a dozen yards away, wreathed in tendrils of darkness. Pure rage emanated from her in palpable waves.

'You disappoint me,' Nagaira thundered. A bolt of lightning lashed at her, but his sister paid it little heed. 'I had thought you were wiser than this.' Suddenly she lunged at him, crossing the space between them in an eye blink. Her fist crashed into Malus and flung him across the square like a toy. He crashed into the wall of a warehouse fifteen yards away, striking the stone hard enough to crack it before rebounding back onto the pavement.

'A wise man would have waited in the darkness for his doom to find him,' Nagaira said. 'But you? You seek it out.'

She swept down on him again. This time Malus brought the warpsword up in a hissing arc and sliced through the witch's midsection. Nagaira staggered with a scream of countless tortured souls, but she recovered almost immediately. Her fist closed about his throat and she flung him headlong through the air.

This time he crashed against the burnt hulk of one of the Chaos catapults. Oaken timbers shattered under the impact, and he landed hard at the siege engine's base.

Nagaira stalked after him. Lightning lashed at her smoky figure again and again, slowing her flight. Still she pressed on, undeterred.

'I could swat you down like a fly, dear brother,' she seethed. 'By all the gods I should! But Tz'arkan must be freed, and so I must content myself with merely crippling you.' She swept down and slapped the highborn's chest with the flat of her hand, cracking his ribs like eggshells.

Malus screamed in agony and buried his sword in Nagaira's chest. The blade burst from the witch's back, drawing a scream of rage. Black ichor smoked from the tip of the blade. She drew back her hand to strike him again – and another bolt of sorcerous lightning struck her, blowing the two druchii apart.

Malus landed hard on his back, biting back a wave of intense pain. Nagaira landed in a heap some yards away. Her body had a grey cast now, and the tendrils of smoke that enshrouded her were all but gone. With a furious oath, she spoke an incantation that rent the air around her and her form regained a portion of its power.

Then a shadow swept over her from above. Nagaira looked up just as Seraphon bathed her in a pillar of dragon fire.

Malus could see her black form wreathed in angry fire. She screamed, spreading her arms wide within the flame, and magical power pulsed from her body. The dragon banked away, but Nagaira's ruined form turned to track it. She pointed a smoking finger at the sky, and a chorus of daemonic howls filled the air. Tendrils of smoke leapt like whipcords from her body, reaching for the armoured form riding atop the swooping dragon.

Summoning his rage, Malus staggered to his feet and charged across the square. At the last moment she saw him, and with a word sent another bolt of black fire through him. He staggered, feeling his guts turn to mush, but the blade sustained him, driving him on. Malus raised the burning blade and chopped it deep into Nagaira's chest.

She howled and writhed around the blade, her unearthly form hissing and sizzling under the weapon's touch. Still she drove the tendrils skyward, reaching for the Witch King. 'You cannot slay me!' she cried. 'The Dark Gods themselves fill me with their power!'

Malus spat a mouthful of ichor into his sister's face. 'And they do not countenance failure,' he said, twisting the blade in her body.

Nagaira screamed again – and the smoking tendrils faltered, just short of their goal. Her body turned grey, once more. Gibbering with rage, she hissed a litany of curses, calling upon the gods for more power. But she had already drawn far too much, and the patience of the fickle Chaos gods was at an end.

Like snakes, the tendrils turned, seeking easier prey. They plunged like arrows, burying themselves in Nagaira's skull.

Malus hurled himself clear of his sister, drawing the burning blade after him. As he watched, daemonic faces took shape all over her body, the mouths working hungrily as they devoured his sister from within. Still screaming, she shrank in the air before him.

The last things to go were her eyes. Nagaira glared at Malus with a look of purest hate. Then she was gone in a clap of terrible thunder.

'Enjoy the favour of the gods, dear sister,' Malus said darkly. And then, like a black wind, Lhunara was upon him.

He never heard her approach. Only the warpsword saved him; it seemed to turn in his hand, reaching skyward just as her bloodstained blades came slicing for his throat. His body moved without conscious thought, striking the twin swords aside in a shower of sparks.

There was no time for fear, or curses, or clever stratagems. She fell upon him like a storm, and it was all Malus could do just to survive.

Her glowing eye gleamed balefully from the depths of her helmet as she drove Malus across the square. The warpsword was a blur, meeting her every stroke with a ringing block that just barely kept death at bay. Already ichor was seeping from a score of shallow cuts on his face and neck.

After several long moments, Malus regained his wits in the face of Lhunara's maddened assault. She said not a word, slashing and thrusting at him with an urgency born of desperation and madness. Where Nagaira emanated rage and power, his former retainer was driven by nothing more than bitter pain and despair. Now he sensed that she knew her chance for vengeance was slipping away.

Her urgency made her sloppy. Lhunara swung for Malus's neck and he ducked beneath the blow, slicing the warpsword through her midsection. The blade parted her armour like paper, the edges turning molten from the sword's heat. Ichor poured from the wound and she groaned... but still she fought on.

The sight stunned Malus. I can't kill her, he thought. Not even the warpsword could slay her!

Lhunara leapt at the highborn and he planted his feet, blocking her twin swords and stopping her rush until she stood nearly nose-to-nose with him. He smelt her foul breath and saw burn scars etched in pale lines along her throat. Within the depths of her helmet Malus could see the deformed cheekbone that had broken beneath Nagaira's blow.

Suddenly he understood. No blade could kill the bearer of the Amulet of Vaurog.

He knew what he had to do. Gritting his teeth, he let go of the burning blade.

At once, Tz'arkan's power tore through his body, filling him with strength and wracking his body with pain. Roaring in agony, he clapped his hands against the side of Lhunara's helmet and squeezed. Face to face, he heard her scream as the steel deformed and bent inwards. She tried to pull away, but there was no room to land a blow, and the daemon's strength was irresistible. He felt Tz'arkan's power growing and wondered how long he had before the daemon regained control of him once more.

Lhunara moaned. Her body spasmed, and bone cracked. Black ichor sprayed across his face.

She drew a wracking breath. 'I... loved you,' she hissed. The words came out like a curse.

'I know,' Malus said, and crushed the helmet flat.

Lhunara's headless body collapsed to the ground. Lightning flickered on the red-gold surface of the Amulet of Vaurog as it rolled free of her body.

Stooping quickly, Malus snatched up the warpsword. For a moment he feared that the daemon would resist him; his fingers trembled, but with an effort of will he seized the hilt and felt the sword's fire hold the raging daemon at bay. Then he grasped the amulet and placed the torc around his neck.

Malus turned his face to the sky, seeking the Witch King. Seraphon was swooping low over the battlements of the inner wall, plucking beastmen from the parapet and flinging them to their deaths. More were racing down siege ladders, seeking to escape the death trap within the inner compound. Already, fleeing figures were running headlong through the darkness to either side of the square. The siege had been broken at last.

Malus wanted to roar his triumph to the heavens, but then he caught sight of a lone figure limping onto the square. The warpsword twitched in his fingers, but then he recognized who it was. Cursing under his breath, he loped across the corpse-choked space just as Hauclir collapsed onto the stones.

His short sword and trusty cudgel were gone, and his mail was soaked in blood. Lhunara had stabbed Hauclir through the chest not once, but twice. His skin was pale, and his breath was coming in shallow gasps. He blinked dully as Malus stood above him. 'I… I think we failed, my lord,' he said.

'No,' Malus replied bitterly. 'You did well, you damned rogue.'

'We held her as long as we could,' Hauclir said. 'Damn, but she was fast. She got Cutter first, then Ten-thumbs. Then she got me. I don't know what happened to Pockets. When I came to, she and that bitch were gone.'

'I'm sure she got away,' Malus said, not believing a word. 'Just rest easy. The troops will be here any minute, and we'll get you to the healers.'

Hauclir looked up at Malus. 'That's about the worst lie you've ever told,' he said. 'You're going to leave me. I can see it in your eyes.'

Malus bit back his anger. 'I have to go, Hauclir,' he said softly. 'I'm out of time.'

Suddenly Hauclir's face turned solemn. 'I know,' he said. 'So am I.' Then he turned his face away, and closed his eyes.

Malus looked down at his former retainer for a long moment, then slowly turned away. Bitterness burned like a coal in his gut. There was nothing he could do.

The dire warning of the daemon still rang in his mind. *He'll have to ride that mount of his to death to make it to the temple in time.* It might already be too late to reclaim his soul, he realised.

And now I'm throwing away the last of my honour as well, he thought.

A dozen paces away he ground to a halt. Slowly he returned the warpsword to its scabbard. As its heat ebbed, he felt the daemon's strength slowly return.

'Damn me to hell,' Malus muttered, then turned and ran back to Hauclir. Gritting his teeth, he knelt by his former retainer's side and unbuckled his sword belt. Quickly he set the sword aside, and the power of the daemon surged.

Malus looked down at his ichor-stained palms and pressed them to Hauclir's wounds. 'Get up, damn you,' the highborn growled. 'Did you hear me, you damned rogue? Get up! You've vexed me for most of a year, and I'll be damned if you're going to die on me now!' Dread filled the highborn, but he focused his will and summoned Tz'arkan's power, trying to force it into Hauclir's wounds.

Hauclir gave a convulsive heave and began to cough. Malus recoiled from the druchii's body, seeing the wounds scabbing over with a dull, black crust.

Malus managed a nervous smile. 'There's your reward. You can thank me later,' he said, and lunged for the safety of the warpsword.

He fell just six inches short. In mid-leap the daemon gripped him in an invisible fist, halting his flight. He landed hard, his fingers outstretched, but salvation was just out of reach.

Agony coursed through him as Tz'arkan swelled into his brain. The pain went on and on, cutting into the depths of his heart and mind.

Pray your precious honour gives you succour on the long ride to come, the daemon hissed triumphantly. And the world dissolved in a haze of madness and pain.

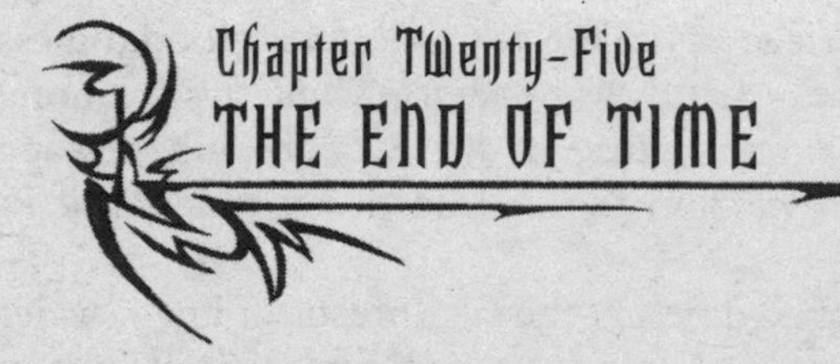

Chapter Twenty-Five
THE END OF TIME

The Chaos Wastes, first week of winter

THE DUST OF ancient warlords slipped from Malus Darkblade's hands, laying out the last segments of the arcane circle that surrounded the daemon's massive crystal prison. Nearly an hour had passed since he'd begun; his skull throbbed with the daemon's blasphemous knowledge and his limbs ached with strain. He'd measured his steps with exacting care, shaping the sorcerous symbols as precisely as he could. Now the great urn was empty, and the complicated ward nearly complete.

As the powdered bone ran through his fingers he felt the final moments of his life slipping away along with it. It slid from his grasp on a tide of inevitability, driven by the daemon's implacable will. As the sorcerous circle took shape around him, Malus glimpsed the vast skein of intrigues and bloody deeds wrought by the daemon down through the millennia, all leading up to these final moments. Empires had come and gone, sorcerers and kings risen to glory and trampled into the dirt and thousands, perhaps *millions* of lives destroyed, all so that he would find himself in this chamber, at this hour, pouring the bones of conquerors upon the stone floor.

He saw what the future held. Tz'arkan had shown him hints of the world to come in the fires of Hag Graef, in the blood-soaked streets of Har Ganeth and the horrific siege of the Black Tower. An age of darkness and ruin was at hand. The daemon would walk among the druchii in the guise of the Scourge and reshape them into a weapon that would drown the world in blood.

Malus looked down at the last threads of fine powder trickling from his hand. We are all nothing but dust in the eyes of the gods, he thought, surprised to feel no sense of rage at the realization. All the heat had gone out of him. His heart was cold and heavy as stone.

Time had run out. All of his schemes had, in the end, come to naught. Tz'arkan had millennia to lay his webs, testing their strands and pulling them taut. Now there was nothing left for him but to take the last few steps left to him.

It was time for Tz'arkan to rise from his ancient prison, and time for Malus Darkblade to die.

The last of the dust trickled through his fingers, landing in precisely the right spot to close the vast and intricate circle. The highborn felt a tremor in the air, as though the final piece of a terrible, cosmic puzzle had finally slipped into place.

That's it, the daemon hissed. It pressed against Malus's bones like a beast pushing at the bars of its cell. *Now the tablet. Read the incantation inscribed upon it. Hurry!*

Stepping carefully, Malus stepped outside the circle and took his place at the foot of the mighty ward. The temple servants rose as one and moved to the five relics waiting nearby. Their ancient bodies creaking and crackling under the strain, the revenants picked up the artefacts and arranged them around the circle, then knelt beside them. The last artefact laid in place was the warpsword itself. The ancient servant placed the long blade nearly at Malus's feet.

The next thing he knew, the servant with the stone tablet was kneeling beside him, hands raised in supplication. As though in a dream, Malus reached out and plucked the tablet from the revenant's hands. He turned to the nearby pedestal and rested the tablet upon its surface. Writing older than Naggaroth, perhaps older than the very world itself, burned their angular lines into his brain. The blasphemous incantation meant nothing to the highborn, but their strange consonants came easily to his lips, thanks to the daemon's brutal tutelage.

The words burned his lips and scarred his throat, but the more he spoke, the faster they burst free. Crackling energies filled the vast treasure vault. A hot wind swirled about the gleaming crystal, pulling at Malus's hair and plucking at the servants' ancient clothes. Agony tore through Malus's chest, but the highborn had no breath to spare for tortured screams. Instead, he spoke the words before him, unravelling the ancient bindings laid upon Tz'arkan thousands of years past.

The wind grew, howling like a tormented ghost in the echoing space. He could feel the nest of snakes uncoil themselves from around his heart and begin forcing their way up his throat. Smoke seeped from Malus's mouth and nose, drawn into the cyclone like oil poured upon the surface of a turbulent sea. It spread like a black stain in the air, hovering before the crystal as the incantation reached its inevitable climax.

As the last lines of the ritual were spoken, the wind grew to a thunderous cyclone. The foul wind buffeted the undead servants, ripping at their rotten clothes and flaying their desiccated skin as it forced them to their knees. The inky smoke writhed and pulsed, lit from within by arcs of pellucid flame as it contracted into an amorphous mass before the highborn's eyes.

Then the last word burst from Malus's throat with a spray of black ichor, and it felt as though his body was being torn apart. The stone tablet shattered into razor-sharp fragments as the daemon broke its bonds at last.

With a rushing sound like an indrawn breath, the cloud of Abyssal smoke contracted further, assuming a terrible, towering form that loomed over Malus's hunched body. The daemon's body was shaped like a druchii's, only broader and far more muscular; it was beautiful, so far beyond the apex of perfection that it was maddening to look upon. Only its broad, malformed head and burning eyes betrayed its birth in the storms of Chaos. Taloned hands reached skyward, and Tz'arkan opened long, misshapen jaws and roared like a newborn god.

FREE! The daemon thundered. Not from the stone, but from Malus himself. The realization did not surprise him. Indeed, a part of him had suspected it all along.

The icy touch of the daemon's power disappeared from the highborn's body in an instant, leaving behind nothing but terrible pain. Malus doubled over in agony, knocking the slim pedestal onto its side.

He knew what had to happen next, and a strange calm settled over him. 'I've done what you asked,' the highborn croaked. 'Now you must fulfil your bargain, daemon. Give me back my soul.'

Tz'arkan, Drinker of Worlds, looked down upon the highborn's pitiful form and showed triple rows of needle-like fangs. 'You shall have all you deserve,' the daemon said with a hateful laugh. 'But first, I must *feed*!'

Too fast for the eye to follow the daemon lunged forward, pressing its massive palm against Malus's breastplate. Deep inside his chest, Malus felt something give way, like a thread breaking, and he felt his heart stop at last. Pain ebbed like a swift tide, leaving only a cold emptiness in its wake.

The daemon drew back, pulling a stream of dark substance through the surface of the highborn's ensorcelled armour. Malus watched Tz'arkan pull his soul from his body and draw it to its gaping mouth. Dying, he sank slowly towards the floor.

Dying, but not yet entirely dead. The ancient sorceries of the temple wards slowed the passage of time in the great chamber. In this one place, a druchii's last breath could take a thousand years to escape.

Lost in its triumph, Tz'arkan began to feed upon the highborn's withered soul. The Drinker of Worlds failed to see Malus's hand reaching for the dark hilt of the warpsword just a few feet away.

His fingers touched the hilt of the burning blade, and felt its warmth kindle the embers of hate in Malus's dead heart. His stained lips pulled back in a bestial snarl.

With hate, all things are possible, he thought, in death as in life. The Warpsword of Khaine seemed to leap into his hands of its own accord, and he swung it in a hissing arc at Tz'arkan's towering frame.

The warpsword tore across the daemon's midsection, igniting its sorcerous shape. A howl of pain and fury tore through the treasure vault, buffeting Malus like a storm wind. It was answered by thin shrieks and wails of terror as Tz'arkan's undead servants cowered before their master's rage.

It was a gamble, perhaps the greatest wager he'd ever made. His calculations pitted the will of Khaine against the hunger of the daemon. The black blade and the sigil in the treasure vault had given him the idea; would the warpsword surrender his soul to Tz'arkan so easily? He believed it wouldn't, not if there was even the slightest hope that he could triumph against the daemon before him.

And if he was wrong, so be it, he thought, drawing back the smoking blade for another blow. He wasn't going into the Outer Darkness without putting up a fight.

The highborn's body felt light and swift as he lunged for the daemon, riding a wave of battle-hunger bequeathed by Khaine's fearsome blade. But before he could strike Malus saw the daemon's blazing eyes fix upon him, and Tz'arkan's thunderous voice spoke words of power that seared the air between them. The daemon's taloned fist clenched around Malus's night-dark soul, trapping it in a cage of crooked lightnings – then it thrust its other hand, palm out, right at the high-born's chest.

Malus felt the air between him and the daemon crackle with invisible power, and he hurled himself to the side a split-second before the bolt of power erupted from Tz'arkan's hand. The black bolt parted the air with a sound like tearing cloth and left a congealed mist of blood and bile in its wake. It licked like a dragon's tongue little more than a hair's width past the high-born's arm, and his skin recoiled from its passage, even within the confines of his enchanted armour. The bolt lashed through the wailing crowd of servants, dissolving their rotted forms with its merest touch. Gold coins melted and ran like tallow. Diamonds and rubies darkened and shattered at the energy's entropic touch. The ravening black fire burned across the length of the treasure vault and scored the thick wall with a crackle of splintering stone.

Tz'arkan still burned as well, the edges of the wound across its midsection curling and blackening like parchment as flickering yellow flames guttered and spat within its unnatural, perfect flesh. The daemon cackled insanely, its voice trembling in pitch between amusement and murderous rage as it pivoted to face Malus once more. Black vapour curled from its outstretched hand. It reached for him as though offering a benediction.

The ebon fire leapt out at Malus again. On instinct, he threw himself flat, his armoured form crashing to the polished stone floor, and once again he barely escaped the spell's all-consuming touch. It withered the pedestal where the stone tablet had rested, then scored a deep furrow along the floor as it tracked through still more of the hapless servants. Their thin screams bubbled and hissed as their bodies collapsed into steaming ash.

But the daemon wasn't finished yet. Tz'arkan continued to turn, lashing the arc of sorcerous fire at Malus like a whip. Pillars exploded at its passing touch, showering the vault with pulverized dust and whizzing fragments. Clay urns burst with sharp bangs as their contents boiled in the blink of an eye. Stands of ensorcelled armour crumpled like foil. Then the ravening fire played back across the floor, blackening the gleaming curves of the huge containment wards and then arcing against the squat, iron tripod that held the daemon's crystal prison. The dark metal sagged like hot wax, and the huge, faceted stone tipped and fell ponderously forward. Tz'arkan's entropic lash struck the gleaming crystal, and for a heart-stopping moment the facets sent tendrils of destructive power in all directions, slashing through the huge room like a storm of irresistible knives. A moment later the crystal blackened from within, a canker growing in its core with frightening speed that swelled until it reached the edges of the stone and burst it apart with an earth-shaking explosion. Malus was hurled forward by the blast, his armoured body pummelled by shards of crystal the size of a druchii's fist.

I can't keep this up, he realised. I can't get close to Tz'arkan now, and any moment my luck is going to run out. For half a moment he contemplated bargaining with the daemon – Tz'arkan needed his body to dwell in so it could return to Naggaroth, didn't it? But even as he considered it, he knew that the time for intrigues were long past. He had to think of something else, and fast.

Ears ringing, Malus cast about for somewhere to take cover from the daemon's ebon fire – and then his eyes caught a glint of brass just a few yards away, resting at the edge of the summoning circle. Of course, he thought! Gathering his legs beneath him he scrambled desperately towards the nearby relic, even as the air behind him crackled with building power.

The highborn's questing fingers closed about the brass octagon even as the daemon's sorcerous power leapt at him. Malus spun, raising the Octagon of Praan before him, and the bolt of ebon fire exploded against its surface. Jagged streaks of energy ricocheted from the amulet, deflected by its power and burying themselves like thunderbolts in the ceiling, walls and floor. Malus felt waves of heat radiate from the relic, and to his horror, he saw sizzling teardrops of molten brass running from the surface of the artefact. The daemon's full power was more fearsome than he'd imagined.

It was clear the amulet wouldn't survive another bolt. Malus tossed the damaged relic aside and sought out the next artefact along the rim of the great circle. The highborn's face turned grim. He was only going to get one more chance, and he had to make it count.

Malus lunged across the smoking floor, reaching for the relic. On the other side of the summoning circle, Tz'arkan's laughter faded. The flames licking at the tear in his chest guttered and went out.

'You insignificant little worm,' the daemon hissed. 'I've torn the life out of you, and still you wriggle. Everything you ever were, everything you ever dreamt of, I have taken all away. And yet still you refuse to accept your wretched fate! It is over, Malus Darkblade. You have been a troublesome servant indeed; at times I despaired that we would ever reach this glorious moment. But no matter how hard you fought against me, in the end you still did my bidding, whether you knew it or not.' The daemon uttered a poisonous chuckle. 'Once I have consumed your soul I will take your disgusting shape and return to Naggaroth, and the reign of the Scourge will begin,' the daemon said. Arcs of dark power crackled along its taloned fingers. 'And I could not have done it without you, Darkblade, weak as you were. And now you shall reap your reward.'

Malus closed his hand about the relic. 'Here's a token of my esteem as well,' he growled, rolling onto his back and hurling the Dagger of Torxus left-handed at the daemon.

The dagger was a dark blur, spinning end-for-end across the battered circle and burying itself in Tz'arkan's chest. There was a thunderous crackling of thwarted energies as the power the daemon was about to unleash was disrupted by the force of the relic itself. Fierce arcs of ebon fire lashed at the jutting hilt of the terrible dagger, carving gruesome wounds across the daemon's own unnatural flesh. The Dagger of Torxus began to blacken as well, its pommel and hilt vaporizing under the sorcerous chain reaction. 'No!' Tz'arkan roared, clawing desperately at the dagger's hilt. Tz'arkan's body began to unravel under the onslaught, skin dissolving and flesh turning to liquid beneath. The daemon's howl of fury grew wilder by the moment. 'You cannot stop me, wretch! This world is mine, now! Hear the words of Tz'arkan and despair! The time of ruin is come! And in time you will – '

The rest was lost in a rising crescendo of concussive blasts, as the daemon's power and the energies of the Dagger of Torxus tore one another apart. With a final effort, Tz'arkan ripped the smoking weapon from its chest – and then daemon and dagger both vanished in a flare of white light and a clap of deafening thunder.

A GROAN BROUGHT Malus back to his senses. He had somehow risen to his knees, the burning blade still clutched in his right hand. Tendrils of smoke rose from his battered armour, and clouds of pulverized stone and metal hung heavy in the dimly lit vault.

Tz'arkan was gone. Destroyed or banished back to its goddess-forsaken realm, the highborn neither knew nor cared. Malus took a deep breath, heedless of the reek of burnt metal and scorched flesh that thickened the air. He felt light, almost weightless within his armour. He'd never realised how much of a burden the daemon's presence really was.

A soft chuckle escaped his torn lips. I won, he thought. *I won.*

His gaze fell to the gauntlet covering his right hand. Setting the warpsword across his thighs, Malus pulled the armoured glove away to reveal the ruby cabochon ring that had mocked him for so many months. With trembling fingers he gripped the ring and pulled. It slid easily from his finger, tumbling from his grasp and ringing faintly as it bounced along the floor. The highborn smiled in triumph. Another weary chuckle turned to a wild laugh of joy. 'I won!' he cried.

Something tugged at the side of his face. Absently, Malus reached up with his free hand to pluck it free. His cheek was cold to the touch.

Frowning, the highborn's fingers closed around a small, jagged shape buried in his skin. There was a dull twinge of pain as he tugged it free and held it out before him.

It was a piece of crystal the size of a gold piece, its edges sharper than any knife. He hadn't even felt it bite into his skin.

Worse, there was no blood on it. There wasn't even a dark stain of ichor. Malus's throat went dry.

He reached up once again and gingerly pressed against the side of his throat. Try as he might, he could feel no pulsing of blood in his veins. 'Oh, no,' he breathed. 'Oh, you damned, infernal bastard. You took it. You took my thrice-damned soul!'

The highborn's cry of rage was drowned out by another ominous groan. There was a crackle of breaking stone, then a thunderous crash as part of the treasure vault's ceiling collapsed. The heavy slabs of obsidian struck the already weakened floor and broke through, pouring a rain of ruined treasure and tons of debris into the level beneath.

Suddenly the air above Malus echoed with ominous groans and sharp cracks as well. 'Mother of Night,' Malus growled. The daemon might yet succeed in bringing the entire damned temple down around his ears.

The highborn eyed the open doorway. What would happen once he passed beyond the reach of the containment wards? Would death claim him at last?

There was sharp report just above Malus, and a chunk of obsidian the size of his torso crashed to the floor just a few feet to his left. That decided the highborn. If he stayed where he was he was as good as dead anyway. He gathered up his gauntlet and the warpsword and ran for his life.

He hadn't taken more than a dozen paces when the rest of the ceiling gave way in a long, grinding roar. Gusts of pulverized stone washed past him, swallowing the highborn for an instant in a smothering, black fog. Gritting his teeth, Malus ran on, aiming for the spot where he knew the doorway to lie. The floor shook beneath him as tons of rubble poured down from the temple ceiling.

Suddenly the floor seemed to fall away from him and he was stumbling headlong through empty space. He fell for a long, dizzying instant, then crashed face-first on a canted stone floor. Again the pain felt like a strange echo of true sensation; he knew he was hurt, but he wasn't certain how badly. Malus felt himself skid half a dozen feet before fetching up against a stretch of level floor. He tried to clear his head with a savage shake, belatedly realizing that he'd stumbled down the long ramp leading into the living quarters on the level below the vault.

The air was still thick with dust and smoke. Malus staggered back to his feet, coughing as he struggled to breathe in the grey-brown murk. The floor continued to tremble beneath his feet, and the sounds of collapsing stone had mingled together into one long, muffled roar. Holding the warpsword out before him he ran on into the haze, navigating by memory as he sought the top of the curving stairs.

Stone fell all around him as he went; he smashed against piles of debris scattered across his path, but each time he picked himself up and drove on. The minutes stretched interminably, until he thought he'd got turned around in the murk and was hopelessly lost. Just as he began to lose heart, however, a gust of air smote his face, and he stumbled into a cleared space kept open by a furnace-like updraft of air. The spiral staircase lay before him, its curving wall lit by an ominous orange glow. 'Mother of Night,' he cursed, hesitating at the top step. Malus shook his head helplessly. 'No way out but down,' he said at last. 'If this doesn't warm my bones, nothing will.'

Taking a deep breath, he rushed down the twisting stair. The heat pressed against his flesh like a wall, but he only felt the dimmest echo of warmth. The air rippled and shimmered like a desert mirage as he descended ever lower towards the lake of fire.

He emerged upon a threshold of melting stone, at the mouth of a seething dragon's maw. Magma raged a hundred feet below; as Malus watched, chunks of rock from the cavern's ceiling plunged into the churning sea, raising plumes of molten stone dozens of feet high. The wings of the daemon at the edge of the plaza glowed white-orange along its bottom edges, dripping streams of melting rock into the lake below.

Malus sheathed the warpsword and pulled on his right-hand gauntlet, then hurried quickly down the stairs. As he stepped on the first of the floating boulders, however, the stairway shifted wildly beneath him. The multi-ton boulder wobbled – and began to sink, picking up speed.

'Blessed Mother of Night!' Malus cried, his dark eyes widening in alarm. He took a running start and leapt for the next boulder in line, and it began its death-plunge as well. Scarcely daring to stop, the highborn increased his pace, leaping from one plunging rock to the next and drawing ever closer to the lake of magma below. Behind him the massive boulders struck the lake and exploded into fragments, hurling enormous pillars of molten stone into the air.

The last section of stairs was little more than ten feet above the lake of fire. When his boots touched it the boulder plunged beneath him, striking the magma almost at once. Jets of steam burst from fissures in the stone, and the boulder burst apart beneath the highborn's feet. Screaming every oath he knew, Malus hurled himself forward and leapt the last few feet to the shimmering stones of the plaza. He landed hard on his knees and elbows, hearing the steel hiss against the burning stone.

The plaza began to tremble beneath Malus, and an ominous rumble started to build above his head.

Clambering to his feet, he charged across the broad plaza, and through the chamber of the Chaos Gods that lay beyond. The faces of the Ruinous Powers leered at him from their pedestals as he passed through their midst. Had he the time he would have gladly dragged each and every one across the plaza and fed them headfirst to the lake of fire.

The rumbling was increasing. Malus felt a wind growing in strength behind him as the temple's collapse accelerated. By the time he reached the temple antechamber he was howling like a madman, expecting the roof to fall in on him at any moment. The ghosts, still trapped in the chamber by the force of their ancient vows, regarded him in silent horror as he abandoned them to their fate.

Malus burst into the snowy night air with a desperate howl, just as the temple completely caved in behind him. The ground shook as though it had been struck by the hammer of a god, throwing the highborn forward onto the frozen ground. The sounds of splintering stone and settling earth went on behind him for many long minutes. When it finally stopped, the silence that stretched though the surrounding forest was deafening.

Slowly, carefully, Malus rose to his feet. He turned, and saw that the temple of Tz'arkan was no more. The huge edifice had fallen in upon itself, settling into the ravenous lake of fire. All that was left were tumbled piles of obsidian stone, wreathed by noxious vapours from the raging magma beneath. He looked upon the devastation and was surprised that he felt no relief at having escaped. Indeed, he felt nothing at all.

Small sounds of movement by the temple gate brought Malus around. Groups of beastmen were approaching, their twisted faces rapt with awe as they viewed the destruction of the great temple. Their leader, the one-eyed shaman, sank to his knees before Malus. 'What does this mean, great prince?' he croaked in his bestial tongue.

The highborn's gaze took in the swelling mob, then came to rest upon the awestruck shaman. His rage was gone. His body felt empty, his bones as cold as stone. Victory, he mused, was not supposed to feel like this.

'What does this mean?' he echoed in a dead voice. 'The end of the world, of course. For you, I mean.'

He drew Khaine's burning blade and showed it to the milling herd. Then he showed them what it could do.

MALUS DARKBLADE SQUEEZED the last drops of the blood from the beastman's heart into the side of Spite's fanged mouth, then tossed it onto the heap with the rest. Frowning thoughtfully, he pulled off his blood-soaked gauntlet and pressed his hand against the side of the cold one's snout. He couldn't tell if the nauglir's body heat was improving or not. 'Come on, damn you,' he whispered. 'There's enough meat here now to feed a squadron of cold ones. You just have to raise that scaly snout of yours and eat.'

The nauglir made no move to the pile of severed limbs Malus had stacked scant inches from its jaws. The war beast regarded him with one large, red eye. Shaking his head, the highborn rose to his feet. 'I've done all I can for you, you great lump of scales. If you're going to die on me now, get on with it. It's up to you. But if you're going to get me back for all the punishment I've inflicted on you in the last few weeks, you're going to need to get your strength back.'

Sighing to himself, the highborn turned away and strode to the roaring fire he'd built from molten stone and piles of severed logs. The ground surrounding the bonfire and for scores of yards in either directions had been transformed to churned, red-tinged mud. Bodies and pieces of bodies littered the earth as far as Malus could see. He'd managed to keep enough self-control to spare the last few dozen beastmen and put them to work butchering their companions and gathering logs for the fire. He'd intended to cut them down as soon as they were done, but while he busied himself feeding Spite they'd slipped away into the darkness. He doubted he would see them again.

For the next hour he busied himself by gathering the bones of his fallen retainers and feeding them one by one to the raging fire. He owed them that much, he believed, though he felt nothing as he delivered them to the flames.

I've become dead inside, he thought, watching the bones blacken in the flame. Dead within, dead without, he thought. A lord of ruin in truth.

Tz'arkan had spoken truly. The daemon had taken everything from him, just when it seemed his deepest desires lay within his grasp. I could return home, he thought. I'm still the Witch King's champion, and after the bitter victory at Ghrond he will have need of strong hands to help secure the kingdom. He could still have his reckoning with Isilvar. He could find Hauclir, if he still lived, and set about rebuilding once more.

And yet... and yet he felt nothing. No hunger. No sense of anticipation, even at the prospect of sweet revenge against his last surviving brother. No hatred for the last, treacherous blow the daemon had dealt him.

No hatred, he thought, shaking his head. This is no way for any druchii to live.

Malus stared into the flames for a long time, watching the molten stones char his retainers' bones to dust. As the night waned, more flakes of snow began to fall. By the time that dawn was paling the sky, he'd decided what must be done.

He turned back to Spite to find the nauglir on its feet, nosing hungrily through the piles of beastman flesh laid before it. The sight brought a grim smile to the highborn's face. While the war beast ate, the highborn checked Spite's feet and tail for signs of sickness or strain. Spite watched its master at work and growled ominously between bites. Malus met the nauglir's red gaze with a feigned scowl. 'I was starting to think you'd given up,' he said. 'Good to know I named you Spite with good reason.'

He let the nauglir rest until well past noon while he formulated his plan and gathered up pieces of meat for the journey ahead. He'd heard that the seer of the Black Ark of Naggor possessed a potent relic that would show the location of whatever the owner wished to find, no matter where – or in what realm – it lay. He would need such a tool if he was going to find where Tz'arkan had gone.

He was going to get his soul back. Malus had no idea how such a thing could be done, but he would do it, or die in the attempt. Wherever the daemon had fled to, even if it lay within the very storms of Chaos itself, Malus was going to find him and reclaim what was his. Naggaroth and Hag Graef could wait. What was the point of revenge, after all, if he had no means of savouring it?

By mid-afternoon, Spite was ready to travel. Malus checked his frayed bags and his fresh rations, and then swung heavily into the saddle. He led the nauglir to the square gate, past scores of snow-covered corpses, and reined in at the site of the long road dwindling into the distance.

'You're out there somewhere, daemon,' Malus whispered into the icy wind. 'And if you can hear me, you'd best prepare yourself. The Lord of Ruin is coming for you.'

Malus Darkblade rested a gloved palm against the side of Spite's scaly neck. 'On, beast of the deep earth,' he said. 'To the Black Ark, to the daemon realms, to the Abyss itself if that is where the trail leads. Our journey is over. Now the hunt begins.'

ABOUT THE AUTHORS

Dan Abnett lives and works in Maidstone, Kent, in England. Well known for his comic work, he has written everything from the *Mr Men* to the *X-Men*. His work for the Black Library includes the best-selling Gaunt's Ghosts novels, the *Eisenhorn* and *Ravenor* trilogies, and the acclaimed Horus Heresy novel, *Horus Rising*. He's also worked on the popular strips *Titan* and *Darkblade*, and, together with Mike Lee, the *Darkblade* novel series.

Mike Lee was the principal creator and developer for White Wolf Game Studio's *Demon: The Fallen*. Over the last eight years he has contributed to almost two dozen role-playing games and supplements. An avid wargamer and devoted fan of pulp adventure, Mike lives in the United States.

THE BLACK LIBRARY

Malus Darkblade

Possessed by the ancient daemon Tz'arkan, Darkblade must undertake a dangerous quest to regain five objects of power or forfeit his soul forever!

REAPER OF SOULS
ISBN 13: 978-1-8416-193-5
ISBN 10: 1-8416-193-5

WARPSWORD
ISBN 13: 978-1-8416-194-2
ISBN 10: 1-8416-194-3

Visit *www.blacklibrary.com* to buy this book, or read the first chapter for free! Also available in all good bookshops and games stores

READ TILL YOU BLEED